PENGUIN

THE BOOK OF STOLEN TALES

D.J. McINTOSH's *The Witch of Babylon* has been sold
in twenty countries, was shortlisted for the Crime
Writers' Association Debut Dagger Award, and won a
Crime Writers of Canada Arthur Ellis Award for best
unpublished novel. It was a national bestseller, an
Amazon.ca Best Book, and was named one of CNN's
Most Enduring Historical Thrillers. McIntosh is a
member of the Canadian Society for Mesopotamian
Studies. She is a strong supporter of Reporters Without
Borders and the Committee to Protect Journalists. She
lives in Toronto.

Also by D.J. McIntosh

The Witch of Babylon

D.J.McIntosh
the BOOK of
STOLEN
TALES

PENGUIN

an imprint of Penguin Canada

Published by the Penguin Group

Penguin Group (Canada), 90 Eglinton Avenue East, Suite 700, Toronto, Ontario, Canada M4P 2Y3

Penguin Group (USA) Inc., 375 Hudson Street, New York, New York 10014, U.S.A.
Penguin Books Ltd, 80 Strand, London WC2R 0RL, England
Penguin Ireland, 25 St Stephen's Green, Dublin 2, Ireland (a division of Penguin Books Ltd)
Penguin Group (Australia), 707 Collins Street, Melbourne, Victoria 3008, Australia
(a division of Pearson Australia Group Pty Ltd)
Penguin Books India Pvt Ltd, 11 Community Centre, Panchsheel Park, New Delhi – 110 017, India
Penguin Group (NZ), 67 Apollo Drive, Rosedale, Auckland 0632, New Zealand
(a division of Pearson New Zealand Ltd)
Penguin Books (South Africa) (Pty) Ltd, 24 Sturdee Avenue, Rosebank, Johannesburg 2196, South Africa

Penguin Books Ltd, Registered Offices: 80 Strand, London WC2R 0RL, England

First published 2013

1 2 3 4 5 6 7 8 9 10 (WEB)

Copyright © D. J. McIntosh, 2013

Publisher's note: This book is a work of fiction. Names, characters, places and incidents either are the product of the author's imagination or are used fictitiously, and any resemblance to actual persons living or dead, events, or locales is entirely coincidental.

Manufactured in Canada.

LIBRARY AND ARCHIVES CANADA CATALOGUING IN PUBLICATION

McIntosh, D. J. (Dorothy J.)
The book of stolen tales / D.J. McIntosh.

ISBN 978-0-14-317574-2

I. Title.

PS8625.I53B66 2013   C813'.6   C2012-908386-0

Visit the Penguin Canada website at **www.penguin.ca**

Special and corporate bulk purchase rates available; please see
www.penguin.ca/corporatesales or call 1-800-810-3104, ext. 2477.

ALWAYS LEARNING   PEARSON

For the children I am blessed to have in my life: Will and Mary
Natasha, Brendan, Christian, Madeline, Devon,
Sarah, Morris, Louis and Jaycee.

And to libraries that open magical worlds to the child in all of us.

The Book of Stolen Tales is Book Two
of the Mesopotamian Trilogy.
It takes place in November, symbolized by Nergal,
Babylonian god of war and pestilence.

In December 1631, Naples fell dark. Mount Vesuvius erupted, sending burning ash and toxic gas onto the settlements below. One year later, plague swept through the city. The origins of that plague are unknown to this day.

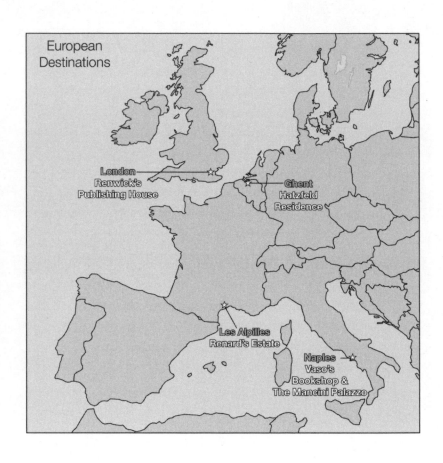

European
Destinations

London
Renwick's
Publishing House

Ghent
Hatzfeld
Residence

Les Alpilles
Renard's Estate

Naples
Vaso's
Bookshop &
The Mancini Palazzo

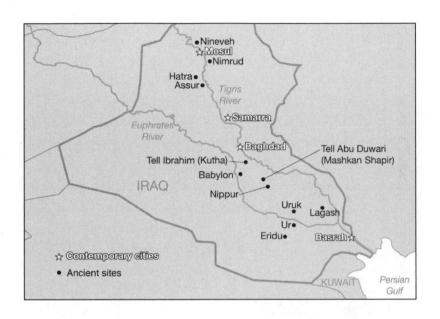

A European Estate,
All Souls' Day

Firelight on the faces of the villagers showed their lust for the burning. They held their torches proudly in front of the captain and his guard. Stunted and malnourished from years spent working in the mines, the villagers leapt at the chance to destroy the noble family's precious property. They fought over who would throw the first firebrand, yearning to see the great estate crumble and burn.

Throughout the day, encouraged by the lord's guard, the villagers set about destroying the garden. They'd ripped up the maze of boxed yew hedges, the cedars clipped into shapes of unicorns and centaurs, and the carefully tended orange trees, bunching them in a ring around the stately home.

The much-admired statue of Eros and Psyche stood under a little arbor thronged with roses, their blossoms long turned a papery brown, but their leaves still verdant after a prolonged summer. The sculptor believed he'd seen the forms of the two lovers in the gray veins of the prized Brocatelle marble. In contrast to the other garden ornaments, this statue had a compelling authenticity. The villagers pried it from its base with brutal force and threw it against the massive entrance doors. They smashed stone outbuildings and piled the rocks on top of the sculpture, demolished wooden stables and added this wreckage to the ring of uprooted trees and hedges. They sealed doors and windows with hot pitch. Enclosed in the circle of vegetation, the great building loomed out of the fog like a pale monument.

The time had come. The captain brought down his hand swiftly and issued the order. His soldiers knelt and raised their muskets. They opened fire. The villagers, unable to comprehend how they had suddenly become targets, froze in shock. Cruel pikes impaled those not felled by bullets. A young man whose wits had not yet left him broke away and tried to crash through the gauntlet of the soldiers' line, but one of the men punctured and gutted the boy's belly with his rapier.

The massacre ended quickly. Bodies lay on the ground like slaughtered lambs. The soldiers heaved them onto the makeshift pyres. The captain's horse, a rare white Camargue tethered to a nearby tree, cried out in terror at the reek of blood.

The captain ordered one of his men to climb through a window broken by the youths and retrieve the prized object. The man returned clutching a small cedar box embossed with a red shield and white cross.

Soldiers added oil-drenched faggots of wood to the mounds of greenery and then joined their captain behind the ring and set it alight. Dense clouds of smoke from the fresh leaves and branches intermingled with the fog, obscuring the red tile roof and grand facade of the manor house.

Pleased by their good service, the captain ordered his aide to gift a gold piece to each member of the guard along with a generous serving of his finest cognac. The aide was permitted to join in, a privilege not normally granted him. The captain toasted his men.

His soldiers threw back their drinks and cheered as the blaze tossed sparks heavenward.

One soldier gripped his throat and sucked in a breath. Cognac could burn when drunk too rapidly but surely not like this. He strained again for air before toppling to the ground. The others followed, stumbling toward the fire, blinded by the poison. Within minutes the entire company lay dying, save one. A soldier who'd cursed aloud when he'd spilled his drink now stood dumbly, gazing at his fallen brothers. The captain pulled a dueling pistol from under his long cloak and shot him through the throat.

The horse flailed in panic, its gleaming white withers slick with sweat, its soft fleshy lips bloody and torn from wrenching at the bit. The captain lashed the animal into submission and mounted, digging his boots into its flanks. He tucked the cedar box into his saddlebag and smiled to himself, anticipating a rich reward from a lord well pleased with the night's work.

The wood was abnormally silent. No rush of wings or predatory growls signaled the waking of its night creatures. The horse, usually a cautious animal alert to the signs of danger, kept up its frenzied pace along the forest trail, focused only on fleeing the smell of murder and fire. A shape like a bloom of ink on parchment spread across their path, darker than the gloom of the night forest and foreign to the natural forms of the trees and plants surrounding it. Both the rider in his reverie and the frightened horse failed to notice the deepening shadow ahead.

Part One

THE PLAGUE
DEMON

Of such great powers or beings there may be conceivably
a survival ... a survival of a hugely remote period when ...
consciousness was manifested, perhaps, in shapes and forms long
since withdrawn before the tide of advancing humanity ... forms
of which poetry and legend alone have caught a flying memory
and called them gods, monsters, mythical beings.

—ALGERNON BLACKWOOD

One

November 17, 2003
London

My brother, Samuel, wrote in his journals religiously, and after he died I kept one of them with me to remember him by. On the long overnight flight from New York to take up a new commission in London, I read his journal again. Although the secrets it held were known to me now, seeing his thoughts and drawings inscribed in his own hand brought his memory close.

If only those first steps my brother had taken during the looting of the Baghdad museum could be undone. Because of his efforts a great Mesopotamian treasure was discovered and saved. But at what price? It was not worth his life or the consequences for the other people I cared about. I wished he'd never gone down that road. It was a fanciful thought, one that comforted me, if only a little. Even our most fervent desires cannot bring a loved one back from the grave.

People always expressed surprise, learning we were brothers, because we looked so different. Our ages contributed to this. I'm thirty-three and Samuel was in his seventies when he died. We had different mothers and I inherited the olive skin, dark hair and eyes of her Turkish forebears. Samuel could easily have been taken for a North European.

I closed his journal just before the plane set down. I'd brought walk-on luggage, so getting through the jungle at Heathrow proved easier this time. I opted to take the tube into the city and pick up a car rental at a place I knew that gave good deals. Despite the long ride on the Piccadilly line, I enjoyed the different faces of the city—farmers' fields in the outlying areas, banks of ivy and holly skirting the tracks, red tile and slate roofs, chimney stacks reminiscent of Dickens, the engaging names of stations as we flew past. Only in London would a station be named Cockfosters.

Once in my hotel room I cast away the sad memories of Samuel and looked forward to my new commission. The promise of a lucrative job had me feeling optimistic for the first time in many months and elated my business had taken such a positive turn.

In a few short hours, I would realize how fleeting this moment of satisfaction was. My good fortune wasn't destined to last long.

Later that night, cold air wafted in through the hotel room window, open for relief from the stifling heat and poor air circulation in the cramped room. Rain fell gently on the pavement outside. The ancient radiators rattled and hissed. I'd shut the lights off even though dusk had fallen, hoping the man outside would give up his post and go away.

I kept out of his sightline, although I doubted he could see anything against the dim background of my room. Five floors down and across the street, the man lingered just outside the yellow arc of light cast by a street lamp. He hadn't moved for hours. Suddenly he looked toward the window as if sensing my presence. What sixth sense did he possess, knowing I watched him?

I'd brushed past him on my way back to the hotel earlier that evening, after acquiring the rare book I'd been hired to bid for at Sherrods auction house.

The man called out to me as I hurried past, "Mr. John Madison, isn't it?"

At first glance he appeared elderly; both of his hands rested atop an ebony cane. A rearing white horse had been expertly carved into the shaft. The horse's rippling withers and powerful legs were meticulously rendered; its flashing mane, arched neck, and head formed the curved handle. In an oddly formal gesture, he bowed and took a few steps toward me. His fluid movements and sure step belied the initial impression of frailty.

"Do I know you?"

"Not yet." His accent was hard to place, but in his voice I detected the faint suggestion of a threat. "My name is Gian Alessio Abbattutis. Perhaps you have heard of me?"

"Haven't had the pleasure. I don't live in London." I pulled my trench coat up to my ears. A light rain began to fall, stirring the dead leaves at my feet.

He indicated my case with the ferrule of his cane. "I think you have in there something that belongs to me." He leaned in and lowered his voice. "Those tales were stolen. I want them back."

"Excuse me?"

"As compensation for your trouble," he added, "I will give you twice what you paid." He dug into his coat pocket and produced a gold coin. It lay in his palm, which was creased with deep lines.

I moved closer. The coin looked familiar. "May I see that?"

He snatched it away, as a magician might. "When you agree to our transaction."

I gripped my case harder and tried to keep the impatience from my voice. "It belongs to my client now. The sale was entirely legitimate. I couldn't sell it to you even if I wanted to. And I don't."

It may have been a trick of the light, the street lamp playing strangely on his face, but his pupils narrowed to sharp, bright pinpoints. "I did not ask to buy it, sir! You'll wish you hadn't kept it. You'll regret this"—he paused—"deeply."

"Good evening," I said curtly and turned away, having had more than enough of his hostile manner. I hastened to the hotel lobby, feeling both a little unnerved at the exchange and annoyed at myself for caring.

The old brick hotel had seen better days. The travel agent neglected to mention shabby corridors, intermittent hot water, and constant gurgles and clangs from the radiators. Convenience won out over comfort because it was close to the Earl's Court tube station. In any event, my stay was for a week—at most—and the room came at a bargain rate.

I unlocked the door with an electronic key card and tossed my trench coat over a chair. Then I poured two fingers of scotch into a tumbler and put David Gray's "Babylon" on the CD player to take my mind off the menacing words of the strange man outside. The solicitor's letter originally proposing my commission was in my pocket. I fingered it, and thinking it might shed some light on the man I'd encountered, pulled it out and read it again.

Dear Mr. Madison,

At the behest of my client, who for the time being wishes to remain unknown, I am writing to seek your services. On Monday, November 17, at 7:30 p.m., Sherrods will offer at auction a rare book. You are being asked to represent my client to bid on it. Details about the item may be found in the enclosed catalog on page 21, item 164. The owner has fixed a price and will not agree to sell the book below that figure. Nor is it available for public viewing beforehand.

Should you be willing to accept this task, funds will be forwarded by my office to cover your travel, accommodation, and ancillary expenses. There is one further stipulation. Once you have concluded the purchase, do not attempt to read the book. My client advises that a repellent history is associated with it and the precaution is for your own protection. Sherrods will deliver the item to the successful bidder in a wooden box. Do not attempt to disturb the contents.

We have set a maximum of 175,000 pounds sterling. My client is unwilling to go beyond that sum; however, we don't anticipate the final price will rise nearly that high. Assuming you are successful, 25 percent of that figure will be forwarded as your commission. Should you decide to accept these terms, please reply by letter.

You are welcome to contact my office should you have any further questions.

I thank you for your consideration.

Cordially,
Arthur S. Newhouse LLP

The solicitor had a swanky Lincoln's Inn address. I made a few inquiries, checked Newhouse out, and agreed to take on the job. Twenty-five percent was very generous in my line of work so I jumped at the chance. After coming close to bankruptcy in recent months, I was in no position to turn down such a lucrative offer.

Other than the reference to the book's dark history and the secrecy surrounding my client's identity, there was no indication in the letter of why the man who'd accosted me would be interested in it. Nor could I recall seeing him at the auction. Not for the first time, I speculated about the repellent history of the book and wondered if it was like others I'd stumbled across. Mina Vanderlin's copy of the *Picatrix*, for example, a grimoire containing spells to summon demons. Or the *Necronomicon* by the mad Arab Abdul Alhazred, although that work existed only in the mind of its twentieth-century creator, H.P. Lovecraft. Newhouse's meaning remained obscure. I couldn't fathom why the old man outside wanted the book so much.

Most of my deals were conducted privately, in the sedate climate-controlled offices and homes of wealthy men and women, but I relished auctions. They had the same drama as casinos. Reading the auctioneer's expressions and gestures, watching whom he'd trade glances with and whom he avoided: the psychological art of the auction shared a lot of similarities with poker. A false showing of your hand, deadpan expressions as tension rose when sums reached astronomical levels, the barely perceptible intake of breath during the count for the winning bid—all were the stuff of legend.

Sherrods was a small auction house specializing in rare books and antiquities, located in the Royal Borough of Kensington and Chelsea. The place was buzzing as a result of a number of spectacular items on the block—a dozen leaves from the Gutenberg Bible, known in the business as "Noble Fragments"; a gorgeous Abbotsford edition of Sir Walter Scott's twelve Waverley novels, including 2500 steel and wood engravings; and ten steatite Mesopotamian cylinder seals circa 800 B.C.

Sleek, well-dressed men and women milled about the Gutenberg display and the Waverley set, catalogs in hand. Some jotted notes in the margins of the item entries; others whispered into their cellphones. In contrast, the object of my attention, ticket 164, garnered little interest. It sat in lonely splendor in its little cedar box adorned with a red shield and white cross.

The catalog details were sparse and their presentation decidedly understated. The entry referred only to a book in good condition printed in the mid-seventeenth century. For that, I was pleased. With fewer bidders I'd have an easier time. I wondered, though, what additional information my client possessed to be willing to pay a high price for such a book.

The more popular items were scheduled to be auctioned at the end of the night to ensure a good audience throughout the evening, so there was still a sizable crowd when my item went on the block. Thanks to my friend Amy, who worked at Sherrods, I'd identified my competitors. A man with a mop of shocking red hair, wearing a navy pinstripe suit, lingered in front of the little wooden box for just a second more than I would have liked. Amy told me auctions were his preferred form of entertainment. Some people took in the opera, others liked the bar scene. He attended auctions. He was notorious for bidding an object up and pulling out before laying any money on the line. Amy smiled at me suggestively when she told me that last detail.

Another agent, Marlee Scott, who often represented rare book dealers in the U.S. and on the continent, was also chasing the book. She would be my major adversary. I caught a glimpse of her in pearls and classic black Dior.

The auctioneer announced ticket number 164 in a posh, clipped accent and the reserve price of eighty thousand pounds. Marlee Scott threw a glance my way, so I knew someone had tipped her off about me too. I smiled and nodded. She picked up the bid at eighty-five thousand and avoided my eye. The auctioneer raised it by a couple of thousand pounds and looked in my direction. I stood pat but Copperhead entered the fray for ninety thousand. I could feel the adrenalin pumping.

I entered a bid at one hundred ten thousand pounds and the auctioneer pushed it up by another couple of thousand. Scott nodded when he looked at her. I snapped up the next bid and out of the corner of my eye watched Copperhead take it after me. He was in a feisty mood tonight. When the auctioneer deliberately slowed the call Copperhead darted a nervous glance over to me, but

I decided to have a little fun and feigned indifference. He squirmed in his seat, afraid he'd taken his game too far. Scott finally raised her paddle, stepping up just in time to rescue him. That was enough for our red-haired friend. He was out.

I took the next bid and noted a wrinkle of worry on Scott's face. She was close to her max. She whipped out her cellphone, stabbed a key with her red lacquered nail, and talked rapidly. She pushed it to one hundred twenty. I upped it by four thousand and held my breath. "One hundred twenty-four thousand. Do I hear one hundred twenty-five?" Silence reigned. I looked over at Marlee Scott. "Fair warning," the auctioneer chimed and scanned the room. "Last chance!" No one stepped up. He waited a few more seconds before giving me a curt nod and announcing, "Sold! To number seventy-eight." I silently cheered.

The book was mine.

Scott raised her delicate eyebrows and gave me a thumbs-up to show there were no hard feelings. I smiled back, appreciating her grace. The book had gone higher than I'd hoped but was still under the maximum. My unnamed client would be pleased.

I closed the heavy hotel drapes and clicked on a small desk lamp before turning back to the book. The written warning not to open it served only to entice me. The antique cedar box inside my case bore no maker's mark except for a coat of arms stamped in its lid—a fat white cross on a red shield. From my research on Peter Vanderlin's European collection, I knew this was the coat of arms of the House of Savoy, the royal house of Italy. That meant the box could date back hundreds of years. Its fitted lid was firmly secured by four small brass screws. As I began to extract them with my penknife I noticed a few tiny scratch marks on the head of one of the screws. Someone had opened the box, and recently too, I guessed. I removed the screws and laid them carefully on the table; then I lifted the lid.

The box was partitioned into two compartments. The larger one held the book; the other was empty. I wondered what it had once contained.

I carefully lifted the book out to examine it. A beautiful object with covers of hammered gold overlaid with black enamel, it was decorated with Arabic-inspired arabesques on both sides and on the front were entwined the initials *T* and *M*. Two clasps held the golden covers shut. The spine was made of silver and delicately banded with gold.

It was in near-perfect condition. The silver was barely tarnished; the metallic finish was free from the dents and splits you'd expect to see from hundreds of years of handling. No dust or moisture had been permitted to mar its perfection. And yet it felt old.

The clasps didn't appear to be locked nor would they budge, suggesting that, unlike the box, the book hadn't been opened for some time. Not willing to risk scratching the metal with my penknife, I spent over half an hour fiddling with the clasps before I succeeded in disengaging them.

The actual volume turned out to be quite slim. Far too small for the size of the covers. I'd seen elaborate metallic covers before on literary Judaica, but nothing nearly so ornate for a book of this size. It measured about five by three inches.

I groaned in disappointment when I saw the first page. It was entirely in Italian. Although I understood a smattering of modern Italian—enough to carry on a limited conversation, or order a decent meal and a bottle of wine—deciphering a complex text was beyond my abilities. Whatever secrets the book contained would remain hidden from me for now.

The book's leaves, further protected with pasteboard, were bound to the metal covers with thin leather ties. Not only were the metallic covers overlarge, they were designed to protect a much thicker volume.

I slapped on latex gloves to protect the old pages from the oils of my skin. The leaves were hand bound and quite stiff. The papers displayed a lot of color variation, ranging from toasty brown to vanilla—not a surprise since older papers often browned owing to their high acid content. I could see, deep in the crease of the spine, they'd once been a beautiful bone white and therefore were of high quality.

The typeface, archaic and elegant, filled the pages almost margin to margin. Centuries ago, books were so costly to manufacture, all the possible space was used. One folio had been cut so closely that part of the text had been severed with it.

I carefully held up the page to the light and spotted a Fabriano watermark—a sign of high value. Fabriano was a prestigious paper manufacturer in the Apennines, in business as far back as the Middle Ages. At one time, anyone who revealed the company's paper-making secrets was sent into exile.

Using my phone I snapped photos of the covers and pages and sent the folder to my email address. It was only wise to keep a record of any item under my care, especially when it had so aroused the curiosity and ardor of others.

I returned to the book and studied the illustrations accompanying the Italian text. They were superb black-and-white engravings. The first few images seemed familiar, reminding me of a popular childhood fairy tale. From there they depicted increasingly dark and horrifying scenes. The second to last showed a woman of middle age dressed in a flowing gown, being forced by two men into a large hearth burning brightly with fire. The woman's flailing movements and the look of sheer terror on her face were rendered so convincingly, they seemed copied from real life. Under this image, the caption read *Gracie a Lo Spagnoletto*. My Italian was sufficient here: *Thank you to the little Spaniard.*

The hair rose on the back of my neck. Lo Spagnoletto was the Italian nickname for José de Ribera, premier printmaker and painter of seventeenth-century Naples. Ribera was one of the Tenebrosi, the shadow painters, who, inspired by Caravaggio, employed heavy contrast between dark and light in their work. A great artist but also a sinister figure in those times, Ribera led the cabal of Naples, a small group of painters who harassed and threatened other artists to beat them out of lucrative commissions. If the prints could be authenticated, the book was worth far more than its auction value.

I flipped back to the frontispiece and checked the title again: *Lo Cunto de li Cunti*. I looked up the words, which translated as *The Tale of Tales*. And then I saw the author's name. I could hardly believe my eyes, but there it was, in clear black type: *Gian Alessio Abbattutis ... 1634.*

Two

The strange man outside claimed to be the author of a 370-year-old book. How could this be? Had he been named in honor of a favorite author? Was he actually related to the original Abbattutis? Perhaps it was a family tradition to name a son after a famous relative. Not impossible. Even probable. But unsettling all the same.

Absorbed in these thoughts, I failed to register the steady pace of footsteps along the hallway or the plonk of a cane striking the worn hall carpet. A hard rap at the door broke through my reverie.

I rushed over to the window and looked down. Through the sheets of rain I could see the man was no longer at his post across the street.

"What do you want?" I called across the darkened room.

He didn't answer. Instead, a moment later he pushed something under the gap below the door. A gold coin—the one he'd shown me earlier—slid across the floor. I walked quietly over, stooped down to pick it up, and took it over to the lamp. There was a reason it seemed familiar. It belonged to me. One of the seven gold coins my brother gave me when I was a child.

Just as I pocketed the coin, his voice boomed through the door. "I have the others just like that one. Don't you want them back?"

I'd entrusted my coins to Evelyn, our old housekeeper. She was like a mother to me and I knew she'd never give them up willingly. I grabbed my phone and punched in her New York number. No response. Flames of fear licked at the back of my mind. I put the book out of sight in the coffee table drawer and yanked the hotel room door open in a fury.

He'd anticipated my anger. He stood in the middle of the hall and held up one gloved hand. "I simply wish to speak with you," he said.

I ripped into him. "If you've done anything to hurt Evelyn, you'll pay for it."

"The lady is fine," the old man interrupted. "I'll warrant she doesn't even know the coins are missing. And I'll give you another one if you let me come in to explain."

I stood aside to let him in. "Prove you're telling the truth—now."

He gave a slight bow, the kind of courtly gesture people made a couple of centuries ago, odd to see in a budget hotel in modern London. "You'll simply have to take a gentleman's word for it."

I hit redial on my phone. Evelyn still wasn't answering. "What happened to the other six coins?" I asked with the phone to my ear.

He strode into the sitting room and sat in an armchair. Again I was struck by the vitality he seemed to possess for someone of his age. And something else bothered me. He had no limp, none of the slow, measured movements of the elderly or infirm who have problems with balance. Why then did he need the cane?

"Lost them I'm afraid. One will have to do."

"Then compensate me for the rest."

With a slight lift of his shoulders—an elegant shrug—he smiled. "Ah. You seek financial returns and here I thought they had sentimental value. We will see. I'd wager, though, you have no real idea of their worth."

True. I'd tried a couple of times to have them appraised. New York has some of the best numismatists in the world but the coins stumped them. They couldn't tell me anything about their origin and, without that, were unable assign an accurate value.

He tapped the floor with the tip of his cane. "They're worth a fortune and I've given one back to you. I didn't have to. Surely that indicates I mean no harm."

"You rob me and you're looking for thanks?" I said incredulously. I ran my hand over my close-cut beard and took his measure. The gargantuan nerve of the man floored me.

His long black coat glistened with raindrops. He removed his hat, shook it to get some of the moisture off, and set it carefully on the floor without answering me. He was short, almost petite, with a thin face and large, dark, alert eyes. I would have called them soulful but his manner was too abrasive for that. His skin, of a reddish cast and puckered like crepe paper, did show his age. I surmised that the color of his hair, cavalier mustache, and goatee, so uniformly pitch black, came out of a bottle. He seemed to give off a kind of repellent dimness, as if his very presence stole the light from the air.

"Again. What makes you an expert on old coins?"

"Let's just say I have an appreciation for history so deep that at times I almost feel as though I'm living it."

From the moment he'd come through the door I'd felt a kind of sluggishness, as if my blood had suddenly turned to lead. Now my heart beat much harder, laboring strenuously to push the blood through my veins. Although the sensation unnerved me, I shrugged it off and moved away from him to the mantel above the electric fire. I leaned against it to brace myself.

His smile lacked friendliness. "What is the oldest currency in the world?"

"The Lydian stater. Handmade from electrum. Stamped with an image of a lion's head."

"Quite right. Staters are very old but not scarce, so they don't command a high price. Your coins came from a remote corner at the intersection of Turkey and Persia, predating staters by at least two hundred years. Your coins may be the only examples left in the world. Very rare and probably priceless."

For some reason he was trying to ingratiate himself with me, to what end, I had no idea. Nothing would be gained by debating currency. "Evelyn would never have let you take them. I'm asking you again. Have you harmed her?"

My remark was greeted with strange, shuddering laughter. "The coins were removed when she was out. I imagine she doesn't even know they are gone. Do not forget. You have stolen my book from me. So we are equal, are we not?"

Once again the bizarre sensation overwhelmed me, strongly enough this time to affect my speech. I gave myself a shake and that seemed to dispel it. "I won the book at an auction legitimately. If you have an issue about ownership it's a problem for Sherrods, not me."

"No, it is a problem for you," he said in a menacing tone.

"What's that supposed to mean?"

He crossed his legs and rested his right hand on top of his cane. "Your brother, Samuel, is dead, I am told. And now the only family you have is the lady you mentioned, your old housekeeper Evelyn, who raised you—is that not so? She is in a wheelchair most of the time. Quite fragile, I understand, suffering greatly from soreness of the joints."

I went to grab the lapels of his coat and shake the truth out of him but felt the sudden assault of another bout of weakness. My actions had no impact and he pushed me away easily. He appeared to be on some kind of mission, determined to have his say. He was well spoken enough although a pedantic quality affected his speech, as if he'd memorized the lines beforehand. "If you care for this lady you will hear me out."

"Go ahead," I said, still trying to get my breath back. "You're not getting out of here."

He scowled at me. "I know her days are spent in predictable ways. She arises early. Goes in her wheelchair across the street to the café. Only she doesn't like coffee; it keeps her awake at night. So she takes her special mint tea with her and they give her hot water for it. She could make it at home but she is stuck in her little apartment too much as it is. She buys a muffin or a roll to go with it. She likes to get out, talk to people. At around four in the afternoon she visits her neighbor, an immigrant like herself, who lives a few floors down. They drink tea together and play poker. They bet only pennies because neither has much money. Friendly games, not serious. Her hands hurt so much she can't shuffle the cards anymore. But she trusts her companion to do it."

I listened with lurching panic. He knew every detail about her life and the implications were obvious. He'd hurt her if I didn't hand over the book. I tried to reach for my phone but found my hand had frozen. A shadow around the man appeared to darken— or was it my own vision blurring? Something was terribly wrong with me. I could utter only incomprehensible sounds.

As if completely unaware of the physical crisis overtaking me, he pulled a round timepiece from his pocket, checked it, swept his hat off the floor and placed it on his head. Then he advanced toward me, locking his penetrating gaze on me as if he could direct the full force of his will through his eyes.

I summoned every ounce of my own energy and failed to move even my baby finger.

He raised his cane and pressed the tip into my neck. He was a slight man but it felt as though the weight of a bull bore down upon me. I felt my skin split and the wooden stock puncture my throat as easily as a stiletto spearing jello.

Then, in one swift motion he flipped the cane back and spun on his heel. He pulled out the coffee table drawer and removed the book in its golden covers. He paused before the door and said accusingly, "You've opened the book. That was a grave error. Have nothing more to do with it. Go back to your homeland or suffer the consequences."

The minute the door clicked shut my breathing and heart rate slowed and my sight cleared. The awful paralysis subsided. I clamped my hand to my neck but could feel no injury. I swallowed, incredulous, expecting my throat to be sticky with blood. My hand was clear. I scrambled to my feet and chased after him.

The lobby door swung shut just as I made it down the back stairs. I pushed it open a crack. The night was misty and gray although the rain had lessened. Directly across from me a short, stocky man hurried down the street, dwarfed by an umbrella so large it hid his head and much of his torso. He looked like an umbrella with legs. The fog was so low I could barely make out the phone box at the next intersection.

I spotted Alessio walking quickly down the sidewalk, one arm holding the golden covers tightly, the other swinging his cane. I stuck as close as possible to the buildings and followed him. As I gained on him, my view of his figure was partially blocked by the angle of the red phone box.

I heard the door creak open. I took a chance and inched toward it. Through the small panes of glass I could see him pluck the receiver from its cradle and push the buttons to make the call. He spoke. I prayed he was contacting whoever was waiting in New York to do Evelyn harm and calling him off.

He hung up. The red door cracked open and he stepped out. I stayed behind the phone box out of his direct line of sight. Cars whizzed past, spraying muddy water onto the sidewalk. He pulled his hat lower and after glancing around the street walked briskly away. I let him get about sixty feet distant before I began to follow him again and reached inside my jacket for my phone to hit 999 for the police.

A car revved its engine behind me. As I turned around, its headlights momentarily blinded me. It mounted the curb. In one horrifying second, I saw it aiming straight for me. I threw myself against a door recessed into an alcove. The car flashed past and braked to a stop beside the old man. He got in and with a screech the car sped off. He was gone and the book with him.

Three

Furious about the attack and still worried about Evelyn, I ran down the misty street to my hotel room. I threw back a healthy dose of Macallan to quell my shaking hands and got on the phone to report the theft to the police. Gian Alessio Abbattutis—I was already calling him Alessio in my mind—would be lost by now in the labyrinth of London streets. There was little hope they'd find him but I gave them a detailed description anyway. A twisted version. How could I explain letting him into my room and the strange paralysis that afflicted me? They'd never believe it. I told them he'd accosted me on the street. They said they'd log it in and instructed me to fax them a report. I'd have to show up in person at New Scotland Yard for an interview.

Evelyn didn't have voice mail. She complained she only got messages from what she called "the spam people," so when I called her again the phone rang and rang. I cursed myself for not thinking to get a neighbor's number in case of an emergency and tried to stave off the image of her lying on the floor, hurt and alone. The memory of the car accident last June and my brother's death only months ago still haunted every one of my days. To think I might also lose Evelyn plunged me into despair.

Chances were I was letting my fears get in the way of common sense. Alessio got what he came for. Nothing would be served by orchestrating an assault three thousand miles away. Still, I needed to make sure. My next call was to Corinne Carter, my only New York friend certain to be home. Except to attend to basic necessities, she rarely left her place.

"Johnnie! Thought you were supposed to be in the U.K. Fantastic to hear from you, babe."

"I am in London, Corrie. I'm worried about Evelyn because I can't reach her. Is there any way you could go over to her place and make sure she's okay?"

She paused. "Sure, I guess that's all right. Do you have any particular reason to worry?"

"I've run into a complication over here, that's all, and I want to be sure nothing's wrong."

"What complication? John, didn't I tell you it was a mistake to accept that job when the client wouldn't give you his name?"

When she dropped the endearments and called me John, I knew her patience was wearing thin. "I needed the money too much, Corrie. You know how far I was stretched. That's water under the bridge right now. I'd really appreciate it if you could check on her." I gave her Evelyn's address and apartment number.

"Of course. Don't think another minute about it. For heaven's sake, keep safe yourself."

"Thanks. What would I do without you? Like I said, I haven't been able to get a hold of her yet, so please call me back as soon as you find her."

I wandered over to the bed and sat down, hoping I'd hear from her soon with good news. I looked at the open, empty drawer. At least I'd had the presence of mind to make sure the book was insured for the gap of time between the auction and its delivery to the solicitor. Toller Art Insurance in Manhattan maintained a twenty-four-hour line. Predictably, when I contacted them a standard recording came on.

I lay down and stared at the old vermiculite ceiling. When my cell rang I bolted up with a start.

It wasn't Evelyn. I didn't recognize the number.

"Am I speaking to John Madison?"

"You are."

"This is Detective Eleanor O'Neil with the New York Police. I believe you're listed as the primary contact for an Evelyn Farhad in case of an emergency?"

My pulse raced. "Yes I am. What's wrong?"

"Sorry to tell you this, sir, she was found by another officer after a resident of her building called in a disturbance. She'd been assaulted and was critical when he got to her. She passed away in the ambulance en route to the hospital."

Four

O'Neil paused. "Sir, are you still there? Did you hear what I said?"

When I didn't reply she waited. She could have waited forever and I'm not sure I could have responded. I was only vaguely aware of more words echoing through the phone before I let it drop.

Time stretched on. The bottle of scotch was empty. I had no memory of finishing it. There was a strange buzzing in my room. A green light flashed on my bed. My cell with an incoming text. The insurance people probably. I didn't give a shit.

It began to rain hard again and gusts of bitter wind hammered the drops in through the open window. Part of the carpet and the back of a chair were already wet. I left it like that.

In the bathroom I threw freezing water on my face, ran my fingers through my hair. My eyes were bloodshot. A vicious, throbbing pain punched away at my head. After throwing back a couple of Tylenol and washing them down with a drink straight from the faucet, I tossed my clothes and sundries into my bag and snapped it shut. The clock on the night table showed almost one thirty in the morning. My plan, as far as I was able to make one, was to head straight for Heathrow and take the next available flight home.

I slammed the window shut, producing a hairline crack in the glass. The door lock clicked on my way out. I left the key card with the concierge and made my way to the underground parking lot to find my rental, getting drenched in the process but beyond caring.

Stepping into the garish fluorescence of the car park, I'd lost my focus so much I couldn't remember where I'd left the car. The place was completely deserted, the cars ranked like silent rows of sentries. Shadows loomed across my path every time I passed a pillar.

I located it on the third level, a steel-gray Toyota Corolla. About ten yards away I hit the button to open the doors but stopped dead at the sight of the destruction. The dash panel had been pried loose and dumped on the front seats. Sticking out from the exposed underside were criss-crossed wires, neatly severed. "Fuck."

The radio and CD player hung by one intact wire. Random violence from kids with nothing better to do? Hardly. Alessio wanted to scare me into submission and stop me from pursuing him.

Back out in the deluge, the gutters rushed with water, the waste of a busy London day carried along like little boats on the tide. Plastic water bottles, a half-eaten piece of pizza, and a chip bag floated along beside me to form a little dam at the storm drain. Rare for London, the city was so pristine. Every time I lifted my head to glimpse a street sign, rain stabbed mercilessly at my eyes. A car slowed down behind me and as I glanced around in the hope it might be a taxi, it sped up and turned a corner.

Thoughts of Evelyn pummeled my brain. Not of her brutal end but how, though she hated winter, she took delight in the rain. The one time I remember her mentioning her homeland she described the end of winter. "When the rains in spring came to my village our world turned green again. So beautiful, you didn't care about getting wet. You wanted to stay outside and dance." I began to weep then, and let the downpour wash away my tears.

A while later I spotted a cab. By some miracle his for-hire sign was lit up. I waved and he pulled up alongside me. "Where to?" he said when I got in.

"Heathrow," I mumbled.

He slid back the divider window and handed me a paper towel. "Think you might need this, mate," he said.

My cell chirped. When I checked the sender and saw Evelyn's number, I stared at the screen, almost missing the call out of sheer astonishment.

"Hello," I said tentatively.

"John, you keep calling me. Is something wrong?"

The sound of her voice spun me into a delirium of joy and it took me a minute or so to calm down enough to speak. "Evie? Have the police been in touch with you?"

"No. I was next door and when I got back, your friend Corinne was waiting for me. She's here now. Why did you want her to come?"

I didn't want to alarm her so I told her only half the story. "Those coins I left with you were stolen."

She gasped on the other end of the phone. "John! I have not touched them since you gave them to me. I should have hidden those things away."

"It's all right. There's nothing you could have done. Listen, Evie, if Corinne's willing, I'd like you to stay with her for a while— until I can get back to New York. The robbery concerns me. I want to make sure you're safe."

"Oh, I don't know." She paused and I knew she was fretting. It would be a major disruption in her life and Evelyn wasn't adventurous.

"Corinne loves poker," I added. "And I'm sure she'd like the company. Can you put her on the line for a sec?"

A minute or so of silence and then Corinne's voice sailed through the line. "Everything's fine here, John. No worries."

"Thanks for going over, Corrie. I have another favor to ask. Some rare coins were stolen from Evelyn's apartment. She wasn't home at the time, but if there's another attempt I'm concerned about what might happen to her. I know it's a lot to ask, but is there any way she could stay with you?"

A moment passed and then she said, "How long for?"

"A couple of days. Until I can get back there."

"Sure I guess, but only on one condition."

"What's that?"

She raised her voice so Evelyn could overhear. "She has to make her great baklava for me."

I laughed. "I owe you hugely. Really—thanks." I got back on the line with Evelyn and managed to persuade her to go to Corinne's.

"Love you, Evie. Goodnight."

In spite of the relief, knowing Evelyn was safe, my anger boiled over again at Alessio's cruelty. Why did he want the book so badly he was willing to hurt an innocent old woman? It wasn't priceless. I wondered again about the book's evil history and the type of man who might want to collect such a thing. And how could tales from over three hundred years ago matter that much to anyone now?

Clearly, Alessio wasn't working alone. He'd arranged the false police call, and the woman he used to play cop was either a New Yorker or a damned good actor.

I tried to let the passions subside and think rationally. When I set out to find the missing engraving in Iraq, I'd done so blindly, stumbling into a situation not of my own making. I'd turned it into a cause and paid dearly for it. Had I the choice again, it would have been far more prudent to leave well enough alone. But the experience taught me that when the stakes are high enough, people will stop at nothing to get what they want. And that's where my problem lay. Slinking home with my tail between my legs didn't guarantee things would end there. If Alessio threatened Evelyn once, he was quite capable of doing so again. Past experience showed me that waiting for some authority to act was a waste of time. And this theft would be only one small item on Scotland Yard's very long case load.

Signs on the M4 glowed with neon brilliance in the night. I tapped on the divider and the cabbie eyed me in the rearview mirror. "Change of plan. I'm not going to Heathrow after all. Can you take me to the Savoy?"

He glanced at the meter. "Got to add on twenty quid to do that, or nearabouts."

"That's fine."

The driver let me out at a bank machine near the Savoy Hotel. I pressed damp pound notes into his palm. The rain had stopped but a cold fog hung in the air. I feared my bank accounts had been hacked too until the machine began spitting out bills. I withdrew my daily limit from the generous advance paid by the solicitor.

I'd been to the Savoy for other art events and dinners with clients and was familiar with its history. Its name came from a deed of land King Henry VIII granted to a count of the Italian royal House of Savoy. I thought of the Savoy insignia on the cedar box that had contained the book, the white cross on a red shield. That emblem still symbolized the pinnacle of power and wealth.

So many celebrities and aristocrats had crossed the threshold, the hotel might as well have a permanent red carpet. And yet for all its storied past it was still centuries younger than the book Alessio stole. With some of the priciest rooms in the city, it was ideal for my purposes.

I crossed the elegant lobby with its imposing pillars, coffered ceiling, and exquisite carpets. At the registration desk the clerk gave me a measured glance, groping for a way, I imagined, to point out the Savoy didn't accept guests who looked like drowned rats. He asked how he could assist me.

"I'd like to reserve a suite for tonight, departing in two weeks' time. Do you have anything overlooking the Thames?" I thrust out my Amex.

He gave me a tepid smile. "I'll just check then, shall I?" His fingers fluttered over the keyboard and he looked up. "We have a suite available. Eight hundred and seventy pounds per night. Will that suit?" He clearly doubted my ability to pay.

"Marvelous."

He seemed more affable once my credit was approved. We concluded our business and he handed me the door card. "Would you like me to call for a valet to take care of your wet things?"

"Great. Thanks." I headed for the elevators. I had not chosen one of London's most expensive hotels out of mere indulgence. Alessio and whomever he worked with had already shown a penchant for vile tricks. They were fully capable of hacking into and freezing my credit cards too. But I counted on the hotel putting a hold on the amount needed for a two-week stay. Loading one of my credit cards to the gills would stop them from getting a good portion of my money. It was only a temporary solution. I'd stay for one night and in the morning tell the hotel I'd changed plans. Then I'd head straight to the bank and withdraw every cent before anyone could get his hands on it.

When I entered the suite the bedside clock glowed 4 A.M. The valet arrived minutes later for my wet crumpled clothing. A long hot shower dispelled my chills and I fell into bed.

Bright mid-morning sunshine poured through the windows. After a message from Corinne that Evelyn was in remarkably good spirits, I could pretend, for a few moments at least, that all was well.

No nation on earth can trump a full English breakfast. The meal arrived with a discreet knock on my door: soft eggs, half a grilled tomato with parmesan, Canadian back bacon, crumpets perfectly browned and dripping with butter, orange bitter marmalade, and a pot of steaming coffee. Just as the valet reappeared to deliver my clothes, fresh and expertly ironed, my phone chirped.

"Mr. Madison," the insurance agent said after he introduced himself, "I'm sorry to tell you this but you're not covered. We can reimburse you for your coins. Not the book."

"There's got to be some mistake then. The policy's watertight. I've used the same one many times before."

"If there had been damage to the property, or accidental loss, yes. But you're not covered for theft."

"That's impossible. Why bother taking out insurance otherwise? I bought the policy from Jack Edison. Can you transfer me so I can clear this up?"

"He's on holidays."

"In November? When's he back?"

"Gone to Australia. Won't be in the office until next month."

My temper rose with each punctilious syllable he uttered. I made one last effort to be civil. "Please check it again. No doubt you'll find there's been a ... misreading or something."

"I have. And there isn't." He cleared his throat. "You're claiming for a rare manuscript I believe."

"It's a codex. A bound book, not a manuscript."

"My apologies." He repeated the description I'd given last night. "We can't accept your claim because it's stolen property."

"Of course it is!" I shouted in exasperation. "That's why I reported it."

"You misunderstand me, Mr. Madison. The book you described

was listed as stolen property *before* it went to auction. We don't cover illegally acquired items."

I set my coffee cup down carefully. "You're telling me Sherrods auctioned a stolen book? It is a highly respected firm. They check and double-check stuff like that."

"The theft was registered with Interpol quite recently."

"How recently?"

"Yesterday afternoon."

Five

November 18, 2003
London

It was entirely possible Sherrods had missed a theft report only hours before the actual auction. After getting the details from the insurance agent, I ended our call. With no clear title, the onus was on the auction house to return my client's money. But if they chose to put up a fight, it could get sticky. Maybe a good lawyer could rescue me; that would cost an arm and a leg. In the meantime, I was on the hook for a small fortune.

At first I found the Interpol description confusing. Not because of the detail—their theft alerts were usually quite brief and accompanied by photos of the item in question. As I read the report a second time, I realized not one, but five volumes had been reported stolen, all listed as authored by Gian Alessio Abbattutis. These five separate volumes, each with different stories, made up the complete book. Now I knew why the golden covers seemed much too large for the one volume I had. Four more of them, roughly the same size, would fill the gilded covers nicely.

Each volume had been published separately and assembled as a complete anthology at a later period. I recognized the frontis-piece of the one I'd won at auction. It was listed as a first edition, the first volume of the five, published by the Neapolitan printer Beltrano in 1634. The second and last volumes were also published by Beltrano in 1634 and 1636, respectively. The middle two had a different publisher—Scorrigio—in 1634 and 1635. That seemed odd. I wondered why two different publishers were used.

As was customary with Interpol's theft reports, the brief didn't name the book's rightful owner. Maybe no individual name was attached. Often enough these valuable items were assigned to a business for tax reasons. The owner's name might prove difficult to unearth.

I sat back in my chair. Breakfast no longer interested me. The fact that four other volumes were listed as stolen by Interpol might help me. I could follow any of those leads if the man claiming to be Gian Alessio Abbattutis threatened the other buyers. And those buyers, I reasoned, might be able to supply useful informa-tion for finding Alessio. Visiting Amy at Sherrods had to be my first priority, though, to learn who assigned the book to the auction house in the first place.

After settling things over the phone with the car rental agency—which meant losing my entire damage deposit—I left a healthy housekeeping tip, checked out of the hotel, and found a bank nearby. I had to haggle with the teller and sign my life away before the man finally handed over the cash. This would furnish me with enough money to manage, whatever lay ahead.

I rented a safety deposit box and placed my gold coin, along with the cedar box that had contained the book, inside. Knowing Alessio could use my phone to find me, I put it in the safety deposit box as well. I bought a money belt and then went to a discount electronics store for an untraceable burner phone.

It felt good to walk in London's crisp autumn air. The strange paralysis I'd experienced last night hadn't returned. The more I thought about it, the more I believed it resulted from some form of hypnosis. I rubbed my fingers over my neck on the spot where Alessio's cane had bitten into my skin. It was tender but the skin wasn't broken. My neck was fine. My imagination was working overtime. My resolve deepened to chase down leads to the other volumes and prove they'd never been auctioned to me in the first place.

Sherrods was located on the same street as Christie's—Old Brompton Road. I found my friend Amy Price, a petite transplanted Australian, in her office and able to spare a few minutes. We were on good terms. On my last visit to London we'd shared cocktails followed by a night out and one thing had led, very pleasantly, to another.

She got up from her desk and I gave her a hug that lingered long enough to be more than friendly. She shook her finger at me in mock disapproval. "Don't be cheeky," she said. "I'm at work." Then her smile faded. "I know why you're here. I'm so sorry. Very bad luck, John. The police contacted us last night after you reported the robbery. It must have been horrible."

"Amy, listen. I hate to tell you this but the book I bought here yesterday was stolen."

She looked at me with puzzlement. "I *know*. That's what I meant. You'd have arranged for insurance, of course. Still, it must be upsetting."

There was no way to break this gently, much as I wanted to spare Amy any trouble. "Don't worry about me, Amy," I said. "The auction house could be in some difficulty. Legally they're obliged to return my client's money because the title wasn't cleared. Have you thought about what you're going to do?"

"What do you mean? The theft happened after you left here.

We're not involved." A hint of worry darkened her eyes. "What are you trying to say?"

"A claim's been made the book was stolen *before* it went on the auction block. There's an Interpol file on it."

"No way. I checked that personally. It was completely clean." She smoothed her brown hair in a nervous gesture.

I wanted to reassure her if I could. "Apparently, the Interpol alert came in right before the auction. You couldn't have known."

"Oh no—are you serious?" She bent over her laptop and frantically punched keys. I could see apprehension clouding her face as she found and digested the Interpol report. When she turned around her voice quavered. "I cleared that bloody thing.... They were about to offer me a permanent position. I'll never get another job in this field." She put her head in her hands and valiantly tried to hold back a sob.

"Not your fault, Amy. You couldn't have known about the report. Besides, these things don't always become public."

She lost the battle with her emotions; when she looked up, I saw her lovely blue eyes brimming with tears. "You know what it's like. The office gossips feed on stuff like this. One of the interns is a nephew of the owner and he's thoroughly pissed he's not getting the job. Wait until he hears."

I touched her shoulder reassuringly. "I'm getting that book back, Amy, and nailing the asshole who stole it from me. I'll do anything I can to help you. But you've got to tell me what you know. The thief said his name was Gian Alessio Abbattutis. He might be a nut job or maybe a descendant of the author. Or just got a kick out of using an alias. I have a feeling that book's at the center of a family dispute. What can you tell me about the author? I've never heard of Abbattutis. It's not exactly a household name."

"John, that's a pseudonym. The author's real name is Giambattista Basile. A celebrated member of the Spanish court at

Naples and later awarded a title—the Count of Torone. He had a great sense of humor and loved anagrams. If you check all the letters you'll see Gian Alessio Abbattutis anagrams almost perfectly to the author's actual name."

So Alessio's use of the name Abbattutis turned out to be a perverse kind of joke. "Why would the real author use a pseudonym?"

"It was pretty common to do so in those days and Basile's writing contains some pointed satire directed toward powerful political figures. Maybe it was self-preservation. He was far ahead of his time because he wrote in the Neapolitan dialect—instead of classical Latin—horrifically hard to translate properly. That's why the book remained obscure until the twentieth century. The anthology's a collection of fairy and folk tales. It's often compared to Boccaccio's *Decameron*."

"Well, that's fitting. The guy who stole my copy looked like he walked right out of one of those old stories."

Amy raised her eyebrows. "The entire book includes some of the earliest versions of fairy tales every kid knows," she went on. "Like 'Puss in Boots.' Some of the stories are pretty violent and there's tons of sexual innuendo, not kid stuff at all. The book's structured with a wraparound story like the one in *The Arabian Nights*, explaining why the tales were told."

I looked her squarely in the eye. "Did you know it included illustrations by José de Ribera?"

"No! That would have increased the book's value astronomically."

"Exactly," I said ruefully. "An incredible find, really. My client stood to make a fortune. There's something else. The book's gold covers are really well executed, with Arabic-looking arabesque designs. Is that unusual for an Italian book? What do you think?"

She thought about what I asked for a moment and said, "I remember now. Except for the initials, the covers are almost a direct copy of a famous design done in 1537 by Hans Holbein the Younger

Design for a metal book cover by
Hans Holbein the Younger

for an English book." Amy bent over her computer and searched for an image and then swiveled the screen for me to take a look.

"That's it, exactly, except for the initials. Why is that ring on top?"

"To fasten the book to a cord or belt so it couldn't be lost or stolen."

"Nice. I'm curious why Sherrods' catalog made no mention of the author's real name or the fact it was a fairy-tale anthology. That would have made it highly collectible."

"The consignor was very secretive and wanted to limit how much information we gave out. Since the owner was represented by someone I know and trust, I went along with it."

"Didn't the secrecy raise your suspicions?"

"Happens all the time. Some sellers can be pretty weird. They would have refused to let us auction it, otherwise. How are you thinking to get it back?"

"By finding the thief. Listen, can you put a hold on the money? If the book does turn out to be stolen your consignor had no right to sell it so he's not entitled to the proceeds."

"We wired the funds this morning—sorry." She bit her lip. She was already thinking beyond the immediate theft and how to protect Sherrods' reputation. "Our lawyers will have a go at it. The house may not be compromised."

"The whole thing might turn out to be a nonissue. One family member accusing another of selling it without permission. It wouldn't be the first time someone made a false accusation of theft."

She brightened up for an instant but her face fell as quickly. "Interpol would have checked all that before issuing the alert."

"Not necessarily. Depends on who made the accusation. If it's from someone powerful, that would influence the police. Look, if I can retrieve it, I'll make it clear you were instrumental in helping me get it back. That should help. Who's the consignor? Where did it come from?"

"I'm right fucked anyway so you may as well know. It came from Ewan Fraser Associates." She sighed as though she were carrying the weight of the whole world on her shoulders.

"Sounds Scottish. Is he from Edinburgh?"

"No, Naples. We've dealt with him in the past. Completely trustworthy source. He's a rare book dealer in his off hours. It's somewhere between a hobby and a real business for him. I met him on a trip once. A big blustery guy."

"Why Naples?"

"He works at the national library there. Moved to the city

because he's always loved the Italian life. And it's a lot warmer than Scotland."

Her face clouded over. I saw she was thinking the same unpleasant thought I was.

"Surely he wouldn't have taken it from the library and sent it here hoping no one would find out?"

"And used his own name? Doesn't make sense. Not rightly."

"Does your consignor still have the other four volumes, or were they sold too?"

"What are you talking about? We auctioned the complete book."

"No, Sherrods didn't, Amy. There's no way. I found only one volume of the five inside the gold covers, the first one published in 1634."

With an exasperated sigh, she fished among some papers on her desk, pulled out a sheet, and handed it to me. "Here's the record of consignment." She ran her finger underneath a sentence. "It clearly states all five volumes were offered."

"I don't give a damn what it says. Your 'reliable' consignor falsified the record then. I *know* there was only one volume. I checked." I clicked on my phone and brought up the photo image of the frontispiece I'd taken. "Here, I took a photo."

She backed away a few steps and crossed her arms. "John, that doesn't prove anything. We're good mates, you and I. But don't try putting one over on me. This situation is bad enough without you … distorting it."

I was on the verge of flinging back a retort when I remembered the tiny scratches I'd seen on the wooden box. "It's customary for any house to check on an article before putting it up for sale, right?"

"Yes."

"And did you in this case?"

"Stop giving me the third degree. Of course I did."

"You just looked inside the wooden box though, correct? You didn't actually open the covers."

Amy wilted, her face falling for an instant; then she sidestepped my question. "This discussion is getting us nowhere." She glanced at her watch. "In five minutes I've got to go on deck. I imagine you'll want to see Ewan to sort this out?"

"Absolutely."

"I'll make sure he'll be at the library tomorrow."

"That's good—thanks."

"I'll let you know, but I can't talk to him directly until I've cleared everything with Sherrods' solicitors. Now I've got to run. I don't want to look a total wreck when I break the bad news to my boss. You'll have to excuse me."

She turned to leave, her shoulders slumped, and said despondently, "John, I'm shattered. And so sorry you're in this position. But now that this is a legal issue it's best we don't talk more about it."

I wasn't happy with Amy's dodging the question of whether or not I had a complete book but my heart went out to her all the same. She gave me a quick hug. "I'm on your side, Amy. Don't forget, if it's in my power to clear this whole thing up, I will."

With a beleaguered smile she hurried out the door.

Six

The sun vanished behind a heavy bank of cloud, and London, one of the most beautiful cities in the world, felt desolate. Amy hadn't actually seen the book itself, of that I was sure. Had she also been warned it was dangerous, or had she trusted Ewan Fraser too much? At this point it didn't matter. It was my word against hers. Amy and I liked each other, but she was in a very junior position. The entire issue would swiftly move to the chief curator and Sherrods' lawyers. If they could divert some of the blame by fingering me, they wouldn't hesitate.

I had no real proof the theft in my hotel room even took place. If anyone had noticed a man lingering in front of the hotel, they'd hardly have paid him any heed. I could see the wheels churning at Sherrods right now. They'd claim that I'd stolen it myself with the intent to sell it on the black market. And worse, with the book gone, who was to say the copy they offered at auction was the same one listed by Interpol?

I had a prearranged appointment with Arthur Newhouse, the solicitor who originally wrote to me, to hand over the book, assuming I was the successful bidder. I hadn't told him about the theft and fully intended to keep the appointment to learn the identity of my anonymous client and unravel this mystery.

En route to his office I stopped off at a couple of bookstores to see whether I could buy a translation but met with no success. At a printing shop I faxed my theft report to New Scotland Yard and did a quick check of my email. A well-intended message came in from a business friend in New York saying word had already leaked out about my involvement with Sherrods and a stolen book.

I swore under my breath. It had been only a couple of hours since I talked to Amy. Bad news travels faster than the speed of light.

My last experience dealing with a stolen relic from Iraq proved to me that once a rumor grabs hold, it's hard to control it even when you're close to the source. From this far away it would be impossible. My only hope lay in recovering the volume that had touched my hands so briefly and finding the other four.

I entered Lincoln's Inn through a gatehouse, a handsome red-brick structure accented with white limestone and two turrets joined by a crenulated wall bearing the Lovell coat of arms.

The Newhouse chambers occupied a prestigious spot on the third floor of a posh bank of buildings at New Square. Framed by a double archway, a wide, formidable iron door buttressed with rivets and topped with sharp pikes formed the entrance. A handsome coach house–style lamp with a flickering gas flame hung overhead. Did all this fortification protect the lawyers from the screaming mobs or the disgruntled clients from their lawyers?

One of Newhouse's clerks came out to greet me in the reception room. "I regret to tell you Mr. Newhouse has been delayed," he said. "He'll be back by 2 P.M." He gestured toward the giant grandfather clock stationed beside an umbrella rack as if I wasn't aware of the time.

"That's fine. I'm happy to wait."

"Glad you're able to accommodate us, sir. Would you take a seat? Might I ask our Jennie to bring you some tea?" Our Jennie, a sharply attractive, narrow-faced young woman seated at the reception desk, looked up without smiling. She appeared to think pouring tea was about as enticing a proposition as doing overtime on Christmas Eve.

"I'm fine. Thanks anyway," I said.

The fellow gave me a brief nod, excused himself, and disappeared down the hall. The only seat on offer was a rose damask settee so uncomfortable it felt as though it had been stuffed with cement. Jennie typed away on her desktop in silence. The grandfather clock chimed the half hour and ticked away the minutes. I wondered whether the police had already told Newhouse about the theft.

On my phone, I launched a browser and searched for the author under his real name. For his work to become a sensation in his lifetime was remarkable enough, but Basile had accomplished the near impossible—his words were still read and lauded centuries after his death. He was both a poet and court administrator, and also, most notably, one of the earliest Europeans to collect and transcribe oral folk tales.

Shunted from one patron to another, Basile was often treated miserably by his wealthy sponsors. He opined that "no life could be more unstable or fuller of anxiety," and "you serve now, you serve later, you serve today, you serve tomorrow and then ... suddenly it's night for you. You're told to turn yourself around and get out!"

I could relate to that. The more I read, the more I found myself intrigued by the man. He was the life of the party wherever he went. His poems and bawdy, comic stories were much sought after. One of his early translators described the anthology as being among the "oldest, richest, and most artistic of all books of popular tales."

Basile wrote literary versions of folk tales in the opulent, overblown Baroque tradition. But some of his fables were scurrilous and brutal, reminiscent of Swift's dark, sharp-pronged satire.

"Mr. Madison?"

I'd become so engrossed in Basile's life I hadn't realized Arthur Newhouse stood before me. I clicked off my phone. We shook hands and he showed me to his office.

The solicitor knew how to make an impression. Although I preferred the flair of Italian design, Newhouse was impeccably turned out in a British-tailored charcoal pinstripe suit and twill silk tie. A cabinet with a computer and files sat against one wall, the only sign this room was actually used for work. He took his seat behind a beautiful Georgian-era mahogany desk that held photographs in silver frames and a quill pen in a holder.

A Francis Bacon painting hung on one wall among several other works by well-known artists. I'd always found Bacon's portraits shocking. He painted the condemned soul, his wraithlike figures with howling mouths and tormented anatomies so convincingly rendered, just looking at them was painful. Bacon suffered from terrifying bouts of asthma all his life. I'd often wondered whether those contorted mouths expressed his own awful feelings of suffocation.

The grotesque image seemed out of place in a solicitor's office; then again, owning an original Bacon was a symbol of status and wealth and perhaps that's what he wanted to convey. It must have set him back millions.

Newhouse opened with an apology. "I'm terribly sorry to be so late. It's not my habit, I assure you. I do hope our Jennie made you comfortable in the interim."

"Yes, of course."

Apropos of nothing he waved a pale hand toward the quill. "Used by Jonathan Swift. The nib broke as he was finishing a passage. You can still see the spray of ink in the original manuscript."

I assumed this was intended to set me at ease and perhaps demonstrate he was a man of means if I hadn't been sharp enough to conclude that from his art.

"That's fascinating," I said politely. "But I'm curious about your client. Why did he choose me to represent him ... or her, as the case may be? Why pay for me to come all the way from New York when there are dozens of talented London dealers?"

He tossed back a sweep of flaxen hair that had fallen across his forehead. "Come, Mr. Madison, your talents are well regarded even on this side of the pond. My client—and it is a 'him'—was very determined, perhaps I could say, even desperate, to acquire the book. And yet his funds were limited. He put aside every penny of his capital to buy it.

"To win the auction he needed someone with a quick mind. A skilled bidder. He'd heard about your success last year when a George Stubbs equine painting was auctioned." Newhouse had rested his arms on the desk. He leaned forward and clasped his hands. "To be perfectly frank, I advised against hiring an American. And you a kebab, no less." He punctuated this slur with a wink as if to show it was all in good fun. "As you pointed out we have a surfeit of talent right here. All the same, my client made up his mind and wouldn't hear of anyone else."

The insult about my Turkish origins proved that for all his expensive trappings, Newhouse lacked class. And I didn't buy his explanation. The Stubbs purchase involved some sleight of hand but it was hardly earth shattering. "He chose me solely because of that?"

"You must have realized my client's desire to remain anonymous already telegraphed a very private nature. Discretion was paramount. He was afraid a London dealer might, well, indulge in chatter, as it were."

Here then was the real reason. "What was so important about the book that your client felt the need to hide his purchase of it?

And the reference to a malevolent history in your letter—what did you mean by that?"

"Afraid I can't tell you. I'm not privy to that information."

It felt frustrating to make so little headway. As Newhouse was my only contact, I'd hoped for more.

In an obvious effort to change the subject, he brought our talk sharply around to the purpose of our meeting. "Were you successful in acquiring it?" His heavy, reddish eyelids blinked rapidly. "I'd be happy to take possession of the article now if it's all the same to you." He opened a desk drawer, removed a small bottle of ink and a booklet, and reached for the quill. "Excuse this little penchant of mine. I like to use the quill for my official signature."

"With a broken nib?"

Coloring slightly, he said, "The nib was replaced. Some time ago."

I smiled. "Of course you realize that by repairing it you've degraded its value—that is, if Swift ever did use it. We kebabs know a fake when we see one."

He ignored my rejoinder and cleared his throat. "Let's get to the business at hand, shall we? What was the book's final price?"

"Well under your client's maximum. One hundred twenty-four thousand pounds."

Newhouse leaned back in his chair and raised his eyebrows. "Very good. We hadn't dared hope for a decent sum. People seem willing to pay anything these days."

The praise felt genuine. I smiled in response to his compliment.

"I'll take possession of it then." He bent his head to write in the notebook. When he saw I hadn't reached for my case, he looked up abruptly. "Well?"

"I can't give it to you. Someone stole it from me last night." I watched his pale eyes closely but didn't find the flash of surprise that should have been there.

He dropped the quill, ink splattering his receipt book. "This comes as a shock, Mr. Madison. Sherrods has our money already?"

"Of course. They wouldn't let the book out of their sight without the funds."

"I see. Now tell me, what happened *exactly*?"

"A man robbed me. He took the book and some rare gold coins. He knew a great deal about me. My name, my occupation, and the daily routines of family members in New York." My voice faltered as I recalled the threat against Evelyn. "How did he know I was your point man for the purchase?"

"I've no idea, I can assure you of that. Perhaps a contact at Sherrods?"

"I suppose that's possible." I remembered how forthcoming Amy had been with me about the other bidders. "I've learned the book consisted of five separate volumes. Was your client expecting to buy the entire book or just one volume?"

Newhouse sat up straighter. "Why, the whole book of course. As it was, the price turned out to be very dear. He'd never pay that much for only part of it."

"Well, he'll be doubly disappointed then. Sherrods offered only the one volume."

"This is a disaster! You've reported this to the police and your insurance company, I hope."

"Of course, right away. I gave the police a preliminary report last night and am due to be interviewed at New Scotland Yard tomorrow morning. As for insurance, you'll have to get in touch with my broker, Jack Edison. He's handling it personally. He'll take a bit of time with this. You know how these companies are. Tons of paperwork. Always is in the case of art theft. In fact, he's out of the country right now."

This time his cheeks flared to crimson; there was no hiding his anger. "All the same, a significant amount of money is involved. I can tell you, Mr. Madison, I've been practicing law for over twenty years. The book was in your possession and stolen or not, you are responsible. I can assure you I'll press the case to its limit. You have my word on that."

"I understand it's a difficult situation all around. The onus should be on the auction house to straighten things out."

"That's a fine thought, Mr. Madison. It disappeared while in *your* possession." He stared at me accusingly.

"Yes, but it was reported stolen by the owner *before* it was even auctioned. I'll be happy to provide you with the link to the Interpol report. Given the circumstances, I'd like to know who your client is, to tell him this in person."

I expected Newhouse to refuse my request outright or at least to express dismay at the new information. Instead, he pulled up his gangly frame, took out his cellphone, and abruptly left the room.

His reaction was unusual to say the least. He hadn't pressed me for any more details about the attack in my hotel room, instead immediately mentioned the insurance money. And despite his fit of temper, I'd sensed underlying anxiety in his voice.

After a few minutes the office door swung open. Newhouse didn't retreat behind his desk this time but faced me, quite agitated. The words spilled out of him. "Ordinarily I wouldn't reveal my client's identity; however, new circumstances have arisen that are troubling indeed. His name is Charles Renwick. My firm has represented his interests for many years. He owns a small publishing company producing high-quality, limited-edition books. Illustrated stories, books in great demand by collectors around the world. They sell for substantial sums."

He paused to sweep his hair back again and I thought what a girlish gesture it seemed. "I've been quite worried about him lately," Newhouse confessed. "That book went to his head. He'd become infatuated with acquiring the damned thing. Utter foolishness. And look where it's got him."

"Well, I appreciate your candor, Mr. Newhouse. Could you arrange for me to see him as soon as possible?"

Newhouse turned even paler. "I'm afraid not. Charles's shop was burgled last night and no one can find him. Terrible business. Blood at the scene. He's feared dead."

Seven

Newhouse set up an appointment for me with Renwick's business partner, Tye Norris, at the publishing house they ran together. Norris reluctantly agreed to meet me later in the day after the police cleared the crime scene. With almost two hours to kill before I met him, I found a pub, and with a draft of crisp Wolf Ale before me, checked Interpol to see whether any of the volumes had been recovered. They hadn't.

I was quickly running out of options. I turned my attention to the topic of fairy tales in an attempt to discover why someone would go to such lengths to possess a rare and early version. The sum total of my knowledge about them is comparable to most people's: I first heard the stories as a child when I wouldn't have thought to question their meaning. Evelyn lovingly read to me from picture books every night before bed. I didn't know at the time that she couldn't read English. She made up the stories based on the illustrations. According to her, the Pied Piper kept rats as pets and stopped them from biting children with his music; Sleeping Beauty died because of her sins; Oscar Wilde's selfish giant was an evil Jinn. I realized how far some of her versions missed the mark only when I saw Disney's cartoons for the first time.

On my cell's Web browser, I used the rest of the time to refresh my memory about fairy-tale authors. People chatted amiably away in the background of the pleasant, old-fashioned pub as I settled into the comfortable leather bar stool, my elbows propped up on the mahogany counter, and began to read. According to one article, the first folklorist to put together a collection of tales was another Italian, Giovanni Francesco Straparola. His anthology, *The Facetious Nights of Straparola*, was divided into sections of twelve stories referred to as "nights," similar to Basile's division of each volume into a "day." Although I'd never have recognized it from the title, Straparola's story "Biancabella and the Snake" was a version of "Beauty and the Beast." This in itself I found interesting. Like most people, I'd thought the famous fairy tales originated with the Grimm brothers.

I was on firmer ground when it came to Charles Perrault and remembered reading somewhere that his inspiration for Sleeping Beauty's castle was the Château d'Ussé overlooking the Indre Valley. His most famous stories included "Red Riding Hood," "Cinderella," "Puss in Boots," and "Bluebeard."

But when I think of fairy tales, it's still the Grimms who come first to my mind. I knew their stories although not much about their lives. The article described the brothers as serious scholars who promoted German culture and shared a mission to popularize folk literature, initially for adults. They collected oral stories from friends and colleagues and began to publish anthologies. Wilhelm did most of the writing and editing and transformed many of the tales by giving them a Germanic feel, adding Christian motifs and elements of pagan mythology. Apparently, the dark and explicit sexuality in some tales caused a furor among many German readers, so later, the Grimms tamed the stories and added moral lessons to them. I found the contrast between the two countries fascinating. Two hundred years earlier, far from offending any of his countrymen, Basile's own book of sensual tales was a runaway bestseller.

A Web search turned up portraits of both the author, Giambattista Basile, and the illustrator, José de Ribera.

Giambattista Basile and José de Ribera

I gasped at Basile's portrait. My theory about Alessio being a descendant of Basile's was spot on. They were mirror images of each other. Clearly, Alessio had stolen an object he considered his birthright.

By now it was late afternoon and the pub lights switched on. I shut off my phone, finished my drink, and headed for the nearest tube stop.

After a long ride on a train crammed to the gills, I arrived at Southwark station and headed to the address where Newhouse told me I'd find Charles Renwick's business partner.

Southwark was so old it was referenced in the *Domesday Book* of 1086. Buildings burned to the ground in the Southwark fire of 1212 and hundreds of people died on the newly constructed London Bridge, caught between raging fires at both ends.

Home to the bawdy and licentious, the area once hosted both the red-light district and the infamous Marshalsea Prison, as well as the Rose and Globe theaters. The new Shakespeare's Globe Theatre and the Tate Modern set off a wave of gentrification. Pockets of rundown buildings remained, not yet assembled by some ambitious realtor. Renwick's business was located near Chancel Street in one of these, a dim corner composed of residences and aged commercial outlets.

C. Renwick Fine Books did not appear to be a thriving publishing house. It was an old two-story structure of bricks so sooty it looked as if the facade hadn't been touched since the Great Fire. The front window was streaked with dust; a dirty white blind obscured the view inside. The nameplate beside the door had the dull greenish tinge of brass that hadn't seen a cleaning cloth for years.

Something else sparked my interest. A small carved stone figure dangled from an aluminum bracket over the door, a Babylonian amulet intended to ward off demons. Strange to see such an exotic charm hanging here. I tapped the enameled horse-head knocker and waited.

I heard a shuffling sound inside. A hand shifted the blind. A gnome-like, white-haired fellow peered out at me and promptly dropped the blind. After much clicking of locks and sliding of bolts the door opened. The man stood to one side so I could enter. "Do come in, Mr. Madison," he said. "I was told to expect you."

In stark contrast to the exterior, the front room was attractive and orderly. A polished oak floor and elegant William Morris Acanthus wallpaper of intertwined leaves fit well with the room's antique furniture. Edwardian lamps with cut-glass shades cast a gentle ambient light. Against the back and east walls handsome walnut display cases held what I presumed were the firm's published books. They stood on tilted wooden stands to reveal illustrated pages. My eye caught an edition of Hans Christian Andersen's *The Little Mermaid*, its gorgeously designed first letter, *F*, with a mermaid ingeniously curled around its tail.

Smashed glass on one of the cases reminded me about last night's violence. Purplish dust lay over many of the surfaces in the room.

Norris saw me observing it. "Newhouse told you about our burglary, I understand. The police technicians have been over everything for fingerprints. That purple stuff will be the devil to clean off. They've cleared it now—the police—and given me permission to get on with things. Not that I have the heart to without Charles, mind you."

I smiled sympathetically, imagining how shaken up the old fellow must be. "Arthur Newhouse told me about the break-in. Is there any news yet of Mr. Renwick?"

The poor man looked as if he hadn't slept for a week. When he spoke, his lips quivered. "No word. Nothing at all. I'm not quite sure what to do." His glasses slipped down his nose and he pushed them back with a weary sigh. "Charles was here at the time of the robbery—that much we do know. I spoke to him on the phone right before it happened. He was just putting on his coat, getting ready to leave." He looked around. "I've not been able to touch the floor, although he would be most distressed if he saw this mess."

Glancing at the shards of glass on the hardwood, I noticed a rivulet of dried blood in one corner. It ran underneath the display case.

"We'd best talk in the shop," Norris said flatly. "I find it too upsetting to stay for long in this room."

Norris locked up and led me through a double set of leaded-pane doors. The "shop," as he called it, yawned in front of us, a vast space at least sixty feet deep. Two massive, antiquated printing presses stood off to one side. Norris explained that a large copper vat sitting on a heating coil was a paper digester. One wall held high banks of narrow metal trays in different sizes. These were shut, so I couldn't see what they contained. I guessed printing plates and movable type. Several large rectangular tables had been placed side by side and stacked with papers of all kinds, colored leather hides, spools, cutting tools, and implements associated, I assumed, with various elements of the printing process. The place had the vaguely musty but pleasant smell of an old bookstore, the only modern touch, rows of Phantom LED linear lighting strips overhead.

"Those lights are the closest approximation to sunlight we could find," Norris said when he noticed me looking at them. "Charles abhorred fluorescents. He believed they distorted one's vision and hence affected the quality of the final printed page. Candescents are just as bad and ultraviolet destroys books." He looked at me over the top of his glasses. "Before we get started, may I offer you a cup of tea? I've just made a fresh pot."

"That would be great. Thanks."

He went over to a small cabinet that held a sink for washing up, a hot plate with a kettle, and a coffee maker. Something about him bothered me. He seemed familiar but I was certain I'd never met him. And then it struck me. He bore an astounding resemblance to Pinocchio's Geppetto. The kindly Geppetto with the black brows, glasses tucked on his bulbous red nose, sturdy mustache, and constant expression of delighted surprise. Norris was practically a carbon copy.

"Did Newhouse tell you about the theft when he called earlier? Of the book I won for Mr. Renwick, I mean."

Norris, I sensed, was normally a cheerful person and likely had trouble expressing negativity; still my question caused him to purse his lips in a slight frown. "Yes, indeed he did. Two thefts in one night. And both associated with Charles. Just awful. Not a coincidence, do you think?"

"Far from it. In fact I think they may have been committed by the same man." I thought of the woman posing as a New York cop and corrected myself. "If not one man then a group working together." The room felt cool and I felt glad of the hot tea. I wrapped my hands around the mug to warm them. "Were valuable books taken from here as well?"

"Just a minute, and I'll show you what they stole." Norris opened one of the lower trays in a cabinet, pulled out a file, and handed it to me. "Not books. But they did take this. One of the valuables Charles had from the time he was a boy living in the Orient—the Near East rather; I suppose that's the correct term to use now. He kept it on display in the front room."

I looked at the photograph. I had no idea what to make of the strange-looking circular stone, although I immediately recognized the markings as cuneiform writing. I held the photograph up to the light to get a better look. "Do you know what it is?"

Norris shook his head. "Can't tell you. Renwick himself didn't know its exact purpose but it was a prized object. He went over there this past August."

"Where exactly?"

"Iraq."

"In the middle of a war?"

"He told me he'd gone to Basrah. Our English soldiers are in charge there, you know, and compared to Baghdad it's relatively quiet. Frankly, I'm not convinced he told me the truth. I suspected he said that to reassure me."

"Curious the thief would take this and leave other valuables behind."

"You're right," Norris said. "A first English edition of Andrew Lang's *Blue Fairy Book* and one of Perrault's original publications from 1855 were both in the front room—worth a great deal. I've removed them to the bank for safekeeping."

"Does that round stone object have any connection to the book I won at auction for Mr. Renwick?"

Norris lifted his glasses to rub his eyes. "I believe it did. Just what I cannot say. Charles was not a talkative man at the best of times. Very close-mouthed about it."

As I drank my tea, I wondered why Renwick had been so guarded about the object. I didn't want to upset Norris any further but had to bring the conversation around to my attacker. "Did Newhouse tell you what happened to me?"

"I got the gist of it. You were assaulted by a stranger?"

"That's right. A peculiar man. He carried a cane with a white horse carved on it. Black hair and mustache. Goatee. Black hat and long coat."

Norris reacted as though I'd struck him. "My goodness! A similar person came into the shop yesterday afternoon. Said he was interested in buying one of our books. I explained we didn't sell them directly. He argued with me. Finally I agreed to let him have a children's fairy-tale book just to get rid of him."

My nerves tingled on hearing this. "Did he say anything else?"

"No. But he had a strange quality about him." Norris's voice grew hoarse and I had to lean in to hear him. "And he didn't even pretend to give me an honest name. At first I thought he was trying to make some kind of joke."

"Gian Alessio Abbattutis—is that what he said?"

"Why, no. Wilhelm Grimm—one of the German fairy-tale brothers, the younger of the two. Can you believe that? Why make up a name I'd recognize as false?"

I mused out loud, "Maybe he came to check your place out because he knew he'd be back later to rob you."

Norris took off his glasses and rubbed his eyes once more. "He waited till after I left for the day. Until Charles was alone. I fear I'll never see Charles again."

"How can you be so sure?"

"The police are still looking but I know he's gone. I'm just waiting to hear where they've found his remains. Charles was a man of … shall I say, determined punctuality and habit. Even though he lived in a flat a mile away, this was his home. He'd arrive every morning at precisely eight. Neat as a pin he was. Dressed in a suit every day I knew him. He'd hang up his jacket as soon as he came in and put on an apron to work in. At seven thirty in the evening, promptly, he'd take his hat, lock the door, and cross the street to the public house for a glass of sherry and his evening meal. His faithful routine, six days a week. On Sundays he'd walk in Kensington Park and take afternoon tea in the Orangery. The only exceptions were regulated holidays and his three-week excursion abroad every August. Set your clock by him, you could."

"How old is Mr. Renwick?"

"Seventy-two. Not that he held any truck with celebrations."

"You've worked together for a long time I gather."

"From well before we set up the business. We met at Eton. We were outsiders. That's why the two of us were naturally drawn to each other."

"Why outsiders?"

"He was the only boy in the school with a disability. Picked up some sort of pathogen as a youth living with his parents in the Near East. The illness crippled his bones and caused a permanent limp. His spine was badly distorted so he had to walk bent over. And his skin was permanently affected. The other boys nicknamed him the dwarf. A nasty slight. Renwick was short anyway and his spinal deformity forced him to stoop. I was his only friend.

"The bullying drove him into his shell. Like a turtle he was after that, always afraid to stick his neck out into the wide world."

Norris's account of Renwick's suffering struck a nerve. I'd witnessed other kids on the receiving end of the merciless treatment my schoolmates doled out to the weak ones. "Kids can be cruel. What about his family?"

"He came from blue blood; his father was a diplomat in the British foreign service—a vice-consul in Persia and later promoted to ambassador to Iraq. Charles regaled me with stories of how his father had to pretend to lose at backgammon when he played with the Hashemite King Faisal II. 'Wars have been ignited over less,' he'd say.

"And I was a scholarship student without a penny to my name. No silver spoon for me. We were both odd types; that's why we sought each other out. That and our dedication to books. From Eton we went on to Cambridge together."

"What did you study?"

"Comparative literature."

"Did that include fairy tales?"

Norris smiled. "Yes."

"Do you know why Renwick wanted Basile's *The Tale of Tales*?"

Norris's eyes brightened. "I can show you more easily than telling you."

I followed him over to the printing presses. Norris ran his hand lovingly over one of the machines. "A Kluge letterpress. Impossible to duplicate this quality nowadays. We use movable iron type. This was Charles's specialty. He had a genius for selecting a typeface that perfectly suited the personality of the book. You can't get the same look with computers. The text they produce is too perfect, too homogeneous. And Charles brooked no mistakes. He almost drove us into bankruptcy once when he destroyed an entire printing of a custom folio ordered by a collector. There'd been a slight error. I insisted we could print a new page and rebind but he wouldn't hear of it.

"The codex, the custom of binding books, is relatively new, you know. Books used to be sold in sections, or quires, as we term them. And customers had to pay to have their books bound themselves. At our shop we bring in an outside expert who knows how to hand bind. Otherwise, everything is done by us."

We walked over to one of the rectangular tables. Norris explained their starting point was always with the spirit of the book. "All the other decisions flow from that," he said. He carefully picked a finished book from a shelf and removed it from its plastic sleeve.

"Charles's pride and joy was our fairy-tale editions. He loved the stories as a child, became a collector of them in university, and went on to publish them." He put the book on the table for me to leaf through. "This is the true tale of Cinderella, based on a story by Giambattista Basile, not the cartoon version children are familiar with today. Perrault must take the blame for that."

"How so?"

"He modified it to make it more palatable to genteel readers. 'Cinderella' is an old story, although not originally European. We think it came from China as an oral folk tale. Giambattista Basile was the first to name the heroine Cinderella."

"What's the other version?"

"Basile painted her as a schemer who hated her stepmother and wanted her governess to marry her father instead. She and her governess conspired to murder the stepmother, plotting to push the woman into a chest and break her neck with the lid. Though the plan worked, her governess turned the tables. Soon after she married the father, she favored her own daughters and forced Cinderella to become a kitchen slave."

"Amazing the story could change so much. Those heroines always seem to be victimized by evil stepmothers or queens."

"That's true, and the men frequently come off as quite passive—taking a back seat to the main action, so to speak. They turn from a frog into a prince at the end," he chortled, "and marry the girl who's done all the work of carrying the narrative. Or a king will start the action by forbidding his daughter to marry her beloved and the rest of the tale is about how she cleverly outsmarts her father."

I laughed at this, not having thought about the stories from that point of view.

"Stepmothers were a later substitute for the wicked mother. The Grimm brothers made that change in 'Snow White,' for example. But the women at the center of these early stories were assertive and quite imaginative in devising ways to escape their fate. Basile's tales were often quite black, full of sexual innuendo. The young women he portrayed were not at all like today's passive princesses. They would ultimately succeed by astutely manipulating the people around them. Quite feisty ladies, I guess you would say."

For a moment Norris appeared to forget I was there as he murmured, "Charles loved what he called 'the tales' the most. One of his few happy memories was being read to by his nan before bed. He believed they were true, you know."

I smiled, thinking of Evelyn. "True? Not just stories?"

"He thought they were based on real events that occurred long ago. Of course, he didn't think that as a child. He developed that theory later, as he began to travel and read widely."

Norris saw me admiring the font they'd used on the Cinderella book. "That's an old Garamond font. One of the originals. Charles searched high and low for the type pieces. Beautiful, isn't it? We commissioned Farrar for the illustrations. The complete printing was sold out before the first book came off the press.

"Our next project would have been an adventure. Charles always wanted to try something original. Sylvia Bellman completed the graphics and we decided to make our own paper for it. Only a month ago we spent several long days gathering willow and cow parsnip for the paper. Autumn is the perfect time because that's when plant cellulose is at its peak. When properly treated, cow parsnip produces a beautiful translucent paper stock.

"You'll know the story—'The Pied Piper of Hamelin,' one of Charles's favorites. The reader will be able to see flora of the meadow like the one the piper led the children through embedded in the pages themselves. I intend to finish it"—his voice trailed off again—"as a tribute to him. It may well be the last book our firm publishes."

"The Pied Piper" was one of the more macabre fairy tales. The cheery piper in his colorful clothes leading children to their death seemed an odd and disturbing choice. "Did Renwick think that story too was based on a real event?"

"Indeed he did. And he may have been right about it. Scholars have devoted years attempting to trace the story back to an actual occurrence. Some think it was an analogy for a case of plague that swept through a German village; others believe it to be an early recounting of a particularly lurid case of pedophilia.

"I think that's why he pursued *The Tale of Tales* so obsessively. He wanted the early versions of the stories so he could find the germ of truth in them." Norris cleared his throat. "He'd talked himself into believing that one of those stories had origins in the Middle

East and linked directly to his childhood illness. He referred to it as a *plague tale* and had himself convinced the author hid some guide or code in the book that pointed to the source of a deathly contagion. Pure folly, in my opinion."

Eight

Norris shook his head, his white forelock bouncing as he did so. "Charles was always a fanciful man, but that theory of his went beyond all bounds of rationality."

I had to agree with him. The notion of a virulent disease having anything to do with a fictional tale sounded preposterous. Still, it helped explain Renwick's warning about the book. "Which story was he referring to?"

"Why, I'd almost think you took this nonsense seriously too. I don't know which title, Charles wouldn't tell me, but it was one of the four famous ones I'm sure. 'Sleeping Beauty,' 'Snow White,' 'The Pied Piper,' or 'Beauty and the Beast.'"

"You said earlier Renwick thought the author included a secret reference to a real location in the book? A map or a series of directions?"

"Yes, something like that; I can't tell you more. I simply don't know because Charles kept it to himself. It wasn't his custom to hide things from me, but something about that book changed him. And it frightened me. 'Better you stay entirely out of it,' he said."

This tallied with the admonition I'd received in the solicitor's letter. "Newhouse said the book had a repellent history. Do you know what he meant?"

I caught a fleeting look of disapproval on Norris's face when I said this. "I have no idea. But from the time Charles first mentioned that blasted book, his personality changed. One day I came into the shop and he seemed higher than a kite because he'd just learned it was to be offered at auction. And then almost overnight, he sank into a deep depression. It wasn't at all like him to display such mood swings. I was very worried and said as much but his behavior continued. He'd come into the shop with red-rimmed eyes and I knew he hadn't slept a wink. Normally he was quite soft-spoken but he'd snap at me for the merest trifles. He began to study the most gruesome subjects—Greek chimeras and medieval exorcists. Those books are still here." He picked a few off the shelf and handed them to me.

All of them looked to date back a century or more ago, reprinted in modern formats. Leafing through them, I shivered a little at the illustrations. They reminded me of José de Ribera's frightening images. Most of the ideas contained within them reflected sheer superstition, but if people actually believed that stuff, I supposed they could do harm.

"One day I found him, just over there"—Norris nodded toward a corner of the shop—"curled up in a ball, shaking as if he'd had the fright of his life. Claimed a monster was hunting him. A demon, he called it. He lost weight after that, and rapidly, at least two stone." He dropped his voice, though we were alone. "Very alarming, it was. You can imagine, I began to fear for his sanity. And then just when he seemed to be tipping into a permanent breakdown, his mood reversed. He learned you'd agreed to bid on the book for him. Suddenly, everything was rosy again."

Norris shook his head ruefully. "It's almost as if the tales he revered all his life began to take over his mind. Had he been a more well-rounded person, had a life outside of work, things might have been different."

"How do you mean? He didn't have any family? No wife or children?"

"I'm afraid not. Excessively shy, he was. Felt he'd be rejected because of how he looked. 'No woman wants a crooked man,' he'd say. My own dear wife, bless her heart, tried to introduce him to several ladies. Lovely women. But to no avail.

"In third form Charles developed an infatuation with a sister of one of the other boys. A beautiful girl, although he couldn't hope to attract her. To his amazement she invited him out to tea one day but she stood him up. One of the boys put her up to it. They ribbed him mercilessly about it."

A moment later Norris added, "Speaking of women, one particular lady appears to have caught his eye. I mention it only because it seemed strange. Again, out of character for Charles."

"Oh?"

Norris pulled out the Cinderella book and took a photo from between the back leaves. "Here she is." He handed it to me.

The photo must have been taken on a cheap camera, perhaps even a Polaroid, because the color had faded to sepia tones. The woman had been caught off guard and was clearly not posing for the picture. She was young, around twenty, and had an enchanting face, although you would not call her classically beautiful. Rosy lips and alabaster skin, enhanced by expressive dark eyes. A wariness in her look and in the way she held her body suggested tension or strain.

An older man stood behind her, his hand possessively planted on her shoulder. Her father perhaps? He too seemed unaware of the camera trained upon him. He had the air of someone always in command and his thin lips were turned down in a slight frown, as if whatever situation they'd been captured in tested his patience.

It may have been due to the faded color of the poor-quality

photo, but his skin, although wrinkle free, looked artificially bronzed, as if he'd applied cheap tanning lotion. It contrasted oddly with his thick helmet of snow-white hair. The background was out of focus so gave me no clues as to where the photo had been shot. I turned it over and saw on the back a note scrawled so hastily it was difficult to make out. I thought it said *Talia, Aug. 18/2000*.

"Do you know who she is?"

"Afraid not. Goodness, I haven't been much help, have I?"

"On the contrary." I smiled, genuinely appreciative of the time he'd spent with me. "You've given me a lot to think about."

I handed the photo back. "Is there any chance he had an English translation of Basile's entire book?"

Norris thought for a moment. "Offhand I'm not certain, but Charles may have done. Let me see."

He ran his fingers along the books lining the shelves above the table and then said, "Ah, here they are." He pulled out two heavy tomes and flipped to the copyright page of one of them. "This looks quite complete. Editor is Norman Mosley Penzer. It's based on a translation from the Neapolitan to Italian by Benedetto Croce. Not terribly recent though—published in 1932, and I believe that might well be the most comprehensive English version."

"Is there any chance I could borrow them for a few days?" Seeing a frown begin to grow on his face, I quickly added, "It would help a lot to get to the bottom of the theft."

Norris hesitated for a moment as he wrestled with my request. "I don't know. Charles was quite possessive about his belongings. But the circumstances are extraordinary, aren't they? I'll have to ask you for a note acknowledging that you have them."

"Of course. I'd be glad to." Norris got a receipt book from his desk and I decided to press my luck. "Given how long Renwick sought the book, I imagine he did a fair amount of research. Are there any records?"

"That's likely. Nevertheless his personal papers must remain private. I wouldn't even dare to go through them unless authorized by his executor."

"Understood," I said. "That would be Arthur Newhouse, I imagine."

Norris nodded. He'd been very obliging. I thanked him and promised to let him know of my progress. He showed me the door and I stepped out into the damp London evening.

My mind spun with all these new revelations. Renwick believed one of the tales in Basile's book contained a clue to the origins of a deadly sickness he'd contracted as a boy in the Middle East. His obsession with the book therefore likely had little to do with its monetary value.

My cell buzzed. A text came from Amy confirming that Ewan Fraser would be at the library tomorrow. The first direct flight I could get to Naples was at one in the afternoon the following day. I'd scheduled the police interview for the morning, so I'd have to bunk in another hotel for the night. I booked a room at a bed and breakfast in Wapping and hopped on the tube at Southwark station.

Much as I loved my home city, I'd exchange the New York subway for the London underground any day. On my first trip to London as a kid I'd savored the rush through that dark, round cylinder. With my nose pressed against the glass, the tunnel walls seemed to fly past only inches away. I'd pretend to be in a rocket, barreling toward the center of the earth. Samuel told me the term *padded cell* came from the early trains that had no windows and buttoned upholstery. London rush-hour commuters probably felt not much had changed since then.

I liked the way each station had its own unique character. Baker Street with the silhouette of Sherlock Holmes printed on a wall; Waterloo with the wonderful spiral of four hundred steps down into the bowels of the city. I'd heard somewhere a ghost station, now closed to the public, underneath the British Museum still had crumbling posters on its walls from its use as a shelter during the Second World War.

I found a seat between a guy with his nose between the pages of the *Guardian* and a woman wearing a full-tilt burka. When I glanced at her she averted her gaze and clutched the shopping bag on her lap a little tighter.

I noticed an old man at the end of the car staring at me. He wore a fifties-style fedora and sat bent over as if he were unable to straighten his spine. Norris's description of Charles Renwick flashed through my mind. Would Renwick suddenly show up like this, knowing the police must be combing the streets for him?

My stop came next. The man got ready to disembark. When he left the train and began to climb the stairs I followed him. At the top of the stairs he turned and raised his hat and then held out his hand, palm up. He gave me a ghastly grin and pointed his forefinger at his empty palm. Not Renwick, but a beggar. I slipped him a quid and hastened away.

London real estate prices had grown so astronomically high, even professionals earning salaries on the lower end couldn't afford to live there anymore. Wapping too had succumbed. A ramshackle collection of maritime warehouses and sailors' shacks had been converted to prestigious condominiums and trendy public houses, its seafaring past now a ripe tourist trap.

The cold drizzle, somewhere between a wet mist and a light rain, hadn't let up. Lamps cast pools of light on cobblestone squares, interspersed with long stretches of gloom. In the distance I heard the forlorn toll of a church bell. The Thames was just ahead; already I could smell the dank water. I followed the road near the river's edge in search of a place to get a meal.

Slanting amber light from the front windows of a pub beckoned me inside. The Prospect of Whitby had an old flagstone floor, blackened wood beams in the Tudor spirit, and a low stone hearth with a merry fire. I felt as if I'd just stepped back into history. At the rear, tall leaded-glass windows opened onto a balcony overlooking the Thames.

The bar woman was in a chatty mood, and she volunteered that a man called Hanging Judge Jeffries used to like sitting on the balcony to watch convicts he'd just sentenced swing on a noose. She pointed out that a noose still hung outside. More benignly, Samuel Pepys and Charles Dickens were fond of taking a pint here. Learning that Turner may have drawn inspiration for his sublime paintings from his view in the pub impressed me. The bar woman told me that the place used to be called the Devil's Tavern in a nod to its nefarious patrons. It even had a smugglers' room upstairs.

I finished my meal and stepped outside. The street was empty, with the exception of a lone man in the distance. As he walked under a street lamp his long dark coat and hat became visible. He held his left arm perpendicular to his body in a curiously formal stance, as though he were offering his arm to a lady or carrying something fragile. And indeed he was. The golden covers of the book. This far away, the horse was a mere white flash on the cane he swung as he walked. I quickened my pace. Even with my case banging into my thigh I knew I could overtake him.

Alessio reached a cross street, stepped lightly to the other side, and ducked out of view. I rushed to the corner and saw a space between two buildings blocked off with a wrought-iron partition. I doubted he could scale it and could detect no sign of him through the fancy ironwork or beyond. I slowly scanned the street again.

Somehow he'd managed to hide because I now saw he'd doubled back and was heading in the direction of the pub I'd just come from. As I gave chase, he turned before he reached the tavern and disappeared once again.

People didn't just vanish into thin air and I soon saw where he'd gone. A narrow passageway between the pub and the building next door led to a flight of steps ending at the river. The stairs were slick with spray and I almost slipped before I reached the bottom and set my case down. The gibbet swinging from the pub's balcony loomed in front of me, its iron fastenings creaking as the noose swung slightly in the wind.

It was even darker down here. Water sloshed on the pebbles and detritus at the riverside. A rat slipped along mossy rocks. The ghostly outline of a stationary barge floating out in the Thames emerged from the gloom.

I scoured the line of the river ahead to my right, but could catch no sign of him. Startled by a noise I spun around. Alessio stood beneath the far end of the balcony, leaning on his cane, still clutching the book's gleaming gold covers in the crook of his left arm. Dim light spilled from the windows of the pub above, casting deep shadows that coalesced around him. The shape of the shadow was unnatural and bore no relationship to the outline of his body. As I ran toward him, I wasn't prepared for his next move.

He heaved the book into the river, grunting with the effort. It disappeared beneath the surface only a few feet from the bank. I kept my eye on the point where it entered and sloshed knee deep into the frigid river, groping about on the slimy bottom. My fingers brushed cold metal and I seized it triumphantly. The book would be badly damaged if water had leaked inside. As I lifted it, the clasps fell open and I cried out. It was empty. Alessio had hidden the volume and baited me with the covers.

His cane smacked my temple with a loud crack. Blood burst over my eye. In desperation, I jammed the metal corner of the covers into his chest. He let out a yell and stumbled backward on the slippery pebbles. I rushed at him in a rage. He whipped the cane against my elbow and swore at me in Italian.

I dropped the book and fell backward into the filthy water.

As he bent to give me another blow I gripped his coat with one hand and pulled him with all my strength into the river. Before I had a chance to deal with him the strange sensation I'd felt in the hotel room returned. All my muscles seized. I could no longer grasp the covers and dropped them. My other hand lost its grip on his coat. With mounting terror I fought against the tyranny of this weird paralysis but remained frozen in place, unable to move even a finger. I could still see and hear and I hadn't lost consciousness.

Alessio snatched the golden covers out of the water and waded farther out into the Thames. The river swirled around his chest— it must have been agonizingly cold—but he never took his black eyes from mine. And then he slipped, crumpling like a marionette whose strings had been severed, beneath the oily surface of the water.

The moment he disappeared from view I came out of my trance and plunged in the direction I'd seen him fall, gagging on the water and struggling against the current. I moved my hands in the water blindly, unable to find him, and after a moment or two, fought my way back to the bank grunting and cursing.

From my place on the shore, I saw his cane and hat bobbing along the surface about thirty feet downriver. The white horse's head gleamed on the wavelets, twisting and turning with the water's flow.

Nine

November 18, 2003
Harlem, New York City

After a brutal stretch in Iraq, Nick Shaheen desperately needed the leave. It was hard to say what had been worse—undercover ops before the war broke out or the uncountable near misses on active duty once it had. When he'd been invited to join Special Forces three years ago at the age of twenty-seven, Shaheen considered it an honor. Not many ethnic Arabs were trusted by the U.S. military, especially in sensitive roles. There'd been no question about assigning him to data interpretation; his skills were needed in the field.

A recurring backache from a spinal injury acquired during these years from hell now followed him around like a malicious stalker. "Phantom pain," the doctor declared. Shaheen downed an OxyContin. Powerful stuff to be taking, really, but the only antidote to the ache in his vertebrae. He ate breakfast at his favorite post, the corner table. The waiter brought his El Cubano sandwich. Hot roasted pork, savory mustard, double pickles.

His phone vibrated. He checked caller ID and got a surprise. His commander, Harry Falk, came on the line. "I'm off, you remember?" Shaheen said with his mouth full.

"I know. Something's come up and they want you specifically."

"They who?"

"Request got forwarded via the DTRA."

"Why do they need me?"

"Didn't provide a whole lotta details," Falk said.

"I get all the luck."

"Apparently you're good at your job. I tried to tell them the truth but they insisted."

"I'm on leave."

"You said that already. It's canceled."

"Anybody else on deck for this?"

"Just you. They referred to it as an 'inquiry.'"

"Tell them I'm indisposed."

"Then I'd be lying."

"Seriously, what's this all about?" Shaheen looked longingly at the half-eaten sandwich growing cold on his plate.

"Can't really tell you, Nick. They're hogging the info. I'm just as curious as to why they want *you* and not the CIA. This is happening completely outside normal command."

"What're the coordinates?"

"Some suit named Leonard Best will pick you up. A civilian consultant. For the duration, you're working with him—you're at Amor Cubano, right?"

"Am I that predictable?"

"Does it rain every time I want to go on a picnic?"

"You've never been on a picnic in your life."

A laugh. "Remember to fill me in. I'll be waiting by my phone."

"Sure. You and Angelina. I've barely started eating."

"Yeah, that's likely." His commander hung up.

Shaheen threw a twenty on the table and rose when he saw a man enter the restaurant and head over to him, getting his hand ready for the shake. Leonard Best was on the short side, with glasses that enlarged his weak brown eyes. He wore a Brooks Brothers suit and nondescript tie. Classic bureaucrat. He looked around fifty. Much older than Shaheen, although considerably less weather-beaten.

"Lieutenant Shaheen, Leonard Best." Best's hand felt soft and tentative.

Shaheen returned the handshake with a solid grip. Best handed him a card. Shaheen glanced at it and put it in his pocket while retrieving the plastic case that held his army ID.

Best waved it away. "That won't be necessary."

"I like to observe the formalities all the same." Shaheen offered it again.

Best took it, flipped open the cover, gave it a cursory glance, and handed it back. "I have a car waiting outside. Appreciate you accommodating us on your leave."

"Not a problem," Shaheen said. "I love working on my time off. Things get awfully boring otherwise."

Best looked at him askance, not yet able to discern Shaheen's sarcasm.

"So you're with the DTRA? What's this all about?"

"Actually I'm a consultant, not an employee," Best replied. "If you don't mind, I'll fill you in when we get there. I've got a car and driver waiting outside. Apologies for the cloak-and-dagger stuff."

"Where are we headed to?"

"Not that far. Over on the West Side."

Ignoring honks of rage, their driver strong-armed his way into traffic. Shaheen caught Best looking at him out of the corner of his eye and could tell what he was thinking. Bringing Shaheen in was a serious mistake. His haggard appearance and his dress—worn camouflage pants, Lil Wayne T-shirt, gold necklaces flopping around his neck, and stringy long hair pulled back in a ponytail—weren't fitting, Shaheen knew, even for an officer on his own time. Best probably thought his attitude stank and that he seemed like a smartass. He would no doubt also wonder about the wisdom of using an Iraqi-American man on such a highly sensitive mission.

"Can I ask why you people wanted me in particular?" Shaheen said.

"We were told you're one of the best they have."

"They just don't want to spare their heavy hitters."

Best forced out a smile. "No point in making this any more difficult, Lieutenant; it's not exactly a party for me either. You'll see what I mean soon enough."

At 120th Street West the 1 train shoots out of its dim tunnel into broad daylight. For the next ten blocks it flies past clusters of mid- and high-rise structures and the hind ends of squat brick buildings whose best days are long behind them. Their driver stopped near an enclosed stairway leading up to the 125th Street station. As they emerged from the car, an unfamiliar stench assaulted them. Shaheen had heard the New York Transit Authority planned to renovate these stairwells. Couldn't happen fast enough, he thought to himself. They crossed the street and continued a short distance north until they reached a padlocked chain-link gate between two buildings. Best opened it with a key and they proceeded to the rear of one of the five-story walk-ups fronting on Broadway.

He led Shaheen to a scarred green door with a buzzer pad fixed to the wall. The level-three reinforced door was new and had been purposely defaced to fit in with the area. It had a multi-locking system; the light fixture above it held a camera that recorded all activity within a three-hundred-foot radius. Best pulled out a customized chip key and inserted it beneath the false buzzer. With a click the door swung inward and they entered a hallway constructed of stubbled concrete.

"What is this place?" Shaheen asked. "Smells like a morgue."

"It's a secure biohazard facility. We don't want to be transporting individuals any farther than we have to if some pathogen threatens the city."

Shaheen couldn't hide his surprise. "A secure facility here? Weird choice."

"Precisely why it *is* here," Best said. "In these matters, secrecy is paramount."

The hallway dead-ended at a second door. Best pressed the flat of his palm against a device in the center and waited. A green light blinked twice and he pushed the door open. All the surfaces on the second floor were constructed of dull sheets of titanium to limit porosity and reduce glare. A doctor wearing a molded face mask and a white one-piece coverall waited for them inside. She was tall and thin with wispy gray hair and glasses. Her hands were gloved in latex.

The doctor gave Best a brief nod. "I'm Dr. Abbott." She motioned toward a cubicle off to her right. "Please change your clothing, including your footwear, in there. Everything has to come off. We want to limit contamination from the outside too."

"What about my gun?" Shaheen asked, noting that Best hadn't introduced him.

"Just leave it on the shelf. You won't need it in here."

They hustled into their white suits and pulled on disposable slip-on boots. When they emerged from the cubicle, Abbott held out their face masks. "These are a devil to put on but they must fit perfectly." The doctor fiddled with the adjustments for a few minutes and then declared both masks fitted well.

She adjusted her own mask, picked up a file folder, and

indicated they should proceed toward a metal door. She unlocked it and they made their way down the hallway. Shaheen noticed her round-shouldered stoop, common enough in very tall people. "Both patients—Loretti and Hill—are incapacitated. You've seen the photographs?"

"Yes," Best replied.

Asshole. Shaheen was irritated at having to come here without any background preparation. It put him at a disadvantage.

"Get ready then," the doctor said. "It's not a pretty sight."

Their boots squished as they walked down the hall; otherwise, the place was as quiet as a tomb. Shaheen detected the vague disinfectant smell again. He'd always hated the combination of false lemon scent and chemical disinfectant. It reminded him of the makeshift latrines in Iraq.

"Do you know how the disease is transmitted?" Best asked.

In a worried gesture, Abbott raised her hand up to her brow, stopping herself just short of touching her skin. "Well, both patients had unprotected contact with a lot of people—soldiers, their families, colleagues, first responder medics. No one else has been affected—yet. If it's communicable, it's not likely airborne. And their wives confirmed they'd had intimate relations since their return from Iraq. It may be too early to tell, but it looks as though it doesn't spread through blood or bodily fluids either. Still, we were surprised you didn't send them to Walter Reed."

"Confidentiality's a primary issue," Best said. "Walter Reed's a big facility: hard to lock down, hard to keep quiet. If it does spread, we'll have no choice. We'll have to involve the major facilities. The subjects returned from Iraq a month ago; we can deduce that whatever they picked up, it came from over there."

Shaheen was beginning to get a glimmer of understanding. The main purpose of this facility was to keep any news of biological threats under the deepest possible cover. That probably meant they had no idea of what they were dealing with, and if it involved enemy action, no clue as to who exactly might be behind it.

"Loretti and Hill are both microbiologists, correct?" Abbott said.

Best nodded. "You received the records, I assume?"

"Yes." Abbott checked her file. "Both of them initially complained of flu-like symptoms. Their doctors assumed they'd come down with a respiratory infection. Since then other symptoms have shown up and now the disease has progressed rapidly. The DTRA code named it 'Black Death' after the plague in the Middle Ages, I assume. Highly unlikely to be related to bubonic plague, if that's what your people are thinking." The doctor sighed. "I wish it was," she confessed. "At least we'd know how to deal with it."

"You still have no idea what's caused it?" Best asked.

"Not yet. But the lab's working 24/7." Shaheen saw the signs of worry in the deep lines etching the doctor's brow. "It's his skin that's causing Loretti so much distress. It's tightening up all over his body and drying out, like his skin's in a slow cooker with an internal heat source. His temperature is very elevated but Hill's is flat. Cortisol, GH, and norepinephrine levels are also very high, but that's a predictable response to the terrific stress Loretti's under. He has significant swelling and soreness in the glans and foreskin, acute blistering on his neck, and a severe case of oral thrush. That could be from a yeast infection he acquired in Iraq. I understand it's a very starchy diet you feed them over there."

Best ignored her last comment. "What about a form of venereal disease?"

Shaheen smirked and Abbott glanced disapprovingly at him.

"Tested negative for all known STDs. He's experiencing hallucinations now too. Hardly surprising given his state."

Shaheen took all this in with growing awareness. Two Americans named Loretti and Hill had acquired some kind of disease, probably in Iraq. Virulent enough that it set off loud alarms. Shaheen had not been involved with the hunt for biological weapons, although he knew Washington placed a high priority on the search and so far had turned up nothing. The international intelligence community privately ruled out any biological threat from Hussein's government well before the onset of the war. Could Loretti and Hill have discovered something after all?

"I wanted you to see Loretti," Best said to Shaheen, "so you'd know what we're dealing with."

They walked down the corridor to a bank of tempered-glass windows. Two white-suited guards, heavily armed, stood on either side of a door. It reminded Shaheen of a high-security prison cell.

"We can't go in," Abbott said. "This is one-way viewing glass. Loretti's been sedated, but even with that he's been tearing at the restraints."

Shaheen was suddenly aware of a light dimming as though some form had cast a shadow over them where they stood. Abbott and Best appeared not to notice.

"When Loretti initially came to us, he tried to tell us something," Abbott said.

"What?" Best asked.

"We couldn't figure it out. He pronounced two separate and distinct words. 'Ersh' and 'gal.' It probably means nothing. Just the product of a disordered mind. He repeated them over and over. We taped him and had a speech therapist evaluate it, but got nowhere. Maybe your people can have a go at it.

"This is what Loretti looked like one month ago." Abbott handed Shaheen a photo of a dark-haired man in his thirties, on the lean side, square jawed, ruddy faced. His appealing smile revealed a row of perfectly even, sparkling white teeth.

"Okay, showtime," the doctor said grimly.

At first, Shaheen could make out only the dim form of a figure sitting upright in a chair of some kind and the vague outlines of cupboards and a counter. An attendant went inside and closed the door behind him. The doctor touched a dial on the wall and the room flooded with bluish fluorescence.

"My God," Shaheen said.

Ten

The patient was propped up in a heavily padded lounge chair that supported his body from head to foot. Its back and head rests were tilted. Restraints had been placed at Loretti's ankles, knees, waist, and neck and at the elbow and wrist of one arm. His other arm hung limp and flaccid by his side.

"Loretti can't lie flat," Dr. Abbott explained. "He's experiencing acute respiratory distress; the fluid in his lungs would drown him. The restraints look cruel, I know, but we need them. Otherwise he'd rip his skin off. Something is causing the epidermis to harden and the entire surface of his skin is tight and intensely itchy."

The man was naked except for a wide gauze bandage covering his genitals. A web of color-coded IV lines and heart-monitor wires attached to various body parts was looped to machines. Padded restraints protected his skin; his neck was swollen and bruised and some of the purplish patches had ulcerated. From Loretti's milky eyes Shaheen realized he'd probably gone blind. His flesh had reddened and was stretched over oddly malformed bones, his shoulders and rib cage so enlarged they were a caricature of masculinity.

"Why is he so misshapen?" Shaheen lowered his voice as if Loretti could hear him through the glass.

"That abnormal bone growth you see occurred over just a few weeks."

Shaheen barely heard Abbott. He was furious. "Can't you sedate him? Put him out somehow? Keeping him like that is obscene."

Abbott bristled. "If we sedate him any more he won't survive."

"Put him out of his misery then, for God's sake. We treat animals better than that."

"My role is to preserve life, not take it," the doctor snapped.

"What about his family? I can't believe they'd want to keep him alive in this condition."

Best nodded to the doctor, effectively ending the conversation. "Thank you, Dr. Abbott. We don't need to see Hill. We'll go."

Shaheen followed Best to the change room. He ripped off his mask.

"Why didn't you want to see the other guy? Is he like that too?"

"No," Best said. "He fell into a coma before the symptoms you saw on Loretti materialized."

"Lucky man."

"He still is."

"Still is what?"

"In a coma. But he'll never recover. He's brain dead now. I'm sorry to expose you to this," Best said. "I wanted you to realize what a dire problem we have on our hands. We need your help. Let's get out of here; we can talk more in the car."

"I don't see how I can assist you," Shaheen said when they reached the vehicle and Best had climbed into the back seat beside him. "You know I'm not a scientist. That's not what I do."

Best extracted a file from his briefcase and set it on his lap. He cranked open his window. "It's stuffy in here."

"Yeah," Shaheen said, "exhaust will help a lot. What the hell caused what we saw in there?"

"We have no idea. As you heard, the medical people are knocking themselves out to find it. They suspect it's a pathogen that's been engineered and the microbiologists either stumbled across it, not realizing what they found, or were deliberately contaminated. You can imagine the implications if that germ starts to spread to our troops over there. Or gets transported over here. We need you."

"For what?"

"To find the infection site."

"Come on. The army's checked every conceivable biohazard location already."

"I know," Best said.

"Yeah. And they got zero. There's nothing to find. Before the war, sanctions were so tight it was hard to import a tube of toothpaste let alone dangerous chemicals."

At this, Best lost his patience. "Perhaps you'll allow me some credit, Lieutenant, since I have a *few* years' experience. I've seen the bloated bodies of the Kurds after Hussein dosed them with poisoned gas at Halabja. Gruesome sights are an occupational hazard for me. Loretti and Hill were sent out to locate evidence of bioweapons and they found something lethal. You're right, we haven't discovered any sites—yet. And we've had our people go over each place the scientists checked officially. Where we've made no headway is with what they did on their own time over there. That will be your job."

Shaheen took a package out of his pants pocket and removed a cigarillo.

"Look," Best said in a friendlier tone, "it takes a different set of skills to pry information out of the locals and that's your forte, right? A new pair of eyes might help. Your record for turning up dependable information is first class; that's why we want you. But there are other connections you'd need to explore too. You'll be going to London first."

"The Brits? They've got infected people too?"

Best shook his head. "No. Loretti's wife told us he'd met with an Englishman, Charles Renwick, in Iraq this August."

"So?"

Best flipped through the report he held and scanned one of the pages. "It looks like Loretti was staying at the same Baghdad hotel as Renwick last August. The wife says Renwick approached her husband with some story about a source of plague."

"Has Renwick been interrogated?"

"He's missing. He may be dead."

"From the same thing that's infected Loretti and Hill?"

"No. Police are investigating a robbery at Renwick's business. They think it went bad. No telling when, or if, this Renwick will turn up. We want you to speak to the London police about their investigation. Get a handle on what Renwick was doing. Oh, and there's another American involved too."

"Who?"

"His name's John Madison. New Yorker. Antiquities dealer. Renwick hired him to buy a rare book and now Madison's reported it stolen. Renwick's lawyer is suspicious. He doesn't believe Madison's story. And Madison was also in Iraq last August."

Best slapped his folder shut. "That will have to do for now. Your flight to the U.K. leaves this afternoon. You'll get your boarding pass, reporting protocol, and all the details by email. You work directly with me."

Best's phone rang. He looked at the screen and held his hand up for Shaheen to wait until he took the call. As he listened, Best grimaced, his lips pressed together in a tight white line, and said, "Shit. When did this happen?"

He listened again and said, "How soon?" And followed that up with, "Okay. I'll come back right away." He ended the call, his face transfixed with worry. "Loretti's wife has come down with the same thing. They're bringing her in now."

Eleven

"Hell, so it's communicable after all," Shaheen said. "Looks that way, although we can't be sure yet. I've got to go back. My driver will have to drop you here. I'll keep you posted."

Shaheen got out and waved down a cab. In the car he pulled out his phone, found his list of contacts, and selected a name. Terry Davis, a former army IT specialist he'd used on past occasions. One of the few older men he knew who could beat the pants off most computer hackers. Terry ran his own company now.

"How's it going, Terry? You very busy these days?"

"Busy as a flea at a dog show—what else is new? You got something for me or you just like hearing my soothing tones?"

"Right on both counts. I'd like you to run two checks. The first is a Leonard Best, private consultant, lots of government gravy going his way." Shaheen checked Best's card. "Company name is BioThreat Analytics. He's likely got security buffers up the yingyang so it may not be easy to find anything. I'll send you his prints asap. And this is totally off the grid."

"Am I getting paid?" Terry chuckled on the other end.

"Dinner for two at Hy's—good enough?"

"Depends on who the other half of the two is."

"Your choice, of course."

"My daughter's in town. She'll love it. Who's the other guy you want me to clear?"

"The second is John Madison. New York antiquities dealer."

"That should be easy enough. Let me see what I can do. When do you want it?"

"In the next five minutes?" Shaheen said.

"Shouldn't have asked. Give me four minutes to get a coffee and it's done. Need you to throw in a couple of Broadway shows for that."

"No problem." Shaheen laughed and clicked off.

Shaheen's ID case came especially equipped with a fingerprint sensor, a handy device he'd used many times in Iraq. With a USB connection, he downloaded a digital copy of Best's fingerprints to his laptop and emailed the prints to Terry.

Shaheen paid the cabbie and mounted the stairs to the friend's midtown apartment where he was staying. He intended to collect his things and wait to hear from Terry.

"You owe me a new desktop," Terry said when he got in touch three hours later. "My computer nearly blew up doing that search for you. Here's what I found. Best is a world authority on biothreat analysis. Ph.D. from Yale in biochemistry. Lots of government commissions. Nice big fat ones.

"About five years ago he dropped off the radar. That's when I ran into issues digging stuff up. It looks like he spent most of that time working directly for the CIA on bioweapons strategy. Can't find any negatives. His profile is sound. On the personal front, he's married with a kid at U Cal. Red Cross board member, regular contributor to Save the Children. All round nice guy it would seem. Clean enough to run for the Senate."

"That was a joke, right? What about Madison?"

"Bit of a checkered past on him. Naturalized citizen, born and orphaned in Turkey. He came to America at the age of three. Samuel Diakos, his elder brother, raised him in New York. Tossed out of a couple of private schools in his teens, then he got hit with some drug charges. Cops could only make one of them stick. Teenage rebellion stuff. Went on to distinguish himself by flunking out of Columbia.

"Pulled himself up by the bootstraps and started his own business, where he's been quite successful. The people I talked to said he was a likable guy. Followed in his older brother's footprints—antiquities—but as a dealer, not a scholar." There was a temporary pause while Terry shifted the phone to his other ear and picked up his notes.

"Who's the brother, Diakos you said his name is?" Shaheen asked.

"Was. An archaeologist specializing in Assyrian culture. Died in a car accident with Madison at the wheel this past June."

"Bad news there."

"Very. I got chatting with one of the ladies I contacted. A Claire Talbot. She said it broke Madison's heart. Claimed he hasn't been the same since. His business troughed. Later on in the summer he got embroiled in a stolen artifact situation—in Iraq."

Shaheen jumped at this news. "Tell me more."

"Wait a sec…. Found it. It's not clear how he got involved. Police say he ended up looking good on that one. Made some risky moves but some smart ones too. They clocked a few bad guys thanks to him. Don't have much else."

"Can you send me a photo and his bona fides?"

Shaheen heard Terry tapping on his keyboard. "Done, pal. Anything else?"

"That's cool. Thanks, Terry. Have fun with your daughter."

Shaheen sat on a daybed near the window, one of the few pieces of furniture in the place. His friend had to work two jobs just to keep a junior one-bedroom apartment. Shaheen loved New York too and wanted to live there, but on a first lieutenant's salary he couldn't even dream about it. The best he'd be able to afford would be a place in the far-flung outskirts and what would be the point of that? He had expensive desires and a thin wallet.

He glanced at the photo of Madison Terry emailed, the kind of professional portrait someone would use on a website. But he'd checked and Madison didn't have one. High-class clients knew where to find him, Shaheen guessed. A good-looking guy, strong jaw line, close beard. His Turkish background showed up in a faint Asian tilt to his cheekbones. He could pass for a westernized Iraqi, Shaheen thought.

Madison had been involved with stolen goods in the summer and within a few short months appeared to be again. That raised flags. Throw in the ties with Renwick and Iraq and Madison warranted a much closer look.

Shaheen powered off his laptop. The involvement of the Defense Threat Reduction Agency caused him some concern. Why not the biothreat infection specialists at Fort Detrick or disease experts in Atlanta? Shaheen hadn't asked Leonard Best about it because Best had assumed he knew. The DTRA's mandate focused on protecting U.S. forces from bio and chemical agents. It also included a proactive element. Countering threats by getting ahead of the curve in developing new forms of bio and chemical warfare. The involvement of the DTRA in the Loretti and Hill situation was entirely justified. Still, it caused a spark of suspicion in Shaheen's mind.

Army life had been rough all the way along. Not the risks—on good days he reveled in those. No matter how much other soldiers respected his work, a line had been drawn in the sand. Whether it was a blatant slur from a guy loaded on uppers and beer or the distance he felt from fellow soldiers, he knew many of the men he worked with didn't like his Arab origins. If he'd been born and raised here, maybe it would have been different.

Since the initial invasion, there'd been a delicate balance in Iraq. Both the south under the British and the north were still relatively calm. Conditions in the central regions were more volatile although under control despite regular flares of violence. But Shaheen knew the edge was tipping dangerously, like a heavy plate spun carelessly on one baby finger. If a deadly disease threw the troops into panic, the whole operation could crash.

He glanced out the window. Two teenagers dressed in designer gear sauntered arm-in-arm along the sidewalk. A homeless man shuffled along behind them, muttering to himself. He wore a thin T-shirt and shorts. Far too little for the cold edge of a windy November day. Instead of socks, he'd stuck his feet into clear plastic bags, secured around his ankles with rubber bands, and shoved them into a pair of dirty runners.

If the toxin spread here, it would affect everyone, rich or poor. And that prospect didn't bear thinking about.

Twelve

November 19, 2003
London

New Scotland Yard occupied a mid-rise rectangle clad in stain-less steel. It looked impenetrable. Shaheen figured that was the idea. The sign outside announcing its name had become a landmark because it revolved fourteen thousand times in a day. If so, that was the building's only distinction. It would have fit right into any industrial park or suburban commercial district. The former Whitehall headquarters, an old brick building of Gothic turrets and domes, seemed much better suited to Scotland Yard's mystique. He felt a vague twitch of disappointment.

A clerk directed him to a sparsely furnished waiting area, sternly functional with white walls and charcoal-gray upholstered seats to match the carpet. The only other occupant, a tallish man with dark hair and a close-cut beard, was smart looking, an expensive dresser, but held himself tensely. He nodded at Shaheen and then bent his head and flipped nervously through a magazine. No surprise given what Shaheen knew about his recent history. The prospect of a police interview had that effect on some people, even if they had nothing to fear from the law. And in Madison's case, he did have.

Shaheen caught Madison giving him the once-over and smiled to himself. With his stringy hair caught up in a ponytail, blatant gold ring, and chains, Shaheen figured he'd been pegged as a street-level drug informant. He liked subverting people's expectations. It caused discomfort and gave him a slight psychological edge.

Madison couldn't hide his surprise when the clerk returned to summon both of them. In the interview room, Shaheen flopped into a chair, took a cigarillo from his pocket, and fiddled with it, stopping just short of lighting up. The door swept open. In walked a prim, no-nonsense–looking woman with cropped blond hair, wearing a plain navy pantsuit.

"Thank you for coming," she said to Madison. "I'm DCI Virginia Wilson, Homicide and Serious Crime Command. I gather you've met Lieutenant Shaheen?" Madison, unable to keep the astonishment off his face, swiveled around to eyeball Shaheen, who handed over his identification.

"Glad to meet you," Madison said. "But why are U.S. Special Forces showing up here for a local robbery?"

Shaheen waved the unlit cigarillo he still held between his fingers. "Renwick spent time in Iraq. He's of interest to us, and the inspector"—he pointed the tip of the cigarillo toward Wilson—"has been obliging enough to let me sit in."

Out of the corner of his eye Shaheen noticed a fleeting look of irritation on Wilson's face when he pointed toward her.

Madison turned to Wilson. "What does that have to do with—"

Wilson put up her hand to silence him. "Did you have any dealings with Mr. Renwick prior to the recent auction you attended on his behalf?"

"As a matter of fact, I didn't even know his name until yesterday."

Wilson raised her eyebrows. "How so?"

"I learned it from his solicitor, Arthur Newhouse, only yesterday."

"That's rather unusual I should think," Wilson said.

"You're absolutely certain you've never met Renwick?" Shaheen chimed in.

"That's what I just said," Madison intoned icily.

Shaheen twirled the cigarillo in his fingers. "Funny. You and Renwick were both in Iraq last summer. Not exactly a prime vacation spot. You're sure you didn't cross paths—"

Madison cut him off. "How many times do I have to say it? The answer is no."

"We've noted your response, Mr. Madison," Wilson said. "Let's continue where we left off. Mr. Renwick wanted you to bid on the book without disclosing his name to the auction house—is that unusual?"

"Far from it. It could even be considered customary, especially for higher-priced items, when a buyer's represented by an agent. But for a dealer not to know his client's identity is uncommon. He offered a substantial commission so I accepted the terms."

"You're claiming the book was stolen from you at around 11:45 P.M.—correct?" Wilson asked.

"That's right. As I said in my report, a man walked up to me outside my hotel, introduced himself, and tried to put me off my guard by starting a conversation. Then he made a grab for my case. We tussled. The case came open and the box fell, spilling the book onto the sidewalk. I bent to get it and he hit me with his cane, snatched the book, and took off." Madison touched his temple with his hand. "I've got the bruises to prove it. I chased him and almost reached him when a car nearly ran me over. He got in and they drove away. Any luck tracking him down?"

"We have alerts out. But no, not at present."

Wilson paused to look at the file she'd carried in with her and read out Alessio's description. "A bit of time has gone by, and you've had a chance to think about it. Do you have anything to add about your assailant? You said the name he gave was Gian Alessio Abbattutis and you referred to him as Alessio for short—correct? Did he have an accent? Any additional distinguishing characteristics?"

"I can only tell you he spoke in a kind of antiquated formal way. I don't think English was his native language."

"And you never met this … Alessio either, prior to him robbing you?" Wilson scrutinized him as she said this.

At the second mention of Alessio's name, Madison looked ill at ease. "Definitely not."

"No sight of him since?"

"He got what he wanted. He's hardly going to seek me out again."

"We're pursuing the stolen book, and it appears to be tied to the burglary at Charles Renwick's shop through the same suspect." Wilson ran her finger down the page in front of her. "There's a major discrepancy in your account, Mr. Madison. The auction house claims you received a complete book from them, the entire Italian anthology. On the other hand you state it was only one volume, the first in the series. How do you explain that?"

Madison's discomfort seemed to ease as the conversation moved off Alessio and back to the book. "There's a simple answer to that. I looked at the item and photographed every page. I record every object as a matter of course with each commission I have. Sherrods didn't record it. Their mistake."

Wilson caught Madison off guard with her next question. "You've told us Alessio accosted you on the street, on your way back from the auction. How could you possibly have had time to take photographs?"

Shaheen expected Madison to stumble but he kept his cool. "I didn't leave the auction house until after ten that evening and hadn't eaten anything since lunch. I stopped off at a restaurant and took the photos there."

"Where?"

"A place across from the Ritz Club casino. Don't remember the name."

"In Mayfair? Why not somewhere closer to the auction house?"

"It was just a couple of tube stops. I like the bar at the Ritz but it was too crowded."

Wilson raised her eyebrows in disbelief. "A gambling man, are you?"

Madison gave her a grim smile. "You could say that. I certainly seem to attract risky ventures." He eyed Shaheen. "I'd still like to know why the military's here."

Wilson ignored this and checked her file again. "Our records show your involvement in the theft of an Iraqi antiquity not long ago. Somewhat of an odd coincidence, isn't it?"

"If you're going to do a background check make sure it's accurate," Madison said testily. "You're referring to an engraving someone stole from my brother. In my business you can't escape stolen items. You need to be constantly on the alert. A lot of antiquities we dealers see have dubious provenance. That's common enough. The American authorities were quite thankful for my help. They're still holding the engraving as evidence for the trial of the thieves."

"And getting back to the book, you had no knowledge it was illegitimate when you won it at auction?" she shot back.

"Of course not. Who'd risk their client's hard-earned money that way? One mistake like that and your reputation is history."

Madison's sturdy self-defense didn't appear to impress her. "You have to admit, Mr. Madison, the circumstances are questionable. You were in possession of a rare book and now it's conveniently disappeared. You were formerly involved with the theft of an antiquity and lives were lost. Both you and the missing Mr. Renwick were in Iraq last August."

She was purposely trying to rile Madison, hoping he'd make some slip, Shaheen decided. He liked her style.

"It's been anything but convenient, believe me," Madison fumed. "Interpol didn't identify the book's owner. Can you give me any further information on who it is?"

"That's not for public consumption, as you likely already know," she said. "It's my task to learn what happened to Mr. Renwick and find the book." She glanced over at Shaheen. "Would you care to ask anything, Lieutenant?"

"Yeah, thanks. Can you describe the book?"

"Physically you mean?"

"No. That's in the report you faxed in. What was it about?"

"A collection of seventeenth-century Italian folk tales," Madison replied. "Quite rare. The Interpol report doesn't give much information, but neither did Sherrods' listing."

"I don't know anything about book auctions, yet that strikes me as odd," Shaheen said.

Madison sat back and relaxed a little, visibly glad to be asked his professional opinion. "It is unusual. The more information provided about an object, the more likely it will garner interest and command a higher price. But I was told the vendor wanted it that way. And now, knowing it was stolen, I can see why. A detailed description might have alerted the real owner sooner than it did."

"Why would Sherrods go along with that?"

"Prominent auction houses like Christie's or Sotheby's have more latitude to turn stuff down. Sherrods is smaller and hungrier. If it means getting a sale they'll go along with what the vendor wants. And they made a nice buck off the commission anyway. They did their job and cleared its provenance beforehand. It was just a timing thing. The Interpol alert came out only hours before the actual auction began."

"Do you know why Renwick wanted it?"

"He had a theory that some of the tales had origins in real events. Thought one of them might be connected to some disease he picked up in the Near East when he was a child—"

Shaheen cut Madison off. "A disease? What kind?"

"Don't know. Whatever it was Renwick caught it long ago—in childhood. It left him with severe physical abnormalities. People develop all kinds of wild theories about things. And they get obsessed with proving them. I tried to find out more from Renwick's business partner but that's all he knew. Renwick was pretty close-mouthed about it, apparently."

Wilson slapped her file shut. "That will be all then. Thank you for coming in, Mr. Madison. We have your contact information and will likely be in touch. Will you be staying on in London?"

Madison stood up with obvious relief on his face. "Not unless the thief's still here. I have every intention of getting that book back."

Wilson frowned. "That's not at all wise. Vigilantes just make matters worse. Leave this to the police."

"If it isn't recovered I may as well kiss my business goodbye; rumors are already circulating back in New York. And there's a legal issue. The book was in my possession and, stolen or not, I might be liable, so there's a better than even chance I'll be on the line for a whack of money I don't have. Plus, the thief didn't act alone. Others are involved. They threatened me. If you'll pardon my frankness, I'm going to pay the assholes back."

Madison took a few steps toward the door before appearing to think better of it and turning around. "About my time in Iraq"—he threw Shaheen a glance—"like you mentioned. Over there I got thrown under the bus. I felt like a pawn in someone else's chess game. I didn't know what the agenda was or who I could trust. I'm sick of that. I'm tired of lowlifes thinking they can fuck me over, ruin my business, and walk away laughing. I'm going on the offensive with this and will bring these people to justice whether it's official or not. I hesitated to say this before because you'd probably think it sounded ridiculously old-fashioned, but this is a matter of personal honor for me. It's no more complicated than that." He threw Wilson a warm smile, nodded to Shaheen, and walked out the door.

As his footsteps retreated down the hall, Wilson said, "The last time I heard someone talk about personal honor was in an old movie right before the dueling scene. I expect that's just bluff. He's not given us the full story. And he didn't sit in a restaurant across from the Ritz snapping photos. Unfortunately, we can't prove it because the night clerk didn't notice when Madison got back to his hotel."

"You're right on that one. Doesn't compute at all."

"I wish we could stop him from leaving the country. Without more evidence we don't have the right to, especially an American citizen. You could, though," Wilson said.

"No worries. He'll be under active surveillance. What do you think about the discrepancy as to whether he bought the entire book or just one of the volumes?" Shaheen asked.

"The book's gone. There's no evidence to support either claim. But I'd side with Sherrods, who told us the entire book was offered. They're an old and very respectable firm."

Shaheen thought about the discussion with Madison for a moment. "Not sure I agree. He strikes me as pretty smart. If he was going to put something past us, I don't think he'd try something so obvious."

"Well, your endorsement is just more speculation. He'll end up being trouble, I can sense it, even though there's nothing we can do to stop him right now. He was attending the auction at the time we've concluded the robbery and possible assault on Renwick took place. And realistically? As far as the book Renwick wanted is concerned, Madison is probably right. Our best chance of finding it will be when it turns up on the black market. That could be years from now."

As she stood up, Shaheen noticed her somber pantsuit had no wrinkles, not even a speck of lint. He'd known a marine like that once. An officer. An older guy. Whenever he wore his dress uniform, it looked as if he'd personally ironed and starched it, and his shoes were polished till the light bounced off them. "Respect for the office. If you don't have respect for what you're doing, what else have you got?" the officer said when Shaheen remarked on his dress. Wilson was clearly of the same mind.

"Madison could just be good at spinning us," Shaheen said after a moment. "But he might be on the level. If it were me, I'd do the same as him—get the job done myself."

Wilson's disapproving look showed his reply didn't sit well with her. "It's highly unusual to include external personnel in one of our investigations but my superiors insisted. I don't care for that kind of murkiness. And I noticed your reaction when Madison referred to Renwick's illness. What was that all about? If there's some public health concern, I need to know."

"That has to stay classified."

Good though she was at keeping her facial expressions neutral, a spark of alarm flashed in her eyes. "God forbid we have to face another SARS outbreak or something like that. If Renwick is dead and his body's lying in some alley and he was a carrier...."

Shaheen held his hand up. "Anything of that nature and we would have told you. If there's something to concern yourself about, you'll know." He quickly changed the subject. "Madison was holding back on something."

Wilson couldn't help smiling. "Definitely. Renwick's solicitor is certain he's involved in the book theft. If he's guilty, when and if the book turns up for sale his fingerprints will be all over it—metaphorically speaking."

"You may not have a long wait. As I said, we'll be keeping a close eye on him." Shaheen eased himself out of his chair. "That is if Interpol doesn't get him first."

"That's not going to happen," Wilson responded.

"Why not?"

"You'd have to steal the *Mona Lisa* before they got directly involved. Investigations are left to local or national police."

"Who does own the book, by the way? Who filed that Interpol claim?"

"A wealthy Italian from Naples, Lorenzo Mancini," Wilson said, "an aristocrat. The Comte de Soissons. It's a French title, although he uses the Italian word—*conte*. He's an investment banker, quite powerful and secretive. Mancini has the highest connections and the lowest, if you know what I mean. Put bluntly, he's a money launderer. Find a mound of dirty money and you'll pick up his trail."

"He's from Naples? You mean he's with the Camorra?"

"No official link but he can call upon them anytime and he's useful to them as well. They don't operate as a tight group like the Sicilian Mafia do. I learned quite a bit about them when I assisted on a case involving one of their men in London a few years back. They follow an ancient tradition. The Greek Cumae settled Naples first and their society was structured around *fratria*, family-based fraternities headed by a patriarch. The Camorra form loose-knit cells centered around their families, similar to the fratria. Almost like tribes."

Wilson gazed at the door Madison had just closed on his way out as if she could see the ghost of his image through it. "Whether or not Madison took that book, by involving himself in Mancini's affairs, he's already a dead man."

Part Two

WITCH IN THE STONE BOAT

This spell I lay upon you, that you slacken not your course
until you come to my brother in the underworld.

—ICELANDIC FAIRY TALE FROM
THE YELLOW FAIRY BOOK BY ANDREW LANG

Thirteen

November 19, 2003
Naples, Italy

My morning interview at Scotland Yard went better than I hoped. The police hadn't found Alessio's body, or if they had, made no connection to me. The story I gave them went down smoothly enough. They would never have believed the truth of how an old man overpowered me or why I let him into my hotel room in the first place. But why was Special Forces there? They didn't waste time on stolen valuables without a compelling reason. Shaheen didn't look fit for army grunt let alone officer rank in an elite outfit. The questions multiplied and I had no answers.

The accusations about my abduction to Iraq last summer really burned me. Amazing how information gets twisted. Just being associated with a stolen artifact made me guilty in their eyes—never mind that I helped put the thieves behind bars. Simply being in Iraq made me untrustworthy. All the more reason to locate every volume of the book. And fast.

Late that afternoon, the plane's wings dipped and banked a

gentle curve to land at Naples' Capodichino Airport. From the air, densely packed buildings fanned out in the almost perfect half-basin cupping the glittering ultramarine harbor. A few freighters piled high with orange containers chugged out of the central port marked by its tall white-and-blue loading cranes. Yachts floated like tiny seagulls on the water. City streets zigzagged in a maze of angles.

They rolled up a movable stair for us to exit the plane like a scene out of *Casablanca*, although in the taxi on the way to my hotel the image of Havana came most vividly to mind. Like the old Cuban city, Naples had hundreds of exquisite Spanish-style six- and seven-story buildings, all with graceful balustrades, painted in pastels or constructed from the famous local yellow tufa stone. Many showed the wear of centuries. The guidebook I picked up in the airport claimed Naples boasted five hundred churches and from what I could see that had the ring of truth. In one block alone I spotted three Baroque beauties. But they were abandoned, their entrances padlocked and barricaded with chain-link fencing.

We battled with Vespas and motorbikes along palm-fringed cobblestone streets. A friend once told me Naples was a city on steroids and I thought how apt a description that was. Wherever I looked, everything was one continuous blur of motion. I took a deep breath, glad to have escaped my woes in London. It felt good to be here. My hotel on the harbor was near Castel Nuovo, a formidable fortress built by French crusader kings. After checking in I wandered across the street to the waterside promenade to take in the view.

Vesuvius loomed over the eastern edge of the harbor, dominating the landscape. Waning afternoon sun lit up the town nestled at its base, the cloak of forest on its lower slopes and the furrows of reddish stone making up the two cones at its peak. I couldn't take my eyes off it. The stratovolcano, once worshiped as a power of Jupiter, possessed the god's legendary temper. I could almost believe a living and vengeful god still dwelled there.

The humpbacked mountain sat placidly in the distance but its peacefulness was deceptive. Almost two millennia ago, clouds of deadly ash, burning rock, and superheated gas shot twenty miles into the sky, suffocating thousands of people. Its most recent eruption was in 1944. No one believed that would be the last.

We all get used to the natural environment we live in and in time take it for granted. Central Park is like that for me, even though I always look forward to walking its shaded paths. I imagined that here it was different; you could never really let your guard down and Vesuvius's presence contributed significantly to the boisterous Neapolitan character. Living here would be like walking blindfolded through a minefield with a whistle on your lips.

I had the evening in Naples to myself because it was much too late to visit Ewan Fraser at the library. At a café on the edge of Piazza del Plebiscito, I stretched out my legs and basked in the sun's warmth, a welcome change from the chill and fog of London. My vantage point served as a prime people-watching spot. The waiter brought me a cup of espresso strong enough to fuel a jet plane. I sipped at it, admiring the parade of gorgeous Neapolitan women with flowing Botticelli locks, tight jeans, fitted jackets, and trim little boots. After a while, reluctantly, I took my mind off those lovely visions and went over all that had recently transpired in London.

Why hadn't Alessio killed me when he had the chance? Why choose to wade dangerously farther into the river? The man had committed suicide in front of me and no matter how I tried, I couldn't make sense of his deliberate and awful end.

Another puzzle—what had Alessio, or Grimm as he'd latterly

called himself, done with the first volume, and why did he want it so badly? I was almost certain the accusation of theft arose from a family quarrel but the issue of the book's "repellent history" still nagged at me.

I'd never experienced anything like the sensation of paralysis that had gripped me on two occasions now. I remember having felt very cold, too, a deep internal cold apart from the frosty drizzle that night. Had those brief sensations of paralysis been the first indication of a serious medical problem? As soon as the thought arose I dismissed it. I'd been poked and prodded and tested after the car accident last summer and the doctors found nothing wrong. If not from an underlying condition then, how had the old man subdued me? A skilled hypnotist might induce such a reaction in his victims; I could think of no other rational explanation.

Tye Norris had been helpful, but our conversation left me holding several threads with no idea how they wove together. In Charles Renwick's opinion, one particularly well-loved fairy tale contained a kernel of truth—of history—that promised to lead him to some revelation about an illness he contracted in the Middle East as a boy. What that was remained a mystery. With all of these queries, I was reaching for filaments, gossamer strands from a deadly web, lingering just out of my reach.

Amy told me Giambattista Basile was brilliant at devising anagrams. In fact, he'd put together an entire book consisting of the anagrammatized names of court ladies. Could the key Renwick sought be an anagram?

As my thoughts drifted, the face of the mysterious woman in Renwick's photo surfaced. Although too prosaic to call haunting, her image had floated into my mind a few times and left a strong impression on me. The more I thought about the tight-faced older man with his hand possessively clutching her shoulder, the more she seemed like a sparrow caught in his talons.

Something clicked and I realized what Renwick's scribble on the back of the photo might mean. *Talia, August 18/2000.* Initially I'd assumed it was a woman's name. Now I thought it might refer to Italia. Renwick's handwriting had been faint and difficult to read so I may just have missed seeing the extra *i*. If I was right, the note meant the photo was taken just over three years ago in Italy on August 18, 2000.

I got out the English translation of Basile's book that Norris lent me. Amy compared it to *The Arabian Nights* and now I saw what she meant. The *Nights* tales were contained within a framing story about Scheherazade, who spun stories for the king to save her life, cleverly leaving him each night with a cliffhanger so she would live to see another day. The original thriller writer, I thought with a smile.

Basile, too, created a framing story for his anthology, a much more ribald account of a princess named Zoza who, finding she'd been cheated out of a princely husband by a slave girl, cast a spell to give the girl an insatiable desire for stories. Ten old crones were summoned to tell them. Each volume of Basile's anthology constituted a day in the telling of the tales. The entire anthology, all five volumes, comprised fifty tales in all.

Which one pointed to the origin of Renwick's childhood illness? None of Basile's titles was familiar except for "Cinderella Cat," and Norris hadn't included it in Renwick's short list. I would have to read through all fifty of them to find the right one so I opened the English translation at the beginning and began to read.

The first two stories were completely unfamiliar and it occurred to me I might be taking the wrong approach. Starting instead with the well-known versions of the four stories Renwick mentioned might provide me with a link to their Italian precursors. All four of these tales were in the Grimm collection: "The Pied Piper,"

"Sleeping Beauty" (called "Briar Rose"), "Little Snow White," and "The Singing Springing Lark," a version of "Beauty and the Beast." None of them resembled any of Basile's titles.

Fairy tales were originally told sitting around the fireside at night, when the sense of magic was most pervasive. When plague and illness visited those hearths, stories arose as a way to explain the devastating events. I went back to the *Grimm's* to see if I could find anything along those lines.

The Grimm brothers' version of "The Pied Piper," called "The Rat Catcher of Hamelin," described a mystical figure hired by the village of Hamelin to rid the town of the rats. After the piper performed his service, the mayor refused to open the village coffers to pay him. In retribution, the piper lured the town's children away with music. They were never seen again. After rereading the story I looked up Hamelin on the Web and was surprised to see that the town actually existed in Lower Saxony. To this day, a local regulation outlaws music and song on the Bungelosen, a street near the Pied Piper's home. A great tourist ploy, if nothing else.

My late brother believed legends and myths were based on real events transformed over centuries of retellings. In the case of "The Pied Piper," this seemed a reasonable possibility. Literacy was a privilege granted to only a few in those times and stories of victory and defeat, humor and horror would have been transmitted orally, changing over time. Some terrible calamity had fallen upon Hamelin's children, its true nature hidden by the repeated narrations over hundreds of years.

Had the village been attacked by an obscure plague that swept away its youngest and most vulnerable? A stained-glass window in a Hamelin church appeared to be an early, tragic record of the calamity. I read about it in a document called the Lueneburg manuscript, circa 1440.

In the year 1284, on the days of John and
Paul, it was the 26th of June, came a colourful
Piper to Hameln and led 100 children away
To calverie on the Koppen Mountain.

The window featured a piper dressed in pied clothing, made up of vividly colored patches, playing a flute. A group of children climbed toward a mountain peak against a curious landscape dotted with villages, trees, and a river. Because of its association with rats, repellent carriers of the Black Death, "The Pied Piper" has been interpreted as a plague tale. But 1284 predated the time that the scourge first afflicted Germany, and as I discovered to my further surprise, the notion of the piper as rat catcher hadn't occurred until much later, in the 1500s. That cast doubt on the story's associa-

August von Moersperg, copy of a glass window in Market Church,
Lower Saxony, Germany, 1532

tion with the disease that took one hundred million lives in the fourteenth century.

Some other type of pandemic then? Through the centuries, unfamiliar pathogens traveled to Europe along trade routes. Epidemics of unknown origin would sweep through a region or town and disappear again as quickly, like the plague that struck Athens in 430 B.C. when the crowded city was under siege by the Spartans. That disease accomplished what the Spartans could not. A third of the population died. I found an account of it by Thucydides, who described their symptoms:

> Externally the body was not very hot to the touch, nor pale in its appearance but … reddish, livid and breaking out into small pustules and ulcers. But internally it burned so that the patient could not bear to have on him clothing … or indeed to be otherwise than stark naked.

If plague caused the disappearance and demise of the children of Hamelin, perhaps it was spread by an itinerant musician.

As I read on, I discovered a link between the long-ago event in Lower Saxony and Kutná Hora, a Czech town. In the Middle Ages, charming rogues traveled throughout Germany luring young people to work in Kutná Hora's silver mines. Was it possible "The Pied Piper" described one of those early charlatans who stole children away to labor in the mines?

Perhaps both versions held some truth. It would be strange indeed for parents to voluntarily see their children exiled to some foreign land. But if a plague swept through Hamelin killing off many adults, the orphans left behind might have been enticed to places like Kutná Hora, never to return again to their homeland, working in the mines their only hope for survival.

Night fell on the piazza. I gave up reading and headed for my hotel. As I walked back along the seaside promenade, I saw the diminishing outline of Vesuvius gradually swallowed up in darkness.

Fourteen

November 20, 2003
Naples, Italy

Next morning a short hike through cobbled streets brought me to the Royal Palace, a sternly functional structure built by a Bourbon king. Giant marble statues of Naples' former rulers—French, Spanish, and Italian—stood in niches within the colonnade forming the ground-floor facade. All who passed by felt intimidated and small in comparison to the pale sculptures draped in their finery. I guessed that was the idea.

The *biblioteca nazionale*, housed in the eastern wing of the palace, was named after one of Italy's last kings, Vittorio Emanuele III. I admired the oversized architectural elements in the building—twelve-foot-high double wooden doors and soaring ceilings. The central arch opened onto a large rectangular courtyard flanked by more colonnades. It was empty and mostly in shade. My footsteps echoed on the flags. This led into another courtyard, also vacant, save for a few parked cars. A perfect place to stage an assassination. Doubtless, in past times it had—a sudden strike from an enemy hiding in the deep recesses of the colonnade.

I had to retrace my steps in order to find the library entrance. A grand marble staircase led to a small high-ceilinged room where glass display cases held beautifully illustrated manuscripts and early books. In the next room several library staff sat behind a glass and wood partition that reminded me of an old railway station ticket counter.

A pleasant-looking woman with a sweep of smooth gray hair and glasses spotted me. "*Prego?*" she said.

I explained I'd come to see Ewan Fraser. She glanced at her watch and said he wasn't expected for another hour. I inquired whether the library had an early copy of Giambattista Basile's anthology. She replied proudly that it did.

After I filled out a couple of forms, another staff member escorted me through the Grand Salon di Letteri. The collection looked fit for a king. Books filled two stories of cases fashioned from carved, burnished wood. Curved wrought-iron stairs in the corners ascended to the upper gallery of shelves. Above this, gorgeous hand-painted scenes adorned the upper walls. This upper level soared to wooden buttresses and a magnificent ceiling fresco. Bright Neapolitan sun shone like a floodlight through the tall windows.

As I stood, caught up in the vision, a junior librarian brought the book out and escorted me to a secure room with a long worktable. At first glance the book appeared almost identical to the volume I'd held in the drab London hotel room. It had the same stiff, browned pages, crowded text, graceful drop caps starting each story, and frontispiece with Basile's pseudonym, Gian Alessio Abbattutis. But it included none of de Ribera's arresting, disturbing illustrations. The librarian agreed to let me snap pictures provided I didn't use a flash. When I finished, I checked the frontispiece again and swore under my breath. In my eagerness to view the book, I'd overlooked the publication date—1637. This must be a second edition, printed one year after the last volume of the original anthology.

A heavyset man who looked to be in his late forties strode into the room. He wore horn-rimmed glasses and sported a full curly blond beard. His longish blond hair was flecked with gray.

I rose and held out my hand to greet him. "My name's John Madison. Are you Ewan Fraser by any chance?"

"Indeed I am, lad." He grasped my hand, nearly crushing it in his firm grip. "Welcome to our library," he said with obvious pride.

"It's magnificent. Had a devil of a time trying to find it though."

"Aye, that's on purpose. Keeps the riffraff out." He chuckled and instantly put me at ease. "I hope you're enjoying Naples."

"Yes. It's a great city."

"You'll hear no argument from me. Many visitors just jump off the cruise ships and head for Herculaneum or Pompei and miss the fascinations of Naples itself. People here are very accepting. They'd have to be after three thousand years of rule by so many different cultures. We're mutts and proud of it. Much the hardier breed. But don't try driving here!" As he shook with laughter I noticed a curious object swinging from the broad leather belt around his stomach: a wide loop of soft yellowed chamois decorated with sparkling gemstones secured to the belt with a kind of topknot.

Fraser saw me glance at it and patted it. "My girdle book," he said. "Belonged to a sixteenth-century noblewoman from Naples. Her book of hours. In those days, wearing a book was a fashion statement and a mark of wealth." He touched the topknot. "This Turk's head knot keeps the book secure. The leather used for the covers is lengthened to form a kind of purse that holds the book. Before printing became widespread, books were rare and valuable so they had to be protected. Monks chained medieval manuscripts to library shelves for the same reason."

"Interesting." I didn't know what else to say. Even though "Turk's head" was a derogatory reference to turbans Turkish men wore, he didn't seem embarrassed to use the epithet.

"And this," he continued, pointing to a silver horn he wore about his neck, "is a charm Neapolitans wear to protect against *il malocchio*—the evil eye. But enough about our local lore. Were you looking for anything particular in our collection?"

"I've just been photographing Basile's *The Tale of Tales*. The staff was very helpful."

After the camaraderie, mention of the book brought him up short. He blanched momentarily then quickly resumed his informative chattiness. "One of Naples' most beloved authors," he said expansively. "He was revered in this city. In tribute, his tombstone was lodged beneath the pulpit at Santa Sofia di Giugliano until it was destroyed. The original palace on this site is long gone. The author no doubt spent much time in it."

"Do you have any idea where I can find a complete first edition of *The Tale of Tales*? The library has part of the handsome second edition, but I'm interested in the first."

"The only one I know of is in private hands." He glanced out the window, a move that seemed designed to avoid my eyes. "If books and art are your interest, there's enough fascinating material here to occupy a lifetime. I doubt you could do justice to all our possessions, even taking that long. We have drawings by Leonardo da Vinci, and rare maps and papyrus scrolls from Herculaneum. After Italy's last king was deposed in 1946, the Royal Palace became a museum. Fitting, isn't it?" He waved his hand toward the rows of book-laden shelves. "What with the digital age upon us, all these will become curiosities, their value as repositories of history limited by the new scrolls we'll be reading on a screen."

"I wish I had the time to spend here," I said appreciatively. "I've just flown in from London hoping to talk to you about an edition of *The Tale of Tales* I purchased for my client at an auction. Apparently it was consigned to Sherrods auction house by you—is that correct?"

At my mention of Sherrods his expression grew less affable. "I was told the sale went smoothly. Is there a problem?"

"You might say so." Out of the corner of my eye, I noticed three students sitting at the table beside us listening to our conversation. "Is there any chance we might go to your office? It's probably best to discuss this privately."

"Very well." He motioned for me to follow him.

The "office" was no more than a cubbyhole with a desk and chair. Beside a computer, file folders and stacks of books littered the desktop. Fraser offered me the seat while he balanced his large bulk against the edge of the desk.

"Thanks for sparing the time," I said. "First, can you confirm Sherrods received the complete anthology from you—all five volumes?"

"Yes. There's obviously some problem. What is it?"

I got ready for his reaction upon hearing the bad news. "Well, there was only one volume, not five, in the wooden box bearing the Savoy coat of arms." Fraser started sputtering and I held up my hand to let him know I had more to say. "And the book was reported stolen shortly before the auction was held."

Fraser's face reddened to the roots of his beard. "That's impossible! Who reported this? Where did you hear it from?"

"Interpol's got an alert out. Unfortunately, I'd already won the auction and taken possession of the book before I heard about the theft."

I came prepared with the Interpol file already selected on my phone. I clicked it on and held it out for him. He took one look at the screen and faltered, as if on the verge of losing his balance. I quickly got up and slid the chair over for him to sit down.

He flopped into it without speaking while he digested my news.

"You've given me quite a scare, sir. I can assure you that the book came from a source that is … beyond reproach. There must be some mistake. We'll get it cleared up." He took out a handkerchief and wiped his brow, stuffing the cloth back in his pocket. "What's become of the book then? Have you turned it in to the authorities?"

"I never got the chance. Someone robbed me before I could. It's gone. And I never had more than the first volume." I didn't tell him I hadn't any proof of that.

"What? This is so strange. I don't know what to make of it all." He rubbed his fingers over his eyes.

"All the same," I said delicately, "the auction house and my client are out a lot of money. I hope you'll be good enough to issue a refund while you're sorting this out."

Fraser threw up his plump pink hands in frustration. "This is a legal matter now. I'll have to confer with the person who entrusted it to me. I have no direct responsibility for any monies exchanged, but I assure you that I do feel a moral obligation. Let me see what I can do." He swiveled around in the chair, picked up the receiver from a handset on the desk, and dialed a number. He spoke rapidly in a dialect I was unfamiliar with.

Dropping the receiver back into its cradle, Fraser scribbled on a piece of notepaper and stood up. "The owner has agreed to speak with you through an intermediary tonight." He handed me the paper. "At this address. Under the circumstances, it's the best I can do."

This seemed an unusual way to conduct business, but then the entire affair had been odd from the start. "And what's his name— the owner?"

"A noblewoman. Her name is Zelladina Margareta Marie."

"That's quite a mouthful."

"Yes. To the few who know her intimately, she's just Dina. She's very jealous of her privacy and will likely refuse to see you directly, hence the intermediary. She lives in the Sanità district. Frankly, I don't recommend you go there." He frowned as if to emphasize the point. "The household Dina lives in has a … I guess you could say, unusual history." Fraser cleared his throat uncomfortably. "Apparently, she suffered some traumatic personal event in the past. It's rumored she has a dire aversion to men."

Fifteen

Distaste for men or no, I intended to seek the woman out. Ewan Fraser gave me her address and warned me again to wait until the evening meeting. He could see I was anxious to get the matter sorted. He was right, but his advice fell on deaf ears. The taxi I flagged refused to take me into Sanità. The driver claimed the street I wanted was too narrow for a car. He dropped me off near the archaeological museum and I proceeded the rest of the way on foot.

It was no surprise a noblewoman had been the owner of the book I sought. I'd met members of European aristocratic families before, a pretty common experience in my line of work. More princesses, duchesses, lords, and counts from old European states exist in this world than anyone can imagine. To stay afloat financially, many sell treasures once sewn into garment linings or otherwise spirited out of countries where war or revolution put an end to noblesse oblige. Emblems of the prestige they'd once taken for granted ended up on the auction block, while they retreated into the ever-diminishing circle of the gentry, unwilling to face the disintegration of their station in life. Some still insisted on using their titles, even though the money and territory they once possessed vanished long ago.

Once, I'd assessed the belongings of a Polish baron whose grandchildren had no interest in the trappings of an archaic social order. He kept up appearances by occupying an Upper East Side apartment. The building was cushy enough, but the apartment's interior looked as though it hadn't been updated since the 1930s, and that included the appliances. He sold off art objects piecemeal to cover his property taxes and living expenses.

I entered Sanità through a street lined with tall buildings so narrow there was barely room for a car to pass through. Perhaps the taxi driver had been truthful after all. As to the danger, no one approached me save for an unshaven man pushing a baby stroller full of umbrellas. It was odd, since there were no clouds in the sky. I suspected some pretty interesting contraband lurked underneath the umbrellas.

He flicked a quick glance up and down the street and gave me an ingratiating smile. "*Americano?*"

I nodded.

He gestured toward his stack of umbrellas. "Snowballs—if you want." He'd figured the only reason a tourist would venture into this area alone would be for a hit. Snowballs were a mix of coke and heroin and heroin had never been on my shopping list. I shook my head and crossed the street.

In this district, only the upper balconies got the benefit of sun; the road's cobblestone surface swam in shadow. At various points, overhead archways bridged the buildings. Off to my right a short strip of lane opened into a courtyard, abruptly dead-ended by a small but imposing palazzo.

In contrast to its closest neighbors the palazzo was in immaculate condition, made of large blocks of stone painted a warm ivory. Bowl-shaped balustrades sat under every window. Grecian nymph statuettes on a ledge near the roofline held up a wide, decorative cornice. Entrance stairs a full story high led to dark-green double doors, a small viewing window in each one. All the ground-level windows were barred and shuttered. It seemed incongruous for such a stunning building to be hiding away in this rough part of town.

A pale face gazed out from one of the fourth-floor windows, a young woman with braided hair. As she watched me, her eyes seemed to burn straight through my bones. The noblewoman appeared to have earned her daunting reputation. That wasn't the most startling thing about her. I'd seen her before. The intriguing woman in Renwick's photograph.

I mounted the stairs and pressed the doorbell, waiting while the chimes echoed. No one answered. I pressed it again. A few minutes passed by. Still nothing. A third attempt was also unsuc-cessful. I stepped back into the courtyard and looked up at the window again. The woman was gone. I walked away, perplexed about what her connection with Renwick could possibly be.

The better part of the afternoon lay ahead of me and I decided the best use of it would be to learn about the curious round stone artifact stolen from Renwick's shop. It took me over an hour to find a printing shop where I could copy the photo Norris gave me and fax it to an archaeologist colleague of Samuel's in Chicago.

I also sent out an alert to a network of art and antiquity dealers I belonged to, asking them to get back to me if they heard of any discreet offers of seventeenth-century fairy tales. A thriving black market for antiquarian books existed, just as it did for art objects. If one of Basile's volumes had been offered for private sale, there was a slim possibility my colleagues might hear of it.

I grabbed a bite to eat at a bistro. It only took a few hours in Naples to realize the city earned its reputation for fabulous food honestly. It seemed this was also true in Basile's time. I smiled when

I resumed reading the English translation and came across his endearing and somewhat sorrowful description of his beloved city, written as he set off to become a soldier of fortune for the Venetians.

> Ah! My beautiful Naples, behold I am leaving you, and who knows if it will be my lot ever to see you again: you whose bricks are of sugar, whose walls are of sweet pastry, where the stones are manna, the rafters are sugar canes and the doors and windows sugar cakes.

This passage was typical of his writing. Full of rich description and metaphors. It reminded me of Gabriel García Márquez's *One Hundred Years of Solitude*, a favorite book of mine. Basile had the same remarkable talent to marry the fantastic with everyday life.

Turning later to other fairy-tale authors, I found a site on Andrew Lang, a nineteenth-century English anthropologist and folklore scholar. He'd assembled over four hundred tales in twelve separate volumes known as the Fairy Books. I found myself drawn in by Henry Justice Ford's haunting, evocative illustrations, just as I had with José de Ribera's earlier ones. Lang even retold one of Basile's stories, "The Snake." Lang's story, "The Enchanted Snake," was little more than a synopsis of Basile's tale and lacked the Neapolitan author's gorgeous descriptions and rich language.

Il Gatto Nero, the club where Ewan Fraser had arranged my meeting, was located off Via Giardinetto, a steep flagstoned street smack in the middle of the touristy part of Naples. Had I not more pressing business, it would have been easy enough to become waylaid by the shops—outdoor markets with fresh greens and local white cheese shaped like pears; seafood stores with trays of fresh mussels, clams, and snails in saltwater baths; confectioners selling pastries so artfully designed it seemed a shame to eat them; Italian leather footwear and custom-made jewelry. I took a few minutes to slip into one of the jewelry stores and buy necklaces with beads made from volcanic stone for Evelyn and Corinne.

They say strong attractions make themselves felt within the first five minutes of a new acquaintance. I felt that way about Naples and wished I had the leisure to get to know it better. It had the same rough edges, chaotic energy, and sudden breathtaking glimpses of beauty as my hometown. Grand though Paris and Rome were, the pulse of this city beat much like New York's. And in the short time I'd been here, it felt closer to my heart.

I arrived at the club half an hour early. A notice stuck to the door stated it was closed for a private party. The proprietor asked for my invitation and I explained it had been only verbal. When I gave him my name, his face lit up immediately. He ushered me to a cramped seat at the bar.

The warm, somewhat fusty trattoria was packed with people, all of whom seemed to know each other. My lonely post attracted some sidelong looks, including several from a couple of quite alluring women. I ordered a Campari and soda and surveyed the crowd. The only other man sitting alone looked like a Mafia enforcer with fists the size of boxing gloves. A white scar ran horizontally across the top of his forehead as if someone had tried to scalp him and quit halfway into the job. He cast an unfriendly glance my way.

The crowd looked pretty well-heeled, everyone talking at once, the volume deafening. Nor did the roar die down much when the musicians, a trio, launched into a tune. Music is my lifeblood. Before I left New York I'd loaded up my phone with some of my favorites, a ton of John Mayer, Jimmy Page, and Mark Knopfler. And yet, the way events played out, I'd had almost no chance to listen to them. It was a real pleasure to take in some music for a change.

After a couple of songs a spotlight clicked on. The guest artist moved into the circle of light. My blood rushed. A gypsy was my first thought, a woman like the one Victor Hugo immortalized. Or Carmen, who drove Spanish soldiers mad with desire. She wore her long black hair unbraided and it fell to the middle of her back. A provocative silky shift swayed about her thighs.

The audience stopped chatting and sipped on their drinks appreciatively, devoting themselves to the feast before them. Ewan's noblewoman had changed her mind. Instead of sending an emissary, she'd come in person.

Later, I learned her Neapolitan songs shared many elements of Portuguese fado, melancholy songs of the heart. I couldn't understand all the words but that didn't matter; her voice embraced and consumed me. When she finished, the guests broke into an uproar of applause. Some called out her name. They obviously knew her. They would not settle down until she gave them two more songs. At the close, she faded away into the dark at the back of the stage. A goddess had come to entertain us and then disappeared like a phantom.

Emerging from my trance, I signaled to the waiter and asked him in Italian who she was. He laughed. "Ah! You have just had a special pleasure—Dina does not often sing. She does so occasionally at private gatherings like tonight, but never joins the guests afterward."

I doubted she'd left yet; it should not be too late to catch her. Beyond the stage and past the kitchen, I found a short corridor and saw a side entrance with a door propped open. I slipped through it. It led to an alcove partly obscured by a high wall. A Mercedes was parked with its motor running, the guy with the white scar I'd seen earlier in the club behind the wheel. Dina—should I call her that?—was pressed against the car, locked in a steaming embrace with a sleek, elegantly dressed man. I ducked back behind the door to avoid being seen but kept it partially open.

The man's back was to me so I couldn't see his face. If Dina was reluctant to talk to me before, intruding on this encounter would get me nowhere. I hoped he'd leave after saying good night to her.

She lifted her head back from the kiss. He turned slightly so he was in semi-profile, pulled her against his crotch, and ground into her pelvis; then he took her bottom lip in his mouth and bit down. He slipped his hand under the short silk sleeve of her dress, caressed her skin, and slowly pulled the sleeve down, fully exposing her breast. He bent his head. She let out a little gasp when he took her nipple in his mouth.

I was looking at the second person in Renwick's photo, the man with the shock of white hair and bronzed skin gripping Dina's shoulder.

The driver's presence didn't seem to deter them at all. Despite that, it was a deeply private moment and I knew I should do the decent thing and wrench myself away from the sight. When I shifted my feet to turn away, the man straightened up abruptly. Had he heard me? He looked around, trying to judge where the sound came from. Dina snatched up her dress. He murmured something to her, opened the rear door, and the two of them got in. The door shut with a solid thud and the car took off.

A wealthy, older man and a young woman—an old story. Any message for me tonight had been forgotten in the throes of passion.

Sixteen

hatever Dina felt about men, it certainly wasn't aversion. I wondered how that rumor got started. Back inside, most of the guests had left and they'd opened to the public. I ordered a couple of shots of Macallan deluxe single malt and lined them up in a row on the counter, western movie style. A little expensive but worth every penny.

Images of Dina and her lover swirled through my mind. He had a cruel, lean face and when he'd glanced around at the sound of my foot on the gravel, I saw his eyes were small and hard like two pale bullets. A man used to ordering people around.

An hour later I paid for my drinks and left. As I trudged along the hallway to my hotel room, I spotted Dina standing against the wall beside my door. Regrettably, she'd changed from the clingy dress she wore in the bistro to a pair of tight Levi's and a conservative navy-blue top. "I see you've had a change of heart," I said.

"I need to talk with you"—she glanced at the door—"privately."

"Well, that's what I'd hoped for. Come in." I opened the door and followed her inside. My room was a comfortable size with a window overlooking the street, a king-sized bed, a wardrobe, and two armchairs. Dina looked around, noting the state I'd left the room in. Not taking the time to unpack properly, I'd flung my jacket onto the bed and dropped wet towels haphazardly on the carpet.

"You have good taste in clothes," she said. "Like that Bugatti jacket. You should have hung it up. It's very North American to buy expensive things and treat them as if they came from your big-box store."

I had to smile at her gibe, imagining she'd never ironed so much as a napkin. "I didn't have time on account of having to rush out for an appointment to meet a lady. I came to the club tonight but you seemed otherwise occupied. Glad to see you now, though."

"Better late than never, no?" When she raised her hand to push a lock of hair off her face, I saw a cut had caused blood to streak down her hand and dry in the crevices between her fingers.

"What happened to your hand?" I said. "Looks like a nasty cut. Can I get you a bandage?"

Dina rubbed the dried blood as if she could make it disappear. "I came to do you a favor, Mr. Madison." She paused. "If you don't leave the city right away, you won't live to see another day in Naples."

"That's a pretty wild opening line." A fleeting thought passed through my mind that this was some kind of ruse to stop me from getting to the truth about the book. But the blood on her hand was real enough and she looked dead scared. "Who? Who's after me?"

She raised her voice a notch. "Lorenzo Mancini." She went over to the window and cast a frightened glance down the street before turning around. "You have to believe me."

"How did *you* find me?"

"I called Enzo at Gatto Nero. You told the bar woman."

"And who's Mancini?"

"I can't take the time to explain right now. His men could show up any minute. He doesn't know exactly where you're staying but it won't take him long to find out. Believe me. You're in extreme danger." She could see the doubt still hovering in my eyes. "You want the book, don't you?"

"Yes."

"Then come now."

Her fear was palpable so maybe her warning was valid. In any event, her promise to tell me about the book was too tempting to resist. I wanted to know more. I hastily packed my things.

Dina led me downstairs and out a back entrance. We passed rows of parked cars and reached a silver Alfa Romero a couple of streets away. She pulled a key fob out of her pocket and released the locks. "Get in," she said, hurrying around to the driver's side.

Except for a couple strolling arm-in-arm, the street was deserted. Still, I was wary of a trap. "My mother told me never to get in a car with a strange woman." I walked back to the corner, calling over my shoulder, "I'll wait for you on the main street."

With an exasperated huff, she swung into the driver's seat, started the car, and reversed toward me. The brakes screeched and she threw open the passenger door. "See? No one else is inside the car. Now *please* get in."

Dina put on sunglasses despite the hour, fumbled in the glove compartment for a scarf, and wound it around her head. She hit a button and the locks snapped shut. Her hands shook on the wheel as she backed out onto the street.

Italians drive like madmen; Dina was worse. She tore along the narrow streets and screeched the wheels on tight turns. Miraculously, she didn't attract any attention. Still, even in a town where rules were made to be broken, her speed seemed excessive. She wove west through the city center, all the time darting frightened glances at the rearview mirror.

"Okay," I said, growing uncomfortable, "stop the car for a minute."

She ignored me and continued driving.

When she was forced to brake for a rush of oncoming traffic I cranked my door open. "I said stop or I'll get out right now. I need some answers before we go any further. Who's Mancini?"

"My tormentor." She pulled over to the side of the road. A horn blared behind us. I shut the passenger door.

"Why's he after *me*?"

"Because you're trying to get the book back. He wants you out of the way."

"It belongs to him?"

"So he claims. I have more right to it than he does."

"Well, he's working with old information. I don't have it. It was stolen from me."

"Yes, Ewan told me." She looked straight ahead, avoiding my eyes.

"Did you also know that only one volume was contained within the gold covers? Not all five as advertised?" She didn't answer. "I'll take that as a yes. At first, it didn't look to me like the covers had been opened. But you must have and removed all the volumes except the first?"

Dina nodded again, still without looking me in the eye.

"So Ewan Fraser lied when he said he consigned the entire anthology to Sherrods. What did you do with the other four?"

She cast another worried look at the road behind us. "Don't blame Ewan. He was trying to help me. Just after Christmas last year I discovered the anthology hidden in the palazzo. I sold four volumes to buyers privately through Ewan. One in February. The next three over the spring and summer. Yours was the only one that went to a public auction."

Finally the truth. It was a straight admission she'd cheated

Renwick and me. "And you didn't think you'd be caught when it became clear the auction house only had the one volume and not the whole book?"

"By the time anyone found out, I planned to be far from here, living under a different name."

"Right. So, you sold a book you stole from your lover to fund your escape. And too bad for the buyer who ended up getting stiffed?"

"Walk away if you want but I'm willing to tell you who I sold the others to. *If* you help me get away from here." The haughty way she spoke didn't suggest much of a guilty conscience. In spite of her beauty, I found her manner abrasive.

"You seemed pretty damned close with Mancini at the bar."

Dina turned to me, hatred blazing in her eyes. "He forces me to stay in the palazzo. I'm guarded always and have no freedom. I can't drive anywhere or even go out for a walk unless one of his bodyguards is with me. They're called bodyguards but they're really my jailers."

"Yet he lets you sing at a club?"

"Only because it was a private party. He likes to hear me sing. His guard was in the room the whole time."

Her words brought back the image of the muscle man sitting alone at the club. "I had hoped to find a way to talk with you there but Lorenzo showed up earlier than I expected." Dina's hands hadn't stopped shaking and now a few tears slipped down her cheeks. I reached over to put a reassuring hand on her arm.

She thrust me away and searched for something in the side-door pocket. When she turned back, she held a small knife with a nasty-looking blade. "Don't touch me again," she whispered fiercely.

"Take it easy. I'm no danger to you. Threaten me again, Dina, and I get out of the car."

She clicked the blade back into its pearl handle and dumped it into her bag. "All right. As long as the ground rules are clear." She put the car in drive, checked her mirror again, and pulled out. "Lorenzo discovered the book was gone a few days ago. At first he thought a servant had taken it. He beat the man nearly to death with his own hands."

"Jesus! You saw him do that?"

"No. The staff talk. The servant's wife was furious about what happened to her husband. Tonight when we got home from the club she pointed the finger at me. He flew into a rage and forced me to tell him I'd sold the book through Ewan. Then he locked me in my room. That's how I hurt my hand. I broke my window to get out."

"Why didn't you go straight to the police?"

A strangled laugh caught in her throat. "Are you crazy? They'd never get in his way. They'd believe Lorenzo over me any day and agree I stole his book."

"You did."

She said nothing.

"Instead you ask a total stranger for help?"

"I had no choice. I'm desperate. But as I said before, I can help you track down the other volumes. Help me get out of Naples, out of Italy, and I'll tell you where they are."

I mulled over her proposition in silence. Her fear was real enough and I couldn't dismiss her claims out of hand. Most importantly, she promised to tell me where the other volumes were. I made up my mind to stay with her, for the time being at least.

"An old man stole the first volume from me right after the auction. He also robbed my client."

"An old man? What did he look like?" Her voice wavered.

"Black hair and a goatee. He used a cane."

"With a white horse on it?"

"That's him." She took her eyes off the road and in them I saw a spike of alarm. Her face had turned white.

"You obviously know who he is."

"He's an … associate, I guess you could say; he does Lorenzo's bidding. If he was able to get that close to you, it's a wonder you're still alive."

I thought back to the episode of paralysis. "This is going to sound crazy, but can he hypnotize people?"

"If I tell you anything more, you won't believe me."

Seventeen

"Ewan Fraser has been keeping my money safe in an account for me," Dina said. "I'm going to meet him now to get the papers."

"Is that wise?"

"There is no choice. He has all my funds."

"Where's the meeting?"

"At Gaiola."

We left the city center and drove west along Via Francesco. Dina pushed the car to its max, speeding past rows of newer condominiums and tourist resorts on the ritzy side of town. She seemed calmer after her outburst. Now that we'd come to an agreement she began to relax a little.

After a few minutes passed she spoke again. "We'll be going near a famous villa built by Pollio, a first-century Roman, called the Imperial Palace. It's named that because he left it to Emperor Augustus. Pollio was a human demon. He cut his slaves into pieces and threw them into stews, forcing the other slaves to eat them while they waited for their own executions."

"Not very charming. Why are you telling me this?"

She shrugged. "It's on the way. We're also going near an ancient navigator's shrine to Venus close to the site of a sorcerer's house—someone I expect you've heard of."

"Sorcerers don't tend to be part of my social register."

"You must know of Virgil, Dante's guide in the underworld. Many believed he was a magician. The house once belonged to him."

Her words reminded me of some of Basile's characters I'd noticed as I flipped through the English translation. They'd met equally gruesome fates. Penta, who tried to rebuff her brother's incestuous advances by cutting cut off her beautiful hands and presenting them to him in a basin. In another story called "The Crow," a queen threatened to blind herself when she discovered the king sacrificed their children to save his brother. The most chilling of all was "The Snake," about a crone who believed she'd become beautiful and win the king's heart if her old skin was shed. She died a horrible death when she had herself flayed. I assumed the author's dire descriptions were the product of his fertile imagination, but perhaps he'd simply faithfully recorded cruel practices from ancient times.

The road climbed. Spread out below the precipitous drop on one side, luxurious villas with their windows alight bloomed like rare flowers in a sea of green palms and pines. "Why meet Ewan all the way out here? Is this where he lives? He didn't strike me as a wealthy man."

"He rents space in a villa overlooking the Gaiola Islands. The owner is a friend who's often away and entrusts Ewan to look after it."

She yanked the wheel and made a sharp left onto a road that couldn't have been more than ten feet wide. High stone walls crested with vines bordered it on both sides. Dina careened down the steep route as if she were on a speedway and not a twisted canyon. The car shuddered when she hit a hole in the worn pavement. In that instant I thought we were done. But she didn't lose control and luck stayed with us the rest of the way. She eventually slowed to enter an open gate, pulling beside several cars parked in front of a stately home. "This is a private villa that takes paying guests," she said. "It'll be all right to leave the car here for a short time." She threw me a long look. "We can't be seen at Ewan's place."

"Understood. Where's the meeting supposed to be?"

"Near the shore." We locked the car and skirted the parking area and side garden to reach a narrow parting in the trees and a lengthy, precarious set of steps. The descent took us at a heart-stopping angle down the slope. Clusters of orange trees permeated the air with exotic scent. The stair ended at a rough pebble path. We followed it, and after about ten minutes I could hear the swish of waves. We emerged onto a kind of low parapet of old brick-work perched on the seashore. Below the parapet, waves washed over smooth black lava boulders. Two islets sat not thirty feet from shore off to our right. Beautiful though the landscape was with its tumbled ruins and lush flowers, fear pricked at my skin.

"Where's Ewan?" Dina whispered, glancing around anxiously. "He should have come by now."

"He's obviously going to be careful and take his time to make sure he's not followed."

"Maybe," she said doubtfully. She paced up and down the stone platform and kept checking her watch.

I looked closer at the islets, barely more than large chunks of rock rising vertically from the sea. Spray shot up as waves collided with the boulders at their bases. Long, angled concrete piers extended from each like a lobster's pincers. The islets were joined by a narrow archway. I couldn't tell whether it was a natural phenom-enon or constructed by human hands. Only a thin span with no railings, it was the most precarious bridge I'd ever seen.

A three-story house stood on the larger islet. A home in the process of decay like the ancient ruins nearby. Strangely, light spilled from the lower windows, just gaps now, missing the frames and glass, as if evil spirits had set up housekeeping there.

"What is that?" I asked when Dina came to stand beside me.

She expressed surprise at seeing the windows alight. "The Gaiola Islands. Someone's over there—that's really peculiar."

"It couldn't be Ewan, could it?"

"No. He'd stay away from it just like everyone else. That place is cursed. Everyone who has owned it has met with a terrible end. A wizard originally built the house and his spirit still haunts it. An industrialist named Hans Braun was murdered in that very spot. His wife drowned in the sea not long after. Another owner committed suicide and more misfortunes followed. No one dares buy it now. Except for a few tourists, people won't go there even during the day. Maybe it's just teenagers on a dare or something."

I walked over to the edge of the parapet and watched the waves break on the boulders below us. Something, it looked like a dead fish, turned in the waves. It fell into a trough and disappeared for an instant; then the force of the water tipped the white flesh up again as the wave crested.

I braced myself and leaned out, peering again at the thing in the dark water. It bobbed up, disappeared, and washed in closer. As it did so, its form became clearer and I nearly slipped with the shock. "Hell! Someone's drowned out there."

The drop was only about ten feet or so. I clambered down, skidding on the boulders slick with spray. Dina whimpered with fear and followed me. Several large waves heaved the body within a few feet of my precarious hold on a flat black rock at the bottom of the parapet. A man floated in the water; I could see that now. His bare torso and arms moved with the waves, giving the absurd impression he was trying to swim. I hadn't noticed his legs before because they were sheathed in the wet dark fabric of his pants.

I stretched my arm out as far as I dared. After a couple of misses I grasped his hand. It felt cold and slick to my touch. I grunted with the effort of pulling the heavy waterlogged body closer. A large wave rolled him toward me and he beached on the flat rock, face up.

Dina screamed.

It was Ewan Fraser. Someone had beaten his face so badly it barely looked human, one of his eyes a mass of pulpy flesh. His blond hair and beard hung like a wet fringe framing his face. The silver charm against the evil eye still dangled from his neck.

On his bloated belly was the bejeweled girdle book he'd proudly shown me at the library. Blood was still visible in the crevices of banded leather that formed the Turk's head knot. Someone had used the large, hard knot as a kind of blackjack, swinging it repeatedly into Ewan's face, and then tucked it back neatly into the belt like some kind of ghoulish signature.

Dina turned her back and sobbed. The scarf she wore blew off in the wind and floated eerily onto Ewan's damaged face before lifting again and drifting out to sea.

Perhaps it was the need to avoid that grim sight that caused me to look at the forlorn villa on the islet. A shadow passed across one of the windows, temporarily blocking out the light. A minute or so later a figure emerged through the empty doorway.

"Who's that?" I said quietly. Dina turned slowly at the sound of my voice. In the same instant, I knew. His black coat and hat, the cane that from this far away resembled a white needle, were only too familiar to me now. Alessio was alive.

Those black eyes bored into my soul as he stared directly across at us. He lifted his cane and pointed it in our direction. It was as if the wizard who'd built the place were warning us with a wave of his wand.

Dina clawed her way back up the parapet.

Eighteen

"Wait!" I called up to her. "How can I get over there? I don't want to lose him."

I may as well have been talking to the wind. Dina pulled herself over the rim of the parapet and ran toward the pebbled path. When I caught up with her, she was quaking with fear.

It was too dangerous to go straight back to the car. I persuaded her to take a circuitous route off the worn paths. We veered off through underbrush and along rock walls, keeping to the shadows and taking care not to make the slightest noise. Security lights flicked on when we came too close to a gated villa. "Is that where Ewan lived?" I asked.

Dina shook her head and led me to a cluster of cedars above where we'd parked. We could see the car's shimmer of metal just as we'd left it beside the other vehicles. Nothing seemed out of place. I picked up a fist-sized rock and heaved it toward the car. It bounced off the asphalt with a sharp crack but I couldn't detect any motion in response, no one alerted to the noise, no voices.

We waited another ten minutes to be sure. "Time's getting

short," I said. "We have to risk it now." We scrambled down the slope as quietly as possible. Dina started the car and drove back down the narrow lane. When we reached the main road, we both sighed in relief. I was amazed we made it out of there alive. And yet just as my heart rate returned to something resembling normal, questions once more crowded my brain. Had Alessio killed Ewan himself, or were Mancini's men involved? If so, where were they? Perhaps they'd attacked Ewan at home and thrown his body into the sea without learning of the meeting. Had Ewan passed out or died before they found out about the plan to meet with us? It didn't matter what Ewan had told them, I realized. Alessio had seen us. And he'd be coming for us. How had he survived the freezing undercurrents of the Thames?

Dina gripped the wheel tensely and fixed her eyes straight ahead, her face wet with tears. I kept checking the mirrors to see if we were being followed, and tried unsuccessfully to rid my memory of Ewan's hideous image.

I broke the silence by saying gently, "We can't just leave Ewan there. We should call the police." I handed her my phone. "My Italian isn't good enough."

She took a few minutes to compose herself and without slowing down, made a brief call, hanging up without mentioning our names. Dina kept one hand on the wheel while she reached for a tissue and dabbed at her eyes. "Now do you believe me?" she said, her voice sullen. "Look what Lorenzo did to Ewan. He tortured him—murdered him—to find out who our buyers were."

She was right about that and I felt indebted to her. "You saved my life by warning me to get out of Naples. It was brave of you to waste precious time to find me."

Dina glanced at me. "I wouldn't have. But this has all happened faster than I ever thought. Someone had to help me and you were my only choice."

She spoke bitterly but truthfully, I supposed. The headlights of an oncoming car illuminated her tear-stained face.

"Have you ever met Charles Renwick? An English publisher who commissioned me to bid on the book."

"I've never heard of this person. Why should I?"

"He took your picture, or at least he had a photo. Of you and Mancini."

"Impossible. The conte is very careful. He hates having his photo taken."

"From your expressions, neither of you realized you were being photographed. Maybe it was at a party or something and you were caught unawares."

"Perhaps. What does it matter?"

"I just wondered why Renwick would be interested in you. He must have known Mancini owned the book he desired." I chose my words carefully, seeing how distressed she was and not wanting to upset her further. "Tell me about Mancini. Where does his money come from? Was it inherited?"

"Yes. He's from an old aristocratic family. His title is the Comte de Soissons."

"Isn't that French?"

"It is. The family had many ties of marriage with the French court centuries ago. He owns an investment bank now."

"What kind of businesses is the bank associated with?"

"I'm not really sure. He has quite a few Middle Eastern clients; I think he finances a lot of Iraqi oil contracts." She took her eyes off the road for a moment to glance at me again. "Please, I'd rather not speak of him now. I just want to forget him."

The car had been climbing steadily through a landscape increasingly devoid of trees and bushes. We seemed to reach the top of whatever hilly terrain we were traveling through. We turned a bend and I nearly did a double take. "What the hell is that? The ground's on fire!" My eyes hadn't deceived me. Smoke rose directly from the earth. A noxious odor filled the car.

Dina answered without even blinking. "We're in Pozzuoli. There are many ancient volcanoes here."

We were on a lonely stretch of road dotted with dilapidated, abandoned structures.

"What happened to these buildings?" I asked.

"An earthquake struck thirteen years ago. The land rises and falls even now. It's very unstable. No one wants to build on it again."

Perhaps Dina had ventured here to best avoid Mancini. We'd soon know, I thought, whether that was the right move.

A little farther on she parked beside an old commercial outlet shut up for the night. Turning off the ignition, she put her arms on the steering wheel and sank into them. The harsh glare of floods at the side of the building lit up her hair and the shape of her body hunched over the wheel. I wanted to console her, but remembering the little knife, thought it best to just give her some space.

After a few minutes she said, "I didn't think we'd make it this far. I've been planning this for months but needed a few additional things to fall into place. Tonight when the conte discovered I was the one who'd taken the book, I could wait no longer."

"How did you get the car?"

"It's my friend's. Luisa knows what I've suffered. We made an arrangement for me to get in touch with her when I decided to leave him."

"And you're using the money from the sale to escape."

"Lorenzo owes it to me—and much more. I'm entirely dependent on him and have no resources of my own. He keeps the jewelry my mother left me in his safe." Her words caught in her throat.

"What about your other relatives? Couldn't they help you?"

"My father's family was aristocratic although in name only. Through hard work and some good connections, Father built up a business in shipping. One of his boats foundered at sea and the other burned due to arson. The insurance company refused to cover either of them so he lost everything. We had to leave Naples and settle on the one piece of land he still owned, a poor farm outside the city."

"How did you meet Mancini?"

Dina wiped her cheeks with the sleeve of the light top she wore. "Lorenzo and his wife persuaded my father to let me come live with them. They preyed on his hardship and paid him to stay away. Now that Ewan's gone I have nothing left. No friends. No money."

It was a shocking story. True? That was another matter. Elements of her story didn't hold water. "Why split up the book? It would have been worth a lot more if you'd kept all the volumes together."

"I hated to. It almost seemed sacrilegious to break the anthology apart. But I had to."

"Why?"

"The book is evil. I can tell you no more."

"You must. People are dying, Dina! Charles Renwick was robbed and probably murdered for it. You saw what happened to Ewan. The book may be rare and valuable. That doesn't explain why a rich man like Mancini is willing to kill people for it."

"You won't believe me if I tell you."

"Try me."

"The book possesses secrets. Terrible secrets that, if discovered, would lead to unthinkable consequences. Lorenzo wants to unravel its mysteries because he's convinced they point to something of great value. I don't know exactly what he seeks, but it has to do with his ancestor in the seventeenth century, Baron Lorenzo Mancini. He was an occultist and a necromancer—do you know what that means?"

"Raising the dead to predict the future, right?"

Dina looked away for a moment as if trying to decide whether to reveal any more. "The conte studied the ancient Italian practice of necromancy. He learned how to summon a demon who can raise the dead. In French the demon's name is Frucissière. It's also called Frulhel or Frastiel. The painter—José de Ribera—you've heard of him?"

"Yes. He illustrated Basile's book."

"He was a follower of the dark arts too. He left papers in the book with instructions on how to raise Frucissière. Lorenzo found them and followed them."

Tye Norris had said that Renwick feared a demon pursued him. We'd both scoffed at the idea two days ago. Now I wasn't so sure. Was this what Renwick's warning about the book meant? "A hardheaded businessman like Mancini actually believes in necromancy?"

"Not all things in this world can be easily explained away."

"I know, Dina, but isn't it more likely just another ruse to scare you into submission? Those old stories are just cultural curiosities now."

She frowned, affronted I'd challenge her beliefs. "If only it were that simple. The well-ordered world you think you know doesn't exist. There is a universe beyond our limited thoughts, things that live beyond our imagining. Forbidden knowledge."

"They're just old legends. Not really true." Even as I said the words, my certainty began to erode.

"Believe me or not. I don't care," she said disdainfully. She fished in her purse and pulled out a folded paper. "Here's an eyewitness account involving Basile and de Ribera. It's more proof I'm telling the truth. You can't let Lorenzo reassemble the book! I don't care what you believe. What matters is that Lorenzo does."

I stuck the paper in my jacket pocket. "Okay. Let's leave this for now. I'm going to track down those other volumes with your help. All right?"

"Yes." She rubbed her hands together as if trying to dismiss her bizarre statements.

I'd had enough of superstitious talk. "Does anything else motivate Mancini?"

"He's scrupulous about keeping track of his lineage and belongs to two of the oldest noble families in Europe: the Savoys and the Mancinis. They go back over one thousand years. He has pretensions to the throne of Italy."

That explained the Savoy coat of arms on the cedar box. But her last words rang in my ears. "That hardly seems credible."

"On the surface maybe."

"How would that even be possible? Italy's been a republic for almost sixty years."

"Yes of course, I know that. The king was exiled and all his property confiscated because he supported Mussolini and the Fascists. Just this year the heir to the throne was allowed to return, although not as a monarch. Two branches of the House of Savoy have made claims to the throne. The conte believes he, too, has a legitimate right, and in the coming climate of uncertainty thinks he may have an edge. He is, in fact, much wealthier and more powerful than the Savoy family."

I'd heard of aristocrats challenging one another for titles, even when those titles lost the relevance they once held. Usually that took the form of prolonged court battles that only made their lawyers richer. "Fighting over a throne that no longer exists. Talk about delusions of grandeur."

She raised her eyebrows. "Now, yes. But Lorenzo has said many times that great financial and social upheavals lie ahead. Under such conditions, people yearn for stability and structure. Royalty stands for that, if nothing else."

"Why does he think he could be a claimant?"

"He says his ancestor, a son of Olympia Mancini, by rights should have inherited the title that led to the establishment of the royal family but it was denied him. That's not actually true. You've probably never heard of the Ordine civile e militaire dell'Aquila Romana—the Order of the Roman Eagle?" she asked.

"Is it a medal of some kind?"

"There is a medal, yes. It's an aristocratic order, like an elite society. Benito Mussolini founded it in 1942. The Italian government quickly terminated it after the Second World War ended. The conte is part of a small coterie of nobles who swear their allegiance to that order."

"All Italians?"

"No, only him, although they all possess true hereditary titles. What they have in common is they're disaffected. Some lost their property and fortunes generations ago. They know the aristocracy has been terribly weakened and seek to restore it. Lorenzo thinks the time is coming to reassert aristocratic dominance. When the Western economies crumble, states will fall apart. And all these men, except the conte, have ties with the police and the military."

"Why not him?"

"He doesn't need them. He has the Camorra. He finances them and washes their money to make it legitimate. They're an army in waiting."

Dina shifted in her seat, rested her forehead on her hand, and sighed, giving me a glimpse of the great burden she carried. "At the time Giambattista Basile lived Naples was one of the most important cities in Europe. It can be so again. Criminal organizations often seize power when societies fragment. That's what happened in Kosovo. Lorenzo's group of nobles share his passion for power and the art of necromancy."

"It's still difficult to fathom," I said slowly.

"I would agree, except it looks like he actually achieved it. He brought Alessio back from the dead."

"Alessio? You can't be serious!"

"I watched him do it."

Nineteen

Her words stunned me. I didn't know what to say. It was a ridiculous notion, and yet a part of me had sensed that Alessio and his power over me were—unnatural. "He's included you in some of those occult rituals, then?"

"No. He never allowed women to participate. I hid and watched it." A shiver ran through her as if she were watching it all over again. "That's why the man you call Alessio terrifies me."

"He's a dead ringer for Giambattista Basile."

"Exactly."

"That only proves he bears a likeness to his ancestor."

"No. He's a product of the conte's sorcery."

I felt my rational mind sliding into a dark place it didn't want to go. I tried one more angle. "Alessio speaks English. It sounded antiquated but almost perfect grammatically. How do you explain a seventeenth-century Neapolitan with the ability to speak modern English?"

"Only a few hundred years ago he lived as one of the best-educated members of the Spanish court in Naples. And he traveled. Of course he could speak English. French and Spanish too."

Challenging her any further would serve no purpose. She believed. It was that simple. Ideas like that could cripple even the most rational people if their motivation was strong enough. And Dina had been exposed to Mancini's warped thinking for years. There was one thing I was sure of, though—Alessio worked for Mancini.

"How are we going to get the rest?"

"I can't approach ... all the owners on my own. I need your help with that. I made a mistake. I should have destroyed the whole book when I first laid eyes on it and never tried to sell it."

"Okay, so who has the other four volumes?"

Dina dug her nails into my arm and cast a startled look behind her. She'd parked the car so it couldn't be seen directly from the road. I hadn't paid much attention to the cars whizzing by, but now I heard what she heard, a vehicle slowing down behind us. Its high beams shot a blinding light through our back window. The car swung in beside us. I opened the passenger door, ready to confront the driver.

A sturdy guy of about twenty-five got out, and without even looking at me strode over to Dina.

"It's all right." Dina's deep sigh of relief was audible. "This is Joachim."

"A friend?"

"The cousin of my friend Luisa. We have to change cars now."

She got out and said, *"Grazie, Joachim."*

"E' arrivat' sta bbuon'. Tutt' a appost'. Luisa sarrà felic."

"Pe' ffavor' ringraziatel' pe mmè. Luisa è na bbon' amica," Dina replied.

He tipped his baseball cap and they exchanged keys. After we grabbed our bags he climbed into the Alfa Romeo and sped away.

The new car looked like a discard from a low-end rental agency.

I volunteered to drive. She handed me the keys and remained standing outside while I shifted into the driver's seat. Then she said, "I'm just going behind that clump of trees over there. I don't want to stop for a restroom on the main highway because we'd be too visible. I won't be long."

I watched her make her way over to a grove of stunted palms and thought about Joachim. At no time had he glanced my way, almost as if he'd been expecting me to be there. I suppose Dina could have told Luisa about me earlier tonight, but even then it felt unusual for the guy not to have at least acknowledged my presence.

Visibility was good thanks to the full moon although not enough to see much in the engine. Being hunted months ago in New York with a tracking device taught me to be vigilant.

I grabbed my bag and quietly left the car, taking out my penlight. I lifted the hood and played the light over the motor. Everything looked normal. Just paranoia on my part, perhaps. I felt carefully along the underside of fenders and finding nothing, bent down and peered underneath. The penlight shone on the mud-encrusted undercarriage and picked up an object that didn't belong under any vehicle. A series of colored wires twisted out of a small package wrapped in black plastic.

I straightened up like a shot and ran toward the palms. I didn't catch Dina dishabille; instead I found her leaning against a tree, talking on her cell. She jumped when she saw me and abruptly clicked off her phone.

"Who were you talking to?"

"Just Luisa. She called to make sure Joachim came on time. Why are you carrying your bag?"

"There's a bomb under the car your friend so nicely lent you."

She let out a little cry. "No! Luisa would never do that."

"Maybe she didn't know. Mancini's people probably tapped

your phone. If you've used your cellphone to talk to her, Mancini could have gone straight to her cousin and forced him to cooperate. Or just crossed his palm with a hell of a lot of silver." I looked right into her eyes. "I'm telling you it's there. I just saw it. Where did you say we're headed?"

"Rome."

"Call her back right now. Apologize for cutting her off. Say I interrupted you. Then let her know we'll be leaving here in about fifteen minutes for Rome as planned."

She protested bitterly when I said we couldn't get her things out of the car and she'd have to ditch her phone, but I managed to persuade her and we took off. They'd figure out pretty fast no one was in the car when it blew and I felt anxious Joachim might park close by, waiting to hit his remote and touch off the explosion. We probably had only seconds left.

My answer came soon enough. We'd just mounted a small hill when we heard a deep *whump*. As we turned in the direction of the sound, a flash seared the surrounding terrain, lighting up the roof-line of the building we'd left, followed by a belch of smoke and the irritating smell of burning plastic and oil. Tires sprayed gravel as a motor started up farther away. We hid behind some trees in case Joachim was on his way back. Thankfully the sound of the engine receded into the distance.

To be sure, ours was a shaky alliance. I had far too many questions about Dina's trustworthiness, starting with that phone call she made. Was she really just communicating with her friend or telling her I was in the car and they could blow it up? "We've got to get off this road," I said grimly. "Is there a highway anywhere near? We'll have to hitch a ride."

"Yes. It will take a while to get there but we can reach it." Dina clasped her arms around her chest and shivered. "I can't believe it. That Luisa would betray me."

"Maybe they didn't give her any choice." I took off my jacket and handed it to her. It was far too big. She looked like a street waif with it draped awkwardly over her slight shoulders.

We cut across several minor roads and found a footpath winding through some kind of park. The trees gave way and we stepped onto a huge gravel plain with a pond near its center. In the distance, smoke poured from crevices in the rock. Dina anticipated my question. "The crater of the Solfatara volcano. Some believe it is the home of Vulcan, an entrance to Hades."

After what we'd just been through a visit to hell seemed somehow perfectly fitting, and it wasn't hard to see where the idea had come from. The air reeked of sulfur. Across the crater, smoke billowed from pits and holes. A weird yellowish light emanated from the fumaroles. Encrusted rocks and minerals surrounded these openings—brimstone, the old-fashioned name for sulfur deposits. In places the soil had burned so it was little more than cinder, all the vegetation scorched off. It was a strange sensation to put my hand on the ground and feel how hot it was, as if the very earth were dying of fever. Not being of a religious turn of mind, I'd never paid any heed to stories about sinners roasting forever in the fires of hell. And yet here, with night closed in around us and the flares of light turning the plumes of smoke an eerie yellow, I could almost be convinced.

We walked at a good clip, anxious to reach the access road to the highway. "Tread carefully here," Dina said. "We're only on a thin crust. It's all boiling liquid underneath."

Fortunately, we'd almost reached the end of the crater when Dina told me that. I burst out laughing. "Thanks for taking me on the scenic route." She made a good choice, though, by coming here. We were totally alone and no one, I now felt sure, was mapping our progress away from Naples.

After a long trek we made it to an interchange for the A56, which led to the E45, the major highway north. As we waited to hitch a ride I said, "Your game plan was to go to Rome—then what?"

"I needed the anonymity of a large city away from Italy, one I could get lost in. Luisa bought me an air ticket to Berlin under her name. I have an old friend there the conte doesn't know about. He'd expect me to travel to London instead because that's where I went to school."

"Did you discuss this with her on your cellphone?"

"I told her."

"Well, that's out then. So, let me suggest this. If we recover even one volume of the five you sold, at the very least, it will give us some leverage. Who has the others? Who did you sell them to?"

"The nearest is in France, a rich businessman named Alphonse Renard. Ewan told me he's a prominent rare book collector but the only contact is through a post box at Les Saintes-Maries-de-la-Mer."

Twenty

November 21, 2003
En route to Les Saintes-Maries-de-la-Mer, France

We landed a ride with English tourists who vacationed every year in southern Italy and chose November to avoid the summer crowds. They were driving overnight to Florence and kindly dropped us off at a junction where we hitched another ride to the seaport town of Civitavecchia. At six in the morning we huddled in a café until we could get a ferry to Marseilles. We ended up having to wait most of the day and finally boarded a ferry that accepted walk-on passengers. The ship had launched only a few weeks earlier; it was brand spanking new and very comfortable. Our trip would last, weather permitting, about fourteen hours. In the passenger lounge we watched the Tyrrhenian Sea turn from shimmering aquamarine to copper to flat mauve in the fading light.

Once safely away from the shores of Italy, Dina relaxed a little and told me more about her family. "My mother had a lot of trouble conceiving," she said, wrapping her hands around a flimsy paper cup full of coffee. "She prayed every day for a child.

She'd almost given up hope when she learned she was pregnant. I came into the world on her fortieth birthday. She died two years later."

"Do you remember her at all?"

"Only from photos. When I was very little I'd stand the framed picture of her I liked best on my bookshelf and talk to her. Pretend it was really her in the room. My nurse scolded me for it and said if she'd died it must have been part of God's plan and I had to accept it. She took all my photos away. I cried for days after that but by then, her face had been imprinted on my memory."

"We have that in common. My mother died in a mining accident before I turned three."

Dina's features softened for an instant. "Oh. Sorry to hear that."

We all have a tendency to think other people's lives are happy and full until we get to know them better. I couldn't be sure that Dina's sad story was true, but I found myself wanting to believe it. I suggested she consider moving to New York, a big enough city to get lost in, far removed from Mancini's influence. Somewhere I could look out for her.

"A city might give me a place to escape to," she said in reply, "not permanently. I suffocate in cities. I much prefer country life."

I nodded, even though I didn't understand the appeal.

I cast around for a way to get her mind off her troubles. "Okay, let's talk about something else. Well, since stories are dictating our lives right now, tell me your favorites when you were a kid."

That cheered her a little and her eyes sparkled. "Oh, that is hard! I like so many of them. I've always loved fairy tales. I guess my favorite is 'The Young Slave.' It's one of Basile's." She rolled her eyes at me and smiled. "It is like 'Snow White,' but much darker. The Grimms' first 'Snow White' was quite disturbing. The king fell incestuously in love with his own daughter, and her mother, not a stepmother, tried to kill her."

I didn't recall seeing 'The Young Slave' when I read some of Basile's stories. "Tell it to me. I'd like to hear it."

"Well, I may not be able to recite all of it but here's how it starts: 'There was once upon a time a Baron of Selvascura who had an unmarried sister....' I can't remember the next lines but she swallowed a rose petal. Then it goes, 'Not less than three days later, Lilla felt herself to be pregnant, and nearly died of grief, for she knew well she had done nothing compromising or dishonest, and could not therefore understand how it was possible for her belly to have swollen. She ran at once to some fairies who were her friends, and when they heard her story, they told her not to worry, for the cause of it all was the rose-leaf that she had swallowed.'"

Dina chuckled and I was glad to see her relax enough to laugh. I thought about the Disney "Snow White" with the sad-eyed queen who wished for a baby girl. The image of her sitting in a window with her embroidery, pricking her finger and seeing a few drops of her blood falling on the white snow, was imprinted on my brain. How much the story had changed from its early versions. "Go on," I said.

"This is in my own words now. The maiden bore a beautiful baby girl named Lisa. She sent Lisa to the fairies, each of whom gave her a charm. The last one put a curse on her—a poisoned comb would stick in her hair and cause her to die. The fairies enclosed Lisa in seven crystal caskets and locked it inside a room in the castle."

"What, no dwarfs?"

"No dwarfs." She laughed again. "The Grimms added them. The girl's mother was so grief-stricken she fell ill, but before she died she begged her brother the baron to keep Lisa a secret. His suspicious wife unlocked the door against his wishes. Jealous, and suspecting the baron kept this beautiful woman as a lover, she wrenched open the caskets and pulled the girl out, causing the comb to drop out of her hair. Lisa awoke. The wife beat her and cut off her hair. She forced her to wear rags and treated her miserably like a slave girl."

"Amazing to compare that with today's version."

"I haven't told you the ending yet. One day, the baron, who hadn't recognized Lisa, returned home from a trip and overheard her crying about her fate. He embraced his niece and banished his wife from the castle. Lisa married happily and the moral of the story is 'heaven rains favors on us when we least expect it.'"

"Let's hope the heavens treat us that well," I said.

A couple sat on our right. The woman curled her legs up on the bench and nestled beside the man. He put his arm securely around her and smoothing her hair away from her face, touched his lips to her forehead. Dina observed them, not with delight at seeing their fondness for each other, but as if they were a pair of alien creatures.

"I can't imagine what it's like," she said, "actually wanting a man to kiss you like that. Do you have a girlfriend?"

"Not now." I thought of Laurel Vanderlin.

"But you have … in the past?"

"Sure."

I didn't sense her question arose out of an interest in me personally. It almost seemed as if she were trying to comprehend how normal people felt.

"I'll never be able to fall in love."

I looked at her with surprise. Her startling admission spoke volumes of Mancini's abuse. At some point, Mancini had ceased being her protector and become her lover. When did he cross that line and turn a kindly act into something sinister? I didn't want to press her on that issue right now. She'd had enough of bad memories. If Dina broke free of him permanently, given time, she might see love differently. She gazed out the window at the gray sea and said nothing more. The only sound I heard escape her lips was the rush of an occasional sigh. I sensed those deep sighs signaled an extreme loneliness welling up from the bottom of her soul.

We sipped sodas and coffees and listened to the low drone of the heavy ship's mighty engine sluicing through the water. Waves slapped the sides of the vessel, the regular swish of the salty sea like a magical soporific marking progress in time but seeming to suspend it as well. Eventually Dina succumbed to the watery lullaby and slept.

In repose her face looked like that of a sleeping child. But the image of innocence was belied by her injury. Although the swelling had gone down the bite on her lip still looked red and sore. Had she been brave, finding the courage to break away, keeping her presence of mind when she'd felt humiliated and afraid? Or had she lied to me?

On the one hand, her natural assertiveness didn't fit easily with the picture of the victim she painted. Especially in this day and age, unless she'd been locked in a dungeon like the abused women in sensational news stories, could anyone really be held against her will for years, even by a powerful tyrant? Why not try to escape much sooner? And why choose this particular time, when she'd just met me, to flee from him? The reason she gave for wanting to recover the volumes she'd sold didn't ring true. She had some other motive, but what it was eluded me. Even if she'd told the truth about her ill treatment by Mancini and his criminal designs, I still believed some undisclosed agenda motivated her.

More than once over the last few days I'd felt caught up in some wild fantasy. And the narrative seemed to grow ever more bizarre with each passing hour. The memory of Ewan's ruined face and bloated body was achingly real. I had no choice now but to see the story through to its end.

With hours stretching before me until we docked, I decided to look up de Ribera. I knew he rivaled Velázquez as the most important Spanish painter of the seventeenth century. The son of a Spanish shoemaker, he rose to incredible heights. His great talent propelled his meteoric rise but two women also played a crucial role. A narrative worthy of any modern-day celebrity. He fled Spain for Rome as a result of a scandal involving a painter's daughter and achieved almost instant recognition when he moved again from Rome to Naples. He had much better luck with patrons than Basile, because he married the daughter of an influential art dealer who championed the artist's work.

De Ribera's fascination with the grotesque was amply reflected in his many images of martyred saints on the cusp of death. I knew he also liked to paint individuals with disabilities and remembered pictures of a boy with a club foot and dwarfs. To my eye he had no intention to mock them but handled those subjects with a keen eye and sensitivity.

After de Ribera's meteoric rise to fame and subsequent wealth, he fell like a shooting star when a serious illness curtailed his work in the 1640s. A decade later he died in poverty. Had his fascination with the dark side of the human spirit led to his interest in necromancy, or was it more personal? I finally drifted off with his pictures still vivid in my memory and woke only when the intercom blared our arrival at port.

Twenty-One

November 22, 2003
Les Saintes-Maries-de-la-Mer

In Marseilles we caught a bus to Les Saintes-Maries-de-la-Mer. White stucco buildings spilled onto flat sandbars at the shoreline. This was a working man's town. Springing up like an oddity at the town's center was a twelfth-century Romanesque church resembling a miniature medieval fortress. The vast green marsh of the great Rhône delta, called the Camargue, swelled beyond the town.

We found the post office with no trouble. The little depot flew the fleur-de-lys, wedged in between a café and a store selling "genuine" Camargue-inspired bric-a-brac. Dina did her best to coax the postal clerk into telling her where Renard lived but didn't get very far. He'd spoken rapidly in French so I had trouble taking it in.

"We may not be able to see the merchant at all," Dina said after we left the post office.

"How so?"

"Renard lives in a remote area and doesn't encourage visitors.

The clerk said we can get into his estate only on horseback or by foot. He doesn't allow motor vehicles on his property. He gave me the name of someone who might help us. Marc Hanzi knows everyone in the area. He lives near Les Alpilles."

"The little Alps?" I asked. She nodded. "Well, there's something to be said for small towns. We'd never have figured that out for ourselves. Hanzi doesn't sound very French."

"It isn't. Bohemian, most likely, Romany. Here, they're called the Manoush, not Gypsies. He's a Gardian. Have you heard of them?"

"A guardian—sure, like a protector."

She laughed. "Sort of. It's spelled without the *u*. Gardians tend livestock like your western cowboys. They're quite famous. It sounds like finding Hanzi will be difficult enough."

Thinking he lived in a village, I asked, "Is it far away?"

"Far enough. We should get started now."

Not knowing what lay ahead of us or how easy communication might be, I checked my email and was reassured to hear from Corinne that Evelyn was in good spirits and they were enjoying each other's company. Evelyn owed Corinne three dollars at poker and Corinne was taking her winnings in baking.

Before leaving town I gave Dina cash to purchase new clothes and toiletries and enough extra that she wouldn't be stranded if we happened to get separated. We also bought knapsacks and transferred our belongings into them, along with some water, wine, cheese, and *fougasse*, a round bread topped with oil and olives. We followed a gritty sand road out of town leading onto the wide stretches of the marsh.

The road became a gravel trail, no more than a berm rising a few feet above the swampy ground. The sea lapped at the marsh edges far off on the horizon. Our path took us northward. The day was bright and clear, cool but sunny enough that we stowed our windbreakers and walked comfortably in our shirts. Even in November the marsh was lush with tall wild grasses, willows, and shrubs interspersed with open areas and pondlets. Flocks of pink flamingos burst into the air as we passed by. Our shoes left prints on the spongy ground. I thought of the Apsu, the watery element Mesopotamians believed lay under the rim of the earth. If the great deltas of the Euphrates and Tigris resembled this, I understood how their ancient surroundings could give rise to such a notion.

A herd of cattle lingered not far off. It surprised me to see a bull among them with no fence anywhere to be seen. "They just let bulls roam free around here?"

"They're only dangerous if you're waving a red flag," she laughed. "These are the black bulls you see in the Spanish rings. They come from here."

"Have you been here before? You know so much about it."

"When you spend hours alone you read a lot. I used to imagine places to run to and this was one of them. Idyllic, no?" Although she still looked disheveled and weary after our mad race away from Naples, when she drew in a few deep breaths of the clean, sweet sea air she seemed at ease for the first time since I'd met her.

We made our way over to the D85A and hitched a ride to Arles. After standing with our thumbs out for more than half an hour, we were picked up by a trucker who took us past the town of Saint-Martin-de-Crau. He dropped us off at a little road that ran north into a sparse plain.

"I hope I got the directions right," Dina said. "This should be Chemin de Archimbaud. There's a little settlement up here. It's supposed to be not too far to walk."

I hoisted my knapsack over my shoulder and we traveled north again. This terrain was radically different from the Camargue. Flat table land stretched as far as the eye could see. The farmers' fields and sparse grasses were cut off in the distance by a gigantic stone massif. The beginning of Les Alpilles.

The place we found was not much more than a collection of farm buildings. A ruddy-faced woman in coveralls greeted us when we knocked at one of the doors. A broad smile crossed her face when we mentioned Marc Hanzi's name and she told us to take a track that meandered farther north across the plain.

We made good time and found his home fairly easily. A low structure of softly rounded white stucco, topped by a thatched roof and capped with a small white cross, it sprang out of the flat landscape like a curious mushroom. Its roof of thatch didn't resemble the English style but was neatly arranged in layers like a flamenco dancer's skirt. A herd of sheep and seven white horses grazed close by.

Hanzi's curious little house had no windows and only a simple wooden door. An enormous pair of bull horns hung over the lintel. No one answered our knock. "Don't tell me we've come all this way for nothing," I moaned.

"Patience is a virtue, I suspect, especially around here. He'll show up sooner or later." Dina's spirits had definitely taken a turn for the better since our arrival in France.

I wandered near the horses. They had squarish heads, short necks, and deep chests. Dina joined me and explained that their black skin and white coat were characteristic of the breed. They were never shod and considered to be very hardy. I knew next to nothing about horses but could tell the Camargues were smaller and stockier than Arabian thoroughbreds I'd seen. As we settled down near some willow brush to wait, hoofbeats drummed from somewhere behind the house.

Horse and rider pulled up in front of us. A genial-looking man whom I guessed to be in his forties dismounted. He was not tall. He wore a black, narrow-brimmed fedora, white shirt, and black vest and pants and carried a trident. A Camargue version of a herding stave, I supposed.

Dina addressed him in French and introduced me as her American friend. He replied to her in English that in the summer he ran riding tours of the Alpilles, and years of dealing with tourists meant he could converse quite well in English. He greeted us warmly at first, but his good humor vanished when he heard our request to hire horses to journey to Renard's. When he learned I wasn't an accomplished rider, Hanzi reacted with outright concern.

Dina remonstrated with him and after a promise to double his payment, Hanzi reluctantly agreed, only on condition that I prove myself trustworthy with the animals.

I was game for anything. And so it was that we spent the rest of the day with the horses.

I grew up in New York City, where, except for a couple of summers of riding instruction at a camp in Lake Placid, the nearest I came to horses were carriage rides around Central Park. Dina, on the other hand, swung into the saddle with ease and held the reins confidently. "We're letting you ride the big stallion. He runs like the wind." She leaned over and spoke in French to Hanzi, who broke out laughing.

I tried to disguise my dismay.

Hanzi, wiping a mirthful tear from his eye, finally addressed me. "No, you have the mare. She is quite peaceful, very, very good—no trouble with her."

I nodded and gingerly approached her. But after I mounted, I gripped the reins too hard. The mare gave a start when she felt the pull on her bit and backed up; I grabbed the saddle with my left hand to steady myself. Hanzi stroked her neck and whispered soothing words. Using gestures, he showed me how to hold the reins in one hand and leave them a bit slack, to pull to the right or left and loosen them as soon as she obeyed. Dina, who rode the stallion they'd jokingly threatened me with, commenced a leisurely walk. My horse followed behind with ease.

Dina and Hanzi spent a long time helping me get used to the feeling of riding, instructing me on proper posture in the saddle, where to position my legs, how to pull back gently if I wanted the horse to stop. Hanzi observed me closely and occasionally muttered instructions to correct my technique. When I could stay in the saddle as the mare broke into a trot, Hanzi decided I'd passed muster.

The setting sun turned the grass to gold. With night closing in upon us, we decided to wait and strike out for Renard's in the morning. For an additional fee, Hanzi welcomed us inside.

Twenty-Two

November 22, 2003
Les Alpilles, France

The interior of Hanzi's cottage was sparse—rough planked floors, rudimentary bathroom, sleeping alcove, and loft with a double bed. The large ground-floor room had a cupboard, a handmade table and chairs, and a counter holding a hotplate with a half fridge underneath. Without hydro wires in the vicinity, I guessed these were powered with propane. Sheaves of herbs and strings of garlic and fat red onions hung from a wooden handrail. Mixed scents of oregano, thyme, and rosemary wafted through the room. Several comfortable-looking easy chairs on a bright carpet were grouped around a potbellied wood stove.

The air grew chilly when the sun went down, so I got the fire going while Dina and Hanzi prepared a light supper. We were starving and, happily, dinner was delectable. We sat down to a hearty mutton ragout—reheated leftovers tasting of fresh herbs—an omelet, brown farmer's bread, and ripe pears for dessert. We broke open one of the bottles of wine we'd bought. Hanzi proved a more than genial companion. He had an engaging laugh and a great, odd sense of humor.

We topped up our wine glasses and sat around the fire. "This place is my work house. Where I come to tend the animals, you know, and lead the holiday tours. My wife and six little ones are at home in town. Here is my escape." He gestured around the small cottage expansively, and we joined him in a good-natured laugh.

"You picked the wrong season, you two," he said. "May is best when people come from all around the world to Les Saintes-Maries-de-la-Mer." He swung a wiry brown arm in an arc around the room as if pointing to the countries of the globe. "Then we celebrate our patron saint—Black Sarah—and the arrival of St. Mary Jacobé, St. Mary Salomé, and La Magdalene, who witnessed Christ's crucifixion and rise. The four fled from Egypt to these shores."

"I've heard of the festival," Dina said. "You stampede the bulls, don't you?"

"After Mass we Gardians lead the procession with relics of the saints to the sea. We ride into the water and the relics are blessed. Next comes a day of celebration—people bring out violins and accordions; we wear our traditional dress. Gardians lead the stampede of the black bulls through the village streets and show our skills on horseback. Then we fight with the bulls."

Dina raised her eyebrows.

"Not badly, you know," he laughed. "In France we don't kill the bulls. Too valuable! And how about you? Why come now? Few inquire in person about Alphonse Renard."

I decided to stick as close to the truth as possible without providing any details. "I'm an antiquities dealer. A client of mine is interested in buying one of the items in his collection and was unable to make any contact, so he sent me."

Hanzi's heavy black brows knit together in a frown. "It is not my place to say but I must warn you, the merchant has a ... poor reputation. I haven't seen his home but I'm told it is very grand. What man lives alone like that? Especially one with so much wealth? We do not care for him. We think he is spellbound and never go near his place."

I assumed the rumors arose naturally from the rural suspicion of outsiders; all the same, this was not welcome news. I'd hoped after what we'd been through, meeting Renard would prove relatively easy. "Can you tell us how to get there?"

Hanzi's face darkened. "Not exactly." He caught Dina's crestfallen expression and quickly amended his statement. "But I can direct you to someone who does. Her name is Pauline Lagrène. An old woman of the Manoush. She once lived on the marsh. I'm afraid she too can be difficult."

"How so?" I asked.

"She is not used to visitors. She is a seer but no one consults her anymore. She has caused harm to people she doesn't like. Several years ago a woman consulted her. The poor thing had lost her only child, a son, and was so stricken with grief she could not let him go. She pleaded with Pauline Lagrène to help her talk to him." Hanzi lifted both hands to emphasize his point. "The mother wanted to reach her son from beyond the grave. She went home delirious with happiness, believing she had communicated with her child. Two days later, she took her fishing net into the reeds and drowned. Lagrène had cursed the woman, so everyone believed. They cast her out from the Camargue. She lives in exile a little north of here. Between Lagrène and Renard there is bad blood. You must convince her to tell you the way. Pay her. She'll pretend she doesn't know, but she does—don't think she doesn't."

Hanzi didn't want to say anything more about Lagrène. He knew he'd said too much already and quickly changed the subject.

He pointed a calloused finger toward the ceiling. His hands were roughened from years outdoors handling livestock. "You saw how my roof is made from bundles of reeds. We get them from the marsh. In the Camargue there are reed cutters. These men who go in dinghies with the *partègue*." He made a motion as if he were propelling a raft with a long pole. "They follow the creeks and little lakes. There, the water shifts. One day it is a narrow creek; the next time you go, a pond. The reeds grow so tall their tufts block out the sun and sometimes you are lost. If you step the wrong way, you sink into the water and it's black so you can't see the bottom. Many have been sucked in and drowned when gathering their bundles."

His words chilled us and we didn't talk much more. Dina, who looked ready to drop in her tracks, said she'd like to go upstairs. I thanked Hanzi for his hospitality and suggested I bed down near the wood stove. He made no objection. I'd noticed him glance quickly at our fingers earlier to see whether we wore wedding rings. No doubt he thought that not being married, we were acting with propriety. In truth, Dina wouldn't want to share a bed with me, and even if she were willing, I'd get no sleep lying that close to her. Hanzi gave her a kerosene lamp to take up with her and she bid us good night.

After digging out some blankets for me from a trunk, Hanzi retired to his alcove. His snores were audible throughout the cottage. Eventually I gave up trying to sleep and crept out of the blanket roll.

When I did so, I heard a sound coming from the loft. Despite pleading tiredness, Dina was still awake. Was she cold? I grabbed one of my blankets and climbed the ladder. As I stepped onto the loft floor I realized what the sound was. She'd pulled the covers over her head. Both arms hugged her pillow like a kid holding a teddy bear, but that couldn't hide her muffled sobs.

"Dina," I said softly.

She raised her head and turned around. "What?"

"Are you cold? I brought you another blanket."

"I'm fine."

Her red eyes and wet cheeks said otherwise. I sat down gingerly at the end of the bed.

"You've gone through a hell of a lot. If there's anything else I can do to help, just say."

"No, you've been great. I feel like I've wrecked so many people's lives. I just can't get Ewan out of my mind."

"I know. That was a huge shock. I barely knew him and it made me sick, so I can't imagine how you must feel. But we're pretty far from Naples now. I have enough money so you can get safely to any major city in Europe, gain some peace of mind. And perhaps see a doctor to help you work things out."

"You mean a doctor for the mind? I couldn't imagine where to start with that. And you don't know Lorenzo. He'll find me wherever I go. Right now I'd rather stay with you. I'll be okay."

"You're sure?"

She nodded.

I tucked the blanket around her legs and went back down. She was quiet after that and I hoped she'd finally fallen asleep.

Still restless myself, I remembered it had been a while since I'd checked my email. I silently cheered when I got reception. I saw a message from an Italian dealer in my network forwarding a notice that advertised the fourth volume of Basile's book, offered by a Naples bookseller. Although it was late, I sent a hasty text to the bookstore proprietor, a man named Naso. To my surprise, he responded immediately:

Thank you for your inquiry. We expect considerable interest in the book but it is still available. Please reply soon if you want to purchase. It is fine to phone.

Though I had no guarantee the volume advertised had anything to do with the specific one I sought, I punched in the numbers the bookseller gave at the end of his message, keeping my voice as low as possible so as not to disturb the other two.

Naso answered.

"My name's John Madison. I just texted you about the book."

"*Si*. It's in very good condition, I assure you."

"I'd like to know a bit more about its origin, if you don't mind."

"Of course. I bought it in a private sale early this summer."

"Has anyone else expressed an interest in it?"

"A gentleman, M. Barbot de Villeneuve. I have not heard back from him again."

"This may sound like an odd request—would you mind giving me a description of him? I think I may know him."

Naso paused, and spoke again with a hint of suspicion. "I suppose. He's an elderly man and he uses a cane. Does that sound like the M. Villeneuve you know?"

My heart leapt. "It does." I chose my next words carefully. If I told him about the theft on the phone he might turn the book in to the police before I got a chance to see it, so I decided to leave that issue until I saw him. "I'd like to buy it from you. It may take me a few days to get there. If I wire you an advance on the price will you hold it?"

I named a decent sum. Since he hadn't heard again from Villeneuve, he agreed. We said our goodbyes. I did not have anywhere near the money needed to buy the book but hoped the prospect of a sale would be enough for Naso to hold on to it until I got there.

When I searched for the name on my cell, I discovered Barbot de Villeneuve was a woman, born in 1695, the original author of "La Belle et la Bête"—"Beauty and the Beast." Alessio's aliases were certainly inventive. First a pseudonym, then Wilhelm Grimm, and now a French fairy-tale author. Then I stopped short. Dina knew about the buyers of the other volumes. That meant she was aware that one volume was with Naso in Naples, and yet she'd said that the closest buyer was Renard. I cursed under my breath. If Dina had told me the truth I'd have Naso's volume already in hand. Even as I thought this, I knew why she had lied to me. She needed to get away from Naples. And she saved my life by bringing me along.

I got the English translation of Basile's book from my knapsack and sat on the floor with my back against the wall. The wood stove threw a soft light sufficient to read by.

The first story of the second volume was Basile's version of "Rapunzel," titled "Petrosinella," about a prince who fell in love with a beautiful young woman locked in a tower by an ogress. Every night Petrosinella would lower her golden braids so the prince could climb up and "feast with that sprig of parsley at the banquet of love." I laughed softly at Basile's incredible descriptions and lewd sense of humor. I read until the firelight dimmed then gave up and, feeling the need for some fresh air, ventured outside.

The night was cool enough that I buttoned up my jacket. Out there, without the interference of city lights, in the clear Provençal air and the landscape flat to the horizon, the sky was a vast indigo plain. The great band of stars in the Milky Way stood out like a dust shower of diamonds. Silhouettes of the sheep and white horses were visible as they stood on the grass.

One of the horses lifted its head and whinnied and I felt an unexplainable jolt of fear. The horses moved closer together, as if in a tight group they could better defend themselves. The sheep huddled in the same way. A cluster of fireflies burst up suddenly from the grass and scattered.

Something had disrupted the tranquil pastoral night. I concentrated hard to detect it. I could hear something moving along the rough ground. A swishing sound, barely perceptible. A black cloud sailed across the moon. I peered in the direction of the sound but the gloom prevented me from seeing anything.

My brother, Samuel, was a scholar of ancient cultures and not given to flights of fancy. A brilliant man who pursued his studies rigorously, he was also open-minded. I'd been thinking about him a lot, especially since Dina had told me about Mancini's interest in necromancy. What would Samuel have thought? The answer came rushing to me then, under the stars, on the edge of this great plain. Once, when I asked him about Babylonian beliefs, he'd said, "Their old gods aren't dead, you know. They've just withdrawn to hidden places." He smiled then as if to make light of it all. "Perhaps I've been spending too much time studying Mesopotamians. And yet on occasion when I'm in remote landscapes where the arid desert seems endless, I sense their presence. They are neither evil nor good and are driven by urges and desires we cannot comprehend. We Westerners like to think our spiritual allies are caught up in our lives, whether to save us or wreak vengeance on us for our sins. But the gods live outside any moral codes. Humans mean nothing to them."

I had the same feeling now. That some formless power existed and I was helpless in the face of it. I tried to snap out of my discomfort, and I began to walk in the direction of the strange sound when my fingers tingled. I tried to flex them but my hand had grown too cold and stiff. A heaviness descended on me as though my body had suddenly filled with sand. I turned around and struggled back to the cottage, my legs dragging so slowly it was like pushing through deep layers of mud.

I managed to wrest the door open and tumbled inside. Hanzi turned in his sleep and murmured. The coals from the fire glowed in the stove. Hanzi's old enamel kitchen clock ticked comfortingly. Our empty glasses sat where we'd left them on the table. Everything was peaceful. The tingling faded but I stayed awake the rest of the night, falling asleep only when the sun rose reassuringly at dawn.

When Dina woke me, Hanzi was already bustling about. The welcome aroma of coffee drifted through the cottage. While we drank it, Hanzi added a couple of hard-boiled eggs to our food cache and ushered us on our way. "You have a long way to go today," he said. "You must start now."

Twenty-Three

November 23, 2003
Les Alpilles, France

Dina sat splendidly astride her horse, her long hair loose, tousled by the breeze. She looked over her shoulder every so often and gave me an encouraging smile. A good night's sleep had left her refreshed. Her sorrow of the night before had vanished and she seemed genuinely happy.

As for myself, despite Dina's good spirits and the scenic landscape, the feeling of trepidation from last night still clung to me. It had nothing to do with the prospect of curses. A malignance hung in the air, a disturbance in the natural order of things. We'd taken every precaution by spending only cash and not using our real names, except with Hanzi. But I was sure that I'd felt Alessio nearby last night.

We crossed local roads and passed through many fields. Vineyards cropped up as the land began to ascend in a gentle rise. We arrived at the little abandoned shack Hanzi told us to watch out for and turned onto the trail he recommended, which descended into a wooded area. The forest was made up of the kind of thick scrubby bush and weedy trees that grow on poor soil. Before long, our route narrowed to a rough path winding beside a stream. I dug into my shirt pocket and found my ballpoint pen inscribed with the insignia of the New York Knicks. I dropped it on the path. When we returned this way, we'd see if anyone was behind us and whether they took notice of it.

Clouds blocked out the sun. It grew cooler. The bush became much denser. I remembered Hanzi's description of getting lost in the marsh and thought, even here, how easy it would be to lose our way. Up ahead, Dina halted her horse and twisted around to talk to me. "The path dwindles to nothing ahead. I'm not sure what we should do."

"Is there any way forward?"

"Yes, but it's marshy. I don't know if the water is just on the surface or deeper."

Without waiting for my reply, she jumped off her horse and led him forward, testing the area gingerly with each step. She appeared satisfied the ground underneath the water was stable and remounted. I remembered Hanzi's advice to trust the horses. When the stallion plunged ahead, I figured we were safe.

We picked our way along, taking a labyrinthine route that headed vaguely northwest, in a strange country under difficult circumstances. Finally, I was elated to see a small rise. I shouted to Dina. She waved and quickened her horse's pace. Indeed, the path magically reappeared as the land rose and we entered a thicket of gorse and willow.

Yellowing leaves rustled behind us as we made our way through the grove. Odd, I thought, since there was almost no wind. We had to hold up one hand to protect our faces from the slapping branches as we passed through. Once we'd cleared the trees and the land was high enough to get a good look at the surrounding area, we'd regain some sense of direction. We might see, as well, whether anyone was tracking us.

We soon broke through the scrub and pulled to a stop. In front of us lay a large lagoon of black brackish water. In the middle of the turgid span sat an island covered with vegetation and debris. The dwelling centered on it brought a gasp of surprise to our lips. An old caravan painted in garish colors—lime green, canary yellow, scarlet, and indigo.

"This must be Lagrène's house," Dina said finally. "But how on earth do we reach it?"

Twenty-Four

The lagoon was smooth as black glass; not even a ripple stirred its surface. Nothing ruffled the plants either, as if the trees and reeds surrounding the little lake had been composed in a permanent tableau. It reminded me of the dead calm preceding a hurricane.

"Is she in there?" Dina asked. "She might not even be home."

The caravan with its absurdly fanciful colors looked abandoned. I couldn't see any movement through the windows.

"She must have some way to get over there." I searched for any sign of a boat or raft on the island or the shore but could see nothing.

"Maybe she flies over." Dina laughed. "I wonder how deep it is."

"The horses will tell us that." I grabbed the mare's bridle and walked her down to the edge of the lagoon. The water looked oily, as if it were thickened with deposits. Yanking off my shoes and socks and rolling up my pants, I parted the reeds and took a few tentative steps into the sludge at the water's edge. It was cold and murky. I coaxed the mare to follow me in. She stretched her neck down to sniff at the water and refused to budge. "Hell," I said. "There's our answer."

The lagoon stank like an open sewer. No wonder the horses didn't want to go near it. The remains of weathered gray tree trunks with tips like broken spears stuck out of the water. They seemed to form a vague double line leading from the shore to the island, and I guessed an avenue of trees had once lined a drive leading up to the rise. If that was the case, the path between the rows of stumps might be more solidly packed than elsewhere underneath the lagoon.

I led the mare to where Dina waited. "Why don't you stay with the horses? If I tie the leads together I can loop one end around the tree trunks. That way, if there are any danger spots I can use the cable to pull myself out."

Dina looked at the still expanse of water and glanced nervously back to the dense clumps of bushes and trees. "I'm not staying here alone."

We secured the horses to the willows. I tied their blue leads together and fashioned a rough noose at one end. We both stripped down to our underwear, leaving only our shirts on; the rest of our gear went into our knapsacks. My apprehension aside, the sight of Dina's lovely bare legs and what was above, inadequately covered by the thin fabric of her underwear, got my testosterone shooting into overdrive. Good thing I'd started out first and she'd be behind me.

When we ventured into the water I tested the first few yards. My feet plunged unpleasantly into muck. It rose over my ankles until I found relatively solid footing. After a few throws I hooked the loop onto the first tree trunk about twenty feet from the shore. Dina pulled the line taut behind me. The water rose to the middle of my calves and then the pond bed seemed to level out. Lifting my feet produced a sucking sound; bubbles and greenish rotted matter floated up to the surface with every step I took. I thought I could feel live things slithering around my feet and my lips twisted in distaste.

As I approached the first tree stump the muck gave way to spongy water plants. My feet sank a little lower into the morass but it provided a kind of soft mat to walk on that was preferable to the mud. I looked behind and was glad to see Dina steadily sloshing through the water. The length of cable lying on the water surface trailed behind her like a long blue snake.

Slogging through the water toward the seer's house, I remembered a story I'd come across when I was a kid called "The Witch in the Stone Boat." It left an indelible impression on me, probably because of the terrifying picture accompanying it. I'd found the story in a book stowed away in the bottom drawer of an old dresser and had no idea how it came to be there. Now that I'd learned more about fairy tales, I knew it was by the English fairy-tale collector Andrew Lang.

I could still recall the description of the witch, stooped over her long pole, her sinister figure in a small boat moving through the mist at night toward the ship carrying the prince and his bride. The witch stole into the young woman's body and banished the radiant bride to the underworld. It terrified me at the time and I insisted for weeks after that Evelyn leave my light on at night. One day the book went missing. I knew she'd thrown it away.

I surveyed my progress. Two more tree trunks and we'd reach the other shore. I pulled the loop off and, casting it toward the next stump, stepped forward. The mat of waterweed underfoot vanished. I plunged deep into muck and this time it swallowed my legs past my knees; it felt like a vacuum sucking me under. Something bumped against my ankle. I heaved my leg out and up came what at first looked like a large ball of wriggling red yarn. I'd stepped into a nest of long red worms and they'd risen to the

By Henry Justice Ford from *The Yellow Fairy Book*

surface, writhing around my skin. I batted them away furiously with my hand, which only dispersed them. They floated on the surface, trying to crawl up my thighs.

Dina cried out when she came up behind me and saw them. We pushed forward through the knots of worms, both of us straining on the rope. Finally I clambered onto the shore at the edge of the island and flopped down onto wild grass growing between the reed beds. I rested my back against a weathered pole with a rusty ring screwed into it and took a few deep breaths.

Dina stumbled out of the water, her face drawn and pale. "One of those things is still on me. Oh God, I don't want to touch it." Panicked, she shook her leg hard. I gritted my teeth and brushed the red worm off her. It lay squiggling on the ground. We did our best to clean our legs with handfuls of grass before putting our pants and shoes back on.

Reeds ringed the island, giving way to bare, damp earth. "She can't be here," Dina said finally. "With all the commotion we're making, she'd have to be stone deaf not to hear us."

The debris surrounding the caravan we'd seen from the far shore was even more appalling up close—traps, cages of all sizes, many with the rotted carcasses of animals still inside. Broken snares with tattered ropes. Heaps of dried bones. I stirred one of the bone piles with my shoe and unearthed snake vertebrae, turtle shells, and the delicate bones of other amphibians I couldn't name—frogs, perhaps. A string of mud-dwelling sucker fish had been strung up against a tree stump, the circle of cartilage that formed their mouths gaping open, ugly hooks still protruding from gills and lips. The stink of rotting fish along with the putrid swamp water was almost overwhelming.

"I doubt she ventures out much," I said. "Lord help her if this is her food supply."

Around back we found a rudimentary oven built with flat rocks and an iron grill. Beside it lay a small boat, a long pole wedged against one of the seats. The boat was made of rough fiberglass with the texture of cement and was covered with green mold up to the waterline. A painter had been fastened to the bow.

A few feet away from us the reeds began to whip around wildly. I grabbed a stick. As I parted the reeds something rubbery slapped at my hand. I swore and jumped back. The long body of a white snake thrashed desperately back and forth. Another flip of its body and I could see its yellow eyes bulging and red tongue flicking in and out. With every movement, its neck was squeezed ever tighter in a snare. It could be venomous so I didn't want to take the chance of freeing it. The snake's movements lessened until it grew flaccid and lay still. We hurried away.

Dina ran her hand over her forehead, leaving a muddy streak on her skin. "Can't say I want to meet her anymore."

I got a tissue out of my pocket and brushed some dirt off her forehead. "Can't have you looking anything less than perfect to meet the fortune teller."

"Thanks." Dina smiled.

As we drew closer we could see the caravan had a set of wheels that had sunk into the ground until only the tops of their rims were showing. The paint, so bright from afar, was chipped and dirty. Incongruously, meadow flowers, rainbows, and birds darting among orange and pear trees decorated the sides. The windows we thought we'd seen had actually been painted on.

We rounded the last corner and found the entrance, a wooden ramp leading to a dark hole about five feet high and three feet wide cut into the side of the caravan. The door was missing. The frame had split, one dingy hinge fixed to it with a nail. Some protection from the elements came from a curtain made of snail shells threaded on strings.

Dina hung back. "You're welcome to go first," she said.

When I knocked on the door frame, the sound echoed inside the caravan. We waited. No one answered. I knocked louder. Nothing.

Dina raised her voice. *"Est-ce personne ici?"*

The doorway was too short for my six feet so I had to stoop. I could see nothing at first in the gloomy interior. Gradually my eyes made out shapes: more wire and wood cages piled on top of each other against the north wall of the caravan. One of them held a large snapping turtle. I couldn't tell whether it was dead or alive. A large piece of plywood rested on crates. On it, an assortment of rusty knives, old tools, fish hooks and lines, a net. I spotted a glimmer at the other end: an old kerosene lamp had been fixed to a bracket on the wall. The burning paraffin oil turned the air acrid and smoky.

A tall stack of rags appeared to be piled in a chair. Until it moved. A bony hand extended from the heap and beckoned me forward. As I approached, the rags shifted again and a woman raised her head. In doing so, the cloth draping her head dropped away.

The dome of her skull gleamed in the lamplight. Under heavy bluish lids she had the sharp black eyes of a raptor. Her face was thin as a cadaver's but her lips were a full and flaming red that could only have come from rouge or lipstick. From her earlobes dangled two large golden hoops. Dina gasped behind me.

"*Mlle Lagrène,*" I began. "*Bonjour. Mon nom est John Madison et ceci est Dina.*" I gestured in Dina's direction. "*Excusez notre présence, mais ...*"

The old woman interrupted. "*Je m'appelle Mme Lagrène et pas Mlle.*" She flicked a glance toward Dina. "*Chez nous il n'ya pas de vierges. Emmenez cette femme!*"

Dina understood the woman's insult and shuffled back, closer to the door.

"*Vous*"—she crooked a finger toward me—"*venez ici.*"

I took a few steps toward her and asked if she could tell us how to get to Renard's estate.

Her lips drew back in a ghostly smile, exposing sore-looking reddish gums. "*Venez, venez,*" she said to me. She glared at Dina again.

I tried to stay beyond her reach, shuddering at the thought of her fingers touching my skin. Her thin arm snaked out. On her middle finger she wore a silver ring with a gigantic ruby solitaire. I'm not exactly sure what happened next—perhaps a beam from the lamp caught the stone at a certain angle—but a streak of light flashed as Lagrène's hand swept toward me.

For an instant, the entire interior of the caravan appeared to transform. In place of the filthy walls and floors were patterns of vines and flowers on brightly colored backgrounds. Instead of the dirty cages, heaps of sugar candies filled sparkling glass containers. The ceiling glowed with hundreds of pinpoint lights, as if the caravan had suddenly opened to a starry sky. Lagrène's skeletal body fleshed out and seemed to grow in stature until she towered over me.

The vision lasted no more than a few seconds. I was once more in an ugly hovel. I shook my head to clear my mind. Lagrène grabbed my hand with a surprisingly powerful grip and pulled it toward her, turning it so she could see my palm. I was about to yank it away but thought better of it. She brought my palm close to her face and muttered something to herself. Then just as suddenly she dropped it.

"Vous cherchez la rue qui mène à la maison du marchant. Je peux vous montrer, mais cela vous coûtera."

I shrugged off my knapsack and got my wallet out of the zippered front compartment, counting out the equivalent of twenty euros and handing the money to her.

She checked the amount and held out her hand again. *"Plus,"* she said.

I handed her another ten-euro note, raising my shoulders and holding out my hands to show I had no more.

Lagrène gave me the directions but lost me after the first sentence. I hoped Dina had caught all that because I certainly hadn't. I turned to check and she gave me a nod.

"Merci beaucoup," I said, turning back to the old woman. *"Je vous remercie de votre avis."* I turned to leave.

"Un moment!" Lagrène's voice rose almost to a shriek. *"Pourquoi est-ce que cet esprit sombre vous suit?"*

Before I could figure out what she said, she spoke again in her high-pitched whine. *"Prenez garde. Elle vous videra en suçant votre vie comme je fais avec mes animaux aquatiques."* She thrust out her finger toward Dina. *"Ne ralentissez pas jusqu'à ce que vous arrivez au monde souterrain."*

Dina stormed out of the caravan.

Outside, I found her pacing furiously back and forth.

"What did she say? Didn't she give us directions?"

"Oh yes. Exact instructions to reach the estate. She said keep on the path leading north toward the mountain then turn to the east and five miles distant we'll find a new road that climbs the cliffs. Do not err by going past it and taking the old Roman one. At the cliff top we'll see two pillars with the heads of horses where the forest begins. The drive running in between the pillars will take us to the merchant's house."

"Good then. Sounds clear enough. What bothered you?"

"She asked why the shade follows you. She said it would suck the life out of you, just as she did to her water animals."

"Alessio? How could she possibly know about him?"

Dina lowered her voice to almost a whisper. "She didn't mean Alessio. She meant *me*, and then cursed me. She said she wished I would not slacken my course until I reached the underworld. Why would she say that, John?"

"Don't pay it any mind," I said reassuringly. "It's just gobbledy-gook from an old woman who's lost her mind."

Dina didn't seem reassured. "Not everything is what it seems. I know that better than you."

We retrieved the boat from behind the caravan. It wasn't overly heavy; Dina and I easily carried it to the shore of the lagoon. She was in such a hurry to get out of there, I think she would have carried it herself.

I knew now what the post was for and tied one end of the painter to the ring so once we reached the other side, the old woman could pull it back.

Dina brought the pole and jumped into the boat. I took off my shoes and with huge misgivings waded back into the water. The slime closed around my feet again. I gave the boat as strong a push as possible, grasped the pole, and hopped in. I stood up cautiously and pushed out. It was heavy going as the pole sank again and again deep into the muck.

When we reached the other side we almost embraced the horses. As we retraced our route back to the main path I kept an eye out for my pen. It was nowhere to be found. It could have been picked up quite innocently by someone walking the trail, but its absence only confirmed the wariness I felt.

By now it was past noon. We turned onto the main path as Lagrène had directed. A wind blew steadily. We'd been pushing the horses at a reasonably brisk pace, making good time, when Dina halted. I stopped beside her. We could see the trail bending to the east at the base of the cliffs; we were about three-quarters of the way there. Dina took in a deep breath.

"I love it here, out in nature. After being imprisoned like a nightingale in a cage I feel as though I've finally been set free."

My own experience tended to the opposite. My first memory at age three was waking in the Greenwich apartment the day after my brother brought me back from Turkey. I can't remember what my life was like in the tiny Turkish mining village, or even the earthquake that split the sides of the tailing pond, drowning our village and my parents along with it. But I do have emotional memories of those early years. Unrelenting tension, discord, and turbulence.

The morning I woke up in my new home, Samuel was still asleep. I wandered over to the window and looked out on the bustling, noisy city. Blocks of buildings stretched as far as I could see; many appeared taller than the Turkish mountains of my home. In my young mind, the water towers perched on some of those buildings looked like witch huts and I trembled in fear. Later, Samuel explored the city with me and explained away all my fears. For the first time in my life I felt safe.

I'm not sure what prompted me to do it—perhaps those childhood memories—but I looked over my shoulder. Far back I could see a figure moving on foot, picking his way along the route we'd just traveled. Something about the way the man moved disturbed me. Shade billowed around him as if his own shadow were blown about by the wind. Dina gave her horse a gentle nudge to get it moving again. "Wait a minute," I said, holding out my hand.

"Why? We need to keep going. We have a long way ahead of us."

"Look."

She turned in her saddle to see what I meant, squinting her eyes and peering into the distance. "A hiker. He's alone. Nothing to worry about."

"Humor me. I'd like to get a better view." After a few minutes his body came into better focus. His pace was slow yet determined. At first it looked as though he had three legs; then I saw a flicker of white as the third leg dipped and swung. The wavering shadow formed into a long dark coat flapping in the stiff breeze. He clamped his free hand on his black hat to keep it from blowing off.

The sun was still high in the sky, almost directly overhead, but as he moved along the path he left patches of shadow like ink blots dropping on the ground in his wake. Alessio's inexorable progress chilled me, as if he knew, in defiance of all reason, that we were powerless to outrun him even with our horses.

Twenty-Five

Dina cried out and goaded her horse into a full, heart-pounding gallop. My mare tore after them. I lost my balance and pulled back hard on the reins, forgetting Hanzi's careful instructions. The mare reared, yanking her head away. I jolted backward, felt gravity pulling me down. My foot slipped out of the stirrup. She reared a second time and wrenched the reins from my hands. With no restraints, she flew like a fury.

How I remained astride I'll never know. Instinctively, I gripped the horse's belly as hard as possible with my legs. Thankfully, she seemed heedless of my hands wound into her mane. I could smell her sweat rise as she heaved huge drags of breath, almost as if she, too, feared the man behind us.

At some point I settled into the rhythm of the mare's gallop. Cliff faces, yawning over the flat pebbled terrain, came into view ahead. The land sloped upward and the mare labored to keep up speed. A bright arc of water glimmered in the distance as a grove of dense bushes gave way once again to grass.

Dina waited for me just ahead. The mare lifted her head and whinnied when she saw them, slowing to a canter. We pulled up beside them. I slid off and nearly catapulted to the ground. My legs shook so much with the prolonged exertion I could barely stand. My groin and upper thighs were numb. Dina leaned down and grabbed the mare's reins. "You did well. Frankly, I'm amazed you made it," she said.

"I know you were frightened"—I had to stop talking for a few seconds to drag in a few deep breaths—"but you took off without even giving me a warning." I fished in the pack for a bottle of water and chugged down half of it.

Unconcerned, she reached for the bottle and threw back the rest.

"We've gained a lot of distance. He must be far behind by now."

Dina looked toward the cliffs. "I want to take that Roman road, not the one she told us to follow."

"What's the point of that? Alessio can track us there just as easily."

"He won't expect us to take it. He'll go to the one everyone else uses."

That imperious tone had crept into her voice again, as if I were one of her servants. I was too wiped to keep the annoyance out of mine.

"Dina, Lagrène said not to deviate from her directions. It could take a lot more time to negotiate the other road. That's a bad idea. Alessio must know the second volume's at the estate. He'll end up there anyway, regardless of our course."

She tossed her hair back. "Renard's wealthy. Once we're on his estate I assume he'll have security and we'll be well protected. We're totally vulnerable out here. But please yourself. Do whatever you want."

I grabbed the mare's reins when Dina dropped them and

trotted off astride her stallion. I mounted and caught up with her. "This will end up being a dangerous waste of time," I said. "But separating is an even worse idea."

We coaxed the horses to keep up a brisk pace and sooner than we'd expected reached the route Mme Lagrène told us to take, a paved road that scaled the rock face at an easy grade. A couple of cyclists wearing helmets, skin-tight black shorts, and bright jerseys rode ahead of us, laughing and collegial. A motorcycle whipped by to make the climb as well. We'd be much safer here with other people around us. It was mid-afternoon and clouds began to build. The air felt cooler. Once again I insisted we use this route. Dina's answer was to ignore me and, setting her lips in a tight line, urge her horse forward.

The Roman track began farther along on a protrusion of rock, like a broad ledge, ascending the cliff at a steep angle. The stone of the ledge differed in color and I reasoned it hadn't eroded as much because it was stronger than the rock making up most of the cliff face, providing a solid base for the road. Its width easily permitted the two of us to ride side by side, although, unlike the new road we should have taken, it had no protective barrier and dropped away sharply at the edge.

The stallion bucked when Dina tried to urge him onto the track and laid back his ears, unwilling to venture onto it. To Dina's credit she didn't force him but patiently coaxed him onto the trail. He finally complied, although he was skittish and walked stiffly. The mare forged ahead and I took the lead.

Climbing uphill at a walk was uncomfortable, so Dina suggested we canter the horses up to the next level. I managed the faster pace with no problem. There was little evidence of others having used this trail recently. No empty soda cans or water bottles, and the spans of dirt we crossed looked undisturbed. We did spot a few intriguing signs from the past. Here and there small patches of symmetrically laid stones appeared. Roman cobble-stones, I guessed.

About eighty feet along, the track widened into a small plateau, providing a good vantage point while we refueled. We dismounted and pulled out the second bottle of water and hard-boiled eggs from our packs. We fed the horses the carrots and apples, their wet, rubbery lips smacking enthusiastically on the treats.

Banks of somber gray replaced the white pillows of cloud. The temperature dived and we heard the first soft rumble of thunder. We put on our windbreakers. Dina held both sets of reins while I walked over to the cliff edge. On a sunny day the view would be magnificent. Weathered white limestone cliffs, scrubby silver-green bushes sprouting from crevices, and below the cliffs, fields and vineyards, the earth like rough corduroy between the rows. Now the threatening skies gave the landscape a menacing feel.

In the distance, beside the narrow gleam of a canal, I spotted movement. From this far away it looked like a dark fly crawling along a window ledge. He moved slowly with that same nerve-racking, dogged tread. I couldn't distinguish his features or even a clear outline of his body but I swear I sensed Alessio honing in on us, perched up on the ridge. A sudden wave of dizziness hit me.

"What's wrong?" Dina asked nervously. "Don't tell me you've seen him."

Before I could answer the ground beneath my feet split apart and crashed into the chasm below. It was all I could do to right my balance and keep my footing. The stallion whinnied. I squatted down to examine the surface where the piece had broken off and was dismayed to see not stone at all, but a composite of organic material and rock rubble impacted into a kind of loose cement.

"Dina," I said quietly, "keep as close to the cliff face as possible. Single file. The entire edge of this road is treacherous."

She moved back immediately. My warning tone frightened her, so I didn't mention Alessio. No need to petrify her even more than she already was.

On the horizon, long vertical bolts of lightning cut through the heavy clouds. The wind howled. We hurried the horses onward. About an hour and a half into our ascent, a crest of limestone shot up from the cliff face. The track curved perilously around it. Once again Dina held the horses while I made my way around to check the other side.

Our rough road continued upward until it was bisected by a crevasse, leaving a substantial gap.

I walked back. "We've got a major problem. Part of the road has fallen away and the gap may be too wide for the horses." I was tempted to say this was why we should have taken the other route but held my tongue.

"How wide is it?"

"About four feet."

She dismissed my concerns with a shrug. "The horses are probably more adept at making the jump than us."

We had no choice but to continue. We led the horses around the rock crest, the wind slashing at our bodies. From this distance, the trees in the valley resembled miniature shrubs. Without question, a fall would kill us.

I tied one of the leads to the mare's halter and threw one end onto the other side of the gap. I patted her neck, more to reassure myself than anything else. I took a run and cleared the gap easily and then pulled on the lead, urging the mare to follow. Her hind hoof slipped on some scree but she righted herself and made it over cleanly. I tied her to a stunted cedar tree farther down the track and went back.

The stallion was balking. Dina stood between his body and the rock wall. She gave up trying to pacify him for the moment, motioning for me to come nearer and reaching into the pack for his lead. She hooked one end of it onto his bridle and threw the other to me. I caught it and hauled it back until it tensed. The stallion still refused to cooperate, backing up, twitching his ears, snorting, and arching his neck. His eyes rolled, showing the whites. He tried to get away and sidled dangerously close the edge. Dina used all her strength to force him away from the drop and gave him a firm slap on the rump. That spooked him. He reared, almost crushing her against the cliff. Then he took off. His powerful muscles bunched and flexed as his front legs bore down to propel his great weight across the gap. My whole body tensed watching him try to make it.

He leapt.

For a few precious seconds it looked as if he'd make it. His front hooves landed solidly on my side. Then his left hind hoof hit the scree and slid into the cavity.

Twenty-Six

The stallion brought all his strength to bear on his front legs and propelled himself forward—far enough to get his rear legs up and onto my side of the track. When he trotted up to me, I hugged his neck for sheer joy. Dina hopped the space and unfastened his lead with shaking hands. "That was very close," she said. "You were right. We never should have come this way."

"We must be getting close to the top. We'll make it." If only I felt as confident as I sounded. We had no idea what to expect at the peak even if we did finish the climb.

To add to our woes freezing rain began to fall, the tiny ice crystals like sharp pins pricking at our eyes, hampering visibility. A constant stream of pebbles and sticks washed down the track as if we were standing in a sluice. And worse, the stallion limped. He could barely touch his left hind leg to the ground before pulling it up again. I prayed the top was not much farther and squinted through the sleet. Ahead, the track appeared to divide around another massive cylinder of rock.

Dina yelled but I couldn't tell what she was trying to say over the roar of the wind. She waved her arm toward the left-hand fork. It seemed the logical way; the ground there was covered with an accumulation of cedar leaves and twigs like a forest path. It would be good to get away from the slippery scree. Although the route she wanted to take was tight, it did offer the protection of the cliff wall on one side and the rock promontory on the other.

As the mare and I entered the left fork I put up my hand to balance against the wall and noticed a mark carved into its surface. A crude drawing of falling water. A warning to travelers not to proceed. I shouted back to Dina, "We need to go to the right!"

She shook her head in reply but I ignored her and led my horse onto the scree. Dina followed reluctantly. Rounding the column of rock we could see the cliff head at last, about fifty feet farther up. On the left, a torrent of water poured into a deep chasm. Had we taken the other route, we'd have been pinned in the narrow passage, unable to turn the horses around.

We reached the top and I groaned. Our rough road separated. On our left it dwindled to a footpath leading down to an immense stretch of dense, overgrown forest. A hidden valley in the barren rock, the wind blowing the forest treetops almost sideways. Straight ahead, the path climbed again, and as the mountain surged higher it was only bare rock. We desperately needed shelter but saw no sign of human habitation, not even a farmer's shack in the valley. The silhouettes of the trees began to blur in the declining light.

I scanned the valley for the pillars with the horse heads Mme Lagrène mentioned but could see nothing but trees. The forest had to surround the merchant's estate. Our clothes were soaking wet and both of us were freezing. We couldn't stay out in the open any longer. The descent proved easy and we ventured into the shelter of the trees.

Once under the umbrella of the foliage I drew in the fragrance of pine and cedar. Here, we were protected from the worst of the storm. The fat, mossy tree trunks of giant oaks suggested a mature forest. Out of the wind it should have been warmer, but the temperature was just as frigid. It began to snow. I'd never heard of snow this far south, even in the dead of winter.

Exhausted from our ordeal and desperate for some rest, we found a huge upturned tree root beside a stream. We tied the horses to a sturdy branch and they waded into the brook for a long guzzle. They cropped at the stands of grass growing on the bank as snowflakes settled on their flanks. Their warm breath was visible in the air.

We huddled underneath the tree trunk on a deep bed of pine needles, damp but soft. Dina wriggled into the extra sweater she'd brought with her and I gave her my fleece sweatshirt to put on over top. It was a tossup whether our wet windbreakers provided protection or added to the problem, but we decided to keep them on. Dina's hands had turned white with the cold so I rubbed them between mine. I pulled out the bottle of Bordeaux from my pack and the little plastic glasses we'd brought. Our bread had turned to mush so we contented ourselves with the brie and washed it down with generous draughts of wine. Dina nestled as close as possible to me, her reluctance to get close forgotten with the frigid weather. Our shared body warmth helped alleviate the cold.

A while later, the flurries stopped and the clouds thinned out, revealing a full moon casting beams through the forest. An owl hooted. The horses swished their tails as they grazed. The scent of cedar, loamy earth, and forest mushrooms pervaded the night air.

"How far behind do you think Alessio is?" Dina asked nervously.

"Maybe he took your bait and used the other road."

She nodded without much conviction.

"Did Alessio ever hurt you?"

She shook her head. "No. Not him. I was the conte's toy to abuse."

I wondered, after spending several years in their household as a kind of ward, whether she'd begun a romance with Mancini willingly only to find he abused her trust. "How did it start—your relationship with him?"

"Relationship? That's what you call it?" Her voice echoed sharply and the sordid history came tumbling out. "I was fifteen, barely even a teenager when he first set his eyes on me. He and his wife seemed friendly and kind in the beginning. With my mother dead and my father barely interested in me, naturally I gravitated to them. It wasn't long before I'd catch his eyes sliding over my body and had to endure hugs that lasted too long. I ignored it but that only encouraged him. He would press himself against me so I could feel his hardness, touch me when he knew no one else was looking. It was a relief to be away at school in London most of the time, but on holidays and over the summer break I had no choice. They made me stay with them. When I turned sixteen and reached the age of consent in Italy, he raped me."

"You were still a kid." My first impression fell apart like a house of cards. The scene I'd witnessed outside the Naples club was just the latest episode in a long pattern of sexual crime.

"At seventeen he forced me to leave my London boarding school. That's when he became much more public about his *relationship* with me. He began showing me off at parties and events. He chose my dresses, always tight, clingy ones, and got secret pleasure out of watching other men eye me.

"When we walked into a room at these gatherings I heard the whispers. I felt so ashamed. And he had a terrible temper. If I did one minor thing wrong he'd—"

"You went through total hell."

"For years and years." Her mood seemed to switch from sorrow to anger. "The only way out for me is to kill him. I'll have to or he'll do it to me."

Hearing her say that froze my blood. "We'll get away from him, Dina. I'll do whatever I can to help you."

Dina drew her arms around her legs, shivering through her clothes. If the cold hadn't caused it, her memories certainly would. "He'll just track me down. He won't let me go—ever. I spent so many years steeling myself whenever he touched me. Panicking the minute I'd hear his footsteps treading on the hall tiles. The sight of him made me sick. The smell of his hair turned my stomach. That becomes ingrained in your brain, you know. I'll never get rid of it now."

"You'll find someone who treats you gently. Who really cares for you." My words were inadequate and I knew it. After such a long period of mistreatment, she might well find it impossible to ever trust another man.

"After what he did, I can't imagine how. It happened one summer night in Naples. I'd invited a bunch of people over for a party. We were passing around joints, drinking a lot, stuff kids do. Partying late into the night. The next thing I remember was waking up, so out of it I could barely move or speak. He'd stripped off all my clothes and lay on top of me. He'd fixed my drink, sent everyone home, and raped me while I was semi-conscious. And his wife knew! She stood aside, saying and doing nothing!"

Her raw words turned my stomach. "There was no one at school to tell?"

"Not in summer. And even if I'd been able to reach anyone there, what could they do, so far away? I ran away the next morning but I had no money. My friends were afraid of him so they wouldn't help. Twenty miles outside Naples his men found me. They tied my wrists, dumped me into a car, and drove me back to the estate. He refused to send me back to school."

Mancini belonged in prison, but the chances of that ever happening were slim to none. My blood boiled at the thought of him getting away with it.

Her story touched a nerve. At my first boarding school an instructor made a practice of being overly friendly to some of the boys. He singled me out for his attention. He chose kids like me without parents watching their every step. Even at that age, I knew something was wrong and lashed out at him. He retaliated with punishments, demeaning me in front of the entire class and whipping me for another boy's mischief. I couldn't imagine trying to explain a sexual predator to Evelyn, who would in any event have been afraid to confront school authorities. Samuel was unreachable, away on a long stretch of field work. I had to cope on my own.

Dina gave me a measured look. "How old are you?"

"I'll be thirty-four on June seventh."

"That means you're a Gemini, a male sign with a dual nature. You're like Mercury—quicksilver—and Geminis fall in love hard and fast. If love is so easy for you, why aren't you with someone?"

"There was a woman I felt close to recently," I said, thinking of Laurel again. "But it didn't work out that way."

Dina scrambled up. "Oh. I'm sorry about that. But you see? Nothing about love is ever simple, is it?" She glimpsed the patch of sky between the trees. "We should get going while the moon is still bright."

Where to go was the question. We had no clear path. I spotted a clearing between the trees, so we gave the horses their leads and they picked their way along it. Dina rode the mare and I led the limping stallion.

We'd gone about a third of a mile when a howl pierced the night. Even though the sound came from far away, it was unsettling. Both horses brought their heads up sharply and twitched their ears.

"What was that?" Dina asked nervously. "Are there wolves in France?"

"Not anymore. Possibly deep in the Alps. Not here. A farmer's dog maybe."

The howl came again. A little closer this time. Not the yelping bark I remembered from wolves in the Adirondacks but a prolonged, mournful wail. The horses yanked at their leads.

Dina let the reins droop while I continued to lead the stallion, hobbling along on his injured leg. The mare needed no encouragement to get going and she seemed to have a sense of the right direction. Aside from having to duck low-hanging branches and stumbling on the odd tree root or rock, we made headway, the horses' hooves muffled as they proceeded along the forest floor covered with a soft layer of snow.

Twenty minutes later we came upon a little glade and the first signs of human activity. Stacks of neatly piled wood stood in the center of the clearing beside a felled tree with a large ax embedded in its trunk. We reeled from a rank smell. I looked behind the wood pile and recoiled at the sight of a doe, its head pointing skyward on a twisted neck, its belly ripped wide open. "How could anyone kill a beautiful animal like that?" I walked away from it in distaste.

Dina shook her head. "You're in the country now. People hunt. You need to get used to that. I think we're on the right route anyway. Look over there. That might be the driveway." An opening had appeared through the trees, a pathway. Under the moon's bright light, the snow sparkled like silver.

The mare turned onto it. She pricked her ears and broke into a trot. I fell farther behind with the stallion.

Deeper in the forest, another howl broke through the cold air, this time jarringly close. The sound of breaking branches spooked the stallion. It took all my strength to control him. Alarmed, I looked behind me.

Moonlight illuminated Alessio's form on the crisp white avenue of snow.

Dina's mare caught his scent and stampeded down the path. The stallion wrenched the reins out of my hand and raced after them, heedless of his damaged leg.

I faced Alessio. I'd matched him in a fight before. I could do it again as long as I avoided the mesmerizing effect of his eyes. But in an instant two forms burst out of the bushes between us—huge hunting dogs, their bodies the size of small ponies, growling low in their throats. They came to a stop and stood stock-still halfway between Alessio and me. Their tails were lowered, their hackles raised.

Alessio stiffened. One of the dogs crept toward him and crouched, its haunches tightened, ready to spring. The other veered off to the left, foiling any chance for him to retreat. Alessio had no hope of escape. He crashed sidelong into the bushes and the dogs tore after him.

Once the dogs finished with Alessio they'd come for me. I ran down the trail. It was a path to nowhere. A few hundred yards along it dead-ended at a wall of trees.

Torn clumps of frost-tipped grass showed the route the horses took when they charged into the wood. Ahead I could discern movement through the trees. Drawing nearer, I saw it wasn't the horses. They'd vanished. Dina sat up holding one arm awkwardly. Her clothing was torn and the snow around her spattered with blood.

Twenty-Seven

I ran to her. As I bent down, I noticed her top had torn, exposing small white scars crisscrossing her stomach underneath her breasts. They looked like incisions made with a small blade. More of Mancini's torment or an act of self-harm?

Dina murmured something in Italian.

"You've had a bad fall," I said. "Do you think you can get up?"

"Hit a branch when the mare ran into the wood."

With my arm securely around her, I helped her stand. She winced in pain. "Try to walk. We'll take it slowly." Her hair hung in wet drapes around her face and she grimaced with every step.

I listened for the sound of the hounds. They must have finished with Alessio by now. The man hadn't even cried out, so fast had the animals attacked him. We had to find shelter quickly. I decided we could do no worse than to follow the horses. To our immense relief, within a short time the wood thinned, ending at a stone barrier. We entered through a hole in a crumbling wall and found ourselves in a garden.

It was a strange garden, tangled and wild, but also a place of rare beauty. Oddly, no snow lay on the ground here. A beam of moonlight on a sundial cast a shadow over the Roman numeral three. It may indeed have been three in the morning by now. I couldn't tell.

Rows of lavender, the flowers dried on their thin stalks, lined a gravel walk, throwing off a sweet, pungent odor. Ahead, life-sized statues of Grecian robed men and women holding flaming torches gave the place a magical air. Farther on we saw banks of flower beds in disarray, huge rose bushes with briars overgrown, blossoms gone to seed.

Beyond the roses was a rectangular reflecting pool, its surface a mat of floating yellow leaves. The pool was surrounded with paving stones almost hidden by plush moss. At one end stood an arbor, also covered with rose vines, where one fragile flower still bloomed. The arbor surrounded a sculpture of Eros, the fluid muscles of his masculine shoulders ready to loose an arrow from his bow, his gaze directed longingly at a slumbering Psyche.

The path led to a short set of broken stone steps, two gigantic iron urns on either side. As we looked higher we could see palm trees and the rising wall and roof of an enormous house. All the windows were shuttered and no light seeped from between the cracks.

Dina revived at the sight. "Thank the Lord. We made it after all."

"Assuming it's Renard's home, who knows if he's even here? It's all shut up."

"Didn't Hanzi say he never goes anywhere?"

"This looks like the rear of the house. Let's find an entrance."

Behind the palms another stone wall emerged, this one about five feet high. It appeared to be the foundation of an old building. A wooden gate kept in good condition was firmly locked. I desperately wanted to find a route past the wall away from the dogs. We walked its length and it eventually opened onto a stretch of overgrown grass with a circular driveway.

The magnificent facade of an estate house rose before us. It reminded me of a Grecian temple, simple and elegant. Corinthian columns supporting a portico ran the entire width of the building. A wide flight of central stairs made from variegated stone ran up to the portico. A coat of arms was emblazoned over the door. Here, as well, blazing torches had been fixed in brackets to each of the pillars.

Two sets of shutters were thrown open on the main-floor French windows. Warm, golden light poured forth. Despite our aches and pains we hastened up the stairs to the massive set of doors. One of them stood open a few inches. Dina stumbled inside. I followed her in and shut the door. The lock closed with a satisfying click.

The entrance hall floor, large squares of black-and-white tile, resembled a giant chess board. A split staircase curved up to a balustrade on the second floor. A *trompe l'oeil* painting graced the ceiling with a fantasy of mythological creatures—a black bull's head on a nude male body with exaggerated genitals brandished an ugly mace, a winged serpent coiled around a staff, a gorgon with a fish tail held a sword. Suspended from the ceiling, an elaborate chandelier supported scores of ceramic candles lit by flickering gas flames.

A brass bell sat on a wooden table inlaid with ivory in Arabic designs. Dina shook the bell. Its ring echoed through the corridors. When no one came, I called out. We waited for ages and tried the bell several more times. Stillness reigned. The absence of sound in such a large place felt ominous and I wondered whether we'd escaped from our adversaries outside only to encounter more dangers in here.

"It's so late," Dina said. "They must all be asleep. He'll probably throw us out for barging in like this when he wakes up."

"Then he'll have a fight on his hands. Nothing could get me outside again." I looked around. "You don't run an establishment like this without staff. Where are they?"

"I don't feel like camping out in this hall; I'm still hurting all over and there's not even a chair to sit in. Let's see what's in here." She tried the nearest door. It swung open.

The drawing room, for that's what it appeared to be, was someone's idea of a Middle Eastern fantasy. A giant hearth with a brightly burning log fire was enclosed by a massive mantel finished with Persian mosaics. Genie lamps placed around the room looked as if they'd come out of a page of "Aladdin"; gas flames shot from their spouts. Kayseri floss carpets adorned the tile floor. The walls sported woven textiles and a faint scent of incense hung over the room. Several low divans had been placed close to the fireplace. Dina winced as she lowered herself onto one of them.

"You should get out of those wet clothes," I said.

"Into what? Our packs disappeared with the horses."

I found a throw warmed by the firelight hanging on a screen and handed it to her. She went behind the screen to strip off her outerwear. Emerging with the throw wrapped around her like a hijab, she lay back down on the divan.

"I'm staying right here," she said, "and not moving ever again."

A crystal decanter containing amber liquid sat on a side table covered with a burgundy cloth. A stopper lay beside it with two cognac glasses. I sniffed the golden liquor and drew in the aroma of fine Courvoisier. I dribbled some into the glasses and handed one to her.

Dina sipped it slowly and when she'd finished pressed her hand to her throat. "Ah, that burned like a fury. It tastes wonderful." She sank back onto the sofa and shut her eyes.

I ambled over to look at several large books displayed on a banquette. They were in French and illustrated. One appeared to be a book of magic spells; it had a handsome black leather cover with an eight-sided star and crescent moons embossed in silver. The other two were atlases, their pages opened to sections on Arabia and Turkey.

Dina was half asleep already on the divan. The cut on her shoulder hadn't been as bad as I thought, but with all the trauma of our day her pale skin looked as white as the forest snow and the damp had turned her dark hair to ebony. Only her lips retained some color.

I left her to rest and exited the drawing room by another door near the fireplace. The kitchen I found myself in had an antiquated feel, with copper pots hanging from a ceiling rack, an enamel sink, a huge trestle table, and a large cooking stove. I retraced my steps to the entrance hall and climbed the main staircase.

Determined to find either the book that brought us here in the first place or our host, I ventured down the hall. Gas wall lights sprang on and I surmised they'd been set to some kind of motion detector. Many bedchambers led off the gallery; the beds, freshly made up, smelled of lavender. Each room had been beautifully decorated with French landscapes. In one room decked out with teal Regency wallpaper and containing a grand four-poster bed, a Poussin hung in a delicate golden frame.

I found a bathroom with a huge clawfoot iron tub with golden faucets. Despite the warmth of the house and the cognac, I was still cold. I always took showers but the temptation to plunge into steaming water was irresistible. Plump, clean towels hung on the rack and a long robe was suspended from a hook on the door. At that moment it dawned on me what must have happened. The entire house felt as if it had been prepared for guests. Hanzi must have found a way to send word to the merchant of our intention to visit. Renard would have known we couldn't make the journey back at night and had his people prepare the house for us. It was clear he intended us to stay. I didn't waste another minute before filling the tub with hot water and sliding into its welcoming depths.

Reluctantly I got out and dried off. Dressed in the robe, my sopping clothes in hand, I walked down the hall and found a little room with a cheery fire burning in the grate. I hung the garments over the fire screen and lay on the couch, intending to take a quick nap until they dried.

The sun's glare dazzled my eyes and I woke to the sound of a bell tinkling somewhere in the hall outside the room. The sweet, clear light of Provence shone in full splendor on the garden outside the window. I felt dazed at first; I couldn't remember where I was. Then I recalled our perilous journey up the cliffside and the attack dogs in the forest. My peace of mind returned, knowing we were safe. Beside the couch, someone had placed a little table covered with a fine cloth. On it was a plate of sweet cakes and a bowl of grapes and oranges. I sighed with relief. This confirmed my impression of last night that our host intended to make us feel welcome and for some reason, perhaps to give us privacy, didn't wish to disturb us by introducing himself. I fell upon the food like a starving man, which, in fact, I qualified as at that point. I hurriedly dressed.

Downstairs, our backpacks sat in the drawing room. Dina was nowhere to be seen. Had she found the horses? I searched for her outside, taking the opposite route from the way we'd come last night, and soon happened upon the stables. Five Camarguc horses grazed within a fenced enclosure. I was glad to see our mare among them but wondered about the fate of the stallion. He turned up in one of the stable stalls, a warm blanket over his back, chewing happily on hay. His hock had been carefully bound with white cloth.

When I returned to the house to find our host, I called out in the foyer but no one answered. I grew tired of waiting and decided to look for the library. Surely, I reasoned, my host's hospitality would extend to his book collection. I hadn't seen a library on my perambulations last night, but Renard was a noted rare book collector, and I hoped to find the volume of Basile's book there. It turned out to be opposite the drawing room. Bookshelves lined the library's interior walls, a moving ladder on runners providing access to the highest ones. Beside each window, niches held classical sculptures—Hermes with his staff, Poseidon with a trident, Zeus holding a thunderbolt. On the ceiling, a painting of medieval scholars reading scrolls surrounded a prancing white horse. Several comfortable chairs and a reading table had been set close to a blazing fire.

I suspected Renard would keep his most precious volumes under lock and key but it was worth a search. If I could find the book and photograph it, Dina and I could be on our way. I'd promised her that I'd prevent Mancini from reassembling the volumes, but clearing my name and proving the missing volumes' current whereabouts and ownership were more important to me at the moment. I spotted a familiar set of twelve books, each a different color: fine early editions of Andrew Lang's Fairy Books.

I began a methodical search starting with the literary titles grouped on the east wall alphabetically, by author name. Most were in handsome covers of leather or pasteboard in burgundy, black, or green, with gold-leaf lettering. They'd been kept in perfect condition, not a hint of foxing. The majority were in French, although I found a number in English and Italian.

I came across a beautifully illustrated edition of Hans Christian Andersen and Balzac's *La Comédie humaine* series. When I reached Baudelaire I ran my fingers back over the titles and found several versions of Basile's *The Tale of Tales*. First was Richard Burton's famous English edition of 1893. An article I came across on the Web claimed Burton's translation was poor. He'd embellished the stories and even added many new words that never appeared in Basile's original. Another edition, published in 1846 and translated by Felix Liebrecht, had an introduction by none other than Jacob Grimm. It sat beside the Burton. And next to that were the two volumes of the English translation like the ones Tye Norris lent me. That was all; not the volume I hoped to find. I cast another look around the room. Renard had thousands of books. It would take days to search through all of them.

Leafing through the English translation, I found "The Young Slave" among the ten stories of the second day. My eyes had just landed on the sentence "There she saw the young girl, clearly visible through the crystal caskets, so she opened them one by one and found that she seemed to be asleep" when a voice boomed behind me.

"I see you admire my library."

I almost dropped the book as I whipped around to see a rough-looking man dressed in a leather shirt and pants. He was tall; he had a few inches on my six feet. A wild mane of chestnut hair fell to his shoulders. His skin was heavily scarred as if it had once been scalded. His brow ridge was greatly pronounced, a cliff of flesh that overhung his eyes; his nose was unpleasantly twisted above full lips.

After tucking the book back in its place I walked over to him. He gave me a curt nod.

"I'm John Madison," I said, holding out my hand. "Not many people would extend their home to complete strangers the way you have. Thanks very much for your hospitality. We were in sore need of it."

He took my hand and shook it firmly. "It's my pleasure. Alphonse Renard." Plainly this was simply a polite, not heartfelt, response.

"Your home is remarkable, M. Renard. I've been admiring your library. The sculptures and ceiling fresco are especially fine."

I caught a glimpse of pride in his expression. "You see Poseidon over there"—he indicated the statue—"who fashioned white horses from surf. A splendid notion, don't you think? Recalls the legends of the mythical ones, Pegasus and the unicorn. White horses were sacred to the Persians, too. Magical symbols, beings who crossed over from other dimensions to our own, from worlds beyond our immediate senses. I make a study of that realm. 'Behold a pale horse'—isn't that the saying?" He looked me steadily in the eye. "But you didn't come here to learn about the ethereal. The book you seek is not in the library here."

"How do you know what I'm looking for?"

"I told him." Dina eased herself into the room and stood beside him. She'd done up her hair. And where had she found those clothes? She had on a calf-length brown skirt with a matching jacket. Renard said something to her in French that I couldn't catch and she responded in kind, gracing him with a brilliant smile. "Yes, Alphonse," she said in English for my benefit, "John wants to see your book. He's come a very long way for it."

"Dina's right," I said. "I'd like to see it. It's the second volume, I believe, day two in the anthology."

"Well, I'll certainly consider that," Renard said.

"I would appreciate it. I'd like to verify its authenticity and photograph it, if you don't mind. For insurance purposes. Did Dina tell you your volume has also been declared stolen?"

She shot me a hostile glance. "Certainly I did. And also that the claim was false."

Renard hastened to back her up. "I've purchased many rare books. I'm accustomed to these tricky issues with provenance."

"Well, you might want to rethink that. Dina's agent for the sale, Ewan Fraser, was murdered in Naples a few days ago. You could be in some danger—and I point that out only because we were able to enter your house quite easily last night."

"I can assure you," Renard said laughing, "no one gets close to my property without my approval. You need have no fears on my behalf. I was in the process of showing Dina the house. Join us if you wish."

Although Dina was still walking stiffly she seemed well recovered, and Renard, quite unnecessarily I thought, took her arm with exaggerated politeness. I wondered whether underneath her cheery exterior she recoiled from his touch, but far from taking her hand away as she had with me, she gave him another dazzling smile.

Renard chose a key from a large metal ring and unlocked a door beside the fireplace. We entered a corridor and passed by a small room outfitted with phones, computers, and a fax machine. The merchant had not entirely eschewed the modern world after all. The two dogs from the night before lay placidly on the floor farther down the hall. One raised its head; otherwise, they remained docile.

We descended a stairway to another locked door, this one built of metal with a keypad. The room we entered astonished me. It had no windows and it would be hard to know what exactly to call it. An armory? A strong room? Glass-fronted cupboards held an assortment of revolvers and pistols. Rapiers, sabers, pikes, and heavy swords hanging from brackets looked as if they'd last been held by a knight in the Middle Ages. A variety of long rifles, some of them old muskets, had been set into wooden wall racks. Not all the weapons were old. A couple of cases held new pistols and rifles with scopes.

"As you can tell, I'm well defended," Renard said. "And this doesn't include the security measures you can't see."

I gathered that the point of this tour was to impress Dina. He could wage a small war with these armaments. Dina's eyes lit up when she saw the weapons. I sensed for the first time since we'd fled Naples that she felt safe and protected from Alessio and Mancini.

Several large glass display cases held a set of solid gold dinner-ware, a vast collection of coins, and jewelry. Ropes of matched pearls, amethyst-encrusted earrings, and a necklace of fire opals were arranged on black velvet trays.

There, alongside the jewelry, sat the second volume of Basile's anthology. "Can I take a look at this?" I asked, indicating the book.

"Possibly," Renard said slowly. "Later perhaps."

I pressed him on it. "I'd also appreciate it if you'd consider signing the photographed copy indicating where and when you purchased the book."

"Let's deal with that later, too," he said again. His less than enthusiastic response bothered me, but I could hardly snatch his keys and open the display case. They dangled from a ring on his belt so I had no chance to get them.

Renard drew our attention to a bracelet of fat pinkish pearls with a little pendant enclosing an enameled portrait. The bracelet was oddly suspended from a light fixture. He scooped it off and presented it to Dina. *"Un cadeau pour mademoiselle. Un petit token."* He fastened it around her slender wrist. She beamed with pleasure and he pointed to the pendant.

"C'est que j'ai utilise pour ressembler à," he said. *What he used to look like.*

He took us to other rooms, many of which I hadn't seen in my wanderings the night before. The first, a glass conservatory filled with exotic plants, doubled as an aviary. I recognized a white cockatoo and parrots with jewel-green plumage; others I had no name for. In another room, he showed off an enormous wardrobe containing ball gowns and men's dress from bygone ages. Silk sashes, leather boots, women's dress slippers, elaborate masks. Costumes, perhaps, from plays and parties his ancestors once staged.

Eventually he excused himself. "I have matters to attend to this afternoon and ask you to join me for dinner at eight."

"A fascinating gentleman," Dina observed after he'd left. "He was handsome once." She held up the bracelet. The pendant showed the face of a young man, in his twenties I guessed, with long chestnut hair, expressive brown eyes, and a strong jaw.

"Strange man, in my opinion. Although you two seem to have become fast friends."

"I certainly hope so! I adore this place. He has marvelous taste, don't you think?"

"Yes, he has. Where did your clothes come from?"

"He keeps them for guests, apparently. There are more stunning dresses too."

"You'll have a much better chance to persuade him to let me photograph the book, Dina. Will you do that?"

"Let's be patient. We can't just storm in here making demands."

"On the contrary, we need to keep moving. Alessio followed us last night. That means Mancini knows we're here."

"Renard can protect us. There's no way I'm rushing away."

This was building toward an argument between us so I relented. "Okay. We can stay a little longer; it won't hurt to rest up. But we don't know whether we can trust him. What happened to his face, anyway? Is he a burn victim I wonder?"

"An accident. He traveled frequently to oversee his family's business. An oil tanker collided with his car and he almost died. He's quite sensitive about it. Since then he's kept to himself on the estate."

Twenty-Eight

November 24, 2003
Les Alpilles, France

A shiftless and unrewarding afternoon ensued. I asked one of the stable grooms to accompany me into the wood surrounding the garden to satisfy myself about Alessio's fate. We retraced the route back to the forest path. I found the trampled bushes where he fled from the dogs easily enough; that was all. I searched the area; there was no sign of his body. No blood on the leaves, no torn clothing. Either he'd survived or Renard's men had disposed of the evidence. Was he alive? And if so, where had he gone? It had been easy enough for Dina and me to walk right into the house. What prevented Alessio from doing so?

The body of the doe had also disappeared. There was no sign of it in the clearing. I wasn't sure what to make of its absence.

I decided to return to the library to find something to read. Renard hinted he was a follower of the occult. He might have some interesting material about necromancy. As I passed by the library window I chanced to look in and saw Dina and Renard sitting side by side. So much for his pressing matters of the afternoon. Dina's head was bent, her long locks curling over her shoulder. She held a book in her hands and appeared to be reading to him. Over his face flitted the most conflicting expressions. Not the quietly attentive look one would expect from a listener. No, his gaze bore down on Dina with a savage lust. She'd look up at him after finishing a passage, perhaps to add her thoughts about the piece, and suddenly the wildness would disappear as if he'd learned to push it away at will.

When I got inside, the rest of the household staff had finally materialized. One of them was kind enough to bring me coffee in my room. I spent the rest of the afternoon reading the English translation and making notes.

When we entered the dining room that evening, Renard was nowhere to be found. Dina looked around nervously while a manservant poured wine. The merchant didn't put in an appearance until the first course was served twenty minutes later. He looked even larger as he appeared in the doorway, his tall figure thrown into relief by light from the huge, five-pronged silver candelabra. Dinner was an uncomfortable affair. Renard seemed tense and spoke little, although I couldn't help noticing the way he doted on Dina's every word. He had little to say to me. Nor did he linger once the meal was over. He rose and bade us a curt good night. I looked at Dina meaningfully but she wouldn't meet my gaze.

Once again, as night descended, the house grew silent as if the two of us were its sole occupants. Dina didn't seem inclined to talk and took up a book to read in front of the fire. I prowled through the chambers once more to satisfy my curiosity about where Renard had gone. I checked the strong room. It was firmly locked and the book within it. Not finding him upstairs, I went down to the kitchen. His two dogs were curled up in front of the hearth. One of them leapt up, growling, hackles raised. I quickly shut the door. Interesting. For some reason he'd kept them inside tonight.

I happened to glance out the hall window on my way back to the drawing room and saw Renard striding across the gravel drive. I slipped out the front doors and followed him quietly, trying to remain unobserved. If he caught me I'd just say I was restless and couldn't sleep.

The moon was as strong as last night. He walked through the avenue of statues with their vividly flaming torches, and as he did, his figure appeared to recede. The depth of shadow and the torch-light must have been playing a visual trick on me. I rubbed my eyes. When I looked again, he'd vanished.

I wandered down the row of statues, looking left and right, thinking he must have veered off somewhere. Soon I came to the ranks of flower beds, but couldn't find any sign of him. The forest lay ahead. I stopped then, having no intention of venturing into it.

Young trees and bushes grew thickly at the wood's edge, their branches interlaced, the moonlight tracing each twig and leaf to compose a silvery web. I sensed a presence in the trees ahead, but could make out nothing more than their limbs glistening with frost. I peered intently at the pattern of branches. They shifted, but not from the wind as there was little breeze. Something was watching me.

A white stag, its antlers hidden among the tracery of branches and twigs, stood among the trees. It was a giant, the tip of its head a good seven feet off the ground. Then it moved, and I saw the head belonged to a tall human form swathed in a long shadowy cloak. A kind of phosphorescent glow seemed to surround the figure, although that may have been the effect of the moonlight.

Its dark eyes glittered with malice. What on earth was Renard playing at? The stag head, magical though it seemed, must be some kind of elaborate ruse. In the still, wintry night I could almost believe the vision was real.

Just as quickly as it had appeared, with a white flash it turned and fled deeper into the forest. Was this a threat Renard concocted knowing I'd follow him tonight? Or had I caught him unawares in some bizarre nightly ritual? His fascination with the occult led him down some strange paths.

We saw nothing of the merchant the next day. One of his staff informed us we'd be expected for dinner again that night. Dina immersed herself in the library, which she exclaimed was so impressive she could spend the rest of her life there.

"During my years at the palazzo," she said, "the few pleasant moments I had were mostly spent in the library. And I went often to the *biblioteca nazionale*, with my guard trailing along, of course— that's how I became friends with Ewan. Except for him and Luisa I had no companions. So books became my friends. I always feel happiest around them."

At eight that evening Renard and I stood at the foot of the staircase waiting for Dina. He was dressed in formal dinner attire but offered me nothing from his "guest" apparel. I suppose if he regarded me as some kind of rival for Dina's affection that made sense. I felt out of place in my sadly wrinkled jacket and jeans.

Dina appeared at the head of the stairs in a silk gown, a deep rose red. Its hem brushed the floor. It set off her pale skin and dark eyes beautifully. Circled around her wrist was the bracelet he'd given her. On her long, slender neck she wore the fire opal necklace.

Renard's fingers trembled when he took her hand. He seemed to grasp it too tightly at first, as if he couldn't help himself. He quickly apologized and released her.

Candles were the only source of light in the dining room, but they provided an agreeable, muted radiance. The dining table was set with linen, crystal, and the gold dinner service. We didn't sit down to eat immediately; instead Dina took her place at the grand piano at the far end of the room.

I watched Renard as he leaned on the piano listening avidly to her play and sing. I loved her voice as much as the first time I'd heard her sing but felt stung by their exclusion. Renard's brown eyes softened whenever he looked at her and his every gesture spoke of complete infatuation. And yet there were also glimpses of that feral nature I'd seen last night. I sensed he was constantly at war with his dark internal instincts.

Because of my brother I grew up steeped in Mesopotamian lore, so my observations were quite naturally often influenced by those old legends. Now, observing a man with violent impulses who'd become entranced with Dina, I was reminded of Gilgamesh and his companion of the soul, the primitive Enkidu, raised by wild animals. Gilgamesh's solution to pacifying him? He asked a woman to seduce Enkidu and teach him the ways of civilized life. I thought I saw something of this nature at work that evening. The relevance of those stories written thousands of years ago never ceased to amaze me.

Dina encouraged Renard's attention by flirting with him pitilessly.

I hoped this might change when we were seated at the table but it was not to be. They addressed each other, frequently in French, barely acknowledging my presence. The dinner, at least, was sumptuous, accompanied by excellent wines. Dina and I did justice to every course except for a serving of venison so rare it swam in blood. Renard ate that but otherwise barely touched his food. After the port, fruit, and a delectable Boursin, our host signaled to one of his staff. A few minutes later the man returned carrying the book. He placed it in front of the merchant.

Renard toyed with it and then eyed me. "I've come up with a proposal."

The day had gone from bad to worse and I had little patience left. I was certainly in no mood to appease the man. Plainly he got a kick out of causing me discomfort. On the other hand, I did very much want to examine the book. "Let's hear it, then."

When he next spoke, he addressed Dina. "I would ask that you stay here. If after a fortnight you choose to leave you'll be perfectly free to do so. Of course I would not bind you to this in any way. But if you remain, at the end of the fourteen days I will not only permit both of you to look at the book, I will give it to you." He leaned back in his chair. "That way there will be no need for me to sign anything."

"You want her to stay here ... without me?"

"Yes, that's what I'd like."

I looked over at Dina before addressing him. "You've been a gracious host, and we owe you a debt of gratitude but nothing more. You're a complete stranger."

He too turned to Dina. "I'll understand if you choose to decline. I know women have remarked that they find my appearance disagreeable."

Dina's next words set me on edge. "You've been extremely kind to us. It would be my pleasure to visit a while longer. As to how someone looks, that matters nothing to me. It's what is in the heart that counts."

"Dina," I said firmly, "let's discuss this for a few minutes, shall we?" I nodded toward Renard. "If you'll excuse us."

"Indeed," he said. "Please take all the time you wish."

"One minute then." I rose.

Dina scraped back her chair and swept out of the dining room. I shut the door emphatically behind us. She was furious with me, but I spoke first. "Surely you don't want to stay here alone.

We know absolutely nothing about him. You just escaped years of persecution from Mancini and that's bound to have left many scars. Wouldn't it be better to find someone to help you with that instead?"

"You're equating Renard with the conte. He's nothing like that."

"How do you know? We've barely spent any time here. And in that short time I've seen some pretty strange behavior."

"You forget, John, I'm *accustomed* to situations that are out of the ordinary. And how long have I spent with you? I don't know you either. We won't be alone. There are servants around all the time."

"Who will do whatever he says and see nothing if that's what he wants."

"I agreed to help you find those books and gave you a start. Really, I didn't even want to go that far. My other plans have been destroyed. I need time to work out what my future is. I'm free now. No one will ever make decisions for me again. If I decide to stay, I will." Her voice was glacial.

"Fine. It's your decision, of course. I'll do my best to return in two weeks."

She flung her next words at me. "Come back to look at the book if that's what you want, but I have no need to see you again."

Without saying another word, I walked away.

Perhaps out of regret for her unkindness, she caught up to me. "Wait, John." She opened her evening purse, took out a piece of notepaper, and handed it to me. "This is where you can find another collector who bought one of Basile's volumes."

The address was in Ghent. "Is there a name to go along with it?"

"The surname's Hatzfeld; that's all I know."

Her true intention had become glaringly clear. She'd written this note before we came down to dinner. She knew exactly what

Renard's proposal was going to be and how I'd react. I questioned whether she'd devised the entire plan to stay here without me. The evening had been nothing more than an elaborate charade, likely planned between the two of them in the afternoon.

Although it was verging on midnight, I wanted nothing more than to get out of there. I had no reason to care about her choice; Dina was entitled to make any decision she wished. Clearly, she saw the estate as a safe haven. And I had to admit, Renard offered her a far better prospect of escaping Mancini than I did. Still, her words cut deeply.

The merchant obliged me by supplying a carriage and driver. Had Renard's accident prompted his fear of cars? Avoiding them seemed like a peculiar throwback. Nevertheless, if I wanted to avoid hours of hiking through the forest in the dead of night, I'd have to accept his offer.

The coach set out through the gloomy wood, its lamps casting menacing shadows on the trees as we passed through the dense wall of forest. I wondered again what had become of Alessio. If he was still alive, I was certain to encounter him again.

Twenty-Nine

November 26, 2003
Ghent, Belgium

I lost time getting to Belgium from the south of France. The trip required a transfer in Paris but I needed to see someone there anyway, an art dealer who made quiet private sales, fronting for heavy hitters in the black market. I'd done him a favor once and he owed me. He was the sort of guy that kind of thing mattered to. Since leaving Naples, I'd had no chance to take steps to protect myself. Now it was a priority.

My friend showed up with the item I wanted when we met for lunch at the bistro outside the train station. I caught the next train and didn't arrive in Ghent until late afternoon. Still, it was worth the delay.

The Hotel de Flandre was pleasantly situated in Ghent's historic district. The medieval city felt like a place where fairy tales were born. The buildings with their unique stepped rooflines, mottled stone, lead-paned windows, and facades embellished with ornate designs looked as though they'd materialized from a child's storybook. I half expected to see a girl with a long yellow braid gazing out from a turret window or a troll emerge from the watery margins of the River Leie.

Gravensteen Castle added to the mystique. Unlike fanciful palaces bordering the Rhine, it had a forbidding air. Modeled on crusaders' forts with small window slits, its thick walls, built below the water line, prevented ancient enemies from tunneling in. The torture chamber, with its early guillotine and iron necklace designed to pierce a victim's neck when he moved, testified to its dark history.

Dina had given me an address on Gewad Street with the surname Hatzfeld. The house had an immaculately maintained historic facade. Art deco sculptures flanked the main entrance in weathered bronze. I walked past, planning my strategy. Six blocks down the street I found just what I was looking for—a flower shop where the attendant spoke French, not just Flemish. A luxuriant spray of white jasmine stood out among the lilies and roses and I bought a large bouquet.

Retracing my steps with one of my business cards in hand, I pressed the buzzer and hoped for the best. A distinguished-looking man opened the door. He wore navy pants, a white shirt with a waistcoat, and a bow tie.

I introduced myself.

He said in perfect English, "How may I help you, sir?"

His dress and demeanor suggested a butler so I took a chance. "I understand Mr. Hatzfeld is a rare book collector and I'd like to consult him about a book I've been searching for, similar to one he may own. These flowers are a gift for the lady of the house."

The man turned momentarily and called out to someone. I detected the barest twitch of amusement at the corner of his lips when he faced me again.

"Mr. Hatzfeld, as you refer to him, is not at home. I'm afraid you've made your visit in vain."

"I see. Can you suggest a better time?"

The twitch materialized again and faded just as quickly. "That is uncertain at this point. Perhaps you have a card? I'll advise him of your interest."

I held the bouquet in the crook of my arm and getting out a pen, scribbled the details about the volume I wanted on the back of my business card. As I handed it to him, a maid in full uniform appeared behind the butler. He motioned for her to take the flowers.

"Good day to you then, sir. I do hope you'll find the information you're seeking." He shut the door firmly.

Dispirited, I headed back down the street, stymied as to how to reach Hatzfeld. About half a block away I heard my name. The butler, in a much less composed fashion this time, was perched at the top of the steps, waving frantically at me.

"Mr. Hatzfeld is home after all," I said when I returned, unable to resist a little jab.

"Not at present," he replied, "but the lady of the house, as you so politely referenced, would be pleased to speak with you."

He led me through a small vestibule and down a hallway. A quick glance of the surroundings echoed the image the house presented to the street. It kept so faithfully to the original art deco designs that it felt like a journey back in time. Yet for all its lovely accoutrements, it had the stale air of a forgotten room.

I'd formed an expectation of who the wife might be. Someone verging on middle age, elegant and imperious, regulation Gucci scarf and Chanel suit. The vision greeting me as the butler swept me into the room was a far cry from that. I barely registered the introductions.

She stood resting one hand on the window ledge, framed by a terrace with a stone balustrade, the back garden greenery, and the glassy surface of the Leie in the distance. Sultry late afternoon light cast an aura around her hair and figure and for a moment I had the impression I was looking at a portrait of a queen. Were it not for her contemporary dress, she'd have fit right into the Renaissance court at Gravensteen Castle.

Such translucent skin required no makeup, although she did wear a touch to accentuate her high cheekbones and long lashes. She was small boned; the simple jersey and slim skirt she wore showed undeniable curves. If she was any older than me, it wasn't by much.

The jasmine had been arranged in a vase, its lush scent expanding through the room. The butler excused himself. The portrait came to life and held out her hand.

"I wouldn't have agreed to meet you, Mr. Madison, except jasmine is my favorite flower. Were you forewarned or was that just impeccable taste on your part?"

"Somehow, I knew you'd like it." A shiver of anticipation ran through me when I took her small, delicate hand in mine.

She released my hand and moved away from the window languidly, the slightest hint of sensuality in her walk. I had the impression of a passionate woman but one long used to holding her emotions in check. She indicated an armchair and sat opposite me in its mate. The rich sea-green walls set off her honey-colored hair and slightly tawny skin. I imagined her in one of those thirties satin evening dresses, instantly glamorous.

"I understand you're seeking a book," she said. "Can you describe it?"

"It's actually a seventeenth-century anthology that includes several well-known fairy tales. Five volumes written in Neapolitan dialect by Giambattista Basile. I was given to understand your husband is an avid rare book collector and may have bought one of the volumes." She had a way of fixing her hazel eyes on me that was very distracting. I glanced away for a moment and said, "It was kind of you to see me, Mme Hatzfeld, on such short notice."

"Please call me Katharina," she said graciously. "I have no need for formalities. I'm not sure where your presumption about my husband came from. I purchased the volume you speak of. May I ask what is your interest in the book?"

"Pardon my mistake then. I'm an antiquities dealer and bought one of the other volumes on behalf of a client. It was subsequently taken from me. I discovered later it had been stolen before it hit the auction block—a kind of double theft, I suppose."

I detected a faint flush on her cheeks at my mention of theft. She paused, assessing how much she wanted to reveal. "And you think it may have ended up here?"

I sensed a hint of annoyance in her tone. "Please don't think I'm implying that. No doubt yours is a different edition or a different volume entirely."

"Whether or not it ever had an illicit history, I assure you mine is now in its rightful place. Are you aware not all of the original volumes even had the same publisher? Which one did you buy?"

"The Beltrano edition, from 1634."

"Then your client acquired the first volume, day one, in the anthology." She got up. "Come. To settle your mind about this, I'm willing to show it to you."

We walked across the hall and entered a study, this one smaller. She unlocked an antique roll-top desk and lifted out the book, setting it down carefully on a pristine white cloth.

The book's title page confirmed what she told me. Mine had a pictograph of a banner superimposed on a tree; hers was different, the third volume, day three, published by Scorrigio. I decided to push my luck and asked if she'd let me take photographs.

"I ordered several copies made for insurance purposes," she said. "I don't see why you couldn't have one of those." She asked me to wait, shutting the door quietly behind her on her way out. In a few minutes she returned with a sheaf of papers in a black file folder.

Before she could show me the copy, a bustle at the front entrance announced a stodgy woman in a print dress holding the hands of two children, a boy and a girl, both toddlers, red cheeked and chattering away in high spirits. The woman bent down and shushed the girl she called Luna and then said to Katharina, *"Scusat' signurì, mo' me ne vacocoè criature."*

"Aspiett' nu minut', Vera. Te voglio salutà." Katharina held her arms open. *"Vien' a ccà."* The little girl ran to her, the boy following much more tentatively. She gave them each a double kiss and shooed them back. The woman ushered the children away. Katharina waited until they were out of earshot. "My grandchildren are leaving to go home after their visit. Vera, my housekeeper, has her hands full with those two. I forget how much energy little ones take."

"You look far too young to be a grandmother."

My compliment brought a smile to her lips. She sat down and with a tantalizing swish of her silk stockings crossed her legs. "Ah, you are very diplomatic, Mr. Madison. It will soon be my fortieth birthday," she said. "What is that phrase you use in English? Almost over the hill."

"Far from that," I said honestly.

She picked up the file and handed it to me. "Here's the copy of my volume."

I thanked her and put it in my case. "That's wonderful. Would you mind if I took another quick look at the original?"

She gave me a cautious look as if to assess my intent. "If you wish." She walked back to the desk and I followed her. She opened the book gently and turned the pages slowly with a thin wooden spatula.

"It's fascinating to think these pages were first read hundreds of years ago. I understand it was an instant bestseller. I've been told some of these stories are based on actual events. What do you think of that?"

She put a finger to her lips. "They're fairy tales—myths— nothing more. If there's any truth to them, after so much time it's no longer recognizable as such. That's even the case for much of what passes for history. You probably think Nero played his fiddle when Rome burned, no?"

"Sure, I guess."

"Well, it's false. The precursor to the fiddle wasn't even invented until the ninth century. And Marie Antoinette never said, 'Let them eat cake.' That came from the mouth of a French queen one hundred years earlier."

"Really? The reason I ask is because there's supposed to be some tie between Basile's tales and an outbreak of the plague. Would you know anything about that?"

"Not offhand. Unless you mean the author himself. He died of the plague in 1632."

"He did?"

"Not the Black Death. The disease that took his life claimed many souls in Napoli. Historians still don't know what type of epidemic it was."

"Wait a second. Did you say Basile died in 1632? But the first volume of the book wasn't published until 1634."

"Didn't you know? What we're looking at is a final printer's proof—like a galley. It wasn't properly checked and you can see mistakes in some of the story titles and formatting. A terrible volcanic eruption occurred in the winter of 1631 and the following year a plague hit the city. Conditions in Napoli grew very grim, so normal commerce was brought to a halt. Only when Basile's sister got in touch with the publishers after he died did they go ahead and publish the book. Without her, his great writing might have been lost to us."

The sole surviving galley for such a famous book would be even more precious than the first edition. I digested this as I leafed through the rest of her book.

Katharina checked her watch. "I find myself at loose ends without social obligations tonight. If you have no pressing business, could I interest you in an early dinner? Not many people are familiar with Basile's anthology. I'd love to talk more about it and there's a pleasant bistro not far away."

She made the offer quite casually, as if it were all the same to her whether I accepted the invitation or not. I was under no illusions, however, and doubted very much she made a habit of inviting strange men to dinner. No red-blooded guy would turn down an invitation like that, and besides, I was intrigued to find out what she really wanted.

The pleasant bistro turned out to be a five-star restaurant. By the end of dinner, after we'd gone through two bottles of Château Poujeaux, I was feeling no pain and didn't care how much it cost. Katharina tried to pry out of me how I found out she'd bought the book. It became clear this was the real reason she'd suggested we go out. I deflected her questions and she didn't insist. When I asked about her husband she said they'd recently separated. Except for her houseman, who didn't strike me as much of a defender, she was pretty much alone.

"I want to tell you," I said, "to be careful. The man who arranged the sale of the book was murdered in Naples. Can you hire someone to watch over you until this affair is sorted out? Will you be all right?"

My warning didn't seem to alarm her in any way; in fact, her lips turned up in a faint smile. "How very sweet of you, John. But don't worry. I'm quite safe."

I thought of emphasizing the point but her reaction suggested it would have no effect.

"I hope you're right. At least consider it."

Rain was pelting down by the time we left the restaurant. Katharina drew me closer under her umbrella. We were both pretty tipsy and in good enough moods not to care about a few drops of rain. By now it was clear she didn't intend for the night to end at her doorstep. When we reached her place she suggested a nightcap.

She brushed my fingers with her lips as I helped her off with her coat. I returned the compliment with a deep kiss. The cognac we had intended to drink became a distant memory.

The street lamp outside cast a glow in her bedroom, highlighting the wet, golden-brown waves of her hair. Rain water trailing down from her hair glistened on her tawny skin. She let her dress slide to the floor. Underneath she wore only a full-length translucent slip that veiled her body just enough to make me want to see more. I lifted her slip and felt the heat of her bare skin against mine as I took her in my arms.

As we lay together afterward she ran her fingers down my chest. "You avoided answering me earlier, but I'd still like to know how you found out I bought the book. Did Ewan Fraser figure it out? Did he tell you?"

I uncoupled from the warmth of her body and reached for my clothes on the floor, putting them on as I sat on the edge of the bed. "It's a long story and I'll tell you, I promise, but first"—I paused to brush her cheek with a kiss—"which way is the restroom?"

"Three doors down the hall. I look forward to hearing your answer when you return."

Visiting the bathroom was an excuse to buy some time to think up a good answer without revealing too much. I walked down the corridor, counted three doorways, and realized I didn't know whether she'd been referring to the left or the right side of the hall. I pushed open the door on my left.

The odd nature of the room I entered struck me immediately. Not square but octagonal, all eight sides different widths. Even the verticals looked skewed, as if the walls sloped inward. It had bare wooden floors and possessed no furniture save for a mirror in a beautifully enameled frame hanging on one of the angled walls. Its wavy surface and the markings on the glass suggested the mirror was quite old.

At first I couldn't understand what I saw—or didn't see—in it. Although the mirror reproduced the room's background faithfully, my own reflection did not appear. Touching the glass without seeing my hand had a strangely disorienting effect. I guessed the phenomenon had something to do with the mirror's placement in the context of the irregular walls.

The only other object in the room was a framed picture with its face turned toward the wall. Unaccountably, this *was* reflected in the mirror. The backing appeared brittle and browned. It had an inscription in Spanish and a date in Roman numerals. I turned it around.

José de Ribera's *Mary Magdalene in the Desert*

It was a portrait of Dina. I could hardly believe my eyes. Not just her mass of dark hair, rosy lips, and porcelain skin, but every feature faithfully copied. Even the painted expression resembled that of the woman I'd so recently left in France: a patrician aloofness softened with a touch of warmth. The oil painting had tiny eggshell cracks—the patina—of a centuries-old original. But how could that be? Faked oil paintings are legion in the art industry and some have fooled even the best scholars. This one looked convincingly aged. It had to be a clever reproduction.

I heard a sound behind me.

"May I ask what you're doing?" Katharina stood wrapped in her bathrobe, disapproval stamped on her features.

"I didn't mean to pry," I said. "I got the wrong room. Then I saw this mirror. It's entrancing. How does it work? Is it related to the angle of the walls?"

"Something like that," she replied sharply.

"Can you see your reflection in it? Mine doesn't show."

"Only that ghastly portrait is caught by the mirror. I saw your reaction to the picture. You know her, don't you?"

Her tone, her entire demeanor, had changed. She held herself stiffly. The room's bright light emphasized the prominent angles of her face and a tiny web of lines around her eyes that I'd not noticed before.

"Yes, I do."

Katharina moved back to let me exit the room; then she pulled the door shut and locked it with a key from her pocket. "Dina sent you here, didn't she? I took every precaution to hide my name when I bought the book from her agent. How did she find out?"

"Dina gave me your address but otherwise left me completely in the dark. I had no idea you knew her, let alone had a portrait of her hanging in your home."

Her lips trembled in the effort to get her next words out. "She stole my husband from me."

The veil fell from my eyes. "You're Lorenzo Mancini's wife."

Thirty

November 27, 2003
Ghent, Belgium

"Legally, anyway," she said bitterly. "I use my maiden name now." Again I was struck by the transformation in her character. While at first she'd seemed so genteel, her eyes now burned with spite. The mere mention of Dina's name set off a torrent of hatred. "My husband prefers young flesh—that is true. I was seventeen when we married, an alliance forced on me by my parents. Dina came to us in 1998. I suppose she told you the sad story about her life? How she was an aristocrat from an obscure family and that her mother died, her father lost his business and essentially abandoned her?"

"Something along those lines." I tried to keep my tone neutral.

"I'm sure you think she's the picture of innocence," Katharina said coldly. "Lorenzo brought her home one day and announced she'd be living with us. He gave me no choice at all. She had no identity papers. She was unable to speak proper Italian, had an unusual dialect I could barely understand. Her manners were hopeless. My husband took her on as a project, a kind of Pygmalion. He wanted to see if he could turn an urchin into a lady."

"She certainly is that now."

Katharina gave me a black look. "She's anything but. From the start I could see her begin to work on his … emotions. I pleaded with Lorenzo, but in the end, had to stand by and watch it happen. Every flirtatious glance she threw his way was like a razor slicing through my veins. There was nothing I could do. Tell me, where does a fifteen-year-old learn such powers of seduction? She was no virgin, even at that young age. He got her from some brothel." Spittle flew out of her mouth as she spoke.

"Why keep her picture then, Katharina, if you hate her so deeply?"

"My husband checks on me. He insists I keep the painting in that exact location and always makes sure it's there. 'A little torture,' he says—to pay me back for leaving him. The mirror was his idea too. A little beauty he picked up in Lohr. Ours was not a great love match but it fell apart when he met Dina. He has a legendary temper. I go along with his wishes to keep the peace.

"Anyway, that's not *your* Dina," Katharina snapped. "It's a 1638 Renaissance portrait attributed to José de Ribera, the illustrator of our little book. One of the painter's earlier works. An almost identical painting by him now hangs in the Prado that dates to 1641. My husband was mistakenly told it was a portrait of Margarete von Waldeck. That proved untrue, since von Waldeck died thirty-seven years before de Ribera was born."

"Who is Margarete von Waldeck?" I said, still reeling from the date of the painting and the name of the artist.

Katharina's angry stance hadn't abated in the least. "How do you know Dina?" she asked shrilly.

"I met her in the course of searching for my stolen volume. How does Margarete von Waldeck fit in?" I repeated. "The likeness to Dina is unbelievable."

I followed Katharina as she walked back toward her room. "Von Waldeck's a young woman with a sad history. Some believe her personal story became the basis for 'Snow White.' Her father's estate bordered a village in Hessen whose poor laborers were small as a result of malnutrition and long hours spent working underground in local copper mines. Hence her association with dwarfs."

Renwick's conviction that the old tales were based on actual events came back to me. Katharina continued, her voice brittle with anger. "Margarete's stepmother was extremely jealous of the young girl's beauty so she sent her away to the Spanish court at Brussels. The family hoped she'd gain a prominent marriage and their plan succeeded too brilliantly. The young prince, soon to be Spanish king Phillip II, fell deeply in love with her. Margarete's father wanted a match with a nobleman but never dreamed of so high a prospect. It was a dangerous alliance for the girl. The Spanish court would never allow such a marriage."

"Was she poisoned like Snow White?"

"She died at the age of twenty-one. And yes, many think court officials poisoned her."

"Pretty difficult to prove when so much time has passed."

"People will believe anything, though—won't they?" The implication of her words was directed more to my defense of Dina than to the poisoning of Snow White.

We'd reached her room. I shrugged on my shirt and jacket and stepped into my shoes. Katharina watched me dress in silence, her arms crossed over her chest.

"I still don't understand how a picture that's centuries old could be a mirror image of Dina," I said.

"You have it the wrong way round. My husband became

entranced with Dina *because* she resembled this picture he so loves. She wormed her way into his heart and ruined my marriage."

"And yet Dina's terrified of him. He abused her."

She hesitated for a moment, trying to pull herself together. "No doubt you've come under her spell as well. Dina must have wanted something from you—what was it?"

"My help to get away from him."

Katharina allowed herself a twisted smile at hearing this. "Well, perhaps she's finally finding that my husband's obsession cramps her style."

"I'll say. She sold the book to fund her escape from him."

"She never had money of her own. I bought my volume anonymously, to help her on her way. Stupid girl. Of course, it was also a way to restore the book to our family."

Quite unintentionally, I'd opened a raw wound and our pleasant interlude had blown apart with the force of a cannon shot. Katharina certainly didn't want any solace from me. She made it obvious she had no interest in prolonging the misery. The best thing I could do for both of us was bid her goodbye.

Back in my hotel room I fell into a troubled sleep, only to be jolted awake with a feeling of dread, the way I often felt in the aftermath of a nightmare. Sirens wailed outside the window. I tossed and turned for the next few hours and, finally giving up, took a long shower to shake off the uneasiness. As I trimmed my beard I noticed the marks where Alessio had pressed his cane into my neck seemed to have grown darker. That gave me a moment of worry until I figured they'd probably just been aggravated by the cascade of hot water.

I packed hurriedly, hoping to grab a coffee before I boarded the train for Brussels. Naso's bookshop was next on my list. I planned to fly from Brussels to Rome and then transfer to the Naples train.

Toxic air hit the back of my throat the minute I stepped outside. A couple of emergency vehicles swept past. Several blocks away a crowd gathered on the sidewalk. As I drew nearer, I could see puddles of water, and fire hoses curled on the wet pavement like fat black pythons. Firemen were winding the hoses back onto the trucks blocking the street.

People chattered in the low, excited tones used for calamities that did not affect them personally. They were kept at a distance by police tape and several officers, but I was tall enough to get a view of the damage. The street-level windows of Katharina's home had been punched out. Soot covered most of the first-floor stucco in an ugly black stain. The door, rocking in the breeze at a crazy angle, had been bashed in. Steam or smoke, I'm not sure which, sifted out the wrecked window and entrance. My gut twisted in dread.

I tried to ask several bystanders whether anyone had been injured but they spoke only Flemish. I was on the point of breaking through the crowd to find a cop when I felt a light hand on my shoulder.

A middle-aged woman wearing a knitted coat thrown over her dressing gown said, "You wish to know about the fire—I heard you asking."

"Yes, can you tell me what happened?"

"It started around four this morning. We woke up with flames turning the street red outside our window. The fire trucks came and we were ordered out of our houses in case the fire spread. Flames were shooting out of Katharina's first floor. They found her inside, dead."

When you fear something, learning that fear is real does nothing to lessen the shock.

"Did you know her then?" the woman asked sympathetically, having noticed the look of dread written all over my face.

"Briefly." I remembered the children. "Was anyone else hurt?"

"Her houseman and the maid are safe. They got out through the garden level."

I recalled Katharina telling me the housekeeper was taking the grandchildren back to their parents. An even greater catastrophe had been narrowly averted.

The woman turned around to chat with her neighbor.

Like a horde of wasps, press photographers swarmed a black limo as it pulled up in front of the house. The burly man with a white scar on his forehead exited the front passenger seat and tried to clear the reporters away. The back door swung open and Mancini emerged. He wore sunglasses and kept his head bowed, but his snow-white cap of hair and hawkish nose were unmistakable. The guard stared menacingly at the journalists pressing in as they shouted questions at Mancini. He batted away at them, yelling back in Italian.

I was glad of the diversion. I faded to the back of the crowd and made my way toward the Ghent railway station, feeling overcome by the horror of Katharina's death. Not for the first time that morning, I wondered what had become of her volume. Was it back in Mancini's hands?

Thirty-One

November 27, 2003
Ghent, Belgium

Shaheen slouched against a stand of multicolored pillars at the
Gent-Sint-Pieters railway terminal main entrance. He'd been
waiting for almost half an hour. The noon train was due to depart
soon. John Madison would be on it and Shaheen intended to inter-
cept him. Shaheen's location gave him a panoramic view of the area
in front of the station. Directly across from him was a drop-off
point for cars, beyond that a busy tramway and a heavily treed
plaza crowded with hundreds of commuters' bikes.

No one paid him any heed and that was how Shaheen liked
it. Just another out-of-work migrant, a scrounger hanging around
to milk commuters and tourists. He fit right in with a local thug
standing nearby, sporting a big belly that swelled like Niagara
over his belt. The guy wore oversized hip-huggers and a hoodie.
Universal uniform of hip-hop. The man's appearance was made
all the more repulsive by the fact that his top barely covered his

stomach; he stretched out surprisingly delicate white hands to the commuters for money.

Shaheen had spent a couple of productive days in London. He'd interviewed Renwick's solicitor and the business partner, Tye Norris. After a request from DCI Wilson, Norris turned over all of Renwick's notes and bills. Described by Norris as a fastidious man, Renwick was anything but when it came to his personal papers. Shaheen had unearthed a jumble of scribblings on torn-off paper scraps, disordered bills, bank charges skewered on an old paper spike, looseleaf notebooks started and never finished, all dumped helter-skelter into large drawers. Renwick kept no private diary so it took two days of pawing through the heap of material to discern what was relevant.

Among the jumble, a few gems turned up.

One notebook entry confirmed Renwick was convinced the source of his childhood disease could be tracked to a specific archaeological site in Iraq associated with a famous fairy tale— unnamed—a story originating with the Mesopotamians.

The second find concerned a piece of lined foolscap paper with a photocopy of a picture stapled to it showing a youthful dark-haired woman and an older man. On the lined paper Renwick had written *Talia, August 18, 2000, in the company of Lorenzo Mancini. Shot photo unobserved as pair emerged from services at Cathedral of San Gennaro. Mancini family believed to have originally possessed complete copy of* The Tale of Tales. *No response from Mancini.*

Shaheen recognized Mancini from the picture because he'd done a check on the Italian aristocrat after Wilson identified him as the stolen book's owner. Somehow, perhaps through a patient search of historical source material, Renwick learned the Mancini family owned a copy of the book. Shaheen thought Mancini merited a close look.

Renwick's papers were interesting but shed little light on his visit to Iraq and subsequent disappearance. Despite mounting circumstantial evidence, there was still no definitive proof that Renwick's interest in the book and time in Iraq were related to Shaheen's mission.

Shaheen sifted through the rest of the material, hoping to find a description of an Iraqi site where Renwick may have led the scientists, or notes about his conversations with Loretti and Hill. He was disappointed. What he did know for sure was that Renwick arrived at the al-Rasheed hotel in the Green Zone last summer, late on the afternoon of August 12, and met the two scientists at the bar that evening. He paid for their drinks. Renwick also made numerous references to a circular stone weight, apparently some family heirloom. Probably the same one listed in the police file on the burglary at the publishing house.

The London office agent Shaheen conscripted to watch Madison failed miserably. He lost him somewhere in Naples. He'd tracked Madison to a Naples nightclub and then back to his hotel room. After that, Madison vanished. No one saw him leave his hotel. No credit card charges or phone calls to his contacts in New York showed up to help pin down where he'd gone. Madison had been clever but he'd slipped up now by using his credit card to purchase a train ticket out of Ghent. And he was booked on a Swiss International flight leaving from Brussels. They had him in their sights once more.

Shaheen checked his watch. It was almost noon. Where was Madison? A second man, posted on the departure platform, waited in case Madison entered the station without using the main entrance. Shaheen got out his phone to check but the other agent hadn't spotted Madison yet either.

Shaheen swept his glance around the street, paying close attention to anyone who disembarked from trams shuttling in and out across from him. He couldn't be absolutely sure Madison would show up at this time, but his flight left Brussels at 3:30 P.M., so if he took a later train he'd be cutting it pretty close.

When he looked around again a figure caught his attention in the plaza. An older man in black sat on a bench, the hem of his long coat dragging on the pavement. He wore a formal top hat. His gloved hands rested on the handle of a white cane. It was a gloomy, cool day in Ghent, the sun entirely obscured by clouds, but strangely, the old man seemed to be sitting in a pool of deep shadow.

Trams whirred into the station, disgorged passengers moving on again after a few moments. The black-coated man remained sitting under the leafless trees of the plaza. Like a flickering early motion picture, the trams blocked sight of him when they pulled in and revealed him when they pulled out. If this wasn't the thief Madison described, it certainly was his double.

Shaheen pushed himself away from the pillar and began to walk toward him as the old man abruptly stood and gazed southward along Koning Albertlaan. Shaheen turned to see what he was looking at.

Madison was heading their way.

He no longer resembled the sharp-looking guy dressed in an expensive jacket and tailored pants at the police interview in London but walked with a dejected air, as if he'd just lost his best friend. He had on a bulky jacket and jeans, a pack thrown over his shoulder.

The black-clad man moved forward haltingly. For a minute it looked as though he was going to step right off the curb into the oncoming trams. He turned his head in the direction of the station and nodded. Toward whom?

Shaheen followed his line of sight and saw the big-bellied guy move on a direct trajectory for Madison. The man held his right arm stiffly, his hand plunged into a side pocket of his loose trousers. Certain sign of a concealed weapon.

Madison ambled slowly with his head down, unaware of the danger, jerking his head up only when the heavyset man got ten feet or so away. Before he had a chance to react, the pistol was in the man's hand. A look of horror crossed Madison's face. He turned on a dime and ran. It wasn't enough. That close, even an amateur couldn't miss.

Madison took the shot square in the back.

The force of the shot propelled his body forward several feet. His foot lifted momentarily as if he were trying to execute a dance step and he crumpled onto the sidewalk. He used his arms to crawl for a few inches then lay still, face down.

The shooter fled, his fat thighs pumping like fury.

Shaheen had made the fatal mistake of training his attention on the spotter in the black coat and noticed the gunman too late. He reached under his jacket for his Ruger LCP-CT and aimed but cars prevented a clear shot. A passerby screamed. The gunman ran into the gap between trams.

Madison lay on his stomach, a hole from the bullet burned into the back of his jacket. Shaheen pocketed his gun and whipped out his phone to call an ambulance. He reached Madison and bent down to turn him face up.

Madison kicked out at him. Shaheen leapt back in surprise. "What the fuck? Are you immortal or something?"

White-faced, Madison turned over. He dragged in a couple of deep breaths and edged himself into a sitting position, clamping his hand to his back. "Shit. That knocked the breath out of me. What the hell are you doing here?"

"Seeing to your protection." Shaheen laughed. "Are you wearing something under that jacket? Gotta be." Shaheen stretched out a hand to help Madison up.

"A friend in Paris gave me a Kevlar vest. It seemed wise, under the circumstances. Always be prepared, I guess."

"Let's get out of here. People are gawking."

Now that the attack was over, commuters who'd initially scattered at the sound of the shot rushed back. One woman shook her finger at them and yelled something in Flemish. Shaheen cast a glance over to the plaza but both the spotter and the gunman were long gone.

Thirty-Two

Shaheen and Madison crossed the plaza and entered the network of streets beyond to find a place to talk. Madison took his time and walked with some difficulty. Shaheen used his cellphone to call his agent still waiting on the platform. He described the shooter and asked the agent to deal with the police, who'd probably be on scene any minute.

"If two people want you terminated in broad daylight they've got to have a compelling reason," he said to Madison.

"Two of them? Who was the other one?"

"Old guy with a cane sitting across from me. The one you described in your report to Scotland Yard. He was acting as a spotter. He knew you, at least what you look like, so we can assume the shooter didn't."

They found a bar just opening for the day, and settling at a table in a dim corner, ordered their drinks.

"My back feels like it's loaded with bird shot."

"The vest'll stop a bullet but you're going to have serious

bruises." Shaheen reached into his pocket and took out a pill box. "OxyContin. I swear by them. Just take one though because they're powerful. Any more than that and you'll spend the rest of the day in never-never land."

Madison threw one down and swallowed. "Doesn't sound like such a bad idea. Do you know who the shooter was?"

"Nope. What's that smell? You been standing around a bonfire?" Shaheen asked. "They must have been burning tires."

"It's from a house fire near my hotel."

"What are you up to in Ghent?"

"Tracking one of the volumes. And the woman who bought it just died in that fire. I saw her yesterday and she gave me a photo-copy of the volume she owned." He paused and tried to shift into a more comfortable position. "Her name was Katharina Hatzfeld. Lorenzo Mancini's wife."

Shaheen raised his eyebrows. "You mean the book's real owner?"

"The same. He's in town right now."

"You're a one-man destruction machine, aren't you? Remind me not to invite you over for dinner. I'd wind up dead."

Madison gave him a grim smile. "I was back in my hotel long before the fire started. You're free to check with the night clerk. The neighbors say it was an accident. I don't believe that. Mancini's desperate to get his hands on all the volumes of Basile's book."

"Okay, point taken. Where were you when Ewan Fraser was murdered?"

"Trying to get the hell out of Naples. I'd been warned Mancini wanted to kill me too."

"Too? You're suggesting Mancini killed Fraser?"

"Not directly. Hired muscle. Mancini's got a history of abusing people. He raped a young girl he and his wife took in. He's a total pig."

"A brunette, longish face, dark eyes?"

"Yes. She's the one who stole the book from Mancini in the first place. How did you know?"

Shaheen thought for a minute. "Saw a photo of her Renwick took. Where's she now?"

Madison shrugged. "On the run, last I heard."

The waiter brought their drinks. Shaheen extracted a cigarillo from his jacket pocket. Madison chugged down his scotch and ordered a second.

"So what's the real reason the military is interested in me?"

"We're checking Renwick's movements. He was in Iraq last August, same as you. And now you're hunting down the book he wanted."

"I never met Renwick in Iraq. Like I told you before, we've never met at all. I can't see why you'd be interested in him; he was just a fusty English publisher."

"Last September in Baghdad he met two individuals who encountered some trouble," Shaheen said. "Americans. People on our side. I need to know what they talked about."

"What kind of trouble?"

"Not at liberty to say. But it's nasty enough." He tapped his cigarillo absentmindedly over the ashtray as if it were lit. "The fact Renwick's missing sends up a big red flag. And now Ewan Fraser and Mancini's wife are both dead. Seems like the book you're chasing is bad luck—wouldn't you say?"

"*Mancini's* bad luck. The guy's a homicidal maniac. Aren't you going to light that thing?"

"Promised myself I'd quit."

"You like tempting fate then?"

Shaheen grinned. "Pretty much describes my life."

"You know something else was stolen from Renwick, right? A circular stone artifact he brought back from Iraq. It was marked with cuneiform writing."

"Saw a reference to it in the police report on the burglary," Shaheen said. "How does it fit in, do you think?"

"No idea. Don't even know what it is, but I'm trying to find out. People develop all kinds of wild theories about things. And they get obsessed with proving them."

"We've been trying to piece together some Iraqi words. *Ersh* and *gal*. Your brother was a specialist in ancient tongues. Do those words mean anything to you?"

"Not offhand," Madison said. "Is it written down? Maybe that would help."

Shaheen got out his ballpoint and wrote the two words on a cocktail napkin, turning it around for Madison to see. Madison studied them for a few minutes. "If I'm right, the word should be written like this. Er-esh-ki-gal. Actually, it's not a word, it's a name. The goddess of the Mesopotamian underworld. Associated with Nergal, the male underworld deity and Babylonian god of plague."

Thirty-Three

Shaheen remained stone-faced despite the bombshell Madison had just dropped on him. Could Renwick have led the scientists to a bioweapon site associated with some ancient plague source? If so, the Iraqis had kept it an ironclad secret. Shaheen couldn't afford to rule out anything at this point. He took back the napkin, scribbled a note, and crammed it into his pocket. "You were heading to Rome?"

"Still am," Madison said. "And then on to Naples to check out another volume of Basile's anthology. The fourth one."

"Isn't that Mancini's home base?"

"Yes. I'm hoping he'll remain in Ghent long enough so I can slip in and out of the city before he returns. Maybe you could help keep him here. You'd probably get a lot further checking him out than wasting your time on me."

Before they parted, Shaheen gave Madison his cell number and wished him luck. As he watched Madison walk away he wondered whether he'd see him alive again. Mancini wouldn't make the same mistake twice.

Shaheen had arranged to have Mancini's movements tracked after the interview with Madison in DCI Wilson's office. He knew Mancini flew to Ghent early that morning but until Madison told him, he hadn't learned why because Mancini had cloaked his phone and computer. The conte was booked into the Duke's Palace Hotel in Bruges, twenty-three miles away. An appropriate place, Shaheen thought, for elite customers. He decided to try a face-to-face. The owner, after all, should know everything about his book.

An expensive cab ride took him to the hotel in Bruges. When the registration clerk called the suite, he got no answer. Since Mancini hadn't checked out yet Shaheen assumed he was still busy with the police and fire officials. Or maybe the grieving husband was just out for a long, comforting lunch.

Ten minutes later, through one of the high, elegantly curtained windows, Shaheen spotted a limousine pulling up. Mancini's tall, angular figure strode through the lobby doors, his guard trailing behind. Shaheen stepped forward. "Conte Mancini," he said, "a word with you? I'm First Lieutenant Shaheen, U.S. Army Special Forces."

It registered for an instant and vanished just as quickly—a glint of fear in Mancini's tight little eyes. Shaheen noticed it before the guard thrust himself between them.

"My ID," Shaheen said, holding it up.

The guard, a well-muscled fellow with a white scar on his forehead, waved the card away rudely. "*Lassatece mò!* Do not bother him now."

Mancini gestured for his guard to back away. He held out his hand for the ID and glanced at it before handing it back. "What is it you want?"

"Just to talk—about the book you reported stolen."

If Mancini was a man in mourning he didn't look it. His expression spoke, instead, of anger. Rage suppressed, but just barely. Shaheen had seen that look before on insurgents right after they'd been caught. A faint odor of smoke lingered over Mancini's clothes.

Nature had not blessed the conte with good looks. He had a craggy nose, hard eyes, and thin colorless lips. But money could banish a host of imperfections. Shaheen guessed he was a well-preserved mid-fifty. His snow-white helmet of hair contrasted oddly with a wrinkle-free face, the smooth skin likely the product of a surgeon. And his suit, expertly cut to hide a paunch, probably cost thousands.

"Surely the American military has enough to do these days, Lieutenant, without chasing after stolen books. What do you really want?"

"I'll admit it sounds like a stretch. It'll take some time to explain. It concerns an antiquities dealer named John Madison. I think you know of him." Shaheen gestured toward the bar. "Can we talk over a drink?"

At the mention of Madison's name, the man's body tensed. Mancini appeared to weigh his options. "Very well. But I'd prefer the privacy of my suite. Come with us." He turned his back abruptly and marched to the elevator. The guard inserted himself between them.

Proof, Shaheen thought, that Mancini was deeply entangled in this whole affair. Anyone else in his position, particularly after his wife had just died in a fire, would have told him to get lost and hidden behind a platoon of lawyers.

When they stepped off the elevator, the guard insisted on a weapons check. Shaheen gave him the Ruger but objected when the guard held his hand out for the cellphone. No way was he about to let someone inspect his contact list or text messages. "Leave it,"

Mancini said and the guard shrugged. Shaheen pocketed his phone and they entered the room.

Mancini's suite lived up to the hotel's palatial past: gold chandelier, large stained-glass window, a king-sized bed discreetly tucked away behind high velvet drapes with braided ties. The guard took up his post near a divan. An attendant in a white jacket and black pants looked up when they walked in and waited to do Mancini's bidding.

Mancini shrugged off his jacket and threw it over a chair. Loosening his tie, he sat on the small divan. "Would you care for a drink, Lieutenant? I certainly need one."

Shaheen chose a chair opposite. "I'd love one, thanks. A dash of bourbon on lots of ice is good." Behind him he could hear the opening of drawers and the clink of ice cubes as the attendant got busy at the bar. "Mr. Mancini, I've been trying to trace the steps of a Charles Renwick, an Englishman who traveled to Iraq this past August. He might be tied into a case we're investigating involving the transport of bioweapons in the Middle East."

"This Renwick fellow—was he an expert in the field?" Mancini interjected.

Mistake number two, Shaheen thought. By now, with his information network, Mancini had to know Renwick wanted the book and who he was. "No. He hired John Madison to bid for your book when it was auctioned in London. He's missing, possibly dead. And the dealer who handled the sale of all five volumes died in Naples a few days ago. I've been told the book has a malicious history. It certainly looks that way from where I'm standing."

"Ah. What a series of tragedies. My book does seem to live up to its reputation. The rumors surrounding it go back to the seventeenth century, to a nobleman, Baron Lorenzo Mancini, my ancestor and a forefather of the Italian royal family. By all accounts, a domineering and intimidating man. It is said the copy of the book my family owns brings misfortune and its history would certainly seem to confirm that. Right from the start it was associated with a catastrophe."

The attendant brought the drinks over, serving Mancini's cocktail first. He poured a shot glass full of amber liquid over frosty ice cubes in a tumbler and handed it to Shaheen.

"It's brought tragedy in its wake again then. As I mentioned, Ewan Fraser was murdered." Shaheen watched Mancini closely, but beyond a slight narrowing of his eyes the man didn't react.

"I wonder where you heard that. The police blamed vagrants for the killing. If you're right, perhaps it was a falling-out among thieves. Rats fighting over the spoils. The book is worth quite a large sum. When that order of money is involved, who can predict what criminals will do?" He tilted his glass and took a sip. He set it down and glowered at the attendant. *"Chist' fa schif!"*

Although Shaheen couldn't speak Italian, it wasn't hard to imagine what Mancini said.

The attendant scurried over, bent to pick up the glass, and dropped it on the floor. When he stooped to gather the broken pieces he cut his finger badly but continued to collect the shards in his bare hands. He scurried back to the bar.

"What a fool," Mancini said contemptuously. "I hope *your* drink is acceptable."

"High-class bourbon," Shaheen replied. "Can't go wrong with that."

"You pay them a fortune and they still don't know how to make a simple cocktail," Mancini grumbled. "Now where was I. Oh yes. One year after our temperamental mountain erupted in 1631, a deadly plague struck Naples. I suppose the first sign of calamity associated with the book is that its author died of this contagion. There've been various speculations as to what the illness was but no one knows for sure. The gullible will tell you the sickness is associated with an ancient demon, birthed in the Middle East.

"Giambattista Basile and the painter José de Ribera had brought gifts to the daughter of a Neapolitan noble on the occasion of her fifteenth birthday. Basile gave her a puzzle, a curious stone weight he'd acquired on his travels as a soldier of fortune in the Aegean, and also a collection of folk tales he'd spent a lifetime gathering and rewriting. The book came in the form of a printer's galley. De Ribera illustrated those tales."

"There's some speculation several of his stories were based on real events. What do you think?" Shaheen asked.

"It's plausible. Basile wrote versions of both 'Snow White' and 'Sleeping Beauty.' Medical researchers have recently discovered a very rare disease called Kleine-Levin Syndrome. Those afflicted with it experience periods of constant sleep for days, even weeks. They must be woken up to take food and water. Who knows? Centuries ago people would explain away an illness like that by saying a spell had been cast on the victim. And someone sleeping for weeks on end would be such a startling occurrence, you can see how a story would be woven about it.

"But you interrupted me, Lieutenant." Mancini allowed himself a crack of a smile when he said this. "I was telling you the history of my family. Both the daughter and Basile succumbed to the plague shortly after her birthday celebration. Since then, the book has been called cursed. And a belief, held dearly by Baron Lorenzo Mancini, clings to it still: that it points to a secret location in old Mesopotamia, an undiscovered landmark that like Tutankhamen's tomb is lethal to anyone who disturbs it.

"The book was originally owned by Baron Mancini's cousin. Since the cousin's only child died of the plague, it was passed on to the baron in the 1640s. He took a special interest in it. He was a master of the occult, studied necromancy and astrology, and taught these practices to his five daughters."

The attendant approached Mancini with a replacement cocktail and set it gently on the side table. Mancini threw the man an exasperated glance and continued. "Through the machinations of their well-connected uncle, Cardinal Mazzarin, one of the baron's daughters, Olympia, married Eugene Maurice, Prince of Savoy and Comte of Soissons, an ancestor to Italy's royal house. At that time, the French court held sway and Olympia was a favorite, some say a lover, of the French king. Her husband died under strange circumstances. It's rumored she poisoned him and engaged in the black arts. Court life in those times was rife with esoteric beliefs—astrology, alchemy, and sorcery. Accused of plotting another poisoning, this time of the king's mistress, Louise de La Vallière, Olympia was forced to flee to Spain for fear of her life after what they'd called 'the Affair of the Poisons.'" He picked up his glass and touched his lips to the drink, apparently satisfied with it this time. "So has mere possession of the book afflicted this family? History would seem to bear that out."

From Samuel Morland,
The History of the Evangelical Churches of Piedmont

"And the Mancinis have owned it ever since?" Shaheen asked.

"Yes. Although the book remained within my branch of the family, since those times the Savoys have indeed been cursed with a brutal history. In 1655 the Duke of Savoy ordered the massacre of the Waldenesians. They spared no one, not even children, drove women through with pikes and burned their homes to the ground. And in 1900, King Umberto I was assassinated as a result of his association with another massacre. This time of protesters."

"A bloody history all right," Shaheen said. "But not much different from a lot of other dynasties. Look at the massacres of Protestants all over France in the sixteenth century."

Mancini nodded approvingly. "Yes. I fear the Italian royalty was treated rather harshly by its people. And worse was to come. Because the Savoys supported Mussolini, they lost the monarchy along with all their property and were condemned to exile. A trail of woe continues to follow them. Whether there's any truth to these beliefs about the book, who knows? Until recently my copy hadn't been opened since the time the baron had it."

"Maybe you're better off without it then?"

Mancini responded with a barking laugh. "Come now, Lieutenant, there is no place for superstition in modern life.... You are aware who actually stole it, I presume?"

"A young woman—your lover, I'm told."

"Betrayals are worst when they're close to home. You're referring to a girl I took under my wing. I gave her everything. No one would describe me as a vulnerable man." He pressed his lips together as if to suppress some unwelcome emotion. "But she's broken my heart and repaid my generosity in a most cruel way. I discovered the book was missing only recently. At first I thought a servant stole it but found mere days ago it was her. And now she's left me."

Shaheen sensed he was genuinely upset about losing her. Mancini paused to collect himself before saying, "These recent events have all come at a very difficult time. My wife just died in a terrible accident. That's why you find me in Belgium. I think, however, you may already know this."

"I'm very sorry to hear about your wife. I know it's a difficult time to intrude. If you'll bear with me a few more minutes. The reference to a location you say is hidden somewhere within the book—any idea where it's supposed to be?"

"I have no time for such frivolous pursuits." Although Mancini said this dispassionately, Shaheen noted how the man's angry spirit now fell away as he spoke. A slight tremor in his voice and a light in his hawkish eyes gave him away. He'd been seduced by the notion of hidden valuables and believed the rumors to be true. Basile's book was worth much more to him than sentiment or family heritage.

"I do intend, though," Mancini continued, "to recover all the volumes and restore the book to its rightful place in my home. And I have a question for you, Lieutenant. Where is Madison? He's intruded into my affairs recklessly. He has defiled my women. I want him stopped." The glass the man held was delicate and Shaheen thought it might break in Mancini's hand. His knuckles turned white under his sudden, forceful grip.

"Last I heard Madison was swanning around Europe, trying to pick up the trail of the missing volumes. But if he does find them, that will only help, won't it? He'll tell the police, who will get them back to you. Maybe you should be paying him. He might even unravel the secret the book's supposed to hold."

"What's your opinion of him?" Mancini asked.

"A troublemaker. On the other hand, he may turn up something helpful to my investigation. As long as he's useful, I don't have a problem with him."

This answer appeared to satisfy Mancini. Visibly relaxing, he sat back and crossed his legs.

"You might have a point there. Perhaps I should not have let my anger get in the way of common sense."

Shaheen decided to push the conversation further. He watched Mancini closely with his next words. "Madison nearly bought it today. Someone tried to shoot him."

"I gather he survived," Mancini responded dryly.

"He did. The gunman was a rookie. Had to be. Head shot's the one he should've gone for. Or if he'd used a Russian Makarov with nine by eighteen AP rounds he'd have got the job done."

Mancini managed a wry smile. "The assailant got away, I assume?"

"Yes, he did." Shaheen set his glass down.

"I admire the work you people do over there in Iraq. Laying your life on the line for such small rewards."

"We're not exactly in it for the money."

"My apologies. I didn't mean to imply anything of the kind. I have business connections in Iraq. My family line has had a long association with the Middle East. Napoli's commercial history is intimately connected with the region. I suppose I too have played a positive role. Easing the flow of money in and out of Iraq is as vital a need as bullets and planes."

Shaheen finished his drink and rose. "Well, let's hope the war's over soon. Thanks for agreeing to talk with me. Much obliged."

Mancini rose, the look on his face almost affable now. "Please leave your contact information with my guard. If I learn anything more, I'll be glad to let you know."

"Happy to."

The guard returned his gun and saw Shaheen out.

Evening had settled in by the time Shaheen left. The air had turned cold and the slender young trees lining the sidewalk bent and swayed in the wind.

One thing stood out from his conversation with Mancini. The

notion that an elderly English book publisher, or book of fairy tales for that matter, could be remotely associated with bioweapons would strike anyone as absurd. And yet Mancini hadn't pointed this out. Had not asked even one question about how they might be related.

Thirty-Four

T he offer came late that night with a knock on his hotel room door. It arrived more quickly than Shaheen expected. The man who stepped over the threshold reminded him of Leonard Best. Nondescript. The kind of mid-level bureaucrat who toiled away behind some office partition, ticking off the days until retirement.

Shaheen listened carefully to what the man had to say. Mancini's name didn't once cross his lips. Shaheen accepted the blank card with a cell number and bank account printed on it. Predictably, the phone number was untraceable; Shaheen made sure of that the minute the man left. The proposal was enticing, no question, and after taking some time to consider it, he answered the man in the affirmative.

What the fellow had to say was short and to the point. That if, in the course of his investigation, Shaheen was willing to share what he'd learned, he'd be well compensated. The amount of money offered made his eyes pop. It was understood his participation wouldn't include any military knowledge that might compromise his mission or any aspect of the war effort.

Mancini, both in character and behavior, was the kind of man Shaheen detested. But Shaheen believed Mancini knew much more than he'd revealed and that prying this knowledge out of him could turn out to be fundamental. Given the enormous repercussions should an outbreak occur, Shaheen couldn't afford high-handed morality when choosing allies. He'd crossed that line in similar ways more often than he cared to remember over the past three years.

In intelligence circles, rumors about what Shaheen had done and what was necessary to achieve it caused some to fear him. Deep trust from his mates, essential to his job, was often missing. More than once this came close to causing a catastrophe.

He had a lot of Arab blood on his hands, literally, not all of it justified. One time, in the baking heat of the desert, he'd gone without water for days after an operation. The blood had dried on his skin like a stubborn stain. He'd spent hours picking off the dry flakes. Those memories caused Shaheen much worse pain than the jagged nerve endings in his spine and he hated them. His contract was up in another year and he'd sworn that would be the end. Shaheen had total confidence the money Mancini offered him would be impossible to trace. Start-up funds for when he was free of the job. He could do worse than that.

The second proposition presented a more troubling concern. Shaheen wouldn't be required to take any action, just stay out of the way when they dealt with Madison. That would happen when Madison ceased being useful. Nothing more than venal retribution on Mancini's part, Shaheen thought. He liked Madison and thought the man had courage. Judged within the wide parameters of such an important mission, even good men were expendable. It was the devil's hand he was holding, but he'd shaken that hand a few times before.

Thirty-Five

November 27, 2003
En route to Naples

While I waited at the airport for the flight to Rome, my cell chirped. Dina's clear tones came on the line. "John, is that you?"

"It is. Are you still at Renard's?"

"No."

"Why not?" I recalled her hurtful words. "You said you never wanted to see me again."

"You don't really think I meant that? We were right outside the dining-room door, John. Renard was listening to every word we said. It was the only way to convince him."

"And the point of going through that charade was?"

"I knew if I was alone with him I could persuade him to let me see the book. And I was right."

"He just let you go freely? He was totally obsessed with you."

"Quite frankly, I wanted to stay there. Renard was an entertaining companion. I loved the estate. He became very upset when he heard I wanted to go but kept his word and didn't force me to stay. I told him I'd return in a few days."

"Is that your plan?"

She didn't answer me directly and said instead, "Where are you?"

"Why do you want to know?"

"You said you were planning to meet the bookseller in Naples—right? I want to go with you."

"No, I didn't, Dina. You never told me about Naso. I had to discover that one on my own. We haven't had the most fortuitous time together so far. Going our separate ways makes more sense at this point. Why would you even consider returning to Naples? I thought you were afraid to go anywhere near Mancini again."

"I couldn't pick a better time. I'm in touch with one of our staff who told me he's still in Ghent dealing with the house and Katharina's death. The last place they'll expect either me or you to turn up is Naples. Anyway, I thought you needed to see Renard's book?"

"Yes, of course I do."

"How were you planning to get to Naples?"

"By train."

"I'm in Rome now. I'll get on the train with you—which one are you taking? I've got Renard's book with me."

She'd been stringing out information bit by bit and I didn't have the patience for it anymore. "Email me photos of Renard's book. If I get them before I reach Rome, I'll agree to go to Naples with you."

There was a pause on the line while she thought about what I asked and I heard her sigh. "Very well. But you'd better be there."

"Why didn't you tell me about Katharina?"

"If I said anything, you might not go to see her. And of course I couldn't cross her doorstep. She used an intermediary to buy her volume but Ewan managed to learn her name. I knew it was her."

"Are you aware of what's happened to her?"

"Yes. It's front-page news. In all the newspapers and on TV. The blaze started in the day room. They think she used some kind of starter fuel and put too much on. When the flames leapt up her clothing caught fire. It must have happened rapidly. Maybe some fuel spilled—I don't know. She toppled into the hearth. That's what they're saying."

A distant image flickered in my mind but I ignored it, too intent on unwinding the rest of the story. "The reports say she tried to light a fire in the middle of the night?"

"You'll never hear what really happened through the media," Dina said. "Mancini killed her. It had to be him."

"Why would he do that?"

"Either Alessio did it or one of his other men."

"And you know this—how?"

"Because he wanted to clear the way to be with me—officially. Divorce isn't possible because they're both Catholic. He'd grown tired of her accusations and complaints. Said she'd become too expensive. That's another reason I made up my mind to leave him."

With divorce out of the question Dina was right; only a partner's death could pave the way for a new marriage. And yet the whole thing struck me as false. I met men like Mancini regularly in my line of work. Wealthy, elite alpha males. Keeping up a good front, maintaining at least the appearance of a marriage, especially with a family, was the norm. A gorgeous mistress—sure. But those men didn't tend to trade their wives in for one. Married with a mistress on the side was practically expected as proof of manhood.

"Katharina had harsh things to say about you."

"Let me guess. She said I seduced Lorenzo and destroyed her marriage."

"You've got the gist of it."

"The woman was insanely jealous."

"If Katharina hated you so much, why keep that portrait? It looks so much like you."

"He makes her do it. He owns the Ghent property and she's totally dependent on him for income."

That tallied with the fury I'd seen on Katharina's face. Jealousy bottled up could drive people to extremes and actions they'd normally never contemplate.

"Six months ago he separated us, forcing her to stay at the house in Ghent, keeping me with him. You can imagine how she reacted to that. White-hot hatred. That made her bitterness even worse. I'm glad she's dead. She enabled him."

"She said you encouraged his attentions."

"She *would* lie about it. To save face."

The boarding call for my flight pealed throughout the airport. I had to make a decision. I told her which train to get on at Rome for the trip south and we agreed to meet at the ticket counter.

In Rome I found a café right outside the railway station. I checked my phone and was glad to see that Dina sent the photos of the pages from Renard's volume. I ordered a bite to eat and found the restroom.

Shaving off my beard felt like a travesty, something equivalent to cutting off my right arm. But it had to be done because it was my most recognizable feature. Not only did I like the look of it, my beard hid the birthmark on my jaw. With it gone my face looked painfully naked and years younger. The birthmark appeared even redder, a strange Q-shaped blight.

Much more alarming, the marks on my neck were a little larger than when I last looked and felt sore. The marks worried me. I'd have to find a doctor soon.

In a nearby menswear shop I picked up a replacement denim jacket and a black tuque. My knapsack completed the ensemble. I hoped people would take me for a college kid on a low-budget European trek.

While I waited for my train, I called Evelyn. She wanted to know when I'd be home. "Soon, Evie," I said, with no real conviction that would be the case.

Despite holding off until the very last minute, I saw no sign of Dina and had to race to catch the Naples train. Thinking she'd already boarded and I'd somehow missed her, I searched through all the cars without finding her.

Had Mancini's people caught up with her in Rome after all? Or did she simply change her mind? If the latter, why bother to send me the photos of Renard's book? Surely not out of the goodness of her heart. If she'd been taken by Mancini's thugs, chances were good they'd brought her back to Naples. But how could I break through Mancini's phalanx of men to find her? I was sure he had a much worse fate in store for her than a locked bedroom door. I thought of contacting the Naples police and then remembered Dina saying they wouldn't intrude on Mancini's affairs, especially concerning an internal family matter. Maybe another solution would come to me.

I mulled over Katharina's revelations as the train sped south. I firmly sided with Dina. She was too young when she first entered the Mancini household to be anything but a victim. Katharina's obsession with her was as sick as Mancini's. The strange portrait and mirror in the upstairs room fascinated me. What was that all about? According to Katharina, the mirror came from a place called Lohr. Had I remembered this correctly? I looked up Lohr on my phone browser and was surprised to find an image of a mirror very similar to the elaborately enameled beauty in Katharina's octagonal room.

The Talking Mirror, Lohr Mirror Works

It was manufactured at the Lohr Mirror Works, a German Renaissance-era company noted for their fine craftsmanship. The article described it as a talking mirror. In one corner, it bore the words *amour propre*, meaning "self-love." The claim of a talking mirror had to be either a fable or an ingenious story hatched to enhance the object's appeal. Intriguing, nevertheless.

As I pulled out the English translation of Basile's anthology, intending to read it during the train trip, a folded paper dropped out. The one Dina gave me after we found Ewan in Gaiola. I'd transferred it from my jacket to the book and completely forgotten about it. Dina called it an eyewitness account of events in the lives of Basile and de Ribera. I looked it over. It appeared to be written nine years after Basile's death by the wife of a Scottish nobleman who'd once been stationed at the Spanish viceroy's court in Naples:

We have been settled in familiar surroundings at Edinburgh for nine years now and with age I have the luxury of time to look back on our adventures in Napoli, so I take up the pen. Word reached me that de Ribera is near to perishing. Would that blight visited upon us so many years ago have finally taken its toll on him? I hear that along with the sickness his fortune is lost. As the son of a shoemaker, he rose far above his station. Well, like returns to like, as they say. It is whispered he practiced the dark arts and hopes that knowledge will lead to his resurrection. His Holiness caught word of this and ordered the book to which he attributed the ritual be destroyed. I doubt the Lord will comply. He will hide it.

Our year of tragedy began when Vesuvius erupted, spilling streams of liquid rock like hot blood down its slopes and blowing deadly ash onto the city. My husband and I barely survived, having narrowly escaped to a barge anchored in the harbor. I swear mightily the heat caused the seas to boil that night. Fish gasped on the surface of the water.

Thus, I now believe that episode ushered in an even more perilous state of affairs, although it would be one year hence before we understood its consequence. It was as if the great force of the explosion had opened up Hades and released a demon into our midst. Certainly the fumes and smell of brimstone spoke of Hell's domain.

After the eruption, those of us with means fled the ailing city for the countryside, which provided safety enough and good provisions but lacked the pleasant diversions we'd become accustomed to. It was for this reason—to stir us from our boredom—that the Lord threw a grand fete to celebrate the fifteenth anniversary of the birth of his daughter, Talia. The evening began as a splendid affair, although its outcome still causes me to quake. Pray, what miracle saved my husband and me from the scourge?

We arrived at dusk. Torches lit the garden, casting a warm glow and turning the reflecting pond to copper. The avenue of orange trees was in full bloom. We drank in their splendid perfume. Inside, all was opulence, from rich furnishings to statuary and portraits draped with garlands of ivy and wisteria. Bouquets of lush pink lilies filled the urns so completely they threatened to topple over. A quartet of musicians delighted us with their playing. Through the salon doors we could see tables piled high with sweets—pignoccate, affile arranged on little silver trays—I could imagine the taste of the sweet jam spilling out from their centers—and Venetian glass jars filled to overflowing with colorful marzipan.

I have always been a person of elevated perceptions and on that night, despite the celebration, I sensed some ominous undercurrent ruled the air. Looking back, I know it would have been too late to act on my suspicions even if I'd paid heed to my fears.

Everyone dressed in their finery, the ladies' garments sporting the new higher waists and billowing sleeves cut to show their chemises, their décolletage so low it was a marvel the cloth covered their teats. How the ladies paused and shifted their eyes to the great mirror in the hall to preen like peacocks as they passed by. The sight of that mirror prompted my memory of a legend about that place, that the Lord possessed another mirror, not so grand as this, but one that was spellbound for it cast no reflection back except to a chosen few, and those, self-admirers. If such a thing existed I had never seen it and I suspected this to be idle talk.

The Lord was stationed at the foot of the grand staircase to welcome his guests, his wife, poised and aloof, beside him. He said a few words of greeting but he was a distant, arrogant man and when he pressed my hand I felt no warmth.

The Captain of the Lord's Guard had joined the party, watching the guests with his sharp eyes. He had a reputation for duplicity and even those beyond his reach were cautious around him.

Two men stood not far from the Lord. The poet and raconteur Giambattista Basile, a short fellow with a strong mustache and soulful eyes. And the painter, de Ribera, his wig of coarse curly locks spilling over his shoulders. Two men who could not be more different. Basile with his remarkable sense of humor, fine wit, and brilliant turn of phrase easily kept us entertained for hours. A gallant little man with a soft heart whom the ladies adored and a gentleman of the highest moral rectitude. For it was said, even after Basile's long travails and finally gaining favor with the Duke of Acerenza who granted him the Governor's position, he refused the illicit spoils such an honor might gain him.

De Ribera was of a saturnine disposition and some believed given to sorcery, although widely recognized as a great and gifted artist. The two men shared a common bond, a deep affection, some might call it adulation, for the Lord's young daughter. Both were well on in years and de Ribera married. In any event their station in life would never have permitted them to move their feelings beyond the realm of desire. But old men can dream as much as women are wont to do, I suppose.

A bell chimed and despite its faintness everyone hushed for they knew what it portended. The crowd turned toward the stairs and looked up. The Lord stood a little straighter and smiled at his daughter, whom he favored above all others. I stole a glance at his wife. Much as she tried, she could not mask the bitterness in her face upon spying the delicate girl who'd just appeared at the head of the stairs.

Talia wore a simple silk gown as suited her age. Her ebony locks were caught up with a garland of flowers. She descended the stairs, the image of grace and sweetness. Her father took her hand and brought her to the guests. His wife followed in their wake, but sourly. As she was his only child, her father had indulged her and she took part in activities that many whispered would spoil a young woman. And for all her innocence, the girl had a calculating side. Even at that tender age she was quite a skilled coquette who managed to persuade all to do her will. I am told she confessed once to her maid that she'd rather have been born a boy.

The musicians struck up a tune and Talia gave us a song; her voice came through as clear and true as the bell that had summoned her into our presence. Soon the hour for gift-giving arrived. We retired to the salon for this purpose. She cried with pleasure as the Lord presented her with her very own white horse. A serving man held up a painting of the beast for all to admire. It was known the Lord favored the white Camargues and had a stable of them. Some felt the keeping of this breed to be a cruelty because their natural home lay in the French Rhone marsh.

Lovely gifts from the guests followed and Talia was quite overcome with joy. De Ribera bowed deeply and offered a folio of his engravings. Murmurs circulated through the gathering; all were impressed with his generosity. Basile stepped forward holding in his hands a little cedar box. He opened the lid and asked her to look inside. A hush ran through the crowd as she lifted out gleaming black enamel and gold book covers inscribed with her initials. He helped her to undo the clasps. Inside lay five volumes, a printer's copy, containing many of the stories she loved.

She thanked him profusely and began to turn away when he said there was something more. He lifted out of the bottom of the cedar box a most curious object, made of some dark stone, circular *in shape with unusual markings on it. Her father's frown signaled his displeasure. It was an odd present indeed.*

Pray that lovely box had never been opened. But it is far too late for such misgivings now.

The account ended abruptly. It took me a few minutes to digest the enormity of what I'd read. Finally the origin of the book—or galley, as this account proved—had been laid bare. It showed Renwick's supposition about a link between a plague and Basile's book was justified. The author had written of a terrible blight and a ritual involving the book. I was getting closer to the truth of all these connections, although much remained to be sorted out. But what to make of the name Talia? Why did Renwick's photograph identify Dina as Talia, the girl who received Basile's galley as a birthday gift?

And where was Dina now? Her unpredictable and capricious nature wounded me once. I wondered again whether she simply changed her mind about meeting me on the train. I hoped so.

Her fear of Mancini seemed genuine. Why risk her life trying to recover the rest of the volumes? It made no sense. I rejected the idea she just wanted to make more money from them. Something much deeper than simple avarice drove her but she had withheld it from me.

In contrast, Mancini's goal was crystal clear. He wanted the entire book back because it contained a key leading to something of immense value to him. I was determined to make him pay for his violent actions and all the grief he'd rained down on us. If his secret lay within those pages, I intended to find it first.

I couldn't let go of the idea of necromancy and pondered again how it fit into the puzzle. On the surface, the grotesque notion of bringing back the dead to foretell the future seemed counterintuitive.

But the concept had captured human imagination. My own brother's given name—Samuel—was associated with the most famous biblical tale of necromancy: Saul asked the Witch of Endor to summon the prophet Samuel back from the dead to predict the outcome of a battle. Many times I'd wished to see my brother again, to talk with him, feel the comfort of his presence. The hole his death left in my life had never been filled and it lingered on. These questions and feelings absorbed me until the train pulled into Napoli Centrale.

Thirty-Six

November 28, 2003
Naples, Italy

N aso's bookstore was located off Piazza Dante. The giant statue of the poet stood at the piazza's center, towering over the crowd, one arm extended as if emphasizing a point in the middle of a speech. Naples, with its smoldering volcanoes and grand literary traditions, seemed a far more appropriate home for Dante than Florence, I thought.

People milled around, enjoying the evening. I bought one of the piping hot pizzas you find everywhere in Naples, small enough to hold in your hand, filled with buffalo mozzarella and sweet tomato sauce. I'd skipped the introduction to the English translation Norris lent me and sat on a bench to leaf through it now. My eyes lit on a short but startling paragraph, written by a chronicler of events in Naples around the time Basile died:

> For the scourges of the conflagration [meaning the eruption
> of Vesuvius] were scarcely extinguished, when the just God,

perceiving that they [the Neapolitans] were not yet repentant,
sent another kind of chastisement, a disease … which proved
so cruel and contagious that it appeared to be the plague and
carried off numbers of people in a short space of time. Among
these were many notable people; and they went on dying day
by day and of those who perished [was] … Giovan Battista
Basile.

It was a harsh judgment on the poor souls of the city who'd
suffered the twin catastrophes of the eruption and sickness and
unfair to the people of warm-blooded Naples. It did, however,
corroborate the Scottish noblewoman's record. Two eyewitness
accounts now confirmed what Katharina originally told me about
Basile's fate.

At seven that evening I slung my knapsack over my shoulder
and walked through a passageway to the booksellers' alley to
search for Naso's shop. A battered blue door marked the entrance.
The sign swinging over it read Publius Ovidius Naso—Libri.
The head and shoulders of a Roman, a classic olive wreath circling
his brow, were painted below the name. I smiled at Naso's wit
when I recognized the proper name of Ovid, ancient Rome's
greatest poet.

A stencil of a pointing finger and the word Libri directed me
up a flight of stairs, where I found an open door. Had I the leisure,
I'd have spent hours in Naso's quaint shop combing through the
old books. Shakespeare and Company was one of my favorite
haunts in Paris and Naso's place reminded me of it. Books were
tucked into every nook and cranny, in stacks, in piles, weighing
down bookcases so the wooden shelves bent like branches of trees
heavy with fruit. A maze of rooms invited exploration. A comfortable chair or two beckoned. Ornate glass lamps gave the shop a
Victorian feel.

At the sound of my footsteps, a figure bending over a cabinet straightened up. A pleasant-featured older man greeted me. He wore a bow tie, a print shirt, and a suit of eye-scorching purple on his chubby frame. Even in his platform shoes, he couldn't top five foot four. A fringe of gray hair ringed a prominent bald spot in the center of his scalp.

"*Buona Serra*—Signore Madison?"

"Signore Naso. A pleasure." We shook hands.

The cabinet behind him contained some curious items. Jars of what looked to be herbs, two short lengths of wood hand-cut and stripped of their bark, a set of antique silver pipes. The cabinet also held a Middle Eastern demon bowl. Inside it, concentric lines of Arabic script circled a crude drawing of a horned monster. Items like this would be buried upside down under thresholds or key points in ancient households to trap demons before they caused illness or otherwise wreaked havoc on the family.

It seemed a macabre interest for a man who looked like a cherub. I introduced the subject of my visit. "You'll remember I inquired about a book? The fourth volume in Basile's anthology. You still have it I hope?"

"*Si*. But not here."

"Good. I have some bad news, I'm afraid."

"You don't want to purchase?"

"No, it's not that. I hate to be the one to tell you but I've learned it was reported stolen." His face fell when I showed him the Interpol report. He took a few minutes to recover from the blow and told me the financial loss would be enormous.

"I'm trying to trace the whereabouts of each volume; I'll help you get your money back if there's any way I can."

Naso thanked me. "I must waive your deposit then. It is too bad I have no sale, but it makes sense now."

"What does?"

"My store was broken into last night. It's why I've taken the book away. Too valuable to leave here after that."

"Any idea who tried to rob you?"

Naso threw up his hands in exasperation. "No one saw it."

"Could we take a look at it now?"

"Of course. We must go to Il Fontanelle for a nice yet long walk—if you wish."

He locked up. We descended the stair into the alley still bustling with people and he directed me toward the old city gate, Porta San Gennaro, and Borgo dei Vergini, "the Virgin's Quarter." Naso explained the odd spelling of Vergini. It was masculine, meaning a place of male virgins, but he didn't know the reason for that curious name. Our ultimate destination lay through the Sanità district and into the Valley of the Dead.

"You know of our San Gennaro, the patron saint of Napoli?" he asked as we passed under the gate.

"I do. There's a big festival in his honor in New York."

"He saved Napoli from the terror of another explosion by Vesuvius but it is an irony. Fate ended his life at a volcano. The pagan emperor Diocletian, seeing Christianity as a threat, condemned San Gennaro to death. First they pushed him alive into a furnace but the flames couldn't harm him. He came out untouched, not a mark on his skin. Next, they tried to feed him to wild bears. The animals lay down peacefully at his feet and wouldn't devour him. Finally, the emperor ordered him beheaded in Solfatara."

I thought back to the crater, the hot chalky gravel plain Dina and I so recently traversed, with its sulfurous pits and holes once thought to be entrances to hell. "What a grisly story. I trod on that very spot myself not long ago."

"The saint's followers salvaged his blood. It is kept in vials to this day. And so we celebrate the miracle of the saint's new blood when our priests hold up the relic and show us how his clotted blood turns to liquid. I have witnessed it many times myself. San Gennaro continues to protect us."

Perhaps because of the macabre topic Naso raised, the warning Ewan gave me struck a chord. "I was advised not to go into Sanità—but you do often and without a problem?"

"Every evening if I have no other pressing matters."

"I should tell you this as well. Others who bought volumes of Basile's book have been attacked, two of them killed. You should return it to the authorities. Get rid of it right away and protect yourself."

"My brother is *o parracchian*—how do you say it in English? Our parish priest. No one will touch me." His shoulders sagged a little as he thought about what losing the book would cost him. "And if it's stolen as you say, then, yes, no matter the consequences I must give it back."

Tiny bars and shops occupied the ground floors of buildings lining Sanità's roadways. Sheets and garments flapped on wires strung between the upper balconies. Roofs swarmed with satellite dishes and aerials. One place, fallen into ruin, was being rapidly taken over by vegetation, green bushes and vines spilling out of the chinks where the mortar disintegrated. It was considerably dirtier here than in the southern part of the city. Stray dogs barked at us as we neared the heaps of refuse they pawed through. We made an odd duo, me in my denim and Naso conspicuous in his bright purple outfit, bobbing along amiably beside me. People cast suspicious glances at me but they nodded to Naso and let us pass by.

It surprised me that despite the constant uphill climb and hundreds of stairs Naso managed to match my pace.

As if he'd been reading my thoughts he said, "You're quite fit, keeping up with me like this."

"I'm like David Lee Roth," I joked. "I used to jog but I had to stop because the ice cubes kept falling out of my drink."

Naso bent over with a belly laugh.

Once he recovered, his face grew grave. "My friend, I will tell you about where we're going—Il Fontanelle. It takes its name from the springs and streams of the terrain called the Valley of Death. It's a cemetery, although unlike any you have ever seen. We are already beyond the ancient north wall of the city. At one time, only fields and woods could be seen from here. It was the custom to bury bodies of nobles in churches but the poor deposited their dead at Il Fontanelle. During the great plague that killed more than half the population of Napoli, bodies became too numerous for churches to hold so they, too, were added to Il Fontanelle. When heavy rains and floods came, all the corpses washed into the streets below. A dreadful sight."

We reached another incline, a narrow street in such bad shape, parts of it had no pavement at all. It was flanked by garages and other commercial outlets along with some homes, all of them in disrepair. Set incongruously into this poor territory was the massive entrance to Il Fontanelle. Two walls of smoothed tawny rock rose dramatically from the ground to form a cavernous triangular-shaped opening almost fifty feet high at its peak.

Naso unlocked an iron gate and motioned for me to follow. "It began as a quarry. Over the centuries, it was fashioned into halls and rooms. The gate must be kept locked because it attracts those who wish to do their business in private. The Mafiosi are known to welcome initiates here."

Like a cathedral in a cave, a long high corridor resembling a nave ran down the ossuary's center and, in place of pews, low white fences stretched along both sides. Behind these, rows of bones were piled with exacting care on top of each other: the long bones, femur and tibia of legs, radius and ulna of arms, stacked like cut kindling. Skulls sat atop these bones like post caps on a fence. Three rough wooden crosses stood at the end of the main corridor, marking an apse. A faint beam of moonlight leaked through a huge hole broken out of the high ceiling. Whether I shivered from the temperature drop inside or the eerie allure of the place, I wasn't sure.

Naso stopped at a transept midway down and took the branch to the right. More skulls were lodged in little wooden glass-fronted boxes, gray with rock dust. On some, worshipers had draped rosaries, pictures of saints, coins, and other mementos. The only light came from flickering candles. The ceiling was so high it faded overhead into blackness.

He waved toward the boxes. "Being close to the spirits, it prompts many strange practices, no? You may think this grotesque but I have heard odd things about English rituals too. Victorian people encased their stone coffins in wire cages to prevent the spirits of those suspected of being demons from resurrection."

"Really? I've never heard of that." I took another look around. "How did all this come about?"

"We are thankful for it. A priest, Father Barbati, encouraged the care of the bones in the nineteenth century, which before that lay scattered and dirty. Then a cult emerged, the Anime Pessentelle, who saw captive spirits in the bones. The arrangements here now were completed by citizens seeking shelter when Napoli was bombed during the Second World War. They brought their children in wartime and felt grateful to the spirits for protecting them."

He stopped in front of what looked like a small mausoleum carved into the rock: pillars topped by a triangular roof with a rectangular hollow in the middle. Set into that, another wooden box held a skull. Naso reached in his pocket for two short white candles and placed them in the hollow. He made the sign of the cross. After a few moments of silence he said, "I lost my wife last year. I come here to remember her dear soul."

Inwardly, I recoiled from the shrine, hoping the skull hadn't belonged to his wife. Now I understood why he wore two wedding rings. "You have my sympathy," I said. "I know how hard that is."

"I'd been solo most of my life," he said, his voice tinged with sadness. "Ladies I liked had no time for me so I never married. One day my shop assistant left. When I advertised for someone new, the woman who showed up captured my heart. Marisa was her name. She taught me to speak English. She was a graduate student, much younger than me, studying rare books in Naples."

He stooped to light the candles. "To this day I don't know what she saw in me. She said she had a difficult life growing up and I treated her with more kindness than she'd ever experienced. Of course, we both loved books. We spent four blissful months together and then we got married. Three years ago this past June we put our names to the wedding record. She looked so serious, as if she were signing her life away, and I suppose in a way she was. We ran the store together until she fell ill. She had a bad fever and couldn't tolerate bright light. By the time the doctors diagnosed meningitis it was too late. She slipped away within the week."

He bowed his head in silence, saying a prayer I supposed. His grief touched me, and I understood how coming here, strange place though it was, gave him some solace.

Naso raised his head again. "I felt as though my own life had been stolen from me. For days I refused to believe she was gone." Then he asked an odd question. "Do you ever feel there comes a point where books become *real* to you?"

"Lately I've been getting that feeling a lot."

"They did for me after Marisa died. Before, I found stories entertaining but only as well-written narratives someone made up. Fiction in the true sense. In the months following Marisa's death I realized many tales are born of deep emotions—like mine. Eros's pain when he searched for his Psyche, Orpheus longing for his Eurydice. Or Edgar Allan Poe's story about obsession. A man who lost his wife, the dark-haired Ligeia. Her death tormented him so badly he sacrificed his innocent second wife to bring Ligeia back from the dead. A truly pitiless and terrible thing to do, really, and in Poe's dramatic style, it didn't end well."

"I can understand that. It's an expression of desperation. Feeling you can't continue without your loved one in your life."

"You've lost someone dear yourself, I think," Naso said.

"My brother and a friend of mine. Not long ago."

"Ah. Sorry to hear it. Take heart they reside with the Lord."

As I listened to him I appreciated how deep his struggle was coming to terms with his wife's fate. His comforting words moved me and I felt grateful to this kindly man for his sensitivity.

"As to Poe's story," Naso went on, "I read the tale long before I ever met Marisa and thought of it simply as an illustration of an obsession carried too far. But when I reread those pages after she passed on, I found a pain as heart-rending as my own. And now I regard fiction very differently."

He glanced away then as if he didn't wish me to look him in the eye. "To take another's life to satisfy your own craving for a lost one is heinous. It's a horrible confession to make but if given the chance, I would be tempted to do the same."

He rubbed his hands together as if ridding himself of the memory. "Marisa died. I'm a rational man but science could not help me. Grief, if it is profound enough, drives us to look for other means. You will find this bizarre, no doubt. I explored the art of necromancy. The cabinet you saw in my store holds the tools I needed."

"And does that have anything to do with why you sought out Basile's book?"

"Yes. I'd heard one of the tales was associated with calling forth a demon who could raise the dead. Yet when I searched the volume, I could find nothing about that and so put it up for sale. After what

you've told me, I'm afraid I will be in a lot of financial jeopardy."
He spoke wearily. Through no fault of his own he'd ended up in
dire straits.

"I've been told one of the tales is based on real events in
Mesopotamia long ago, and that somehow the story was trans-
formed over the centuries into one of the fairy tales we know today.
A plague tale."

Naso thought about this for a moment. "If the story retains
some glimmer of past events, it might be worth considering other
examples."

"I'm not sure what you mean."

"We look to science for explanations now; in ancient times,
however, metaphor was used. Consider the biblical plague that
caused the Nile to turn red, followed by the plague of frogs.
Scientists tell us the Nile did turn red in the thirteenth century
B.C. at the city of Pi-Ramses in the Nile delta. A period of extreme
drought caused virulent algae to thrive, called Burgundy Blood.
Mats of it turned the water red. Frogs couldn't tolerate the oxygen-
deprived water so they jumped out on land. Plagues attributed
to an angry God were a way to explain an ancient environmental
catastrophe."

I was aware of the biblical plague although not the scien-
tific explanation for it. "Like the myth of werewolves explaining
outbreaks of rabies?" I offered. He nodded. "What about more
recent epidemics?"

"It's the same. When illness proved resistant to the cures of
the day, people blamed it on witches or warlocks or bad fairies
casting spells, so the effects of widespread disease were expressed as
a plague tale."

"There's something else related to this," I said. "I was warned
about the book and told not to open it because it was dangerous.
I assumed that referred to the treacherous knowledge it contains.

You know old books much better than I do. What do you make of that?"

I'd hesitated to mention this to Naso, thinking he'd just make fun of the idea, but his face darkened as he listened to me. "And did you ignore the warning and open the book?"

"It was too tempting."

Worry spread across his features. "How long ago?"

"A few days—why?"

"Did you touch it?"

"Yes, but I wore latex gloves to protect the old papers." Then I remembered I'd handled the golden covers with my bare hands.

"I too looked inside the volume I bought, not knowing about this prohibition," Naso said worriedly. "Did it never occur to you to take the warning literally? Saturating pages with poison was an assassination method during the Renaissance. You lick your finger to turn the page and ..." He drew his finger across his throat. "*The Arabian Nights* includes a story on that very subject. By now, though, I should be dead since I opened the book months ago without any protection. We can conclude that is either not what was meant or the volume I bought was safe."

He bent down and reached behind the box set into the hollow of the little mausoleum and then straightened up like a shot, a panicked look in his eyes. "It's gone!"

"What?"

"The book!"

"I thought no one could get in here."

"Only the caretakers who've been employed here for many years. They know this is my shrine to Marisa. They would not take from me." He rubbed his plump hand over his face. "What am I going to do? This has become a disaster."

I tried to reassure him. "Don't worry. I know who did this. The same man you described on the phone to me. He probably took your copy like he took mine. I've documented as much of this as possible. You're not alone."

"M. Villeneuve?"

"Yes, him. That's just an alias. One way or the other, I'm going to find him."

"All the same, I'll have to tell the police."

"Go ahead. That's the right thing to do."

I walked partway back with him to give him some comfort. By the time we bade each other good night, he seemed calmer. I promised to stay in touch and let him know if I made any progress.

Without Naso by my side, I hurried through the streets searching for a place to get a drink and figure out my next steps. Naso had purchased the fourth volume, day four of Basile's anthology. With no proof and without knowing what happened to the final volume, I'd run out of leads.

It hadn't been pleasant to deliver the bad news to Naso, or to anyone else for that matter. What seemed at first like a righteous hunt for a criminal over a simple book theft had fanned out into deadly consequences for Ewan and Katharina and now probably Dina too. My guilt bubbled up again. Where was she? What happened to her?

When I drew close to Via Santa Teresa and could see its bright lights I leaned against a store window and got out my phone. I checked to see if Dina had left me a message. Nothing. Then I remembered I'd never received an answer to my inquiry about the round stone weight from Samuel's colleague. Even though it was late I could try to catch him at home. I was relieved to hear him answer. He'd recognized the weight and told me what it was used for. I thanked him and hung up, thrilled at this unexpected reversal of fortune. Finally, one key piece of the puzzle Renwick set in motion was solved.

Thanks to his information, I now also knew which fairy tale

Renwick sought. That brought me one step closer to the secret he coveted.

The streets were still lively; all the same, an uneasy feeling stole over me. An alley angled off to my right. I looked down it hoping to spot a sign for a bar or café. Instead, I saw a wavering shadow. One I knew well by now. Alessio, leaning heavily on his cane, shuffled over the cobblestones in my direction. His dark coat clung to him like a shroud.

Part Three

THE LAND OF NO RETURN

To the land of no return, the land of darkness,
Ishtar, the daughter of Sin directed her thought,
. . . .
To the house of shadows, the dwelling of Irkalla,
To the house without exit for him who enters therein,
To the road, whence there is no turning,
To the house without light for him who enters therein,
The place where dust is their nourishment, clay their food.
They have no light, in darkness they dwell.
Clothed like birds, with wings as garments,
Over door and bolt, dust has gathered.

—EXCERPT FROM "THE DESCENT OF THE GODDESS ISHTAR
INTO THE LOWER WORLD," A BABYLONIAN MYTH

Thirty-Seven

He kept his head down, oblivious to his surroundings, as if off in his own world. As far as I could tell Alessio was alone. I dipped into a doorway and held my breath, waiting for him to pass, afraid the crippling paralysis would once again seize my limbs. I flexed my fingers. No tingling or sense of heaviness.

I pushed out from the alcove and trailed him. He walked haltingly along the roadway without once looking back.

He turned north, going deeper into Sanità. I kept my distance, lingering in doorways, keeping to the shadows. As I followed him through the old district, I felt transported in time and Naples' magical history came alive. I fancied that the Prince of Sansevero, a Rosicrucian and alchemist, prowled Sanità's pathways again. Some claimed the prince perfected the metalization of human bodies and produced eternal light from the pulverized skulls of innocent souls he'd abducted. I imagined, too, medieval doctors moving through the alleyways in their cloaks and long-beaked masks to protect against the plague, or the richly festive costumed celebrations before Lent. It struck me that Basile's fantastical characters and flamboyant descriptions were not so much an invention as a faithful record of his beloved city.

A sweet, pungent odor hovered in the air. When Alessio turned a corner, a man swinging a copper censer brushed by him and smoky incense billowed about his cloak. A throwback, perhaps, to the days when plague victims and detritus lay in the streets. As he passed by me I had to cover my mouth and nose, overwhelmed by the perfumed vapor. Knots of men smoked outside the tiny bars lining Alessio's route. They cast sidelong glances at him and looked away. They might have threatened me had I been alone, but just as Naso's good spirit protected me on the way to Il Fontanelle, Alessio's wraithlike presence shielded me now.

He stayed close to the buildings and stopped frequently, putting a hand against a wall to balance while catching his breath. He dragged his right leg and leaned heavily on his cane. Before long, I recognized the streets. He was heading to Mancini's palazzo, where I'd first seen Dina.

I assumed Alessio would take the short laneway leading to it but he continued on. I gazed at the ivory walls of the palazzo, half expecting to find Dina framed by a window. She was nowhere to be seen. No light shone from within the house. It had the still and ominous feeling of a home abandoned.

Alessio turned at the next intersection and made his way down a road barely the width of a car. The block's entire east side was occupied by one long building made of a rougher, darker stone than Mancini's palazzo. No wrought-iron balustrades spilled bougainvillea here—the structure had only a glazed black door flanked by two ancient twisted orange trees. Alessio leaned against the doorpost and fished in his pocket for a key. His hands shook as he inserted it in the lock.

I rushed toward him, shoulder down, and pinned him against the door. He cried out with the blow and crumpled beneath me.

As he fell, I realized this was not the same man who'd shown up at my hotel room. Alessio now seemed as I'd originally perceived him that evening in London—frail and elderly. His face had reddened and puckered so badly it was almost unrecognizable. Only in those dark, expressive eyes did a hint of his former vitality still lurk.

"You stole Naso's book." I wasn't sure he even heard my accusation as he wheezed with the effort to pull in air.

When he lifted his head to speak I could see the bruises on his neck had ulcerated to become fiery-red open sores. "There is no theft when the volumes have been restored to their rightful owner."

"You mean Mancini? Neither of you has any moral right to them now after killing for them."

"I had no part in that. Lorenzo Mancini is the one with blood on his hands. And now he comes for you."

For a moment I feared Alessio meant Mancini had returned from Ghent. "Is he back already?"

"Not yet." His effort to shake his head caused a burst of coughing.

"You work for him. Why are you telling me this?"

"I am more his enemy than you. I set myself against him."

"By trying to kill me? A strange form of retribution."

"You are alive, are you not? I wanted only to find each volume and keep them out of the conte's hands. I did not wish to take your life! I let you live. I went so far as to endanger myself in the London river to stop the demon from overwhelming you. And in France, when Renard's dogs would have torn you apart, I lured them away. I came back here to seek my final rest, not expecting to see you again. It is good, though, that we meet here."

"You'll have to come up with another reason. Superstitions won't sway me."

"It is the truth. The demon would not leave me. It was wedded to me like my own flesh. Only now, because I am weak and sick, has it gone."

Was it possible? Dina had warned me about the conte's desire to raise a demon named Frucissière and from the first, any point of contact with Alessio had an abnormal quality. I dismissed the thought as soon as it arose; it was too incredible to believe. And yet Alessio spoke the truth: when he could have finished me off, he'd waded into the cold Thames. My brother's words drifted back to me: "The old gods aren't dead; they've just withdrawn to hidden places."

Alessio tried to get up and fell back. My anger with him diminished and I felt a wave of pity for the tired old man. "You're very sick. Let me take you to a hospital." I bent down and slipped my arm around his back to help him rise.

His head drooped slightly and he took a moment to drag in a breath. "No. I must finish what I started, even if none of it came about from my own will. I was Mancini's instrument. He sent me out to recover the book, yes. Even though it is not his. The book belongs to the woman."

"You mean Dina? It *did* belong to her all along? That's how you found out I was in Naples, wasn't it? She told you."

"Yes, she did. Lorenzo Mancini's men captured her in Rome and brought her here. I must take you to her for I haven't the strength to help her myself."

"Where is she? In the palazzo?"

"No. The other place. Where no one dares go."

"What other place?"

"I will show you." He lifted his cane to indicate the door but managed only to raise it a few inches off the ground.

"Are they keeping her in here? How many are guarding her?"

"None. Only one was left to keep watch over her. He is no longer a concern, as you'll see."

"If she's in trouble we have to call the police."

"This building is owned by the conte. They will not enter without his permission."

With all that had gone before, I was still wary of him and had no intention of walking straight into a trap. "You're going to have to prove she's in there. I'm not going in just on your word."

With no fight left, he simply nodded. "I understand." He reached inside his coat and brought out a pearl bracelet. The pendant with Renard's image dangled from it.

Dina would never have parted with that willingly. "Show me where she is," I said.

Alessio took one last long look around. His eyes lit on the square pavers of the roadway, the dirty stone facade of the building across from us, the clouds above bruised yellow from the lights of the city. Not the most beautiful sight, but to him, irreplaceable. In his sorrowful eyes the longing was unmistakable. He knew this would be his last night in the city he loved. "She has not changed so very much, my dear Napoli. If not for the cars and the electric lights I would hardly notice the passing of years." He turned the key in the lock. "Please push the door open," he said. "I fear I haven't the strength to do so."

We stepped into a warehouse. Once my eyes adjusted I could make out a large space filled with packing crates, cardboard boxes, and dozens of pallets. Dull, bluish light from the weak fluorescents overhead gave the area a sinister, chilly feel. Alessio led me down a corridor created by walls of crates and boxes at least ten feet tall on either side. The air carried a stench of mold and decay.

The bad air affected him and he wheezed heavily between coughs. He paused to get his breath back. "This building adjoins the palazzo on the other side. It is the only way to gain access to where Dina is being held."

We continued to a sturdy wall on the far side constructed of large stone blocks. Set into it were huge double doors made of oak.

This differed dramatically from the other warehouse walls and I guessed we'd reached the ground floor of Mancini's palazzo. The same one I'd seen from the outside with its windows boarded shut.

Alessio sat down heavily on a crate. "Before we go in, I must rest." He took another shallow, noisy breath. "I will tell you about the place we are about to enter. The old estate has always stood on this spot. Centuries ago it lay outside the city walls—a country manor surrounded by fields and a forest. When plague struck in 1632 a terrible misfortune befell the household. As you'll see, my own tale transformed into a nightmare. My words came to life in a way I never imagined possible."

Thirty-Eight

"Long ago a great lord celebrated the birthday of his daughter, Talia, with a grand fete. People flocked to the manor, needing respite from the destruction wrought by the eruption of Vesuvius the year before. Not long after the celebration, plague struck down the revelers.

"Talia was the first to succumb. Soon everyone else fell ill and I too began to develop a great fever and weakness in my lungs, my throat so sore it was as if claws raked it from the inside. My skin burned and itched, grew red; my very bones felt sore. I was barely able to walk to the chamber pot to piss. In the end, of those who'd stayed on after the celebration, only the lord himself, the captain of his personal guard, and the painter de Ribera were spared.

"Raging with grief, the lord declared the villa cursed and ordered it burned to the ground. He told the captain to have his soldiers rip up every piece of combustible material in the garden, destroy the outbuildings, and build a ring around the property to set it on fire. Villagers recruited for the task were happy to oblige, believing the house and all who'd touched it had been condemned by a demon's spell.

"At the last moment, the lord had misgivings. Instead, he chose to abandon the estate and keep it hidden forever from human eyes. With his captain, he hatched a terrible plan to massacre both the villagers and his guard lest they reveal the secret of the house. A fire was set, used only as a funeral pyre for the bodies. The captain and his horse were found some days later, dead in the forest of some mysterious cause."

He put his head in his hands. Again I asked if I could take him to the hospital and again he refused. "Thorn trees were planted around the house. Over time, the forest crept right up to its doors and mingled with the thorn trees to form an impenetrable wall. Local people, fearful of the estate's history, stayed well away."

·   "Fearful because of the plague?"

He didn't answer me, but said, "I will start at the beginning. For her birthday, I'd prepared two gifts for Talia. One was the printer's copy of five volumes of my tales encased in the golden covers and a cedar box.

"The second item I presented to her that evening at the manor as well. On my posting to Candia as soldier to a nobleman of Venice, I'd met an Ottoman trader who spied for the Venetians. He journeyed all over the mystic East and possessed a round ring of stone with strange writing on it. He told me it was very old and came from a temple. He said the ancients used it as a weight, ballast for spindles in the weaving of flax. I thought the weight a fascinating relic and fashioned a pretty box to present it together with my book. When I gave the gifts to Talia, I explained one of them contained a puzzle and challenged her to decipher it. She mistook my meaning. Believing the spindle weight was the puzzle, she pried off the seal with a knife. Inside she found nothing but a fine gray powder. I know now, to my despair, these were the seeds of the plague collected by the ancient ones. Unleashed, it spread throughout the party like a flame set to dry fields.

"She, at least, did not suffer but fell into a deep sleep from which none could rouse her. Others fared much worse. And so it was that one of the tales I penned came to life in the most horrifying way. In spite of the lord's efforts to contain the disease, its deadly fingers caught hold of the populace of Naples."

My mind raced as I bent again to help him up. The fairy tale and the story of its origins that Renwick sought so avidly was "Sleeping Beauty." Alessio had just confirmed the conclusion I reached after talking to Samuel's colleague. He interrupted my reverie. "Now I'm dying for the second time from that accursed disease. I've seen how my story became famous over the ages yet changed almost beyond recognition. I give no thanks to the conte for raising me."

I felt sorry for the man, so mired in his delusions. "Why keep up the pretense? You couldn't possibly be the author."

Alessio raised a trembling hand to silence me. "Can you not see what's right before you?"

"I'm sure what you've told me is true. Any historian with access to the Mancini family records, however, could piece together those facts."

A faint smile hovered over his lips. "I have no concerns if that is what you wish to believe; my purpose is not to convince you. Would you care to know how the story ends?"

"Of course."

Alessio steadied himself by gripping his cane tighter and continued. "Over the years, the manor deteriorated. The population of Naples swelled and the city took over the farm fields and woods. The new generation of Mancinis realized the force of this growth into the countryside was irresistible. They feared to raze the old house completely because, in that event, a stipulation in the will would give the property to the church. As a compromise, they demolished only the upper stories of the manor and built a new grand home on top. The first floor of the house was sealed off and the windows blocked. The doors were never breached until the present conte allowed his curiosity to prevail and dared to enter it.

"Once, the estate garden was spectacular. It had a pathway made from the black lava stones of Vesuvius bordered by magnificent orange trees. In spring, the luscious scent of their flowers drifted on the air for miles around. An ingenious maze offered hours of delight. A grand fantasy for all who beheld it. After the tragedy, for many years the villagers avoided going anywhere near the house, except perhaps for a few adventurous youths who were caught by the thorny branches. Their bones still lie beneath us somewhere." Alessio pointed to the wall. "The stone here differs from the rest of the warehouse because it's the original exterior of the ancient estate."

The way Alessio wove an age-old tale into a historic event impressed me and I had no reason to doubt the story's veracity. He'd tripped himself up, though, in taking on the guise of being an author he could never have known. "How could you know about all this history, after the plague took you?"

"That which I did not witness was told to me by the conte when he brought me back. We had a mutual goal—to regain the volumes Dina had dispersed. I played upon his desires and agreed to assist him for the opposite reason—to destroy the revelation they held forever."

"That still baffles me," I said. "You've just said the weight was deadly, not the book."

Alessio shook his head. "The book is even more dangerous."

"In what way? What's the secret?"

Alessio scowled. "Did I not just say I want to keep it forever unknown? For this reason, I have destroyed the covers and all the volumes I gathered. Lorenzo Mancini wanted one more terrible thing of me."

"And that was?"

"To look into his future. Prophesize his fate and forecast whether he would live to see the outcome of his plans. I told him I did not know when or where he would meet his end. Nor whether his plans would be successful. I said only that he would die under the hooves of a horse. He owns Camargues—the white horses—a tradition in the Mancini family, and keeps them in the country near the village of Domicella. My prediction threw him into a fury for he loves nothing more than to ride. I must have convinced him. I believe he has not gone near his horses since that day. If this indeed turns out to be his fate, it would be a just one, for the cruel man is his own executioner."

These were nothing more than the meanderings of a demented mind. I felt sure of this now. That Alessio was highly intelligent was obvious. And he had a dogged spirit anyone would admire. He was likely a distant relation of the author Basile, as I'd originally thought, perhaps also a gifted scholar Mancini hired to trace the family legacy. His mind had become affected in the process, maybe as a result of his illness. It didn't really matter. He'd concocted a tall tale with a lethal effect on real lives.

I was still trying to convince myself of that when, a few minutes later, he regained some strength and took me on a harrowing journey through the hidden house.

Thirty-Nine

The entrance led directly into the palazzo's shuttered ground floor. He pressed several buttons on a plate fixed to the wall and the doors swung inward. It was pitch black inside. "Mancini installed some lights," Alessio said. "There is a switch over here." He indicated the wall to his right.

I swept my hand down it and flicked on the switch. A rudimentary line of bulbs had been strung down the hallway, revealing that the once grand windows had been roughly sealed with bricks.

On either side of us stood two statues. One of Eros pulling back a taut bow and the other, a sleeping Psyche. Judging from their broken edges, the two pieces of sculpture had been whole at one time.

"A glorious place, is it not?" Alessio said. "This was the proudest possession of the Mancini clan until the dread day when the demon crossed its threshold."

The dim, sad space looked anything but grand to me. Down the hall a fresco showed an old woman, tiny as an infant, locked inside a jar suspended from a hook high up on the wall. Noblemen dressed in scarlet and purple robes stood before her. The Cumaean Sybil. Painted along one edge was a pitchfork with two tines. A bident, the symbol for Hades. Underneath the fresco, in gold lettering, were the words

Noctes atque dies patet atri ianua ditis.

"The doors of hell are open, night and day," Alessio translated. "Attributed to the Sybil by our great poet, Virgil. Apollo granted her one thousand years of life in exchange for her virginity. The god fulfilled his part of the bargain but the Sybil denied him her body. He got his revenge by granting her a thousand years of life without preventing her from withering with age. Eventually she shriveled up to nothing more than a voice within the jar."

It was his own fascination with the underworld and necromancy, I thought, that must have attracted Mancini to the Sybil.

Alessio, moving at a snail's pace, stopped in front of the fresco. "It is suitable we meet again in the Sibyl's domain. Like her, I have lived far too long and wish only to die. My association with this house has been a source of deep regret."

"How so?"

"Because I brought the demon upon them. Quite unwittingly, it is true. I bear the responsibility nevertheless."

We ventured into a rotunda. Alessio surveyed it with his hooded eyes. "Nothing here has been touched," he said.

Cobwebs festooned a row of baroque ceramic chandeliers like dusty fishnets. The webs held a macabre catch, hundreds of desiccated insect bodies. Nests of cobwebs draped elaborate cornices and ran in fine strings from the ceiling to the lamps, as if purposely strung to anchor the lights. More statuary, strange ethereal figures, representations of legendary beings, stood on marble plinths in rows on either side of the hall—Pan with his

Marcantonio Raimondi's *Il Morbetto*

pipes and goat legs, a young girl riding a unicorn, a minotaur, and others I couldn't name. Dust in such heaps it had turned to soil gathered in the corners. I stood in amazement taking it all in. Who wouldn't try to imagine the strange circumstances that befell this place?

Alessio gave the entrance hall one last look before heaving a sigh. "Come this way," he said. Off the rotunda we emerged into a large salon. Portraits hung along its back wall. They'd once been splendidly painted and framed but mildew had crept upon them. All the walls were blackened with damp and mold. In many places the plaster had completely disintegrated and fallen onto the floor tiles. The brilliant scarlets and cobalts of the Turkish carpets underfoot had long since faded. This room must have served as both a place of entertainment and a library, I mused, because the cabinets contained dozens of books. Some of the shelves had broken, spilling ruined books onto the floor. Moths had made a feast of them as well as the wall tapestries and brocaded upholstery on the chairs and settees of the room.

Despite the revulsion and fascination I felt with the fallen grandeur of the house I couldn't afford to waste more time. "Take me to Dina now," I said. I might have added *if she's really here.*

Alessio leaned against a settee and with the tip of his cane pointed toward a door. I rushed over and pushed at the creaking timbers until they gave way beneath my weight. I gazed in fear at what the open door revealed.

Bodies lay where they'd dropped, clustered in a foul final embrace on rotted straw. I'd seen the mummies of Capuchin friars in the Palermo catacombs, still dressed in their robes, dried out with ceramic pipes and cleaned with vinegar. Those dead monks didn't compare to the horrors I saw here.

Nobles still in their finery lay curled up like babies on soiled covers. The once rich silk-cut velvets, yellowed lace, and bejeweled satins of their garments had slowly rotted away.

Something—plague?—had left their bodies dry and desiccated. And yet their glassy eyes were still gruesomely intact and their reddish, rubbery skin had shrunk on their bones. Some had abnormally enlarged ribs and twisted spines.

One died much more recently than the rest. He was dressed in modern street clothes. Blood pooled beneath a gouge in his neck. The guard Mancini sent to watch over Dina.

Dina lay on a couch near the guard's body. I dashed over to her. Her mouth was slack and her breath came in slow, shallow waves. I put my arm under her and raised her to see if that would help her breathing. I tried to use my phone to call an ambulance without getting a signal.

Alessio's coat swished as he came up behind me, his cane ponging on the tiles. He reached my side and lowered himself to the floor when I swept Dina up in my arms. "I have destroyed the books and the stone weight for fear they still held the contagion. Before you leave me, you must take back your coins. I am sorry to have caused you so much suffering." He reached deep into his pocket, held out the six remaining coins for me, and sank into a heap on the floor, his coat fanning out around him like a black pool.

Alessio panted again with the effort to pull oxygen into his lungs. "The man you see before you now bears no resemblance to the person I once was. I loved the fullness of life whether the wind blew fair or foul. This shadow life holds no pleasure for me. I will not last the night."

I saw a glimmer of a smile in his expression and sensed a gentleness I'd never noticed before. "I welcome the end," he said, "and ask only one thing of you."

"Of course. What can I do?"

"Keep my stories alive, but let me die here in peace."

"If that's what you want, you have my promise." I took one last look at the wizened wreck of a man before me and around at the ruin of the once elegant home before turning my back on him with Dina in my arms.

Although she was slight I struggled to carry her as I made my way through the warehouse and outside onto the street. Her eyelids fluttered when I reached the intersection but she didn't respond when I called her name. A middle-aged woman walking alone with her dog saw me carrying Dina's limp body; the look on my face was enough. She pulled out her cellphone and dialed emergency.

An ambulance soon arrived with a blare of its siren. In my broken Italian I told the attendants I was a tourist who'd just landed in the city and had found the young woman lying in the gutter as I passed by. Dina started to come to then and spoke a few words in Italian. The fact that I was American and spoke only primitive Italian seemed to convince them. The attendants wrapped her warmly, put her on a stretcher in the ambulance, and left.

A few streets away I found a church and went inside. The sight of that gruesome place and Alessio's terrible suffering were hard to shake. So were his incoherent ramblings about demons and plagues. And now Alessio had taken the secret of the book to the grave. While I'd traced three volumes to Renard, Katharina, and Naso, none of them had witnessed my photocopies and those alone weren't enough to convince the authorities of my innocence. I was still on the hook for the entire book and perhaps even a suspect in Katharina Hatzfeld's death.

Worse, Mancini could return to Naples at any time and check the hospitals. Dina was unsafe. I could think of only one person who might help. When I called, it was a great relief to hear his voice come on the line.

"I'm on my way to Baghdad," Shaheen said. "I want you to meet me in Kuwait."

"Whoa, hold up a bit. Why Kuwait?"

"The last volume of Basile's book is in Iraq."

"Are you sure? How do you know?"

"I'm certain. It was one of the first volumes purchased—last February. An Assyrian scholar apparently donated it to something called the House of Wisdom—know where that is?"

I'd grown up with an expert in Assyriology but had never heard of the place. "No," I said.

"Finding it's our first task. As to the rest, I'll fill you in when I see you."

"What do you mean 'our'? You're saying we're working together now?"

"You're the one with the knowledge about the book and the history of how Renwick got tangled up with it. And we may need your expertise in archaeology too."

The prospect of returning to Iraq had about as much appeal as dropping into a snake pit. The thought of it turned my stomach. Added to that I felt like I'd been hit by a train. I was exhausted and feverish. No surprise really, given I nearly froze on the way to Renard's. Probably just a case of the flu. But the red marks on my neck had worsened overnight and I couldn't rid my mind of the image of Alessio dying in that foul place.

On the other hand, Shaheen's proposition gave me bargaining power and a way out for Dina. I had to decide. "I'll consider it on two conditions. Dina's in the hospital. Guarantee she's protected and once she's recovered, find her a safe place out of Mancini's reach."

"Done. What's the second thing?"

"Explain why Special Forces are involved in this. I was never told."

"That's classified. Like I said before."

"Then I'm not coming."

"Okay," he said. "Email me when your plane is due to arrive. When you get there, if you agree to sign your life away, I'll fill you in. I'm not saying anything over the phone."

If I wasn't satisfied when I met up with him in Kuwait, I could always leave. It was worth a flight there and back to safeguard Dina. And it would be quite different from my experience last August. This time I'd be in Iraq under the protection of the American military.

"We're good then," I said and clicked off.

Forty

December 2, 2003
Kuwait

Shaheen led me to a beat-up Jeep Cherokee in the Kuwait airport parking lot. He'd discarded his street wear and gold chains and cut his hair shorter. Now he was in combat uniform.

"You've lost your street cred," I joked.

He grinned. "All the better to fit in. Wearing my off-duty gear I'd stand out here like a male stripper at a church supper. I see you've transformed too."

I rubbed my hand over the couple of days' stubble on my jaw.

"You all right?" Shaheen asked. "Looks like you've been on a bender."

"Jet lag's catching up with me. I've caught a cold or something and the past few weeks haven't exactly been a party."

"You need any pills or anything just say the word. I'm a walking pharmacy. And if they don't work I can get whatever you want."

Before I left Italy I wanted to see with my own eyes that Shaheen had lived up to his word. At the hospital I was satisfied to find a security guard posted outside Dina's door. That also gave me the opportunity to see a doctor. He told me I'd come down with a simple cold and dismissed my worries about the marks on my neck, declaring them to be a harmless allergic reaction. He gave me some salve to apply to my skin and a mild antibiotic for the cold.

"I'll keep that in mind." When we reached the car, I asked, "Will it be just the two of us going in then?"

"Yep. No worries, you're in good hands." Shaheen opened the trunk and stuffed my pack in; he grabbed a Kevlar vest and helmet and tossed them to me. He opened the flap on a bag inside and took out two metal boxes. Gun cases. Shaheen withdrew a pistol, shutting the trunk with a click. "Take the back seat, if you don't mind."

"I prefer shotgun, Lieutenant."

Shaheen grinned again. "So when an IED blows your ass off because you blocked my view—then what?"

I could see his point and got in the back. Shaheen jumped into the driver's seat, jammed the key in the ignition, and peeled out of the parking lot.

We found a McDonald's a few miles down a dusty stretch of highway and ordered Big Macs and Cokes. Shaheen picked a table near the window. "This place goes back to 1994," he said. "On opening day the lineup was seven miles long. Got my first taste of American food here."

He'd brought a briefcase with him. He reached into it and took out a form and a pen and plunked them down in front of me. "Sign on the dotted line," he said.

The form, entitled "Classified Information Nondisclosure Agreement," had my name already printed in bold at the top. Below the type, my social security number appeared, along with spaces for me and a witness to sign. I was surprised to see it was only two pages long. I'd figured I'd have to wade through a small book. One sentence stood out: releasing information without authorization was a criminal offense. Translation? If I breached it, I'd be an old man before I ever made it back to New York. If I survived an Iraqi prison cell, that is. I signed and handed it back to him.

"Okay, Shaheen. First, tell me how you tracked the last volume here. All my leads dried up—or died."

"Mancini told me," Shaheen said. "He was still in Ghent after you left and I interviewed him. He does a lot of banking business in Iraq and can't afford to get on the wrong side of the U.S. so he agreed to cooperate. Mancini's source was Ewan Fraser. He revealed the name of the first buyer, a wealthy Assyrian named George Bakir from Baghdad. The volume was sold to Bakir last February."

I could hardly believe it. "Then you've got him for killing Fraser! He admitted it?"

"No. He sidestepped it and I didn't press him. That issue's outside the purview of my job."

Not mine, I thought grimly. I couldn't stand the prospect of him getting away with the murders and his treatment of Dina. If Mancini had discovered that the fifth volume was in Iraq, maybe Renwick had too—it made a rough kind of sense. Renwick must have learned the volume was here, hence his visit to Iraq last August. "Why would Bakir be interested in an old Italian book?"

"For a very good reason. He's a world authority on another set of tales, *The Arabian Nights.* Bakir was interested in tracing the tales and believed some of Basile's stories came from *The Nights* and originated in Baghdad."

"And you know where we can find him? But if Mancini knew who it was, why not get the book back himself?"

"He tried and failed," Shaheen said. "Since the war started, Assyrians have come under attack. Bakir had to flee with his family and leave behind the collection he'd spent a lifetime assembling. He donated his collection to the national library of Iraq before he left."

My heart sank. I knew what happened to the library. The volume had probably been destroyed some time ago, if not looted and cast to the four winds. "Did Mancini think Bakir's collection survived?"

"That I don't know. Apparently it had been assigned for safekeeping—to the place I told you about called the House of Wisdom."

"Okay, pal. I've been patient. Now tell me why the army's involved."

Shaheen shifted closer in his seat and chugged down some Coke. "We sent two microbiologists named Loretti and Hill to Iraq to search for bioweapon sites. They turned up nothing. Back home they came down with plague-like symptoms. We know they picked up something in Iraq but not where or what caused it. Did they stumble upon a production site or was their illness just a fluke? All we're certain of is they had a number of meetings with Charles Renwick in their off-hours and there are several coincidental links with Renwick's theories about plague and folk tales. The job now is to figure out whether Renwick actually found the location he believed Basile hid in the book and if he told Loretti and Hill."

"Can't the scientists tell you? Where are they now?"

"Dead. And Loretti's wife's close to dying now too."

"It's something you can catch then?"

"Looks that way. You can see we've got to get on top of this."

My skin crawled and I touched my neck gingerly. I'd had direct contact with Alessio *and* with the book. "How long did it take for their symptoms to show up?"

"That we don't know for sure. Loretti and Hill arrived in Iraq last May, shortly after we took control of the country. If the contagion is just some kind of weird virus, they could have picked it up anytime after that. No symptoms showed until a couple of weeks after they'd gone back home."

I first met Alessio two weeks ago. I tried to reassure myself with the knowledge that the doctor at the Naples hospital gave me a thorough going-over, so surely he would have caught anything serious. "Why include me in all this? That's something you could find out more easily yourself. I know next to nothing about locations in Baghdad, and if you need archaeological advice, any number of experts are better than me."

"You're more familiar with Renwick's line of thought and the particular role that book has played than anyone else at this point. If we need to fill any gaps in your knowledge, then, as you say, that's easy enough to do. There must be a lot of unemployed museum staff in Baghdad these days."

I looked out the window at the golden arches with the MacDonald's name in Arabic script underneath. You could travel thousands of miles from home and some things never changed. I decided to trust Shaheen and dropped a present in his lap. "I know what the round stone artifact is. The one stolen from Renwick's shop."

"Really?"

"It's a spindle weight, believe it or not, called a whorl. It helps moderate the movement of a spindle as fibers are pulled and made into thread. Mesopotamians used them when they wove linen textiles made from flax."

"So how does this fit in, do you think?"

"If the Babylonians wanted to preserve lethal grains of a virulent strain and keep them perfectly dry, a hollow spindle whorl sealed with pitch on its underside would have done the job nicely."

Most border crossings have an ugly air about them. Utilitarian buildings, glaring warnings, lines of idling vehicles, drivers cranky from long waits. The Kuwait–Iraq border was even less appealing than most. The buildings were dirty and makeshift and looked as if they'd been damaged in Desert Storm and never repaired. Large signs in Arabic clustered on both sides of the main highway. Other than the buildings, they were the highest objects in sight. Vast stretches of wasted brown soil extended flat out to the horizon. Gas fumes and exhaust from the ranks of trucks and U.S. army vehicles waiting to cross hung in the air. Many were fuel tankers. Ironic that in a country with one of the world's largest supplies of petroleum, fuel had to be trucked in.

The border crossing itself was a breeze thanks to Shaheen's bona fides. We hooked onto the back end of a convoy headed to Baghdad. Much safer traveling in their company.

We spent the early part of the drive debating the various options ahead of us and working out what our first step should be. Later, I found a treasure trove in the back seat. In an old plastic case Shaheen kept a killer CD collection of mostly seventies bands. AC/DC's *Highway to Hell*, the Allman Brothers, Van Halen's debut album, and music by the little alien, the great Joe Satriani. As frosting on the cake, at the very bottom I found Dylan's *Highway 61 Revisited*. More or less the perfect choice for the road we now traveled on.

Cranking Shaheen's boombox up to full throttle, we sailed through the brown wastelands, getting high on the music. By the time we reached the outskirts of Baghdad we were both in great moods.

Reality hit home at the first checkpoint, a mountain of sandbags and lines of orange cones. Gun turrets swiveled toward us on two Bradley fighting vehicles. Soldiers took long hard looks at our Jeep. Shaheen held up his ID. They gave it a thorough scan and waved us on.

"Damn dangerous road we're headed down," Shaheen said. "Although take your pick. They're all bad."

He stopped talking and sped up. His head turned ever so slightly as he glanced rapidly to the right and left. As fast as our vehicle was going, a black Ford SUV overtook us. All four men inside carried weapons and wore flak jackets and wraparound sunglasses.

Farther along an Iraqi man and his wife stood at the side of the road next to a cart heaped with melons for sale. The SUV slowed. One of the men stuck his M1 out the window and yelled, *"Imshl, Imshl!"* He shot at the cart. It exploded, showering the couple with wood splinters and red melon pulp and rinds. The woman shrieked then stumbled and fell. Her husband struggled to lift her up.

"Assholes," Shaheen said over his shoulder.

"Who are those guys?"

"Mercenaries from Sierra Leone or some other goddamned place. More and more of 'em flooding in here every day. Makes it hell for the rest of us."

It felt bizarre to be back in the city with its frenetic traffic and blasted-out holes where buildings used to be, people passing by the craters as though they'd always been part of the streetscape. I'd spent some of the worst moments in my life here, but I'd also come to appreciate why my brother loved it so.

Our destination, the Palestine Hotel, was a monotonous eighteen-story slab with a colonnade of salmon-colored arches at ground level. The parking lot looked like a Saturday-morning flea market. Dilapidated cars crowded the lot with trunks full of used CDs, DVDs, and cellphones, useless now that most electric circuits in Baghdad were dead. Open side doors on vans revealed boxes of chocolate bars and soda. Some vendors threw carpets onto the asphalt and set cardboard boxes on top with huge pear-shaped bunches of fresh dates. Two green donkey carts piled high with more fruit stood off to one side. They looked like miniature gypsy caravans on truck wheels. One of the mules brayed loudly and a boy in a long white *dishdasha* standing between the animals jerked hard on its tether to quiet it.

The hotel lobby was packed. Sweaty-faced cameramen lounged next to piles of equipment; hotel staff scurried by with messages on trays and mounds of luggage. A woman journalist in D&G sunglasses, a tight-fitting tank top, and jeans held out a mike to some military honcho.

We registered and went into the hotel restaurant. I would have sold my soul for a steak and salad. On the limited menu were hard-boiled eggs, dried figs, and a bowl of lukewarm goat stew. Shaheen tucked in with appetite after our food was served.

"Do you know what the world's oldest recipe is? It's on a tablet."

"No idea," he said with his mouth full.

"You mix up snake skin, plums, and beer then cook it."

"Sounds wonderful."

"It's got all the key nutrients."

Shaheen chuckled between forkfuls. "Not on this menu though," he said. "Wonder why."

After leaving the restaurant we went up to our room on the top floor. A room like this was a luxury in Baghdad. It had twin beds and a colorless shag carpet. Shaheen flopped down on the right-hand bed and waved toward his pack. "We probably can't get TV reception. Help yourself. There are some great X-rated movies in there. One of 'em's got a chick with a rack the size of two water-melons. And you should see what she can do with—"

"Have to check it out for sure," I laughed.

I was hot and dusty from the long trip. I went into the bathroom for a wash and ran my fingers through my hair. When I opened the bathroom door, Shaheen had the window curtain pulled back and the balcony door partly propped open.

"You like the view that much?" I joked.

Shaheen motioned for silence and peered out the window. "Shit!"

He dove toward me, crashing me backward into the bathroom. I had no time to defend myself and cracked into the side of the tub. Shaheen kicked the bathroom door shut.

A thud followed by the rapid shattering of glass and the room exploded. The force of the blast blew the bathroom door off its hinges, bringing with it missiles of scorched plaster and flaming carpet. Shaheen soaked a towel and shouted at me to put it over my mouth and nose. I grabbed my pack as we fled the room, hacking on the toxic smoke flooding into the hallway.

Forty-One

December 4, 2003
Baghdad, Iraq

Shaheen's sharp eye saved us. As he looked down from the hotel balcony at the parking lot, he'd noticed the boy tending the donkeys had vanished. No one in Iraq left their goods untended. The merchants selling their wares scattered rapidly too, overturning baskets of vegetables and knocking piles of CDs to the ground. The blast had two immediate consequences. It delayed our plans by a day and changed my opinion of Nick Shaheen for the better.

Once we settled at another hotel I set about locating the House of Wisdom. One of the staff working at the museum knew my brother and laughed when I asked him about it. "You're about twelve hundred years too late," he said. "Mongols destroyed it when they attacked Baghdad. Some walls still exist. It's adjacent to the national library."

At the same time, Shaheen focused on the scientists' activities outside their regular work hours. He took me with him to see the woman in charge of Loretti and Hill's security detail to fill in the gaps.

"She's waiting for us in the Green Zone—ever been there?" Shaheen asked.

"Nope."

"It's sort of like Valhalla dropped into the middle of Purgatory. If there's time we can have drinks with a few party girls around Saddam's palace pool."

I didn't hate the sound of that. Maybe this would end well after all.

Once we were underway, Shaheen loosened up even more. Cracked a few jokes. I responded in kind. The guy had an in-your-face style, no question. He was as rough as sandpaper. But he also had a quick mind and he'd already proven that he had my back.

Gaining access to the Green Zone took ages even with Shaheen's ID. Fittingly, the formal gate we passed through looked like a Disneyfied version of a medieval keep.

The area was like a prison, cut off from the rest of the city with inmates happy to be incarcerated. Formerly a collection of wealthy residences, institutions, palaces, and ponds, it was a place ordinary Baghdadis knew to keep their distance from. Nothing, therefore, had changed.

After keeping us waiting for almost an hour, Corporal Evers, a steely-eyed soldier who looked like she could bench-press two hundred and fifty pounds in her sleep, greeted us. Guiding us through a jumble of partitioned blast walls and barbed wire, she told us she was currently assigned to protect one of the civilian lawyers.

Once we'd reached a place where we could talk comfortably, she said, "Not sure how much I can help you. I was only on security with the scientists' official team when they assessed sites and I'm told you've already been briefed on them."

Shaheen nodded. "Yes. Unfortunately they didn't keep records of their off-time."

"There wasn't a whole lot of that. We worked twelve-, fourteen-hour days. And we spent that wearing hazmat suits during the summer when the heat was a bugger. So when you were finished all you wanted to do was drink gallons of water, have about ten showers, and sit with a fan blowing in your face until you hit the sack."

"Loretti and Hill did have time off, though?"

"Oh yeah. Usually we'd work straight through a couple of weeks and then knock off for three-, four-day stretches. They stayed in the al-Rashid in the zone here. You probably heard. It got hit with rocket fire a few weeks back."

"We just got nailed the same way. At the Palestine," Shaheen said. "Tell me, what were the scientists like to work with? Did they have any particular interests? What did they talk about?"

"Loretti was an extrovert. Cracked jokes, kept trying to hustle me in a fun way, stuff like that. Nice guy. Hill was the quiet one. Didn't have a lot to say. Kind of got the impression he looked down on us. He was scared shitless to be here, that was obvious."

"They never told you what they did in their time off?"

"No. But Loretti did mention something that struck me as odd. Asked if I knew where he could find the House of Wisdom. I thought it was another one of his jokes and then realized he was serious. Loretti was kind of a history buff. Always talking about how civilization began here and shit like that." She cracked a smile. "Not too civilized these days."

"Did he ever tell you he'd found it?"

"What?"

"The House of Wisdom."

Evers thought for a minute. "Not that I can recall."

"Anything else?"

"Word has it the two of 'em picked something up over here and are in a bad way. That true?"

The last thing Shaheen wanted was to fan the flames of gossip about nasty viruses in the country. "They're recovering from pneumonia. Just being extra cautious because of the work they were doing over here."

"Okay," Evers said, drawing out the last syllable. "Then why couldn't they tell you what you want to know themselves?"

Shaheen looked annoyed at her comeback. "They were pretty sick for a while, and their memory's hazy. We're just double-checking everything."

"All right then. Good." Although Evers saw through Shaheen's hasty coverup she didn't push the issue. She hesitated as if weighing her next words. "I don't want to disrespect them or anything. You appreciate that, right?"

"Whatever you say stays with me."

"Okay. Loretti wanted to see some archaeological sites. He tried to get access to the museum. They turned him down flat on that one. He was pissed. Let's face it, old objects are lying around everywhere. Pieces of jars and things. Nothing worth anything. He wouldn't be the first guy to want a souvenir, if you know what I mean."

"Of course." Shaheen thanked her and we said goodbye.

"She caught you out pretty good there," I said as we walked away. "If you're going to lie, always best to have a plan first. Take it from an expert."

"I had to think of something. What did you find out about that House of Wisdom?"

"One of the first libraries and research centers in existence. Parts of it still remain."

"Where?"

"In the old city. The Crusades destroyed all the power structures in the Middle East and left it wide open to Mongol raids. In

1200 they sacked Baghdad and the House of Wisdom along with it. It was never rebuilt. You grew up here. How come you've never heard about it?"

"I wouldn't exactly call it growing up; surviving's more like it. Lived on the streets from the time I was five. With that kind of pedigree you don't exactly get to visit the cultural hot spots."

"How did you end up in the U.S. then?"

"I was just entering my teens when the Gulf War broke out. Found a way to make it into Kuwait because I heard with so many Americans there, money was flowing. Got a job at a residence with a major general and his wife. They ended up taking me back to the U.S. They had no kids of their own. Great people. I got a scholarship to West Point but they paid for a lot of stuff the army doesn't cover."

The man was chock-full of surprises. "Do you want to check out the House of Wisdom?"

"Sounds like the only move we've got right now. We have to make a detour first though."

"Why?"

"If I'm going to do double duty as a translator we need to pick up a guy for a second pair of eyes on the street."

Shaheen made a call and after a tortuous half-hour route south pulled up in front of an aging Soviet-style apartment block. A squat, tough-looking man waited outside the entrance. Shaheen got out to open the trunk and opened one of the metal gun cases, handing an M4 Carbine to the man who jumped into the rear seat beside me.

"Meet Ali" was all Shaheen said by way of introduction. Ali, chewing a fat wad of gum, grinned, exposing both the gum and a gold-capped row of brown teeth. He patted the gun. "Safe with me," he cackled and grinned again. My trust in Shaheen dipped a little.

As we drove I looked out the dusty window and saw what I thought was a kid playing on a handmade wagon. His mode of transport was a flat piece of plywood tied onto the frame of a baby stroller. He lay flat on his stomach on the plywood. From the knees down, he had no legs. His skin had been crudely stretched over the stumps and tied off like the ends of sausages. On both hands he wore a pair of battered sneakers to propel himself along the cracked pavement. He was covered in dust.

Shaheen stopped the Jeep and spoke to Ali in Arabic while handing him something. When Ali jumped out of the car the kid looked terrified and held up both shoe-clad hands as if to ward off some new misery. Ali spoke to him quietly and gave him a fifty-dollar bill.

"Don't usually do that," Shaheen said after we took off again. "Some things you just can't let go."

Forty-Two

In the golden Islamic age, the eighth century, Baghdad was the global seat of learning, the Athens of its day. The House of Wisdom, Bayt al-Hikma, boasted the first university and a library that rivaled Alexandria's. We strolled through a tight trapezoid-shaped passageway of well-preserved baked brick. It reminded me of the cloistered corridors in ancient monasteries. I touched the walls as we passed through, awed to think that along these hallways the greatest scholars of the world once walked. In the Baghdad library proper, we found a skeleton staff engaged in cleaning and repairing the damage incurred during the April invasion.

When Shaheen handed around photos of Loretti and Hill and asked about the scientists, the librarians shook their heads. My mission was to trace the fifth volume of Basile's book, and in that I had a smidgen more luck. The staff knew of George Bakir, the Assyrian scholar. They told us that to find out anything more we'd have to talk to Syed Al Asiri, head librarian at the time of the invasion.

Syed lived farther south in Dora District. Shaheen was less familiar with this part of the city and it took him some time to locate the man's home. A wind kicked up when we got out of the car. The all-pervasive ash blew into our faces, making even the short walk to Syed's building unpleasant. Late in the afternoon, the sun was a faint bronze circle low in the sky, shrouded by the fine soot stirred up by the winds.

Two four-story buildings, throwbacks to the sixties, faced each other across the street. Considered upscale before the war, the twin buildings now looked unkempt. Their upper floors cantilevered over recessed ground-level shops, many with grates firmly shut over their front windows. Sheets and clothing hung from balcony railings to dry. We climbed a dirty stairwell that smelled unpleasantly of decomposing garbage. Dull light in the hall leading to Syed's apartment made it hard to see.

Shaheen knocked. Someone spoke in Arabic through the door and moments later we were let in. Ali remained on guard outside. Syed introduced himself and pointed across the room. "My father-in-law and daughter," he said. A single bed, surrounded on three sides by a makeshift frame hung with curtains, stood against the east wall. A girl who looked around twelve lay half propped up on the bed. Beside her sat an older man dressed in a traditional white *thawb*. On his head he wore a richly embroidered *taqiyah*. He'd been reading to the girl from a large, colorful picture book. When the old man saw us, he glared.

Clearly the apartment had been without electricity for some time. Weak light seeped in from windows overlooking the balcony. A kerosene lamp and tallow candles were placed in holders around the room. None had been lit and I assumed they were being conserved for evening. A large clear plastic jug of water sat on the counter beside the kitchen sink.

Syed motioned for us to sit at the table and got a bottle of sherry and three tumblers. "I brought this back from England," he said, "when I attended a colloquium at Cambridge, my old school, last winter. I planned to serve it when my British colleagues came to visit me." He smiled ruefully. "I think it will be quite some time before my guests arrive."

He offered cigarettes from a crumpled pack. I thanked him and declined. Flicking on his lighter, Shaheen lit Syed's cigarette and plucked a cigarillo from his breast pocket.

"How may I help you?" Syed asked politely.

Shaheen took a drink. "We're interested in a book left with the national library in a collection donated by a professor, George Bakir."

"I know of Bakir. Can you describe the book?"

"Italian fairy tales, published in the seventeenth century. The author's name is Giambattista Basile."

Syed took a few drags of his cigarette and sat back, crossing his legs. "Yes. It came in with Bakir's collection."

I sensed this whole thing might be breaking our way. "We'd like to look at it. Could you help us find it?" I said.

"I'm afraid not."

"Why?"

"For a very good reason. Surely you know what happened to our library. Looters made off with many precious things. The Koranic library fared far worse. It was deliberately set on fire. So many precious books, some going back to the twelfth century, all burned. Pages of ancient Arabic script floated like dead leaves on the wind. A colleague of mine was killed when he ran around trying to gather them up. Whole shelves of volumes that look perfect but, when you touch them, fall away to ash. I can't bear to go there anymore."

I hadn't heard about the arson. It sickened me to think anyone would deliberately burn books.

"When the Mongols attacked Baghdad they destroyed the House of Wisdom," Syed continued. "All the precious scrolls and manuscripts were thrown into the Tigris. It's said the number of books destroyed caused the river to run black from the ink. At times I like to imagine that all those words were pushed together by the river currents and have pooled in some still lagoon, waiting to be discovered and turned into books again. Just a silly fantasy, of course." He'd taken pains to remain polite yet couldn't keep the resentment out of his voice. "Tell me, why are libraries always targeted? We can't seem to wait to destroy what makes us human in the first place."

With a grunt of impatience Shaheen said, "Getting back to the Italian book—what happened to it? Was it burned too?"

"It was among the library possessions we moved for safekeeping to the Ministry of Tourism in early March, right before the war. The building was very secure; doors to the rooms where we stored the archives were welded shut. Despite the precautions, looters broke into that building too and damaged the door, causing a water pipe to break. George Bakir's entire collection ended up submerged in the water along with many rare manuscripts. The only way to save water-damaged paper is to freeze it right away." He gestured with his hands. "Out of the question for us, without electricity. There is a slim possibility the book was taken by looters before the collection was moved, so you have a slight chance of finding it on the black market. It's not in the library."

We'd gotten our hopes up and just as quickly they'd been firmly dashed. Shaheen put his unlit cigarillo to his lips. I could hear the old fellow slowly pronouncing the words of the story in Arabic to the girl in the background. I looked across at them. She seemed listless, barely heeding what he said. She looked ill and I wondered whether she'd been sedated.

Syed flicked a glance at them and focused his attention on us once more. "This must be a prized book. In August some other men approached me about it. Two Americans and an older Englishman.

What's your interest?"

The brown paper envelope Shaheen carried crackled as he took it from his jacket pocket. He pulled out the photos of the two scientists and laid them on the table in front of Syed. "These men—right?"

"Yes, that's them. Loretti and Hill. The Englishman was Charles Renwick. They came to me with a bizarre notion. Renwick subscribed to an odd theory. He thought one of the fairy tales in the book originated as a Mesopotamian legend. And that it held some clue to the source of an ancient plague. My reaction was, to say the least, one of strained disbelief."

"Was that all he said?"

"No. As I listened to how he made those connections, I began to appreciate his rationale. Plagues did sweep through old Babylon. Often in times of turmoil or when the climate changed and drought or flood brought on poor harvests and malnutrition among the people. Medicine was well advanced by the time the late Babylonian kings reigned. Even in Hammurabi's time tablets described long lists of illnesses and their treatments. An *ashipu* would be summoned to identify the demons causing a disease and administer rituals and incantations to drive the evil spirits away."

Syed tapped his ash and thought for a minute. "We smile at this nowadays but the tablets also described symptoms and herbal treatments, even surgeries that approximate modern medical practice. Extremely sophisticated, really. And they had one fascinating idea. If a surgeon failed to cure a prominent patient, he risked having his hand severed. If he cured his patient, though, he was handsomely rewarded. This was actually written into Hammurabi's code."

"Would make you think twice before going into medicine," I commented.

Syed glanced over again at his father-in-law and daughter. I noted the signs of deep worry in his eyes. Then he appeared to shrug off his feelings. "Charles Renwick took the whole thing one step further."

"How's that?" I asked.

"He thought the Babylonians may have employed disease as an instrument of war."

Shaheen put his cigarillo down on the saucer that served as an ashtray and leaned forward. "Did he think an old plague germ had been resurrected? Perhaps as part of a program carried out by the Hussein regime?"

Syed shrugged. "My field of expertise is books. I'm not a doctor or a scientist. I do know a form of germ warfare is reputed to have been used by the Hittites. Some claim they introduced rams infected with tularemia into enemy villages in Western Anatolia. That happened around 1350 B.C., so the Babylonians might have known about it. If so, there's no record I'm aware of. I do know there have been prolonged outbreaks of tularemia in the Middle East. It causes virulent sores on the body and severe pneumonia."

Syed's father-in-law stopped reading and fixed us with a hard stare so pointed, it seemed to have tangible power. Glancing at the old man, Syed stubbed out his cigarette and got up, walked over, and spoke to him in a rush of Arabic. The man cast his eyes down but held his body rigidly.

"Please excuse my father-in-law," Syed said when he returned. "He is not always well in his thoughts."

His daughter stirred on the bed and kicked off her covers. The father-in-law spoke to her while gently trying to push her back down. Syed leapt up again and rushed over to the kitchen to snatch a bottle of pills from the counter. He poured a glass of water from the jug and perched on the edge of the bed, putting his arm around the girl to support her and holding out the pills for her to swallow.

From the knee down, her leg was a mass of festering raw flesh.

Where skin was still visible it had a frightening blue tinge. The girl whimpered and resisted the pills, weakly pushing her father away. As Syed insisted, she became more upset and knocked the water glass out of his hand. He turned to us. "Please. I'm afraid I must ask you to leave now. My daughter is very ill."

We thanked him and left the apartment, joining Ali outside.

"The girl belongs in a hospital. She could die if she stays here," I said.

"Do you have any idea what hospital conditions are like? They barely have a skeleton staff left. Doctors are targets even in their own homes. No drugs. Infection rates are soaring. Believe it or not, she's better off at home," Shaheen said.

The apartment door cracked open and Syed's father-in-law poked his head out. He pointed to Shaheen and said something in Arabic.

"What does he want?" I asked.

"He says Syed has something else to tell me. He forgot to mention it."

I waited while Shaheen walked back down the hallway, Ali behind him. Shaheen drew closer. The old man pulled a knife from the folds of his tunic. The blade flashed as he thrust it with all his force at Shaheen's neck.

Ali moved fast, his body a blur. He hit the old man's arm so hard the knife clattered to the floor. The old man screamed a volley of words as Ali crushed him against the wall.

Shaheen and I hurried out of the building. The knife had grazed his neck above his collar bone. "That was damn close," I said. "Are you okay?"

He pulled out a tissue and held it to the wound. "You let your guard down for a minute in this hellhole and you're fucked. You'd think I'd have figured that out by now."

"Are you going to send someone to arrest them?"

"And what happens to the kid? That would pretty much be the end of her, wouldn't it?"

A few minutes later Ali joined us. He spoke to Shaheen briefly in Arabic before getting a first-aid kit out of the trunk and bandaging him up. As we drove off, Shaheen related what Ali had told him. "Syed apologized for his father-in-law and pleaded with Ali not to arrest him. Apparently Syed's wife died in a bomb blast when she was driving to visit family on the other side of town. That's how his daughter was injured too. It affected the old man's mind. He blames Americans."

Forty-Three

A thin thirteen-story tower rooted in a massive bed of junk concrete slabs and twisted metal beams was the most prominent landmark in the area we drove through. A blast wall separated the wreckage from the street. The tower was actually the concrete shell of a stairwell.

Shaheen flicked his finger toward the structure. "All that's left of the Mamoun communications center. Burned to a crisp."

We crossed the river to al-Maidan Square, crowning glory of al-Rashid, Baghdad's most famous commercial street. The al-Haydar Mosque soared like a beautiful blossom in a ruined garden, its minaret and two domes of intricate arabesqued tile accented with green and gold, the colors of paradise. It contrasted oddly with the disorder surrounding it. Shaheen squeezed our vehicle into an impossibly small space and we set out on foot. To find the book on the black market we'd need to start with antique shops in the district. The wind had died down and the streets were crowded with people. In some respects it felt like an ordinary day even though a number of the shops were barred and others burnt-out holes. Heaps of refuse created artificial lakes of filthy gutter water. Neither Shaheen nor Ali spoke. Both of them were on the alert and ready to act if things turned bad.

We didn't know if Loretti and Hill had actually come here. Nor would a store owner necessarily remember them or tell us if they had. It seemed a hopeless quest. After canvassing several shops where proprietors shrugged or shook their heads when shown the scientists' photographs, Shaheen suggested we take a break.

The mustard-colored tile walls in al-Zahawi café were inset with depressions holding narghile pipes. In one of the recesses a TV blared. Arabic speech pumped out from its sound system but the screen was snowy. Ali brought three steaming cups of coffee to the table. I fanned away blue smoke.

"Famous place," Shaheen said. "Used to be a hub for poets, educated people. To argue, discuss politics … important issues. A gathering place."

I glanced at the men smoking their bubble pipes amid the low buzz of conversation. "Looks like we're sunk. We've canvassed almost all the stores."

"Let's finish the rest. If they don't pan out, we'll go to the Rashid Hotel where Loretti and Hill stayed. See if any of the staff know something. They always—" Shaheen stopped in mid-sentence and jumped up, walking over to the server. They had an animated conversation; then Shaheen handed the man the photos. The server said something to him and gave the photos back.

Shaheen returned to our table. "I should have realized earlier, at one time or another everyone ends up at this café. The waiter recognized Loretti. The store we want is not that far. Let's vamoose."

As it turned out, the shop on a back street near the square sold both antiques and books. Hanging carpets covered the storefront except for a narrow gap. We pushed aside a rug to enter while Ali stationed himself outside. A bell tinkled as the two of us walked in.

Around the circumference of the small front room, objects sat on shelves—tall brass tea carafes engraved with traditional designs, serving trays, old clocks, lamps, and oil paintings. Among these were a few clay pots and tablet fragments. I wondered whether they'd been looted but figured they wouldn't have been so prominently displayed if that were the case.

The owner, dressed in slacks with the tails of his long-sleeved shirt hanging out, rushed up, singling me out immediately. *"As-salamu alaykum."* He extended his right hand. I shook it and smiled a hello.

"Wa'alaykum salaam," Shaheen replied and made introductions. He explained that I spoke only English.

"I can speak it a little. We used to get many tourists here." The man shook his head. "Not for a long time now. My name is Khalid. We have valuable goods here. Old." He swept his hand around the room. "So many fled when the bombs started. You can see here. Shelves are full and my store empty of shoppers. Only thieves visit now."

"Dark days, Khalid," I said. "The damage to the city is heartbreaking."

The man shrugged. "Yes. We don't know if we will stand here tomorrow or join the cinders."

"Your goods—they're beautiful." I glanced around the room again and saw an antique *Sindar kilij*, the characteristic broadbladed Ottoman sword, sharp enough to slice a human head like a ripe melon. Strings of prayer beads made from polished amber shone in the light; some amateurish paintings were propped against the walls. I picked up an exquisite silver box with a lid enameled in bright colors. Persian. I saw a mirror on the underside of the lid and imagined a sultry woman lifting out her cosmetics, reminding me of Dina. Shaheen promised to make sure she got to a safe place after she left the hospital. I wondered how she was and whether I'd hear from her again.

Khalid hovered one step behind me as I examined the goods. "Many wealthy families sell in order to leave our country. Rare things you cannot find easily," he said.

"Do you sell books too?" Shaheen gave him a smile.

The man's eyes lit up. "Certainly, certainly. Up the stairs." He motioned for us to follow him. We brushed through a drape at the back of the store into another chamber filled with cardboard boxes, Arabic script printed on the sides. A flight of grooved wooden stairs led to the second floor. Khalid's slippers slapped noisily as he led us up.

On the upper level large brass trunks had been set against three walls. Above them, shelves were piled high with books and loose-leaf manuscripts. An electric typewriter sat on a desk in an alcove beside stacks of paper. Many of the books had yellowed pages and worn, hand-tooled leather covers. The dust made me sneeze when I flipped through them.

Shaheen, judging that we'd established a nice rapport with the shopkeeper, pulled out the photos. "These men visited your shop in August. Do you remember them?"

When he spotted a spark of recognition in the man's eyes, Shaheen pressed a little harder. "You do remember them—don't you?"

Khalid hesitated before replying, "Yes, they came. One moment." He went over to the desk and rummaged in a drawer, taking out a small card that he handed to Shaheen. "His name."

Shaheen held it up for me to see. One of Loretti's American business cards.

"Did he buy anything? What was he looking for?"

The owner held up two fingers. "Two books. One I had; the other not." He extracted a huge ring holding keys of all sizes and shapes and squatted to open one of the brass trunks. He cleared a space on the desk and placed a book on it for us to see. It had an elaborate cover of intricate Arabic designs that reminded me a little of the golden covers containing Basile's book.

"Not this one but one like it he bought," Khalid said. "He wanted to know about the jinn." He looked up at me. "Many types of jinn exist, some beneficent and others evil—like ghouls."

A fleeting memory came back to me. Something Samuel once mentioned. About nomads who'd journeyed the desert for decades, unaccountably vanishing and their bodies turning up, ravaged by some unknown predator. Evil jinn were blamed, demons born of fire who crossed between the earth and the spirit world.

"The jinn play pipes at dawn to draw unwary travelers into the desert. After the traveler becomes lost the jinn attacks it to take possession of his soul. Many stories have been written about this. Some can be found in this book here," Khalid said.

Shaheen pointed to the title in Arabic script: *Kitāb alf laylat wa-laylah. The Thousand and One Nights.*

By Henry Justice Ford from
The Book of a Thousand Nights and a Night

"You know this?" Khalid said, looking at Shaheen. "Our most famous tales from far back in history."

"What other book did they want?" Shaheen asked.

"Italian one. Same kind. Tales for children."

"Why would they think you'd have an Italian book?"

He shrugged his shoulders. "The Englishman was very sorry when he found out I did not have it."

I knew how Renwick must have felt. Shaheen gave me a commiserating look.

Khalid caught the expression on my face and said brightly, "But now I do."

"You mean the Italian book? You have it here?" I held my breath in anticipation.

He walked over to another trunk. I heard the ancient lock clicking as he turned the key and pried open the lid. He bent down and withdrew a package wrapped in an Arabic newspaper and handed it to me.

I peeled off the layers of newspaper with trembling fingers and almost shouted with joy when I saw Basile's book. I opened it to the title page. It was the one we wanted. The last volume—the fifth day. I gave Shaheen a quick nod.

"Where did this come from?" I asked Khalid.

The shop owner spread his hands out. "From a Syrian I deal with from time to time. Where did he get it? You know how these things are. We do not always ask." He gave me a pointed look. "Do you wish to buy it?"

"How much?" I said. The expression on my face told him how excited I'd been to see the book but I thought it prudent to bargain a little.

He asked for one thousand American dollars, an astronomical sum to him. It was ludicrously cheap and a fraction of the book's real worth. I was on the verge of accepting when Shaheen intervened. A discussion ensued in Arabic with much gesturing and waving of hands. At one point Khalid shook his head indignantly and I shot a glance at Shaheen, afraid he'd pushed the proprietor too far.

The conversation stopped abruptly when Shaheen reached for his billfold. He peeled off four hundred-dollar bills and handed them to Khalid, who smiled broadly.

The deal concluded, I thanked the shop owner for his time. As I turned to go, Shaheen spoke up. "Did those men want anything else?"

"Yes. They brought with them a very old object." Khalid made a circle with his hands. "A round stone with a hole in the center. They wondered if I knew what purpose it had. I did not know its use but recognized it from descriptions in old stories. I told them it carried a dreadful curse."

"Why did you say that?" I asked.

"This object was possessed by one of the most fearsome beings—Nergal of the Babylonians who reigned over the under-world. The god of plague. Anyone who possesses the object may ...." His face twisted in frustration as he sought the right English word. "May help the god to wake from his long slumber."

"Did they say where they got it?"

"I did not wish to know." He glanced quickly at Shaheen and then back at me. "The old Englishman did say one thing. They wanted to visit an ancient site."

"Did he say where?"

"Oh yes—Babylon."

We'd hit a wall for certain this time. The site of Babylon covered almost a square mile. I couldn't believe the scientists would have been allowed to do any excavating there. Even if they had, it could literally take years to investigate the entire site in detail. Without being able to narrow down the specific location the quest could end right here. Unless I was able to unravel the secret held within the volumes of Basile's book. And that still looked doubtful.

Forty-Four

December 6, 2003
Baghdad, Iraq

After the explosion, we'd moved from the Palestine to the Ishtar, formerly a Sheraton hotel. The Ishtar had once been a fine place but two wars separated by a decade of poverty had taken their toll. At one point its second floor had burned. The ghost of the fire still haunted the inn, though the staff had done their best to air it out. Everything smelled of melting polyethylene and burning plastic. Even the drinks tasted of it.

Following our visit to Khalid's shop I spent a day and a half in our room with my photocopies of the volumes, racking my brains to discern some pattern I'd missed before.

Now that I knew which story Renwick pursued, based on the spindle whorl and the hidden house underneath the palazzo, I turned to Basile's version of "Sleeping Beauty," titled "The Sun, Moon and Talia." The tale appeared in day five, the last volume, the one we'd just bought at Khalid's shop. I scrutinized the story but could see no indications, by way of marks or other printing features, that set it apart from text in the rest of the volume. As with the other volumes, if the clue resided in the story's Italian text, I'd need a translator to sort it out.

I possessed photocopies of three volumes and the one original we'd just bought. Alessio said he destroyed Naso's volume so I was forced to work with what I had. I taped the paper photocopies up on the wall in their proper sequence. My inability to read the Neapolitan dialect initially proved helpful because it made it easier to compare the books and search for hidden maps or symbols.

The volumes yielded nothing as obvious as a map. And there were no unusual symbols in the thin margins. I became increasingly frustrated, unable to find any sign pointing to a physical location. Hiring someone to translate all this material from the old Neapolitan dialect into English would prove time-consuming and expensive. And, so far removed in time from the original book, the English translation that Tye Norris had lent me would be unlikely to help.

I examined the fifth volume carefully. It was in the same pristine condition I'd found the first one in: stiff, browned pages that could easily be spoiled. An engraving of a noblewoman surrounded by scrollwork appeared on the frontispiece. It differed from the others in that it had only nine stories and no eclogue, all of it incomprehensible to me.

Scanning each of de Ribera's illustrations with equal care again I was struck by his vibrant, provocative images and yet they gave me no discernible geographical clues.

Shaheen had been gone all morning, leaving Ali to stand guard. Though he appeared unkempt and casual, Ali always kept a sharp eye out. He stationed himself near the door, occasionally pushing aside the curtains to look out the window and sweep his gaze over the grounds. I began to wonder what had become of Shaheen. When I asked Ali he answered with a smile and shrug. I'm sure he knew and had no intention of telling me.

Toward 11 A.M., I heard Shaheen's voice outside. Ali let him in.

He breezed in carrying a can of Coke, gave Ali a grin, picked his way through the line of my papers, and plunked himself down on the bed. "Loretti and Hill," he said, shaking his head.

My mind was still half immersed in Basile's volumes and I barely registered his remark.

"What about them?" I asked absentmindedly.

"Just got off the phone with Leonard Best, the contact back in the U.S. I'm working with on this. We finally know what killed them."

I looked up. "What?"

"Cryptococcus gattii."

Forty-Five

"It's a spore-forming fungus. Ever been to Brazil?"

"Just a beach holiday."

"Assuming you stayed away from the Amazon, you'd have been safe. It likes warm, moist environments. They call it a killer fungus because the death rate can reach 25 percent for people who come into contact with it. An even more dangerous strain is on the U.S. West Coast. Fatalities there hit 40 percent—that's already close to mortality rates for the Black Death. The fungus our medical people just identified? Through a microscope it looks like a distorted human hand—a spongy palm with four fleshy fingers extending out from it. It's what they call hyper-virulent, meaning it kills over 90 percent of lab animals exposed to it. Loretti and Hill never had a chance."

"How's it transmitted?"

"They're speculating it's airborne but don't know for sure. It lives in soils; in that environment it's practically undetectable."

"So you're out for a hike and you reach down to pick up a flower, your fingers stir up the dirt and you get hit with it?"

"And weeks later you're dead. The spores we're dealing with seem to have properties that are both more acute and different from the spore-induced sickness you find in the western U.S. They haven't seen the skin and bone infections out there for one thing. It's primarily respiratory.

"Saddam had some clever researchers. Now we're wondering if they found a way to tweak this damn thing chemically to kill everything it came into contact with. If so, where the hell were they doing it?"

"If it's undetectable in soil, how would you know? Sounds like an impossible task."

"You've got that right. Our only shot is to figure out where the scientists went. There's still one more lead to check out. Another contact turned up," Shaheen said. "A guide at Babylon. Apparently she gave Loretti, Hill, and Renwick a tour." He popped the lid of his Coke and drank some. "You made any headway with your brain teaser?"

"No. I'm at my wits' end with it actually. I've been staring at it too long. It's got to be something in the text itself. It would help if I could narrow down what I'm looking for. A map? Words buried in the text of one of the stories? There's just not enough to go on. Not to mention I'm totally hampered because I don't know either Italian or the Neapolitan dialect."

Shaheen got up and walked over to the wall. "Aside from the one volume you don't have, is all the material spread out here?"

On the point of saying yes, I realized I hadn't laid out the photos of the gold covers. I hastily removed the images from my case and moved over to the window, shifting the curtains to get better light.

"Watch that," Shaheen said sharply. "You forgot what happened last time?" He pushed me out of the way and looked out. "It's okay, I guess. But don't take long."

I held the two pages up to the light and scrutinized the

arabesque designs. There'd been no wind today to stir up the dust and the sun burned through with crystal clarity. Whether it was the particular quality of Middle Eastern light or the way I held the pages, I saw something I'd missed before. With a tremor of excitement, I shifted the angle of the pages and peered at them again to be sure. I was right.

As a last check I pulled up the picture of the cover design for the English book Amy told me had been copied for the gold covers of *The Tale of Tales*. Aside from the different initials, I now saw that the arabesque design was altered on the Italian version. A slight but significant change.

The original image of the gold covers was archived in my email account, so if need be, another copy could be printed. I got a pen and sat at the small table with the pages in front of me, tracing the outline of what I thought I'd seen. Shaheen came over to observe. I held up the tracing. "These aren't just designs. It's Arabic script. The arabesques cleverly hide several Arabic words."

Shaheen took the paper from me. "I think I see what you're getting at. I can't tell what the words are. They're unfamiliar to me. Almost looks Persian."

"We need to find a computer with broadband access," I said.

That task proved easier than we imagined. The hotel was flooded with journalists and it didn't take long to find one who knew a Jordanian specialist in Arabic calligraphy. The reporter used his satellite-linked laptop to send the image of my tracings to his colleague and got a reply back within the hour. It turned out to be a sacred script called *Jeli Diwani*, characterized by artful, elegantly entwined letters. Turkish sultans once used the writing for secret documents.

"The script makes up three words," I said. "*Mesopotamia, temple,* and *Jahannam*. All this time Basile's secret hadn't been hidden in any of the volumes but on the golden covers in plain view."

Shaheen's eyes lit up when I mentioned the last word. "*Jahannam*—the Arabic word for 'hell.' Did the author ever spend time in the Middle East?"

"He served as a mercenary on behalf of a Venetian noble, Andreo Cornaro, in Candia—an early name for Heraklion, the capital of Crete—and got the stone spindle whorl from an Ottoman trader he met there. Do you see the connections? *Temple* combined with the word *Mesopotamia* and a third word meaning 'hell' indicates a temple dedicated to the god of the Mesopotamian underworld."

"Well, that should be a piece of cake to find. After all this effort, we end up with nothing more than a fictitious reference to hell."

"Actually, it may not be so difficult," I said. "Several sites were devoted to Nergal, the god of the underworld, and his female consort Ereshkigal. The word Loretti was trying to say. Two of them are primary. Tell Abu Duwari, the ancient site called Mashkan-shapir, is associated with Ereshkigal. It's about an hour and a half southeast of Baghdad. The other is Tell Ibrahim, an important cult center called Kutha, between the ruins of Babylon and Baghdad. Nergal's temple site. Those are the main ones I know of; there may be others."

Shaheen looked doubtful. "The book dates to the seventeenth century. How could an Ottoman trader possibly learn about any of those sites when in his time they'd have been long buried?"

"Local people would have known. A temple dedicated to the god of the underworld would retain enormous power in the local memory. The word for 'hell' in Sumerian mythology was *Irkalla*. Quite a different place from the fire-and-brimstone dwelling of demons with pitchforks that we think of. The Babylonians named it something like 'the land of no return' in their beautiful poetry— 'the house without light.' Dry and dusty although not a place of punishment. Souls lived on for eternity suspended in something like a state of purgatory. Our best bet would be to start with the two main cult centers at Mashkan-shapir and Kutha."

"We'll give it a go," Shaheen said. "After we stop off at Babylon."

"You think that's where they found the stone?"

"I'm not sure. But that guide who gave the scientists a tour of the ruins might know."

Babylon's colors struck me first. That and the ever-present dust. Pink-ocher earth tones defined mud-brick walls and buildings; moss-green palms and scrub trees dotted the landscape. As we drew nearer to the famed city the full reality hit me. This was no desert outpost but a major armed camp complete with requisite blast walls, concertina-wire rolls, heavy vehicles, and dozens of ribbed aluminum prefabs. Like giant black dragonflies, helicopters dipped and hovered above the site, the grinding drone of their rotors so loud they shook the earth. As we drew nearer we could see soldiers in full battle dress having their pictures snapped against the backdrop of an ancient statue.

In 539 B.C. the victorious Persians marched into Babylon, taking the city without force and putting a permanent end to Mesopotamian rule. Almost 2500 years later our own troops controlled it, treading the same path as the Persians.

At the height of its powers, Babylon was the most glorious city in the world. Small wonder that Alexander, even after seeing many splendors in the Aegean and the Near East, chose it as his favorite city.

In ancient times the Euphrates bisected Babylon. Now the river ran along one flank and much of the western portion had been submerged. I could only imagine what finds awaited archaeologists should that underwater cache ever be excavated.

The great Babylonian kings Nebuchadnezzar and Hammurabi built a supremely beautiful capital, one that never deserved its modern reputation for profligate evil. With walls many feet thick, it proved impenetrable to enemy armies. Iron gates constructed at the entrance and outflow points of the river blocked invading soldiers. Cleverly, the Persians actually diverted the Euphrates and when the water levels fell, squeezed under the gates while the Babylonians were celebrating a festival. As I gazed on its forlorn remains I wondered whether someone many years into the future would be thinking the same thoughts about the dry husk of my Manhattan.

A strange landscape made up present-day Babylon. Saddam Hussein's extensive re-creation—an Ishtar Gate of gleaming peacock-blue tiles, new fortified walls, and temple buildings—was set against the sad refrain of the original city's crumbling ruins. On a hill, Saddam Hussein had commissioned a reproduction of Nebuchadnezzar's palace, now falling into ruin itself. All of it— the army camp, the replicas, the wasted beauty of a once great empire—seemed like a place frozen halfway through a time warp.

By now I was prepared for the interminable wait to enter a military station, but the situation here presented even more difficulties. We had to wade through checkpoints manned by soldiers from multinational forces—Polish, Italian, Romanian, and Spanish— none of whom knew each other's language. This on the same ground as the Plain of Shinar, home to the infamous Tower of Babel. A prescient omen, I thought, for the ultimate fate of the invasion.

In addition to Ali, who'd driven us to Babylon, Shaheen brought along two others, both private contractors, a brawny young guy named Ben and an older man who'd seen action in both Iraqi wars. I didn't catch his name. They followed us in a Humvee, a chase car for extra protection. The three men stayed with the cars while Shaheen and I went in search of the tour guide.

We approached a collection of buildings that once housed a museum and study facility. Thieves had made off with plaster renditions of Babylonian antiquities. The library and archives, however, did contain many genuine documents.

A pleasant-featured woman dressed in a hijab gave escorted tours, almost exclusively to military personnel. Doubtless she'd kept her job because she could speak English. She confirmed she'd given a tour to the scientists and Renwick.

"Do you remember where you took them?" I asked.

"I have a standard route. It was the same for them."

Our own tour came with a running commentary, not so much about Babylon's history as the damage caused by converting parts of the ancient city into a military base. She led us along a grand processional pointing out paving stones destroyed by tons of heavy metal driving over them. "They dug eight long trenches, piled up the soil, and filled thousands of Hesco containers and sandbags with it. The soil contained many artifacts, pieces of brick with Babylonian inscriptions, ceramics. A helicopter pad three hundred feet from the Ninmak temple caused a major portion of it to collapse."

Gouges were visible in nine of the molded reliefs of the chief Babylonian god, Marduk, the creature with a scaled body, snake head, and eagle-taloned feet. "This damage occurred long after the Baghdad museum was looted," the guide said.

"Did the scientists or Charles Renwick attempt to dig through any of these areas?" I asked her.

She shook her head. "No. They took my tour like everyone else."

"What about this object?" I showed her the image of the round stone spindle whorl. "Did they question you about it?"

She frowned in concentration. When she answered she refused to look either Shaheen or me in the eye. "You put me in a difficult position. I have only this job. My husband lost his. And you wish me to speak ill of Americans so you can accuse me later?"

Shaheen gave me a nudge and spoke to her in Arabic. She twisted her hands as she answered him, darting the occasional glance at me. Then she walked away, our tour abruptly terminated.

"What did she say?" I asked Shaheen.

"Loretti did show her the weight. He believed it was an ancient puzzle of some kind. He told her he planned to remove a seal on the underside of the stone. She knew he'd taken it from an ancient site and was afraid to accuse him of looting it."

"Shit. That means he didn't admit to where they found it?"

"In a manner of speaking he did. He told her he'd just come from hell. The underworld. They called it Meslam—have you ever heard of that?"

"That's Nergal's temple district. At Kutha."

Forty-Six

The road to Kutha ran parallel to the Tigris for some time. Every now and then white patches lined the riverbank like the last vestiges of snow melting under a spring sun. Except here it never snowed.

"It's salt," Shaheen explained. "Crystallizes out of the earth when the ground dries."

As we veered away from the river, rows of derelict tanks and trucks dotted the roadside like rusty hedges, as if a huge scrap yard had been disassembled and strewn along the edge of the road. We passed an oil tanker flipped on its side, the fronds of rubber on its tires mere threads now, waving in the wind like seaweed.

Shaheen's phone buzzed a few times. After taking one of the calls he said, "Strange vibes all around today. You ever heard of Samarra?"

"One of the oldest cities in Iraq, pre-Mesopotamian with unique pottery. I think that's where the great mosque is, isn't it? With the famous minaret like a high cone curling in a spiral. Why?"

"Big battle there yesterday. So ironic."

"Why's that?"

"Oh, you know the story. A Baghdad merchant hears a prediction he'll die and flees to Samarra to cheat the prophecy, only to realize that's where his death is supposed to take place. So saying you have an appointment in Samarra is like saying you've got an appointment with death."

The approach to Kutha cut through farmers' fields of flax and corn, the remnants of the harvest pale and brittle in the weak late autumn sun. In the distance two low hills rose about twenty feet high from a barren expanse of earth and scrub surrounded by a few trees, more fields, and scrubby bushes. When we reached the site we pulled off the road into a slight dip at its edge.

A wide depression separated a smaller mound from the larger fan-shaped Tell Ibrahim, the site of Kutha. The depression marked a canal that had once extended all the way from the Euphrates to the Tigris, an astounding example of Mesopotamian engineering. Ali negotiated the route slowly, trying to mitigate the damage to the site and limit the view of our vehicle from the road. The Humvee bumped along behind us.

The atmosphere was disturbingly quiet, its apparent peacefulness anything but benign. Not even the drone of insects could be detected, with one exception. Large clusters of flies. It was as if the god of the underworld still ruled here, and all life, save the buzzing harbinger of death, had abandoned this territory to him.

Shaheen and the other men unloaded a small arsenal from the cars. "Who would ever believe we'd find hell on this dusty ground in the middle of nowhere? Lead on, Madison, you're our expert—so far as we have one."

As a kid I'd dreamed of one day doing field work like my brother and felt a burst of pride knowing they were relying on my knowledge alone. "The site hasn't been investigated by archaeologists since the mid-nineties," I said. "Both mounds produced very antiquated material. The smaller one, Tell Qadir, includes pre-Mesopotamian objects." I pointed at the smaller mound where the workings of an old archaeological dig were still evident. "Iraqi antiquities officers along with an American team found a buried temple here with some remarkable wall paintings. Artifacts on Tell Ibrahim are a little younger but still date back six thousand years. Neither produced abundant material in recent excavations. Don't expect to find one of Nebuchadnezzar's palaces. Looters pick richer sites although with the total absence of security, they've probably hit this one as well."

As the other three men were out of earshot I said, "Speaking of security, why use contractors instead of bringing regular soldiers with us?"

Shaheen jerked his thumb toward them. "I'm used to working with them. Those guys are worth a whole squad, believe me."

"We don't know for sure whether Loretti and Hill found the weight here," I said, "but if they did, it wouldn't have been just lying on the ground. After two months, signs of any digging will be hard to spot. All the same, that's pretty much our only hope. Let's circle the perimeter."

Shaheen kicked at the dirt and crouched down, brushing his hand over the soil. When he got up, he took a good look around. "One thing's clear anyway. This was no hidden bioweapons site even if they concealed the entrance cleverly. The earth would be covered with ruts and tire marks otherwise."

"Should we continue on then?"

"No choice. I've got to find the source of the spindle whorl. Can't return empty-handed."

I took them back to our starting point. While Shaheen got two spades out of the trunk I checked the ground. Kutha was three-quarters of a mile long; we began at the lowest point of the mound and went in a westerly direction to take advantage of the better light on that side. If that didn't turn up anything, we'd have to climb the mound in concentric circles.

We didn't find what I expected. No holes hacked in the soil, not even small ones. Shaheen and I used the tips of our spades to sift through some surface soil and found nothing but rubble and small, loose stones beneath.

It was like searching for a needle in a whole country of haystacks. As we moved on we grew more dispirited. The place looked completely untouched. We did spot a few perforations. Those could easily have been made by water runoff.

Shrubbery dotted the landscape and all of it had to be checked in case the vegetation obscured any pits. In this location too the earth looked undisturbed. The bright blue of the sky softened rapidly and grew dusky. We'd lost good visibility. A village appeared in the distance as we rounded a curve in the mound. Not unusual for eastern archaeological sites. Entire neighborhoods occupied part of the site at Nineveh. Neither Shaheen nor I wanted to go any farther; the risk of being seen was too great. We decided to leave the section to the last if all else failed.

Shaheen took a swig from his water bottle. "So how do you explain this? Thought you said all the known sites were being attacked by looters."

I looked toward the village and thought about his question for a minute, suddenly realizing what had happened. "They were afraid to. It's the domain of the underworld. Even thousands of years later, people fear this place. It still has a powerful impact on them."

Despite the lack of evidence of recent excavations we decided to finish the search. As evening came on Shaheen argued for returning to Baghdad. Ali disagreed, saying that it was best to stay off the highways as much as possible. Since our vehicles were black and covered with dust, he said they'd be nearly invisible if we parked them here at night. I wanted to rise the minute the sun popped over the horizon to begin looking again. Shaheen reluctantly agreed to stay.

We drank cans of soda and munched on cold cheese sandwiches we'd bought at the base that tasted like slices of latex between slabs of wallpaper paste. I joked that the line from the poem "where dust is their nourishment and clay is their food" described our supper perfectly.

The contrast between the ancient grandeur of this site and the deserted wasteland of today stirred my imagination. Kutha was once a powerful cult center. Daily rituals would have been observed at a richly decorated temple—the house of a great god. The Mesopotamians called it the dark house—Irkalla. And I wondered whether the canal that once bisected it, now a dry bed, held deep meaning, like the River Styx, a boundary between the living and the dead. Nergal, originally a sky god, was condemned to fall to earth and inhabit the underworld after quarreling with the other deities. Another ancient story recycled in Christian lore.

We leaned against the car and traded swigs of scotch from my flask while Shaheen and Ali shared stories about growing up in Baghdad. They'd been fast friends from an early age.

I had some pretty hair-raising stories of my own but Shaheen wanted to hear more about the mythology of this place. While the stars began to appear in the night sky, I told them about Ishtar's terrifying descent into the underworld.

"She passed through six gates," I said. "At each one a demon stripped the goddess of her belongings—lapis lazuli beads around her neck, egg-shaped beads on her breast, even her mascara. By the time she reached the seventh gate she was naked and the demon Namtar brought her into the throne room to face her sister, Ereshkigal.

"Ereshkigal herself was a frightening sight." I paraphrased the old poetry. "Her breasts sagged, she had nails like a pickaxe and hair bunched up like leeks. Out of spite, she showered the beautiful Ishtar with diseases."

Shaheen and the other men chuckled at this description. All the same, I picked up on a nervous edge to their laughter. Most people have a superstitious side even if they never confess to it. And although none of us would admit it, this place, dedicated to the worship of the king of the underworld, felt ominous. As night fell and we huddled together, the dark aura of Kutha stole over us.

"What happened next?" Shaheen prompted me. "Come on. You've got to tell us the ending."

"Ishtar's carcass was hung on a hook to rot. After she died, the earth became barren. Ea, the God of Wisdom, fashioned two beings like demons who took on the form of flies, to travel to the underworld and persuade Ereshkigal to let her sister live again.

"Ishtar revived and traveled back to the land of the sky gods, but Ereshkigal demanded a substitute to replace her in the underworld. The goddess chose her husband, Dimmuzi, who'd been enjoying himself thoroughly in her absence and hadn't missed her at all. So in the end, the prince rescued his lover just like in the old fairy tales."

The night air grew chilly. We were all tired. Ali and the other two men did sentry duty while Shaheen and I each took a back seat in one of the vehicles to get some sleep. Despite the drugs, my cold had grown a lot worse. All the exertion hadn't helped. I quaffed a couple more painkillers and immediately dropped into a deep slumber.

I'm not sure what woke me. I remember the clear view out the Jeep window and my awareness of the dead silence outside. I couldn't see Ali, Ben, or the other man anywhere. My headache had returned with a painful throbbing at my temple. That wasn't what alarmed me.

I couldn't move.

Forty-Seven

December 7, 2003
Tell Ibrahim, Iraq

I was fully awake but my body had shut down. My heart rate zoomed into the stratosphere. I summoned all my energy to break out of it. My limbs finally responded and I bolted upright, drenched in cold sweat. It had been the aftermath of a nightmare; I couldn't recall the details. Still, it left me with a deep sense of foreboding.

It was at that point I noticed the muted strains of music, the notes at once gentle and pervasive, as if the air itself had filled with sound. Had I not known differently I would have thought it came from the car radio. The tones of some kind of flute were immediately recognizable, a mournful melody. An elegy or lament.

I cracked open the door and stepped outside. Almost immediately Ali was beside me.

"Do you hear that?" I asked.

"What? I heard only you coming out of the Jeep."

"Listen." The song rippled through the air again. Barely perceptible now. Sweet, haunting notes.

"You must still be in your dreams," Ali said. "You need coffee to wake up but the café is still closed." He laughed softly.

The sound shifted away from us and now emanated from somewhere farther down the shallow depression. In the east, the skies had lightened into a flat non-color, neither blue nor the deep indigo of night but something more muted, in between the two. The light that heralds dawn. "Wake Shaheen," I said to Ali. "We have to get moving."

Shaheen was up by the time I'd drunk from the water canteen. I handed him the rest to finish. He shook his head to dispel his drowsiness. "What's this about music?" he asked.

"Maybe just a villager," I said. "Sound travels far when it's this quiet."

They stopped talking and strained to listen. "Don't hear a thing," Shaheen said.

"It's coming this way." I began walking down the shallow gully. The music pulled me forward, seducing me. Memories of Khalid's words about the evil jinn returned, the demon from desert wastelands who lured innocent travelers with their pipes.

The melody abruptly stopped about one hundred feet down the depression. Although the light was still low, I could see signs of digging halfway up the rise to my right. We got to work sifting through every hole and cavity, repeating the search in case we'd missed something. Nothing of any interest turned up, nor did I hear any more music. Once or twice a truck barreled down the road and slowed as it neared the site but soon sped away. We'd been fortunate not to have been spotted so far. Our luck wouldn't hold for much longer.

"You're hearing things now," Shaheen joked. "You're not long for the funny farm I'm guessing."

Normally I'd zing one back at him. This time I felt too dispirited. I descended the slope, stopping just short of the bottom. A collection of small rocks had been piled around a shrub as if they were anchoring it. Beside them was the faint outline of a boot. I bent down to examine the imprint more closely. There was only one footprint and the surrounding soil was relatively smooth and free of rubble, as if it had been swept clean.

I kicked one of the rocks and realized it was actually a clod of reddish earth.

Shaheen squatted beside me. "Anything here?"

"Probably nothing but it doesn't hurt to check." The two of us heaved the hunks of hardened earth away. A large pile of debris had accumulated when the remaining clods collapsed inward. We could hear them tumbling down some recess. It sounded like stones falling down a cistern.

A hole not much bigger than a groundhog tunnel opened up. Shaheen shouted for Ali to bring the gear. He and Ben ran back to the cars for our equipment. If Loretti and Hill had picked up some toxin here, no one had any intention of suffering the same fate. Pulling on hazard suits and gloves, we began chipping away at the packed soil forming the tunnel sides. After almost an hour of this we'd cleared a deep depression to a diameter of about two and a half feet.

"If this is the entrance to hell," I said in frustration, "it sure is a damn anticlimax."

"It's probably just a rabbit hole or something." Shaheen waved toward the fields in the distance. "With all that corn and flaxseed out there, there're likely lots of critters around."

"You're probably right." I stood up and slammed my spade down in frustration.

A dull crack like a rifle shot sounded. It felt as though the ground were under pressure, as if it had been subjected to a powerful tectonic thrust. Buckets of earth cascaded into emptiness below. The opening itself hadn't grown a lot; still, we could tell that under the surface it widened into a bigger area. We couldn't see much when we peered into the abyss.

"I think you just struck gold." Shaheen slapped me on the back. "Well done!"

Shaheen and I carried empty Gore-Tex knapsacks and donned our helmets. We kept the spades with us, as well as strong jacklights. The satphones would be useless underground so Shaheen took communication devices from the Jeep. We'd be connected to each other and to Ali, who would stay as sentry aboveground.

"Having second thoughts?" Shaheen asked.

"I don't know. The cavity might be really unstable." I tried to make a joke out of it. "It's not that I'm not afraid of death—I'd just rather not be there when it happens."

"You and Woody Allen," Shaheen laughed. "All right, my friend. Let's get moving. Down the rabbit hole." He squeezed through first on his stomach because he had a thinner build than the rest of us. The older guy stayed on top with Ali; Ben came with us.

I almost called a stop to the whole thing then and there. We were damaging an important historic location and I felt extremely guilty. My brother would have been scathing about our hacking into a sacred site. Despite knowing this, I felt compelled to continue. We'd come so far, after all.

We had no idea what to expect or whether the tunnel would close in ahead. Shaheen turned his light on as I shimmied after him. His head and upper body wriggled comically as he propelled himself along, wormlike. I could hear Ben crawling along behind me. He moved more slowly because he was carrying a length of cable.

At this point the tunnel was barely a foot higher than our supine bodies although wide enough to give us a decent amount of room. Bowels of the earth would be a good description of the environment we pushed ourselves through; it reminded me of the tunnels in ant colonies. My greatest fear was the whole thing collapsing in on us.

Soon we arrived at a square opening framed in stone. Shaheen got through easily. My bigger shoulders and chest made it a harder go for me. Ben, brawnier still, almost got stuck. The tunnel here hadn't widened any but it was higher and changed from natural earth to manmade mud brick. I flashed my light on the surface. It seemed to have been smoothed out somehow, as if it had been planed or sanded. "I think we're in a culvert of some kind," I said. "These bricks have been smoothed by water flow."

Several times we passed large cavities in the sides of the tunnel. Shaheen flashed his light into them. Beyond a few feet the gaps appeared dead-ended. We made slow progress for more than half an hour before Shaheen suddenly quit moving.

We heard his voice through the communication system. "There's a void ahead," he told us. "Hold on." A few minutes later he asked Ben to run a length of cable over to him and told both of us to grip it. There were no projections in the walls of the tunnel to tie it to and we feared the stone wall would split if we hammered a spike into it.

Shaheen grasped the rope. I saw him sit up and direct his light down. The cable tugged hard as he slipped off the edge. When it went slack I shifted my body sideways and carefully inched over. The mud bricks dropped off sharply. I trained the light down.

He grinned up at me from a space about thirty feet deep. I tossed my light down to him and rolled onto my stomach, easing myself over the edge. Ben grunted as he braced himself, trying to cope on his own with my weight.

The room had clearly been constructed by human hands. The chamber floor and walls were surfaced with compact rows of baked brick, glazed to create a polished effect. A mosaic of a Babylonian griffin in red, white, black, and blue had been affixed to the back wall. Cut into the fourth wall, a sizable opening acted as an entrance to a flight of stairs. Rubble sealed the lower part of the stairs. We both stared at what lay on top of the rubble. Heaps of human bones.

"Would this have been a tomb?" Shaheen asked.

"Likely part of a building of some kind, not a tomb per se," I said. "These mounds were built on repeatedly over thousands of years. When new structures were erected over old ones and they themselves disintegrated, rubble hid what lay underneath. But someone has cleared this out. Loretti and Hill wouldn't have had the time or equipment to do it so it was probably looters from long ago."

"Well, this ends our own expedition."

"Maybe," I said. "Keep your light trained on the stair for a minute longer so I can see better."

"Maybe—are you serious? We'd need a couple of centuries to *remove* all that debris."

I examined the entranceway in detail, especially the joins where the brick face met the floor. "Do you notice anything?" I asked.

"Pretty straightforward, isn't it?"

"We're looking at a clever deception." I passed my hand along the wall. "Anyone who dropped into this room would be drawn immediately to this fourth wall. It may look like a gateway but I think it's a trap."

"You start down the steps and you're cut in half by swinging scythes or spikes coming out of the walls? Come on."

"Nothing that dramatic. They've told us, actually. It's called 'the land of no return, without exit.' If this really is a gateway, where are the doors?"

"What would they be made of?"

"Wood—cedar, most likely."

"And you expect that to last six thousand years?"

"Nebuchadnezzar built Nergal's temple in the mid-500s B.C. And, yes, wood lasts that long. Not necessarily intact. There should at least be remnants and these bones are the only organic material here. And another thing." I clicked on my light and trained it on the other walls. "Without cable how do you think we'd have made it back? Those walls are polished smooth; there are no hand- or footholds."

Shaheen gave the walls a measured glance. "You're right."

"Even standing on your shoulders with my arms fully extended I wouldn't be able to reach the rim of the tunnel. People in those days were a lot shorter. Once they'd discovered these stairs led nowhere, they'd be caught in here, temporarily at least. The bones prove it."

I redirected my light to a perfectly round hole positioned close to the ceiling. It resembled a kind of drain, but if that was its purpose, it was in a very strange position. No water from rain or natural seepage from the water table could be drained away from that location. Rather, the water would pour into this chamber. It wasn't a drain at all but a conduit. Did it extend all the way to the ancient canal? I looked at the bones again. They weren't scattered helter-skelter around the stair. I could see them bunched up in a pile against the barrier of rubble. *As if after drowning, bodies had been pushed against the rubble by the force of water.*

"Here's what I think. People, early grave robbers or whatever, got trapped in here, unable to get out quickly because of the diffi-culty of climbing back up those walls. Then, someone activated a triggering mechanism and water poured in to drown them. Even if they floated to the top, the rising water would have inundated the entire tunnel and that would have been too far for them to get out without oxygen. This chamber is a blind, a false route."

"That means we truly *have* reached a dead end."

"Maybe not. Let's go back into the tunnel."

We hitched up the rope and made our way back up the tunnel

until we reached one of the cavities we'd noticed before. It proved to be only a hollow space created when a fissure caved in. The second opening we came across was different, an empty space extending inward at least six feet before it appeared to bend. When I ventured into it and shone the light around the bend, another flight of steps appeared.

I had a chance at that point to tell the other two it held nothing of interest. The foreboding I'd felt hadn't left me since we climbed into the tunnel, and here it was greatly magnified. Deep in my bones I knew we were not meant to see what lay ahead. At the same time, the pull to go on was almost irresistible. I made up my mind to tell Shaheen I could see nothing here, that this route too was blocked. But it was too late. He appeared at my shoulder and shone his light on the stairs.

"You've found another entrance," he said. "Let's get in there."

I knew he'd go in without me anyway so I hoisted myself into the gap and swung my legs down to touch the top of the stairs, which ended at another gate, this one with doors. *Doors* was a misnomer. Although bronze hinges held some of the organic material in place, the doors were barely more than deteriorated strips of wood with a prominent gap torn through the middle. Niches in the walls surrounding the gate held fired-clay cones.

"The Mesopotamian version of a lantern. These would have been filled with oil and set alight," I said to Shaheen as he squeezed through the gap.

Some of the wood splinters from the ruined door fell away in a puff of dry wood dust, releasing a faint scent of cedar. "Another set of stairs here," he said. A minute or so later he exclaimed, "What do you know!"

When I reached him, the cause of his excitement was plain. At his feet were a couple of discarded plastic water bottles and energy bar wrappers.

Shaheen pointed to them. "Army issue. Loretti and Hill were here. No question." Ben, who'd come up from behind, voiced his agreement.

A cloud of black flies hovered around me as we descended the stairway. They seemed to have materialized out of thin air and hung persistently near my head even though I waved my hand around to bat them away. I suddenly felt overcome with apprehension, much more acutely this time. Aboveground I could dismiss the underworld gods as relics of a primitive age. Quaint emblems of the past. In this dim warren the powerful mythic realities felt overwhelming. We'd broken into territory that ancient people held sacred and also greatly feared. Who was I to ignore their wisdom? The warnings about what lay ahead swung back to me with an alarming ferocity.

The thrill of discovery had left me. I felt gripped by sober second thought and instinctively recoiled at the thought of going any farther. We had no business being here. I knew that from the moment we started digging. Too late for misgivings. Shaheen had already crossed the threshold of the first gate and had a mission to find the source of the stone weight. He had the instincts and tenacity of a pit bull and backing off wasn't in his vocabulary. Whatever lay ahead, I wouldn't abandon him.

Forty-Eight

It was a considerable surprise, then, when Shaheen instructed us to wait. The three of us crouched together, poised at the top of the flight of stairs. If we were going in, despite my apprehension, I wanted to get it over with. The suits were hot and uncomfortable; the helmets made it tough to breathe. My throat ached. I couldn't understand Shaheen's reluctance.

"Why are we stopping?"

"Waiting for reinforcements," he replied. "This is the real thing and I don't think three of us is enough. John, why don't you get ahead of me? Your knowledge of these old sites is much better than mine."

We changed positions. In hindsight, perhaps I let false pride obscure what should have been obvious. Even when I heard the rustle of someone making his way toward us, I didn't suspect a thing. There had been signs, though, and I'd been oblivious to them. Shaheen had spoken into the intercom system right after we left the false chamber and I couldn't figure out why I didn't hear what he said. He must have had a second line of communication, closed off to me.

Another sign. Shaheen's reluctance to go the official route, not using military personnel to stand guard while we explored the site. And who were Ali, Ben, and the other contractor, really? I had only Shaheen's word for it that they were on America's side. Shaheen's insistence on taking me to Iraq when he could have called on any number of archaeological experts for this expedition was another red flag. Now I knew why.

A man made his way toward us and edged through the opening. He was suited and booted like us. When he lifted his head my body went rigid with shock. Mancini.

Shaheen had his pistol out, aimed at me. His voice sounded harsh through the intercom. "I'm a good shot even from much farther away. And *my* bullets will work."

"You bastard," I raged. "You're a total scum. A fucking traitor. Shoot that thing off in here you'll just bury us all."

His tinny laugh sailed through the speaker. I couldn't hear Mancini but saw his sly smile through the Plexiglas plate of his helmet.

"They're hollow points. They'll cut up your insides so bad it will look like someone put them in a blender. They won't leave your body, so no impact on the surrounding walls. Don't put it to the test. Get going. You're our front man in case there're problems ahead."

"Forget it. I'm not moving."

He tightened his fingers around the grip. "You've got about ten seconds."

He calculated I'd be too unnerved by the sight of his gun to try anything so I took him by surprise when I bashed him in the chest with my jacklight. I tried to knock his gun aside with my right arm, but I was up against all his military training. He deflected the blow and jammed the gun barrel into my neck. "You get one stupid move, not two. Move it."

The only hope I had was time. If I slowed down and stayed alert as we descended the stairs, there was a minuscule chance some opportunity would present itself, another cavity perhaps, or a new branch I could run into. I clammed up and moved at a snail's pace toward the first entrance.

This flight of stairs differed dramatically from the one above. It had the same polished brick on the floor and roof as in the false chamber but the walls were plastered, probably over a similar type of brick. Most of the frescoes here were intact, startling and stunningly well executed—frightening hybrids, chimeras the Greeks had called them. Vulture-headed lions with claws extended; fish bodies with human heads and feet; thick, coiled snakes. They were intended as warnings. Altogether too late for me.

The frame of the first gate had been made of wood. The second was constructed of stone. Half of the set of doors had been ripped clean away. The other side remained intact. Shaheen pointed at the floor and I saw a circular stone door jamb, shaped to allow it to pivot easily. The presence of this type of door indicated a high-status structure. An ancient bronze bolt dangled on the other side. Debris fell in a trail down the next flight of steps.

"Who would have destroyed these doors?" Shaheen asked. "Loretti and Hill?"

"Unlikely. A thick layer of dust has accumulated under the intact door," I said tersely.

Mancini played his light over the third flight of stairs.

"We must be almost fifty feet underground now," Shaheen said. "How much farther do you think will this go on?"

"Not until we reach hell, where you belong. If you're counting, we'll probably pass through seven gates."

Just as I predicted, we entered three more gates, one finished in copper, green with age, and one of bronze. What remained of the fifth was black with tarnish, which meant it had been faced with silver. The flies stayed with us all the way, swarming around our heads, searching for a way to penetrate our suit fabric and nest in our eyes and ears. As we made our way down, my head cleared somewhat and I kept a close eye out for tunnels that might have been excavated off to the side. I couldn't see so much as an alcove, nor any culverts to drain away water flow.

It was extremely dry. No sign of water runoff or drips from the ceiling. In ancient times, this close to the canal and with periodic, if slight, rainfalls, there would have been a good deal of moisture underground. The early builders must have constructed the tunnel we'd first shimmied through to drain water away from the site much closer to the surface. The fact that it was so dry now meant their engineering still operated effectively.

Each foot we dropped, a greater and greater pressure descended on me. The murky surroundings and progression of ominous chimeras covering the walls added to my fear. I picked up the tones of a flute again, very faintly. Mesmerizing music with all the joy stripped out of it. Each step I took felt blacker and I knew I was indeed on a one-way road. There was no way I was getting out. Shaheen would execute me once we reached the end, of that much I was certain. His betrayal cut me so deeply I could still barely comprehend it.

Shaheen faced life-threatening conditions all the time. If you confronted your fears every day on your job, you found a way to cope. He seemed able to meet every setback or precarious situation with some wisecrack as if he were indestructible and the sheer force of his personality would see him through. And remembering what he'd endured growing up, I thought he wasn't far wrong. You could either take life on the chin or be swamped by it. Early on, he'd chosen the former.

His ability to stare down adversity had also warped his human side. There were only so many times you could kill, even to survive, before it permanently altered your soul. Mancini had obviously found a way to get through to him.

At the seventh gate the stairs bottomed out to a flat, square platform. Here, small polychrome terracotta cones had been applied to the gateway wall to produce remarkable geometric mosaic designs, and the gateway doors, completely intact, stopped even my three opponents in their tracks. The doors were covered with sheets of hammered gold.

On the right-hand wall, early craftsmen had painted an image of a winged demon, Namtar, guardian of the gate to the throne room I was sure lay just beyond the doors. Ben set his jacklight on the floor and in the odd configuration of light, the demon's form appeared to move. Mancini motioned to Shaheen. In a recess below the image of Namtar sat a collection of around two dozen stone rings identical to the weight Alessio had stolen from Renwick.

Mancini bent down and scrutinized them. He glanced up at Shaheen and said something on their private communication channel.

This was where the scientists had found the pathogen, contained within the ancient collection of spindle whorls. I hoped the fungus was still firmly locked inside them.

Shaheen ordered me to sit with my back against the wall. I refused. What difference did it make? I had little time left anyway. In my throat, I could feel my heart beating raggedly. They planned to leave my body here, where it would never be found.

"Load them up and for God's sake let's get out of here," Shaheen said to Ben without taking his eyes off me. Ben shrugged off his backpack and unzipped the flap. Pulling on an extra pair of gloves, he crouched down and began dumping the weights into a polyethylene bag inside the pack.

Mancini went over to the doors and ran his hands across the gold surface. He put his head against one of the panels. I imagined he was hearing the same music I could detect, barely audible through my helmet.

While Mancini's attention was distracted by the doors, Shaheen motioned with his gun again for me to get down. The hell with that. I'd run out of options, I knew, but I could still run for it. I eyed the opening we'd just come through and tried to gauge whether I could sprint up the stairs before Shaheen fired off a round. The fear curdling my gut told me otherwise.

Shaheen's eyes shifted. Almost as if he were directing me toward the stairs. Engrossed in his examination of the doors, Mancini had his back to us. In a moment of blinding joy, I understood.

It was not me he planned to execute.

I crept over to the stairway and Shaheen gave me a slight nod.

Still oblivious, Mancini pressed against the doors. The thin melody of pipes suddenly swelled to a deafening wail. Ben dropped his knapsack and stared at Mancini in alarm. Mancini put his palms flat against the doors and pushed with all his might. There was a loud click. He braced his shoulder to the golden surfaces and shoved again.

The doors burst open like plywood shutters breached in a hurricane.

Forty-Nine

Mancini's light radiated off a huge room, every surface a shimmering, translucent blue. A blue so iridescent it mimicked the shafts of sunlight underneath a tropical sea. Every part of the interior—floor, walls, ceiling—was fashioned from sheets of the royal gemstone, lapis lazuli.

Against the back wall were two immense thrones of inlaid ivory and hammered gold. They were reflected, gold on blue, in the mirror-like walls and floor. On the wall behind the thrones mosaic tiles had been used to create the life-size image of a white horse.

In the midst of this splendor, the protracted disintegration of thousands of dead creatures stunned us into silence. Cruel hooks hung from the ceiling and on some of these rib cages still swung, the cartilage having dried and stuck like glue. The rest of the bones, long ago detached, had fallen to the floor. They'd been severely damaged—skulls flattened, long bones snapped in half, others crushed beyond recognition. They lay in cascading heaps reflected in the ceiling and blue walls rising above them. We stared at the sight. Khalid`s haunting reference to the jinn, the desert demon who feasted on rotting flesh, came back to me.

Mancini and Ben ventured through the doors and then halted as if they'd hit an invisible wall. Shaheen raised his gun again but dropped it and put his hands to his head. Mancini tore off his breathing mask and flailed his hands as if to ward off some threat. His voice broke and I realized he was crying. Ben ripped his mask off, jammed his hands over his ears, and screamed.

A shadow grew on the back wall, not phantom gray but deep maroon, the color of a spreading bloodstain. Amorphous at first, the shadow enlarged and split into two. The shapes began to take form.

One of them grew an abbreviated snout that widened into a viper's head with dark red pits for nostrils. Its body took on the thick muscular form of a predator; wings sprouted from its shoulders and raptor's claws curled out from its back feet. It wagged its snake head back and forth, like a cobra hypnotizing its prey. The image of Nergal.

The other curved into the hour-glass shape of a woman with horns on her spiky head and talons for feet, the sharp killing tools of the owl: Ereshkigal.

The things had a ponderous, dull quality and appeared to be without consciousness as we would understand it. Primordial figures from a time much deeper in history, before humans took their first great journey from Africa to Arabia.

None of the other men moved, either overcome by extreme fear or locked into paralysis as I'd been in my struggles with Alessio. But as if I had passed through Hades and come out the other side, the apparitions hadn't affected me.

The shadow forms began to advance sluggishly, like newborn animals taking their first wobbly steps. The viper head raised and locked eyes with me. I turned away from its gaze and caught

Shaheen just as he began to topple over. Wrapping my arms around his torso, I hauled him back across the threshold. The shadow figures reached Ben and Mancini and tore away at their white suits. The viper's head slowly lowered onto Mancini's neck.

I knew fear would soon paralyze me, whether or not the spirits embraced me too. Shaheen's body, although thin, was dead weight and I felt like I was heaving a ten-ton truck up each riser. My mind kept focusing on what was coming behind me. I tried to shut those thoughts down, summoning every ounce of my strength to drag him up to the sixth gateway. If being hauled over the mud bricks hurt him he didn't react. I screamed his name but got no response. He'd pulled off his helmet in the throne room and the flies clustered around his face and neck. I swatted them with my free hand. They swarmed again the second I took my hand away.

Dragging him slowed me down too much. I propped him up against the wall and maneuvered his body over my shoulder like a sack of coal. My ascent was faster but my heart beat so hard with the effort I thought it would burst. I could still make my left arm work—for how long I didn't know as it was starting to go numb. My breath came in huge gasps and whatever light spilled out from the sacred chamber had all but disappeared. I had to feel my way up the steps in blackness.

As I passed the fifth gate and started the next climb I stumbled and lost my footing. Shaheen slid from my grasp and fell. Precious minutes slipped away as I painstakingly shifted him into a sitting position against the wall and hauled him over my shoulder again. I broke out into a cold sweat. I didn't see how I could make it to the top. And yet I made it through the next two gates.

I'd just reached the second gate when I felt what seemed like a gentle tug, as if Shaheen was being pulled off me. I staggered backward. If I'd been on the stairs I would have fallen again. The flies flew off Shaheen's face in a furious buzz.

Despite my heavy burden I bent and squeezed through the opening in the door and labored toward the next steps. The sense of pulling, of some powerful force reaching for Shaheen, grew stronger. At the same time I felt faint. It took all my strength to maintain my balance. My climb slowed almost to a crawl. I was weakening quickly and there was nothing I could do about it.

A realization flashed through me. The force I'd felt wasn't pulling Shaheen away; rather, it was invasive, flooding into him, *consuming* him. His body convulsed. I threw him through the next door.

The convulsions that wracked his body stopped while leaving his whole body rigid. He groaned. One step at a time now. Each one was agony. At the head of the stair we'd left a light behind to show the way and I could finally see the last gate. Tantalizingly close. But I was no match for the hungry force behind me. Deep pressure like a tidal wave bearing down forced me to stop.

I took Shaheen's second gun and crawled up the remaining steps. As I reached the door I turned and aimed high, past Shaheen, firing off a round. I prayed Ali would somehow hear it and that the earthen roof over the stair would suffer most of the damage, not the tunnel ahead of us. The shots reverberated in the enclosed space as if the blast had gone off inside my head. Mud brick and clods of earth split from the staircase roof, tumbling into the gap. I scrambled back down and threw myself on top of Shaheen, holding my breath.

The answer came moments later. Ali called out. I could hear him only faintly because I still had my helmet on. Soon he came into view. He took one look at Shaheen and grasped him under his arms. With him pulling and me pushing we got Shaheen through the gap and into the tunnel. My ear caught the faint sound of water rushing somewhere below.

By the time we reached the top, Shaheen was coming around. I told Ali that Mancini and Ben were dead. Light rain sprinkled down as we emerged from the tunnel. Soldiers waited for us topside, summoned by Ali as soon as Mancini had entered the tunnel. A Black Hawk stood by. Shaheen's eyes flickered open when he felt the cool drops on his face. He managed a few words and tried to give me the high sign. He said he wanted to walk on his own but a couple of the soldiers picked him up and rushed him into the helicopter. The rain had turned the site to rusty muck. The helicopter rose, its rotors deafening, whipping mud across the mound.

Ali, the older contractor Shaheen had brought with us, and I went back to the tunnel entrance and kicked the chunks of hardened earth we'd removed into the hole to hide the entrance. We raced back to the Jeep. The remaining soldiers commandeered the Humvee, as well as the car and driver Mancini came with, and drove off.

Ali took me back to Baghdad in the Jeep. It was all I could do to make it to my hotel. I felt as if I had nearly lost my life, not Shaheen. I got a carafe of strong coffee from the bar and struggled up to my room. Downing some painkillers, I collapsed onto the bed.

What happened in the pit of that seven-gated hell had to be a hallucination. I'd never experienced a hallucination before, let alone a *collective* one. Yet I knew extreme fear could do strange things to the mind. All kinds of dangerous gases built up in sealed underground spaces. I'd heard of hydrogen sulfide and other chemicals being released. Had Mancini and Ben succumbed to something like that? No doubt I was suffering their delayed effects too.

The mild symptoms I'd first noticed in Rome had worsened. My throat felt like someone had scraped a razor over it. I couldn't clear my lungs. My skin was red and felt tight all over my body, as if it were somehow in the process of shrinking. Red welts now covered my neck and there was no feeling in my arm.

Those spores must have infected me. They were microscopic and would have been no more noticeable than grains of dust or lint. Had they been contained within the book? Did that explain why it had been kept untouched in that cedar box over all those centuries—because its originators knew it carried a contamination? Or had some toxic agent from the journey into the underworld condemned me? It was impossible to tell.

Fifty

December 8, 2003
Baghdad, Iraq

By the time Ali returned to pick me up at the hotel I couldn't walk a straight line.

Shaheen, remarkably recovered, met us outside the Green Zone and ushered me in. We pulled up in front of the Ibn Sina hospital, a prestigious treatment facility for the wealthy in Hussein's day, now a trauma center for U.S. personnel and the occasional Iraqi civilian. The gray-veined white marble floors and teak reception desk at the emerg entrance told of its luxurious history. On a back wall hung a huge American flag, bulletin boards, and army banners. Shaheen indicated a set of doors. We pushed through them to a corridor and passed a room where medics furiously worked on a soldier whose uniform had turned to bloody shreds. His bloated skin was black with severe burns. I turned my eyes away and kept them focused on the corridor after that. Shaheen helped me into the exam room.

The doctor showed up not long after. He gave me a careful going-over before sending me for X-rays and blood work. Shaheen told me he couldn't stay and Ali would drive me back to the hotel afterward. An hour or so later the doctor returned. His first words weren't exactly encouraging.

"Do you have medical insurance? You won't be charged for any limited treatment I give you now but you need to get home immediately. To start with, how did you get that bruising on your back?"

I wasn't about to tell him about the shooting in Ghent. "I had a fall."

He frowned and looked up at the ceiling lights then walked over to the wall and flicked the switch on and off.

"That's funny," he said. "It seems dim in here. Our generators are supposed to be working full tilt." He shook his head. "You've given me quite a bit to work with. A scar on your thigh that appears to have been professionally stitched. Broken ribs, although they've healed nicely."

"Those were from before; I'm not worried about them. I had a car accident."

"How long ago?"

"Last summer."

"I see. Are you a drinker, sir? You've got a lot of injuries for a man your age."

"Not the way you mean."

He touched my jaw and gently turned my head. "How did you get the cut on your scalp?"

"A bar fight. I intervened to help someone."

Disbelief was written all over his face. He smirked. "I've treated combat soldiers with less damage. Whatever your lifestyle is I suggest you switch and take up something safer like skydiving or free solo rock climbing."

"What's that?"

"Skittering up the side of a mountain without a rope."

"Doesn't sound too enticing."

"The good news is you're not quite ready for the grave. The bruising on your back may look nasty. You'll see it heal soon enough. I'm more concerned about long-term damage to your arm. You've hurt it recently, causing a hairline fracture in the ulna—that's your arm bone—and ligament injuries. It's been left unattended and now the bone's infected. There's nerve damage. It could turn out to be permanent."

I remembered the crack Alessio gave me with his cane when we wrestled in the Thames.

"You've also acquired a severe respiratory infection. It's bacterial so we can treat it with antibiotics." He hesitated as if searching for the right words. "There's something else we *can't* explain. An anomaly in your blood work." *Anomaly* was one of those words medical people used to cloak the ones that really got you scared.

"You mean a problem with my blood cells—like leukemia or something?"

"No. Your white blood cell count is a little elevated yet consistent with a respiratory infection. It may be genetic. I don't know what to make of it." He checked the medical history sheet I'd filled out. "You left the section about your parents blank. Are they both still alive?"

"No. They died in a mining accident in Turkey. I was cared for by my older brother. Don't know much about my birth parents and nothing about their medical history."

"Is your brother still alive?"

"Half brother—and no. He died in an accident. Was very healthy before that."

"That's unfortunate. Quite frankly I've never seen anything like it before. Has your doctor in New York told you about this previously? Mentioned any kind of inherited disorder?"

"Not that I'm aware of. Could it affect me in the future?"

"There's a good chance it will. Is it ultimately life-threatening? It might be but I couldn't tell you that. I'm a trauma specialist. You need a hematologist. It requires a much more thorough investigation. And you must get that arm taken care of. I can patch you up for now. As soon as you get home you need to seek out medical attention."

He shot me full of antibiotics, gave me Prednisone for my skin, and fitted my arm with a temporary sling. I walked out the hospital door at ten that evening with two new reasons for alarm: the dimming lights that seemed to follow me around and my blood problem.

I explained the shadow away by thinking that likely it *was* just a poor electric connection. And New York had the best specialists in the world; they could treat my blood problem. Still, the doctor's remarks stirred up my fears about having been contaminated and I couldn't get it out of my mind.

Ali took me back to the hotel, where the heavy-duty sedative the doctor gave me knocked me out for the next twelve hours. The next morning I took a hot shower and downed a jug of coffee. The drugs sat uncomfortably on my stomach. I managed to swallow some bread anyway and felt well enough to think about the immediate future. It became a lot clearer when my phone rang and a familiar voice came on the line.

"Congratulations, you're not dead yet. I hear the doctor said you'd live to see another day."

"Where are you, Shaheen?"

"Decided to revisit hell. A very quaint place when all's said and done."

"Get off it."

His laugh came through loud and clear. "You need have no fears about anyone else getting in there."

"You have it protected? Good."

"The marines signed it as a contaminated site. They stationed a permanent guard. No more looting; they won't even let the antiquities people in. A lot of their work was accomplished before they even got there. You won't believe what happened."

"Try me."

"The whole thing, the tunnel, everything, ended up completely submerged in water. Water ran out the entrance hole as if a spring or something suddenly popped up. The flow is slowing now but it washed all the way down to that depression we parked in and turned everything into a river of mud. Thanks to the powers that be it held off until we got outta there." His voice dropped. "That meant we couldn't retrieve the bodies."

The old canal, still in use, was a couple of miles away from the site. I couldn't imagine how there would be any connection to it. Was it groundwater then? I thought about the ancient myth how disturbing the balance of the world by entering the god's domain would release Apsu, the great sea Mesopotamians believed lay underneath the earth's thin crust. The effect of that much water suddenly flowing through a centuries-old dry environment would cause numerous cave-ins. The mud filling the tunnel would eventually harden like concrete, a next-to-impossible task to excavate.

Mancini had ended up buried in hell beside the image of the Babylonian white horse, just as Alessio predicted. And the stone weights along with him. A strange ending to the tale.

"Leonard Best is none too happy about my failure to retrieve the stone spindle whorls. Lots of black marks all over my record now."

"What ever happened to the one Loretti and Hill found?" I asked.

"Loretti's wife told the doctor before she died. Once her husband opened it, he had enough presence of mind to put it in a secure container. After he got sick, his wife went through his things and found it. She didn't tell the authorities. She'd read news stories about people being charged for stealing relics from Iraq and was afraid Loretti would be accused of theft. They have an old oil furnace in their house, so she threw the spindle whorl into the firebox. That destroyed all the spores and reduced the soft stone to ash."

I was tempted to ask whether Shaheen really would have shot Mancini, but I knew in my heart he would have.

"Why did Mancini want the weights so badly?" I asked instead.

"A joint project he planned with a South African biochemical firm. Those fungal spores were highly virulent and, as opposed to other toxins like anthrax, there's no effective treatment. Their real value is simplicity. The main challenge with current biological weapons is effective disbursement. In contrast, the fungus easily seeds itself. It would spread like crazy in moist areas, just like it did in Babylon's wet flax fields."

"Then people would flee to drier regions where the fungus couldn't survive."

"You're right, a desert would be safe. Anywhere that supported agriculture and livestock would be affected by it. There'd be huge food shortages."

Mancini was a harsh customer. Still, I found it hard to imagine how someone even as amoral as he could contemplate a scheme that monstrous. He'd actually become a demon of the human variety. "Didn't you tell me the fungus can be found on the West Coast? Why not just use that?"

"Extremely difficult to collect. You'd have to destroy forests and sift through thousands of acres of soil to get enough. On top of that the spores hidden in the stone weights are way more lethal."

"Why wait so long to ... confront Mancini? You'd have been able to throw away the key on him after everything he admitted to you."

"I tried and got stopped. A man like that, he had super-powerful connections. You don't funnel money out of the country without the right people turning a blind eye. I was told to back off in no uncertain terms."

"What about Dina?"

"We put her in a safe house. Not in Italy. After a couple of days she left. Vanished into thin air. We haven't heard from her since." Shaheen asked me to hold for a minute. I could hear him talking to someone in the background. He came back on the line. "Looks like I hafta run."

"Do you get leave? Maybe we could hook up in NYC."

"They owe me time off, ten times over. So soon, God willing. Keep a Coors cold for me for when I'm back in the motherland."

I promised to do just that. We clicked off.

Was the idea of enclosing the spores within spindle whorls where they'd be kept perfectly dry and preserved an early attempt to fashion a crude biological weapon? Had the Babylonians actually used them against their enemies? That will never be known. How ironic that our military, hunting for modern weapons of mass destruction, ended up finding ones some 2500 years old.

I never did hear back from Shaheen. A few months after I returned home I got a terse email from Ali to say Shaheen had been declared missing in action near Najaf. The news hit me hard. He'd seemed to me to be indestructible, to have the kind of spirit that burned too brightly to be quenched. Another good man the war chewed up and swallowed whole.

I stopped over in London on my way home. Sherrods had indeed fired Amy, as she predicted. She wrapped her arms around me when I told her about finding the last volume of the book in Baghdad.

My promise of financial help would allow her to stay in the city while she looked for another job.

Of Renwick, there remained a mystery never to be solved. Somehow he'd pieced together the whole story. Enough to point the two scientists toward Kutha. How he achieved that, I had no idea.

I retrieved my phone, the wooden box that once held Basile's book, and the gold coin from the safety deposit box. My intention was to see Tye Norris that afternoon and get an overnight flight back to New York. When I tried I couldn't reach him. That prompted me to contact Arthur Newhouse instead, who gave me the most surprising news.

The police had arrested Tye Norris for the murder of Charles Renwick. Norris had told the truth: Renwick's poor handling of the business and his expenditure of their remaining capital on Basile's book would likely leave them both bankrupt. What Norris neglected to mention was the provision in their business partnership leaving Renwick's share of the building to him. With London property values soaring, Norris stood to gain a small fortune. Newhouse related the terms of the business agreement to the police. In a phone tap they caught incriminating discussions between Norris and his wife, giving them enough grounds to conduct a second search of the print shop.

The book Norris described, intended to be the firm's crowning achievement and a tribute to Renwick—*The Pied Piper*—he'd completed in record time. The copies were snapped up because collectors knew it would be the firm's last book and for that reason its value was greatly enhanced.

Norris pointed out their paper digester when I visited the shop. Paper digesters employed powerful alkaloids to break down plant material. I remembered his sly reference to wanting to incorporate plants to mimic the natural elements in the meadow the piper led the children through. Along with the vegetation, the alkaloids would liquefy human tissue. Renwick's bones had been found in the paper digester, the huge copper vat of slurry that provided the base for the paper Norris made. While tests would be run, there was little doubt they'd found Renwick's skeleton because of its twisted spine.

So Norris, who seemed the gentlest of men, proved to possess a very macabre turn of mind.

And Renwick, who loved books, had in the end himself become one.

Fifty-One

December 23, 2003
New York

No matter how much I enjoyed trips abroad, I was always glad to get home. This time, reaching New York's terra firma felt like stepping onto hallowed ground. I saw the city with new eyes. The street life and the familiar shops, bars, and restaurants I frequented hummed with vitality. New York was more exciting than ever, almost exotic. I invited my neighbors over for drinks— no heavy conversations, just shooting the breeze. It was heaven.

To my great surprise a letter from Dina turned up in my mailbox several weeks later.

John,

I hope this letter finds you well. I haven't been able to find out for sure whether you're even back home. You must wonder what became of me, that is, if you still care to know. What I want to say more than anything is how terribly sorry I am for having misused you. While I cannot excuse my methods, I hope you will agree at least that the reasons for my actions were honorable. I use the plural—reasons—deliberately, for there are two: my children, Luna and Sol.

You'll recall I said that some time after the conte began his assaults on me he refused to allow me to attend school. In fact, I couldn't go back to school because by then I was pregnant, as it turned out with twins. Katharina was barren, which ignited her jealousy. Had I only needed to look after myself I would have tried to leave Lorenzo long ago, but once my children passed the stage of infancy he separated us, allowing me to visit with them only occasionally. He swore that if I tried to leave him I'd never see them again.

Shortly before I met you, word came to me the children were being cared for in Belgium by Katharina's housekeeper. This was the final spur I needed. Katharina was planning to take out her vengeance on them. As you know, I sold the book through Ewan volume by volume to raise the money I required. And that's when chance—or was it destiny?—brought you to my doorstep.

I could tell you saw through the reason I gave for wanting to recover the books after I'd sold them. I don't think you guessed why. I planned to use them to bargain with Lorenzo for my freedom and that of my children. A desperate and unrealistic hope, I know, yet I clung to it at the time.

I'm writing, also, to make a confession. Lying to others does not bother me overmuch, as long as it does no one else harm. Conversely, I think to lie about one's past plays with fate in a dangerous way. The truth is I have no memory of my early years before I entered the conte's household. This has preyed on my mind over the years and I can only conclude that he must have administered a drug that curdled my brain and banished my memories. I have much, therefore, in common with elderly people in the grip of senility. And

I think rather grimly when my time for that comes, it will seem a natural state of affairs.

Mancini made one generous gesture, perhaps the only one in his life. He acknowledged his natural children and left his estate to them. In the end, Alessio did not destroy the four volumes of Basile's anthology he repossessed. I retrieved them, enclosed once more within their golden covers, from that terrible den underneath the palazzo where you found me. As the children's trustee I am making a gift of them to you. You have earned much more, my friend. I hope you will accept them along with my apologies.

I write to you from Renard's home in France, where I now reside with Luna and Sol. When I arrived here I found the estate in disarray. Renard had dismissed his staff; the house was unkempt, quite unlike the light-filled splendor you and I beheld that first night. He was nowhere to be seen. I finally came upon him in the garden, sick at heart and ailing fearfully, convinced I'd never return.

I liked you far more than I ever let on and will miss you a great deal. If I had a more adventurous spirit, I'd be by your side now. You live in a different world. In my soul I'm European and I couldn't imagine living anywhere else. All my adult life has been spent under the yoke of Mancini's hard treatment. Renard understands what it is like to live with adversity and he offers us freedom from it. I don't know how long we'll stay here. For now, we're content.

Forgive me and wish me well ...
Dina

I folded the letter and slipped it into a compartment in my desk. It made sense to me now, all those times I'd wondered if she was keeping something from me. And what greater motivation could anyone have than protecting her children? I was glad she'd found some peace. I'd harbored the idea of seeking her out and persuading her to come home with me once I was settled back in New York. I felt sad to realize that dream would come to nothing.

A few weeks later a small carton arrived. Dina was as good as her word. It contained all four remaining volumes of *The Tale of Tales* enclosed within their golden covers. Together with the fifth one I already possessed, the book was complete. The authorization Dina provided along with the book also meant I could finally clear my name with Interpol and the London police.

I believed Dina's version of Mancini's abuse. On the subject of her origins, it was a different matter and I was inclined to agree with Katharina. Where Dina really came from was a mystery. Even before her letter arrived I'd reached this conclusion by reflecting on the facts she'd given about her parents: her mother, desperate for a baby, who'd died when her daughter was very young. Her distant father, a trader, bankrupt after losing his ships, had ended up exchanging a luxurious lifestyle to eke out a living on a poor farm. What were these but memories cut and pasted from fairy tales. To hide what? Had she really lost her memory, or was her background too painful for her to face?

Giambattista Basile's version of "Sleeping Beauty," called "The Sun, Moon and Talia," was the one tale Renwick avidly pursued. I read the story again. Life imitates art far more than art imitates life—wasn't that the saying? Basile's tale told of a lord's daughter, Talia, who had been raped by a nobleman during her long sleep. Twins were born as a result of the rape. When she woke, the king began a long liaison with her. I remembered de Ribera's illustration, the one of the woman being forced into a fire I'd seen when I first opened the book. In Basile's story the lord's angry wife threatened to kill the children and feed their remains to her husband. She was burnt in an oven in retribution. Although earlier versions of the tale influenced Basile, he brought his own rich imagination to it. It began thus:

> There once was a great lord who, on the birth of a daughter—to whom he gave the name Talia—commanded all the wise men and seers in the kingdom to come and tell him what her future would be. These wise men, after many consultations, came to the conclusion that she would be exposed to great danger from a small splinter in some flax. Thereupon the King, to prevent any unfortunate accident, commanded that no flax or hemp or any similar material should ever come into his house.
>
> One day when Talia was grown up she was standing by the window and saw an old woman pass who was spinning. Talia had never seen a distaff and spindle, and was therefore delighted with the dancing of the spindle. Prompted by her curiosity, she had the old woman brought up to her, and taking the distaff in her hand, began to draw out the thread; but unfortunately a splinter in the hemp got under her fingernail, and she immediately fell dead upon the ground. At this terrible catastrophe the old woman fled from the room, rushing precipitously down the stairs. The stricken father, after having paid for this bucketful of sour wine with a barrelful of tears, left the dead Talia seated on a velvet chair under an embroidered canopy in the palace, which was in the middle of a wood. Then he locked the door and left forever the house which had brought him such evil fortune, so that he might entirely obliterate the memory of his sorrow and suffering.

Despite Alessio's dismay about his story being distorted by later versions, I learned that Basile, too, had based his Sleeping Beauty on a much earlier narrative found in a medieval French anthology: *Perceforest,* and its story of a knight, Troilus, who raped Zelladine after she fell into a deep sleep.

The grain of truth in all the tales was clear. A warning about a deadly contagion, a fungus that grew in the moist flax fields of Mesopotamia, was first embedded in a myth by the Mesopotamians. That myth was the legend of Ishtar, who died from disease inflicted upon her by her sister, a metaphor for the experience of a real plague.

The story of a young, desirable woman struck down through the jealousy of an older woman, her apparent death, and her resurrection at the hands of a male consort had a long history. It traveled through human imagination from the Mesopotamian goddess to Persia and Egypt and on to the Greek legends of Eros and Psyche. The story was transformed again by Europeans: Basile's Talia, Perrault's Aurora, and the Grimms' Briar Rose. It had been duplicated in folk tales around the world. In each epoch the tale changed according to the milieu and imagination of the teller.

Norris said the four stories that especially interested Renwick could be interpreted as plague tales. I realized they could also be seen as tales of necromancy. In each case, despair over the loss of loved ones ran deep enough to inspire an obsession with their resurrection.

It hadn't escaped me that several of those stories mirrored my own experience, as if some unseen force had pulled me inside the pages of Basile's book. The characters I'd read about since I opened the first pages of that remarkable book seemed to have stepped out of fiction into real life. Alessio believed the tales had been stolen. Not just by the actions of Mancini or Dina, but in a larger metaphorical sense. Perhaps, though, the great tales of other ages circulate through the generations just as our ancestors' genes swim within our blood.

I sold the second, third, and fourth volumes to compensate Amy and Naso and Renwick's estate. I held on to the first and the last volumes—days one and five in Basile's anthology—along with de Ribera's brilliant illustrations. I couldn't part with those.

Fifty-Two

Over the last six months I'd been through two nerve-shattering experiences. Because of them, my business was hanging by a thread. I seriously considered leaving the profession altogether. The lure of the East was seductive but it had certainly taken its toll. For as long as I could remember I'd emulated my brother, Samuel. My only thought had been to walk in his footsteps. I knew now it was time to leave his influence behind. Hunting for rare books might be a new horizon for me, one I wanted to continue to pursue.

While I grappled with my future, my sleep was frequently disturbed. The episodes of immobility continued. Awakening at night with a rush of panic, I couldn't move a muscle for several long minutes. This occurred more and more often. It was as if I'd internalized the terrible violence I'd witnessed over a few short weeks and the war was still going on inside me. While I hoped this would dissipate over time, my fears finally drove me back to the doctors.

Months of blood tests to identify the anomaly followed. I finally called a halt to them when a specialist in internal medicine tried to coax me into a formal clinical study. After all that effort they hadn't been able to provide a diagnosis of any more merit than the one the trauma doctor in Baghdad gave me. If I wanted answers about my genetic heritage I'd have to begin my own exploration.

Just before Christmas I took Evelyn on an outing to a location in Central Park we loved to visit when I was young. We'd come from viewing the Fifth Avenue Christmas store windows, which always delighted her. Entering through the Lehman Gates I looked back and saw them superimposed black against a sapphire December sky, the immortal wild boy dancing beside his goats on the curled briar. Snowflakes sparkled like winter diamonds, reviving the feeling I'd always had as a youngster of entering a magical realm.

Evelyn sat in her wheelchair wrapped with a comfy blanket. She wore the down coat and warm gloves I'd given her last Christmas. Her arthritis, always worse in winter, bothered her less that day. At the children's zoo we watched a handler reach into his pouch and throw some fish into the air. Two seals, their bodies wriggling like shiny black rubber tubes, leapt out of their pool. Fish flashed silver and disappeared down their throats. The seals barked their approval. Children pressed against the pool's railing, laughing and clapping, their breath clouding in the frosty air.

My past experience at Nineveh and the recent one at Kutha taught me things are never what they seem on the surface. Friends became enemies and fate turned them into friends once more. Alessio and Shaheen were antagonists who became allies. Evelyn had been different, steadfast from the time I was a boy. I felt immeasurably grateful and lucky to have her in my life. And as to the future, I was certain of only one thing—I would discover the true story of my origins, no matter what the consequences.

As Evelyn and I sat in companionable silence enjoying the winter park, my thoughts slipped back to what had gone before. Rational explanations existed for everything. I was convinced Alessio was a descendant of Giambattista Basile and also a skilled illusionist. He'd likely suffered from mental delusions and talked himself into believing he was the long-dead author. I'd also put the terrors of Nergal and Ereshkigal's underworld domain behind me, believing what occurred to be the result of a toxic gas unleashed when Mancini burst open the doors.

Only one thing bothered me that I couldn't explain. If a poisonous vapor felled three men, two of whom were fit and used to the rigors of war, why not me? As we fled the underworld chamber, I sensed Shaheen being consumed while he was unconscious, somehow taken over. Yet he recovered quickly. Had it really been Shaheen who was attacked—or me?

I'd locked away at the back of my mind the memory of the look in the viper's eyes right before I dragged Shaheen away. I'd done so because to confront the truth was too disturbing. The viper's look now came flooding back with a vengeance. Not the cruel gaze of a hunter, nor the cold fixed stare of an animal closing in for a kill. No. More like an unspoken communication between two souls deeply entwined. It was a look of *recognition*.

Notes

To set the record straight, no printer's copy of Giambattista Basile's *The Tale of Tales* exists, to my knowledge. Nor is there any evidence I know of to suggest that José de Ribera illustrated Basile's book.

Part One Opener
Of such great powers or beings there may be conceivably a survival.
> Opening quotation by Algernon Blackwood in "The Call of Cthulhu" by H.P. Lovecraft, first published in *Weird Tales,* February 1928.

Chapter Six
No life could be more unstable or fuller of anxiety.
> N.M. Penzer, editor, introduction to *The Pentamerone of Giambattista Basile,* translated by Benedetto Croce (New York: E.P. Dutton and Company, 1932), xxvi.

You serve now, you serve later … and get out!
> Giambattista Basile, in the Introduction to *Giambattista Basile's Tale of Tales, or Entertainment for the Little Ones,* translated by Nancy L. Canepa (Detroit, Michigan: Wayne State University Press, 2007), 6.

Chapter Thirteen

In the year 1284, on the days of John and Paul ... Koppen Mountain.
> From the Lueneburg Manuscript, 1430–1450, as shown on the
> website *The Legend and the History of the Pied Piper of Hameln,*
> www.triune.de/legend

Externally the body was not very hot to the touch ... than stark naked.
> Thucydides' (455–411 B.C.) account of the Plague of Athens
> from the website *Thucydides 2.47-55: The Plague,* www.perseus.
> mpiwg-berlin.mpg.de/GreekScience/Thuc.+2.47-55.html

Chapter Fifteen

*Ah! My beautiful Naples, behold I am leaving you ... windows sugar
cakes.* N.M. Penzer, editor, introduction to *The Pentamerone of
Giambattista Basile,* translated by Benedetto Croce (New York:
E.P. Dutton and Company, 1932), xxii.

Chapter Twenty

There was once upon a time ... the rose-leaf that she had swallowed.
> Giambattista Basile, "The Young Slave" (Day 2, Tale 8), N.M.
> Penzer, editor, *The Pentamerone of Giambattista Basile,* translated
> by Benedetto Croce (New York: E.P. Dutton and Company,
> 1932), 192.

Heaven rains favors on us when we least expect it.
> Giambattista Basile, "The Young Slave" (Day 2, Tale 8),
> N.M. Penzer, editor, *The Pentamerone of Giambattista Basile,*
> translated by Benedetto Croce (New York: E.P. Dutton and
> Company, 1932), 195.

There she saw the young girl ... asleep.
> Giambattista Basile, "The Young Slave" (Day 2, Tale 8),
> N.M. Penzer, editor, *The Pentamerone of Giambattista Basile,*
> translated by Benedetto Croce (New York: E.P. Dutton and
> Company, 1932), 193.

Chapter Twenty-Two

Feast with that sprig of parsley at the banquet of love.

> Giovan Battista Basile, in N.M. Penzer, editor, *The Pentamerone of Giambattista Basile,* Vol. 2, translated by Benedetto Croce (New York: E.P. Dutton and Company, 1932).

Chapter Thirty-Six

For the scourges of the conflagration ... Giovan Battista Basile.

> N.M. Penzer, editor, introduction to *The Pentamerone of Giambattista Basile,* translated by Benedetto Croce (New York: E.P. Dutton and Company, 1932), xxx.

Part Three Opener

To the land of no return, the land of darkness ... dust has gathered.

> Mesopotamian myth, "The Descent of the Goddess Ishtar into the Lower World," in Morris Jastrow, *The Civilization of Babylon and Assyria* (Philadelphia and London: J.B. Lippincott Company, 1915).

Chapter Thirty-Eight

The cruel man is his own executioner.

> Giovan Battista Basile, in N.M. Penzer, editor, *The Pentamerone of Giambattista Basile,* Vol. 2, translated by Benedetto Croce (New York: E.P. Dutton and Company, 1932), 129.

Chapter Thirty-Nine

Noctes atque dies patet atri ianua ditis.

> Virgil, *The Aeneid,* Book 6, line 127, in J.B. Greenough, editor, *Bucolics, Aeneid and Georgics of Vergil* (Boston: Ginn & Co., 1900).

Chapter Forty-Six

Her breasts sagged, she had nails ... like leeks.

> "Inanna's Descent to the Nether World," *The Electronic Text Corpus of Sumerian Literature,* Oxford University, 2001, http:// etcsl.orinst.ox.ac.uk/section1/tr141.htm

Chapter Fifty-One

There once was a great lord ... of his sorrow and suffering.

> Giambattista Basile, "Sun, Moon and Talia" (Day 5, Tale 5), N.M. Penzer, editor, *The Pentamerone of Giambattista Basile,* translated by Benedetto Croce (New York: E.P. Dutton and Company, 1932), 130.

Bibliography

I wouldn't have been able to write *The Book of Stolen Tales* without the wealth of information provided by Nancy Canepa in *Giambattista Basile's The Tale of Tales, or Entertainment for Little Ones*. Her expert translation brings Basile's stories—lost treasures in themselves—brilliantly to the forefront. So, too, *The Pentamerone of Giambattista Basile,* edited by N.M. Penzer and based on the introduction and Italian translation by Benedetto Croce. Although a relatively rare book, it's well worth the search.

Books

Abbattutis, Gian Alessio. *Lo Cunto deli Cunti.* Vol. 1. Naples: Beltrano, 1637.

Beecher, Donald, editor, and Luigi Ballerini and Massimo Ciavollela, general editors. *The Pleasant Nights by Giovan Francesco Straparola.* Vols. 1 and 2. Toronto: University of Toronto Press, 2012.

Canepa, Nancy L. *Giambattista Basile's The Tale of Tales, or Entertainment for Little Ones.* Detroit, MI: Wayne State University Press, 2007.

Heiner, Heidi Anne, editor. *Sleeping Beauties: Sleeping Beauty and Snow White Tales from Around the World.* Nashville, TN: SurLaLune Press, 2010.

Lang, Andrew; illustrations by Henry Justice Ford. *The Yellow Fairy Book.* London: Longmans Green & Co., 1894.

Lyons, Jonathan. *The House of Wisdom: How the Arabs Transformed Western Civilization.* New York: Bloomsbury Press, 2009.

Penzer, N.M., editor; based on the introduction and translation by Benedetto Croce. *The Pentamerone of Giambattista Basile.* New York: E.P. Dutton and Company, 1932.

Peterson, Joseph H., editor and translator. *Grimorium Verum: A Handbook of Black Magic.* Scotts Valley, CA: CreateSpace, 2007.

Pullman, Phillip. *Fairy Tales from the Brothers Grimm: A New English Version.* New York: Viking, 2012.

Riverbend. *Baghdad Burning: Girl Blog from Iraq.* New York: The Feminist Press, 2005.

Articles and Websites

Allen, Christopher. "Into the Inferno of the Art of Francis Bacon," www.theaustralian.com.au/arts/review/into-the-inferno-of-the-art-of-francis-bacon/story-fn9n8gph-1226531228863, December 8, 2012.

al-Hadi, Laith. "Baghdad's al-Rashid Street—from Perfume and Music to Motor Oil and Mortars," *Iraq Updates,* September 3, 2011,www.iraqupdates.com/free-news/culture-tourism/baghdad's-al-rashid-street-from-perfume-and-music-to-motor-oil-and-mortars/2011-03-10#.UUhwhb-uGjo

"Al-Maidan Square—A Tale of Baghdad's Times," *Iraq Updates,* January 26, 2008, www.iraqupdates.com/free-news/culture-tourism/al-maidan-square-a-tale-of-baghdads-times/2008-01-26#.UUeNib-uGjo

"Alpilles, Provence," *French Moments,* 2012, www.frenchmoments.eu/?p=1836

Ashliman, D.L. "Sleeping Beauty," *Folklore and Mythology Electronic Texts*, May 5, 2009, www.pitt.edu/~dash/type0410.html

Ashliman, D.L. "Snow-White," *Folklore and Mythology Electronic Texts*, April 11, 2011, www.pitt.edu/~dash/type0709.html

"Babylon," *Global Security.org*, September 7, 2011, www.globalsecurity.org/military/world/iraq/babylon.htm

Barbot de Villeneuve, Gabrielle-Suzanne. "Beauty and the Beast," *Amalia*, n.d., www.maerchenlexikon.de/texte/te425C-007.htm

"Beautiful but Cursed Island of Gaiola," *Travelogue of an Armchair Traveller*, February 8, 2011, http://armchairtravelogue.blogspot.ca/2011/02/beautiful-but-cursed-island-of-gaiola.html

Biblioteca Nazionale di Napoli home page, 2013, www.bnnonline.it

Black, J.A., G. Cunningham, E. Fluckiger-Hawker, E. Robson, and G. Zólyomi. "Ningishzida's Journey to the Nether World: Translation," *The Electronic Text Corpus of Sumerian Literature*, Oxford, 1998–, http://etcsl.orinst.ox.ac.uk/section1/tr173.htm

Brothers Grimm, en.wikipedia.org/wiki/Brothers_Grimm

Cartwright, Garth. "Partying with the Gypsies in the Camargue," *The Guardian*, March 26, 2011, www.guardian.co.uk/travel/2011/mar/26/saintes-maires-gypsy-festival-camargue

"Castle of the Week: Gravensteen Castle, Ghent, Belgium," *Heraldic Times Blog*, July 26, 2012, www.heraldicjewelry.com/2/post/2012/07/july-26th-2012.html

"Chesapeake PERL to Produce Nerve Agent Bioscavenger for DTRA," *PR Newswire*, October 24, 2012, www.prnewswire.com/news-releases/chesapeake-perl-to-produce-nerve-agent-bioscavenger-for-dtra-175659501.html

Davis, John K. "The Story behind Snow White," *Suite101.com*, February 9, 2009, http://john-k-davis.suite101.com/the-story-behind-snow-white-a95097

Deeb, Mary-Jane. "Report on the National Library and the House of Manuscripts," *The Library of Congress*, October 27–November 3, 2003, www.loc.gov/rr/amed/iraqreport/iraqreport.html

"Diwani," *Wikipedia*, February 26, 2013, http://en.wikipedia.org/wiki/Diwani

Elf Presents Alf Layla Wa Layla (A Thousand Nights and a Night), n.d., www.arabiannights.org/index2.html

English, Sandy. "Unesco Report on Babylon," Red Ice Creations, August 19, 2009, www.redicecreations.com/article.php?idc7677

"Finger Licking Poison," *TV Tropes*, n.d., http://tvtropes.org/pmwiki/pmwiki.php/Main/FingerLickingPoison

"Fontanelle Cemetery," *Napoli Unplugged*, 2013, www.napoliunplugged.com/location/fontanelle-cemetery-naples

Gray, Richard. "Biblical Plagues Really Happened Say Scientists," *The Telegraph*, March 27, 2010, www.telegraph.co.uk/science/science-news/7530678/Biblical-plagues-really-happened-say-scientists.html

Greenway, H.D.S. "The War Hotels: Iraq's Palestine Hotel," *GlobalPost*, February 27, 2009, www.globalpost.com/dispatch/worldview/090103/the-war-hotels-part-v-iraq

Heiner, Heidi Anne. "Fairy Tale Timeline," *SurLaLune Fairy Tales*, www.surlalunefairytales.com/introduction/timeline.html

Hendawi, Hamza. "Baghdad's Antique Shops Tell Sad Story," *The Guardian*, July 14, 2009, www.guardian.co.uk/world/feedarticle/8607102

Hilton, Ronald. "Iraq: The Burning of Libraries," *WAIS Forum on Iraq*, April 17, 2003, http://wais.stanford.edu/Iraq/iraq_burningoflibraries41703.html

"History and Traditions of the House of Savoy, the Royal Family of Italy," *Regalis*, n.d., www.regalis.com/savoy.htm

"Jusepe de Ribera," *Artble.com*, 2013, www.artble.com/artists/jusepe_de_ribera

"Kutha," *Wikipedia*, February 26, 2013, http://en.wikipedia.org/wiki/Kutha

Langewiesche, William. "Welcome to the Green Zone," *The Atlantic*, November 1, 2004, www.theatlantic.com/magazine/archive/2004/11/welcome-to-the-green-zone/303547/

The Legend and the History of the Pied Piper of Hameln, February 2006, www.triune.de/legend

Lloyd, Seton, Fuad Safar, and H. Frankfort. "Tell Uqair: Excavations by the Iraq Government Directorate of Antiquities in 1940 and 1941," *Journal of Near Eastern Studies*, vol. 2, no. 2 (April 1943), pp. 131–158.

Mari, Francesca. "Shelf-Conscious," *The Paris Review*, December 27, 2012, www.theparisreview.org/blog/2012/12/27/shelf-conscious/

"Mashkan-shapir," *Wikipedia*, February 27, 2013, http://en.wikipedia.org/wiki/Mashkan-shapir

"Olympia Mancini," *Wikipedia*, February 26, 2013, http://wikipedia.org/wiki/Olympia_Mancini

Matthews, Jeff. "Virgins," *Around Naples Encyclopedia*, October 2009, http://ac-support.europe.umuc.edu/~jmatthew/naples/virgin.htm

Mendola, L. "Italian Titles of Nobility," *Regalis*, 1997, www.regalis.com/nobletitles.htm

National Earth Science Teachers Association. "1631 Eruption of Mt. Vesuvius," *Windows to the Universe*, www.windows2universe.org/earth/interior/Mt_Vesuvius_1631.html&edu=high

"Nergal and Ereshkigal," *Lykeion Regis*, August 10, 2008, http://lykeionregis.blogspot.com/2008/08/nergal-and-ereshkigal.html

"Nergal: Lord of the Underworld," *Gateways to Babylon*, n.d., www.gatewaystobabylon.com/gods/lords/undernergal.html

Nurse, Paul McMichael. "Why Has the Arabian Nights Proved So Enduring?" *The Globe and Mail*, August 14, 2012, www.theglobeandmail.com/arts/books-and-media/bookreviews/why-has-the-arabian-nights-proved-so-enduring/article4480676

Park, Alice. "The 'Killer Fungus': Should We Be Scared?" *Time*, April 23, 2010, www.time.com/time/health/article/0,8599,1984337,00.html

"The Pied Piper of Hamelin," *Dark-Stories.com*, April 29, 2007, www.dark-stories.com/eng/the_pied_piper_of_hamelin.htm

Reeves, Phil. "True Story of the Battle of Samarra," *Arab News*, December 7, 2003, www.arabnews.com/node/241235

"Saturday Stroll—Through the Valley of the Dead," *Napoli Unplugged*, May 24, 2010, www.napoliunplugged.com/saturday-stroll-through-the-valley-of-the-dead-html

Spessart Museum, Snow White—a native girl from Lohr am Main, www.spessartmuseum.de/seiten/schneewitchen_engl.html

"1655: Massacre of the Waldensians," *ExecutedToday.com*, April 24, 2011, www.executedtoday.com/2011/04/24/1655-massacre-of-waldensians/

"Thuc. 2.47–55: The Plague," *Perseus Digital Library*, n.d., http://perseus.mpiwg-berlin.mpg.de/GreekScience/Thuc.+2.47-55.html

"U.S. Troops Accused of Damaging Babylon's Ancient Wonder," *CNN.com/world*, July 31, 2009, http://edition.cnn.com/2009/WORLD/meast/07/31/iraq.babylon.damage/index.html

Waugh, Liz-Anna. "How to Pick Your Own Paper," *Northword*, fall 2002, www.northword.ca/connections/Past_Issue/fall_02/howto.html

Credits

Map of contemporary cities, ancient sites (Dino Pulerà, Artery Studios, Toronto)

Map of European destinations (Dino Pulerà, Artery Studios, Toronto)

Babylonian horse (Permission from Made 4 Museum, California, U.S.A.)

Frontispiece, *Lo Cunto de li Cunti* (E.P. Dutton and Company, 1932)

Design for metalwork book cover (Hans Holbein the Younger, 1498–1543; public domain, Wikimedia Commons)

Portrait of Giambattista Basile (E.P. Dutton and Company, 1932)

Portrait of José de Ribera (Public domain, Wikimedia Commons)

Mesopotamian spindle whorl (Permission from Barakat Gallery, California, U.S.A.)

Pied Piper (August von Moersperg, copy of a glass window in Market Church, Lower Saxony, Germany, 1532; public domain, Wikimedia Commons)

"The Witch Comes on Board" (Henry Justice Ford, illustrator, *The Yellow Fairy Book*; public domain)

Mary Magdalene in the Desert (José de Ribera, 1641; public domain, Wikimedia Commons)

Waldensians Massacre (Samuel Morland, *The History of the Evangelical Churches of Piedmont*, 1658; public domain)

The Talking Mirror of Lohr (Public domain, Wikimedia Commons)

Il Morbetto (Marcantonio Raimondi, 1515–1516; public domain, Wikimedia Commons)

The Book of a Thousand Nights and a Night (Henry Justice Ford, illustrator, Richard Burton, translator, 1850; public domain, Wikimedia Commons)

Acknowledgments

I imagine you, the reader, like me, have a collection of books that were precious possessions in childhood, evocative of the time our imagination first spread its wings. This second novel—the middle child in the Mesopotamian Trilogy—was a real thrill to write, in part because it took me back to those childhood stories and introduced me to a fascinating historical character, the gallant and courtly writer Giambattista Basile.

A whole team of people have devoted generous amounts of time, attention, and care to bring this "middle child" to life. President and Publisher Nicole Winstanley and Senior Editor Adrienne Kerr bring out great books time after time and have helped so many Canadian authors start out on a firm footing. Adrienne's sales intuition and admirable editorial skills are a rare combination in our world of books.

It is a privilege to work with the publishing team at Penguin Group (Canada), one I'm very grateful for. Don Robinson and Penguin's superb sales staff; Beth Lockley and the talented marketing and publicity staff: Charidy Johnston, Robin Dutta-Roy, Laura Meyer, Phil Clarke, Rachel Geertsma, Giselle San Miguel, and

Amy Smith. Copy editor Marcia Gallego and Managing Editor Mary Ann Blair, who does such a grand job on the production side. A real pleasure to work with you all.

Special thanks go to Victoria Skurnick (North America) and Elizabeth Fisher (International) at the Levine Greenberg Literary Agency. Gifted agents I feel so lucky to have.

The sage advice of friends, family, and supporters made all the difference to me on this second journey to publication. Thank you for holding my hand through the roller coaster ride: my sister Ellen Wall and daughter Kenlyn Hughson, Max Allen, Pat Armstrong, Jan Armstrong, Cathy Astolfo, Jayne Barnard, Martha Paley Francescato, Ilkona Halsband, Jane Burfield, Barbara Callway, Madeleine Harris-Callway, Melodie Campbell, Donna Carrick, Vicki Delany, Lisa De Nikolits, Warren and Christine John, Tanis Mallow, Rosemary McCracken, Teresa Pagnutti, John Pendergrast, Lisbie Rae, Jan Raymond, Robert Rotenberg, Linda Smith, Martha Tracey, Christine Von Aesch, Rob and Caroline Wall, and Denise Wilson.

Many thanks to Stephen Mader of Artery Studios and Dino Pulerà for his excellent illustrations.

Fayez Barakat of Barakat Gallery in Beverly Hills, California, has been most generous in allowing me to use his image of the Mesopotamian spindle whorl. I also greatly appreciate the help of Marodeen from Made 4 Museum in Claremont, California, who provided the Assyrian horse image.

Getting to know the city of Naples, Italy, was a real bonus in the writing of this book. One of the highlights of my trip was a one-day custom tour by Limo Service of Naples. I recommend them to anyone traveling there.

Libraries play an important role in this novel and in real life—the Toronto Public Library has been such a useful resource. Finding a rare copy of Norman Penzer's English translation of *The Tale of*

Tales and holding an even rarer edition of Straparola in the library's Osborne Collection were both essential to my work. So, too, the magnificent Biblioteca Nazionale Vittorio Emanuele III di Napoli, where I saw Giambattista Basile's book firsthand. Whether owing to destruction during wartime or economic and ideological pressures, libraries around the world are facing many challenges. May they remain strong.